ANCIENT
GUARDIANS

The Uninvited

Book II

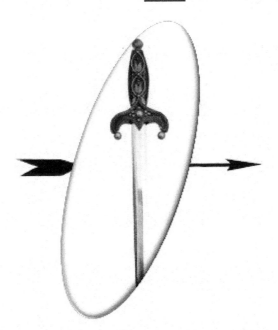

S. L. MORGAN

Pasidian Press 2014

ISBN: 9780615946634
ISBN: 0615946631 (Pasidian Press)

Introduction

Darkness was still on the lands of Pasidian Palace when Levi, Harrison, and a group of Guardians finished their combat drills in the training unit. After all of the chaos of dealing with the Council of Worlds, and preparing Reece to take up permanent residence in Pemdas, Levi was relieved to be in his normal routine again.

"How is it that you were able to counter my last attack so efficiently?" Harrison asked as he swallowed a gulp of water.

"Why would you believe that I would be incapable?"

1

Levi questioned. "You completely gave yourself away with your conceited smirk, as you always do before you attack."

Harrison shook his head. "It was obvious your mind was somewhere else! I knew I had you."

Levi reached for his water, "I have told you time and time again, your arrogance will always give your opponent the upper hand."

"Arrogance!" Harrison huffed, "I prefer to think it is merely extreme confidence."

"My point has been made." Levi said as he took a sip of the water. "And even though my thoughts were indeed otherwise engaged, I still was able to counter your stealthy attack."

"Regardless, I figured I'd have you on that particular attack—especially now that you are betrothed."

"Betrothed?" Levi scoffed. "I will never understand your way of thinking, nor will I try to. How could Reece accepting my hand in marriage serve as a distraction in combat training?"

"Love is weakness, my good friend." Harrison clapped him on the shoulder before turning to clean up their equipment.

Levi followed him, picking up sparring weapons, "And that is where you will always be wrong," he glanced at Harrison with a knowing smile, "as it was that particular emotion that served to enhance my fighting skills this morning."

Harrison sighed, "Nevertheless, I am exceedingly happy for you and Reece. Have you determined whether or not you will go through a Pemdai ceremony, or will you choose something from Earth's cultures?"

"I think that answer was obvious when I reported to our training." Levi said with a laugh. "Reece would have woken up in my arms today, had I chosen the Pemdai ceremony."

"If you ask me—" Harrison said as he smiled wryly at Levi.

"I'm *not* asking you," Levi interrupted, "or seeking your relationship advice." There was no point in taking part of a discussion like this with his cousin. Harrison's views about relationships differed immensely from Levi's, and any topic of conversation over the matter would be pointless. "I will honor the traditions that Reece is most familiar with. She is sacrificing a lot by being forced to live here and adjust to our customs. The least I can do for her is to give her a ceremony that she is more accustomed to."

"Forced?" Harrison said with a laugh. "I saw the look in her eyes when your father ordered that she should live in Pemdas for her safety, and she hardly seemed upset about it."

Levi studied Harrison for a moment. "Well, the least I can do for her is to give her a ceremony that she is accustomed to."

"A *true* romantic!" Harrison teased as they left the building. "Well, get ready. I am quite confident that the palace will turn into a whirlwind of chaos as frantic, female emotions commence preparations for such an event."

"I'll find my way out of that!" Levi grinned. "I am *merely* the groom."

"Yeah, right!" Harrison said mockingly. "We have witnessed firsthand how women on Earth deal with such events, and we've greatly pitied those *grooms* as well! You will be lucky if you are able to return to your duties, as Reece will need your opinions on—"

"Fortunately," Levi smoothly interrupted him, "having paid close attention to her throughout the years, I know perfectly well that she is not one to over react over such things."

Harrison said nothing as they entered the palace, but the

expression on his face told Levi that he was about to discover a whole different side to the woman he loved. Levi smiled in return. Harrison's opinions about women and social affairs were always ridiculous; and no matter what Levi said to defend any of it, Harrison would never listen.

They walked into the command center to retrieve their assignments from Samuel. There was a larger group of Guardians reporting than usual, and Levi was concerned as to why.

"Gentlemen," Samuel said as the men took their seats, filling the large conference area. "It appears as though Emperor Navarre and I were correct to assume that guarding Earth would consist of us needing more men. The Emperor's final demands to the Council of Worlds have led a few domains to challenge our obligation to protect Earth."

Harrison sat back in his seat and crossed his arms, "Do they not understand we revel in a good challenge?"

A tiny grin drew up in the corner of Samuel's mouth, "Apparently not. Either way, they are taking their humiliation out on us by trying to harm and terrorize the humans, and it is up to us to prevent their contact. We are dispatching more men to Earth than usual until it quiets down some."

Vincent, Samuel's chief advisor, stepped forward, "The military leaders from Earth have permitted the use of our aircrafts, so long as they remain invisible to the human eye. If any of these species try to frighten those of Earth by making their presence known through their space crafts, it is your duty to transport their crafts back to their realm and permanently disable them." He looked over at Harrison and Levi, "You men will head up this operation until we have familiarized more Guardians with the process of removing the unidentified crafts from airspace." Vincent addressed the rest of the Guardians, "If these realms seek to argue with the disabling of their crafts, you will take action against the beings as your training commands you."

Levi exhaled in frustration. The last thing he wanted to do was to leave Reece the morning after he asked for her hand in marriage. He nodded in agreement, but resolved to speak to Samuel about it after the meeting. Harrison, of course, was beaming with excitement that they had the opportunity to use the Pemdai aircrafts on Earth.

"We are not in a state of emergency," Samuel said, "but they are definitely making us work for our cause."

A few other men interjected their thoughts, but all-in-all the meeting went smoothly and was concluded quickly. When the meeting was adjourned, Levi followed Samuel into his office. "Commander."

"Ah! Levi." Samuel said as he approached him. He held out his hand and shook it, "Congratulations are an order for you and Reece." He walked back over to his desk and sat down, "I must say, your father and I just discussed your seeing the map to stone...extremely intriguing." He stated confidently, "And helpful as well, although, I am quite confident we will never have use for its powers."

"I agree, sir; however, aside from that, I am here to request leave for at least one or two days."

Samuel smiled, "Granted! I'll have Vincent assign another instructor in your place; however, I am sure Harrison will give you a hard time about this."

"He'll get over it."

"Enjoy your leave, and extend my well wishes to the future Mrs. Oxley as well." Samuel said as Levi turned to leave.

On his way out of the command center, Harrison left the group of men he was speaking to and followed Levi.

"Where do you think you're going?"

Levi never stopped, but continued to walk back toward his room with purpose. "Daylight will be in an hour, and I have plans for Reece and myself."

"And so it begins," Harrison taunted.

"What begins?"

"Your backing out of your duties to be with a lovely lady." Harrison stated with a knowing smile.

Levi glanced over at him. "I'm sure you'll survive."

"Indeed, I will," Harrison boasted. "But I am still perplexed as to why you would back out on a rare opportunity to use our aircrafts."

"Perplexed?" Levi said with a laugh. He stopped and faced his cousin, "Harrison, Reece and I haven't had any time together, period." Levi answered and then continued walking toward his rooms, "Besides," he added, "Her Excellency has been summoned to the palace; my father wishes to learn more about how I was able to unlock the map within Reece's mind."

"Well," Harrison started while continuing to walk at Levi's side. "I'll give you that, I'm curious myself." He nudged Levi with his elbow, "So," he said mischievously, "Where's the stone?"

Levi looked over at Harrison, "Do you remember where the Ciatron set up their domain on Earth before the great battle?"

Harrison seemed intrigued, "Atlantis?" He questioned in disbelief, "It's hidden there? Don't you think that would be an obvious place to hide the stone?"

"Yes."

"Well then, we must relocate it to a place that Reece's ancestor may have not been able to get to because he was human; but, with our talents, we can find a place that is more inaccessible."

Levi smiled impishly, "There is no need for that."

"What? Why?"

Levi glance at his cousin's puzzled expression amusingly. "Because the stone is not hidden there." He said haughtily.

Harrison gazed at Levi darkly, "So you *will* hold to your word. Do you not even trust your closest friend?"

"It is not that I don't trust you, but there is a reason Reece's mind only opened to mine. Until we learn more, I believe it is safest for all of us if I am the only one who knows the location."

"Well, is it vulnerable in any way?"

"Harrison, quit prying; I am not saying a word." He went to turn up the stairs to his rooms, "Let's just say, I am quite surprised that Paul Xylander, with his human limitations, was able to hide it in this location." Levi laughed at Harrison's expression of confusion, "Have fun on Earth, I'll see you in a few days."

With that, Levi turned and hopped up the steps, excited to make arrangements for his and Reece's day together.

Chapter 1

Reece ran at a rapid pace through the forest, out and away from the palace grounds. The exhilarating feeling of running freely through this majestic land so early in the morning was particularly therapeutic.

She slowed into an easy jog as she entered a clearing. As she slowed, she grasped her hips and began to catch her breath. An early morning run was definitely what she needed to help calm her nerves of excitement. She laughed quietly, wondering if she would lose sleep every night over the idea of becoming Levi's wife. She had tossed and turned all night, her mind endlessly replaying the images of him proposing to her the previous evening. Reece knew that she was remarkably fortunate not only to have such a man in her life, but also to live in this magnificent and intriguing world with him.

She walked over to a billowy mound of grass and sat down, overwhelmed with happiness and contentment. She tilted her head up and admired the iridescent purple sky glistening above her. The temperature was surprisingly warmer since before their return to Earth, leaving only small traces of snow on the ground. She gazed out at the illuminating foliage that surrounded her. The glowing, multi-colored blooms, along with the iridescent, fluttering insects that danced throughout them, were absolute serenity. Reece couldn't have asked for a better start to this new day in Pemdas.

She inhaled deeply of the crisp air as she thought dreamily about how significantly her life had changed since the first day she was brought into this dimension for her protection. It had been close to two months since she was escorted into Pasidian Palace on Levi's arm, clearly overwhelmed by the reality that other worlds existed outside of Earth. And now, here she was, permanently living in a new dimension, and engaged to be married to the only man who had ever stolen her heart.

Reece was happier and more settled in her life than she had ever been. Before she met Levi, she thought she had a clear vision of where she was going in life. She planned to finish medical school, and after that, live out her career as a pediatrician. It was funny how things had changed so unexpectedly. Falling in love was the last item on her to-do list for the future. In fact, before Levi, she never allowed herself to be distracted by such emotions towards any man. Somehow, everything within her changed when she met him. Perhaps it was the simpler way of life that the Pemdai embraced that allowed her to slow down, and appreciate the value of living. She'd only ever known a fast-paced life in which she strove to be the best and the brightest; little did she know that her life truly hadn't begun until she came into Pemdas.

As her thoughts became consumed by images of Levi, her heart began racing again. The sun started to rise, turning the sky a rainbow of glimmering colors. Captivated by its beauty, yet unable to sit any longer, Reece stood up and proceeded to head back to the palace. It was a new day, a new life, and Reece could hardly contain her joy. She jogged along the bank of a stream, and followed a trail back to the palace grounds. As soon as the magnificent structure came into sight, she beamed. The groundskeepers were already out tending to the palace's gardens, while servants were bustling here and there. Reece stopped and admired the view of her current home. She bit her bottom lip, somewhat overwhelmed, but also rejuvenated, as adrenaline started coursing through her body. She knew it wouldn't be long until she was back in Levi's arms.

Once in her room, she found her maiden, Jasmeen, preparing Reece's clothes for the day. The maiden was nothing if not passionate about ensuring that Reece was styled impeccably on a daily basis. After a hot shower, Reece took her tea into the vanity room so Jasmeen could begin styling her make-up and hair.

"Master Levi is awaiting you in the sitting room," Jasmeen said while placing the curling rod on the counter.

Reece's heart fluttered with excitement. "He's already here?"

Jasmeen walked back to Reece. "Indeed, he is," she said as she positioned Reece's hair to cascade over one shoulder. "There, now let's get you dressed," she said with a warm smile.

After Jasmeen finished helping Reece slip into an exquisite gown, she dismissed herself and went about the rest of her duties for the day. Reece walked into the sitting room while she clasped the arrow bracelet that Levi had purchased for her. Adrenaline surged through her when she glanced up and saw Levi stand up from the sofa to greet her. *I certainly won't have a problem seeing this face first thing every morning,* she thought as she inhaled, besotted by his image.

Levi had an air about him that commanded any room he was in effortlessly. He was the perfect definition of nobility and absolute sophistication. His tall, masculine frame was always impeccably dressed. His dark hair brought out the brilliance of his jewel-like, sapphire blue eyes, while his strong jawline gave an impressive definition to his handsome face. Reece's lips curved up into a proud, adoring grin. Her emotions were shameless, but she didn't care. Reece couldn't be more grateful that this man was hers.

Levi's eyes brightened as a beaming smile lit his face. He approached where Reece stood silently admiring him. He reached for her hand and brought it to his lips. His eyes never left hers as he tenderly kissed the back of her hand. "You, my love, look utterly ravishing this morning." His thumb absently brushed over the brilliant center stone of the ring he had given her, bringing his attention to it. He twisted the ring as he examined it. "This appears to be somewhat big on your finger. We'll have it fitted more properly when we visit the city today."

Reece glanced down at the ring that Levi was studying. How many times had she stared into the exquisite aquamarine stone since Levi had placed the ring on her finger the night before? The circular ring displayed the brilliance of the round cut, deep blue gemstone that was surrounded by tiny black diamonds encased with outer layer of tiny, sparkling white diamonds. On each side of the platinum band ran two rows of more tiny white diamonds, with a ribbon of blue stones in the center. The ring she wore was incomparable to anything she had ever seen, and she was absolutely entranced by the design of it.

He smiled as his eyes returned to hers, "Would you be up for a journey to Casititor today?"

Reece recalled their private lunch together before she knew about his feelings for her, "Tomato basil soup sounds wonderful!" she replied with a vibrant smile.

Levi brought her hand to rest in the curve of his arm as he led her from the room. "I have arranged to have our breakfast taken alone on the balcony this morning."

As they strolled leisurely through the upstairs corridor, Levi brought a hand up and lovingly covered Reece's. "I haven't had an opportunity to inform you about the history of your ring," he said, as he glanced down at her with an affectionate smile. "My grandfather, Alexander Oxley, acquired this ring for my grandmother while serving as Guardian on Earth. When it was given to me as an heirloom, I had never considered the idea of presenting it to my future wife as a wedding ring." He softly squeezed her hand. "However, being that my intended wife is from Earth, I could think of no other ring that would suit you better."

Reece leaned closer into him. "To wear your grandmother's ring is an honor, and its history makes me love it that much more."

Levi looked down at her. "It delights me that you feel that way," he said with a proud grin.

As they turned down the passageway that led to one of the outside balconies, Levi's expression grew somewhat somber. "I informed my father about the rather unique occurrence that took place between you and me last evening. He's curious to find out more about how I would have been able to see the location of the stone from inside your mind."

"I hadn't really thought about it until now, but does having that knowledge put you in jeopardy in any way? Will you be able to continue to serve on Earth?" Reece asked with concern.

"My mind is already protected from beings that can alter or read minds. So long as I do not proclaim to everyone that I have the information that they are all seeking, I will be perfectly fine."

"That's certainly a relief," she replied. "Does anyone else know besides your father?"

Levi nodded as they strolled out onto the landing. "Harrison, my mother, and Samuel are also aware of it. We agreed that it would be best if I keep the location to myself, as there must be a reason that your mind opened solely to me."

Levi guided Reece to her seat at the table that was prepared for them. He pulled her chair out for her, and he smoothly pushed it back up to the table after she was seated.

As Levi took his seat, the servants brought out breakfast, filling the crisp morning air with the aroma of freshly baked bread and breakfast cakes. After the staff filled their cups with tea, they left the couple to dine in privacy.

"Did your father have any insight as to why this would have happened between us?" Reece asked, before taking a sip of her tea.

Levi spread some preserves on a piece of bread and handed it to Reece. "He is as perplexed as I am, and that is why he wishes to meet with the one person who will know more about the situation."

"Who would that be?" Reece asked, before tasting the

warm bread Levi had given her.

"Her Excellency, Queen Galleta. She is a special and unique individual. She and those in her kingdom are from another dimension that was destroyed many years ago. They have very unique psychic abilities and other diverse talents; Galleta has the strongest of all these talents. My father and Samuel rely on her abilities and knowledge in situations that warrant them."

"Psychic abilities?" Reece asked, somewhat concerned by who this woman was.

Levi's mouth quirked up with a grin before he continued. "Yes. She and her kind have a special ability to read and mentally alter minds." He studied her for a moment. "Do you recall me telling you that your mind is protected to where no one can read it?"

Reece nodded.

"Well, with her unique ability, Galleta will be able to read into your mind and give us answers as to why I was able to see the map to the stone."

Reece's eyes widened, and she swallowed hard. The thought of having her mind read was a little unnerving.

"Reece, I understand this may be—"

"Levi," Reece interrupted him. "I'll be fine."

The expression on Levi's face told her that there was something more to this woman, and he was attempting to figure out how to make Reece aware of it.

"I get the feeling there's something else I need to know?"

Levi smiled sympathetically while he swallowed a bite of food. "You may need to have an open mind for this next part."

He had her attention. "Go ahead," she said with an encouraging smile.

"Queen Galleta knew your ancestor, Paul Xylander." He

paused. "Personally," Levi said in a low voice.

Come again? Reece sank back into her seat, striving to grasp the concept. "How is *that* possible?"

"This is the part that you need to keep an open mind about."

Reece took a sip of her tea. "Obviously."

"When the Pemdai rescued Galleta and her people from the destruction of their dimension, they brought them into Pemdas to take up residence. They stopped aging the moment they left their domain; it was as if their bodies froze in time."

Reece looked at Levi with disbelief. "Impossible."

"Unreasonable, maybe, but it is interesting; and yet, very convenient for the Pemdai while we have been protecting Paul's ancestral line for all this time."

"How did she know Paul personally?"

"Galleta's mind-reading abilities were greatly needed when my ancestors fought the Ciatron during their invasion of Earth. When the Guardians were made aware that Paul had created the stone, Galleta was brought in to consult with him. She advised him to trust the Pemdai with his protection, and the protection of his genetic line. Fortunately, he trusted her; and therein, trusted us to protect him and his cause. Because of her friendship with Paul, he revealed the information regarding the genetic imprint he created to pass down through his bloodline to her. Because she is the only living person who knows the details of that imprint, we believe that she will know more about why your mind opened up to me as it did."

"Well, this should be interesting."

Levi nodded in agreement. "What makes this all peculiar to me is the fact that I was not seeking the information from your mind when it was delivered into mine."

"So if Queen Galleta can read my mind, can she read

yours as well?"

"Not unless I allow her to."

Reece straightened. "So when do we meet with her?"

Levi touched his napkin to each corner of his mouth before placing it on the table. "She arrived at the palace close to an hour ago. Once we have finished our breakfast, we will meet with her in my father's study." Levi leaned in for the teapot and proceeded to refill both their cups. "Oh," he said with a mischievous grin, refilling Reece's teacup as she held it out to him. "I almost forgot...I fear I must be the bearer of bad news for you this morning."

Reece watched as Levi tried to maintain a somber expression. She took a sip of tea. "Bad news?" she asked innocently.

He nodded. "Indeed," he said in a low voice, "and on a day which you and I should be celebrating our engagement." He sighed dramatically as he feigned disappointment.

Reece stared at the expression on his face amusingly. "Seems pretty bad, Levi. Go on; I hope I can handle this."

"It appears that your good friend, Simone, has departed from the palace abruptly. Apparently, the note she left for her maiden has forced Catherine and Lillian to leave as well. They both left first thing this morning in order to be supportive of her."

Reece rolled her eyes and let out a laugh of disbelief. "Well, there went my maid of honor," she said sarcastically.

Levi grinned. "It will be difficult, but I am sure you will find a way past this dreadful news."

"We'll see. Hopefully my newfound depression won't be a distraction for Queen Galleta as she is trying to read my mind in the meeting this morning."

"Indeed, that may be a problem." Levi teased.

When they finished their breakfast, they walked to

Navarre's office to meet with the queen. Upon entering the room, Reece saw that Navarre and an older woman were sitting on a sofa in the corner of his office, engaged in quiet conversation.

Navarre stood and greeted the young couple as they entered the room. "Your Excellency," he said as they approached where Queen Galleta sat formally on the sofa, "allow me to introduce you to Miss Reece Bryant."

Queen Galleta was much older than Reece had imagined. Her coronet of hair was silver, and her skin was pale, thin, and wrinkled; but she sat very straight, and her topaz eyes glowed. "Good morning, Miss Bryant," the queen said with an endearing smile, "How do you do?"

"I'm very well, thank you; and please, call me Reece."

They sat on sofas arranged around the fireplace in Navarre's office. "Reece, I'm sure Levi made you aware of the fact that I knew Paul Xylander." Queen Galleta stated simply, "If you don't mind, I would like to use my abilities to see what's happened."

This is it! Reece thought as she inhaled, struggling to stay focused. "Go ahead," Reece answered, not knowing what to expect. Levi softly squeezed her hand, which brought Reece's attention to him. When she looked at him, he gave her a reassuring smile that helped ease the extremely awkward situation.

"Very interesting," said Galleta. She eyed Levi. "It appears that you are carrying a copy of this genetic imprint within your mind."

A copy? How is THAT possible? Reece thought in total confusion.

"Were you able to see the location of the stone?" Levi asked, with concern in his voice.

"I'm not able to see the location of the stone; I can only see what transpired between both of you." Galleta turned to Navarre. "The information is protected within both of their minds." She looked back at Levi and Reece. "The information has been so well-guarded from any kind of a psychic intrusion that I am unable to see exactly why it is that this unique occurrence took place." She smiled warmly at Reece. "I was, however, able to read both Reece and Levi's emotions at the time the information was transferred into Levi's mind, and it appears that Reece formed a strong attachment with Levi at that particular moment."

Reece felt the heat rush to her cheeks as she glanced subtly at Levi, but her embarrassment faded when she observed that he was still watching Galleta, waiting for more answers.

"Paul created a fail-safe," Galleta continued, "and because of this, the only other people who could ever possibly be able to see the location of the stone, without harm to the Key, would be the Pemdai. They were the only individuals he could trust with the stone, and also with the protection of his ancestral line."

Levi looked at Navarre and then placed his arm securely around Reece's shoulders. "It is interesting how it all happened. One minute my mind was otherwise engaged," he glanced knowingly at Reece, and then looked back at Galleta, "and from out of nowhere, I was seeing images; it was as if Reece's mind were projecting them into mine."

"That was when the information transferred and opened up to you, Levi," Galleta informed them.

"Can you access the information now, Levi?" Navarre asked.

Levi nodded, "Yes."

"I must know, in your opinion, do you believe the stone's location should be watched? Is there any way that it can be found?"

"Paul was an interesting man. I can safely say that there

is no reason to guard the stone. I do not believe it is possible for anyone to come across it without this map."

Navarre sat back and studied both Reece and Levi and let out a laugh, "It is remarkable this has occurred." He looked at Galleta, "The information will continue to pass genetically through their children, correct?"

"Yes." Galleta answered, "Nothing in Reece's mind has been altered. It will be interesting to see if any of their children will have the Pemdai capabilities of seeing the location within their own minds." She looked over at Levi, "Such as Levi has."

"Very interesting, indeed." Navarre said as a servant entered the room.

"Emperor Navarre," the servant said as he stood rigidly at the door, "Samuel has come with imperative information."

Navarre and Levi stood. "Send him in," Navarre said.

"Emperor, please forgive my interruption," Samuel declared with a sense of urgency.

"It is fine, Samuel; tell me, what news have you?"

"I have been informed that Michael Visor is missing."

"Missing?" Levi interjected, alarmed.

"He's found a way to escape his confinement," Samuel replied.

"Dispatch troops to search for him at once," Navarre ordered, and then turned to Galleta. "If you have nothing further, your Excellency, this matter requires my immediate attention."

Galleta and Reece both stood. "Emperor, unless you have any additional questions, I have nothing further to add," Galleta responded politely.

Navarre nodded and looked to Levi. "I will need you to assist Samuel in planning the search for Michael."

"Very well." Levi answered.

Navarre offered his arm to Galleta. "Allow me to escort you to Allestaine; she wishes to speak with you before your departure."

With that, the room was cleared, leaving Levi and Reece alone. Levi turned to face her. "Well, there went my plans for taking leave." Levi muttered, mainly to himself.

Reece's forehead creased in humor, "Plans?"

"I requested leave this morning in order to spend a few days alone with you." Levi's lips twisted as he gazed deeply into her eyes, "Either way, I still intend to take you to Casititor, if only for a few hours. I'm sure you have many questions about everything Galleta revealed to us; perhaps we can speak about it on our journey into the city this afternoon."

Reece let out a soft laugh. "I'm not sure our trip will be long enough to cover all my questions," Reece teased as she wrapped her arms around his waist. "So long as you and your father understand it all, I'll go with that."

Levi's lips quirked up in humor, as he bent to place a light kiss on Reece's lips. "I love you," he said in a low voice. He rose up and offered his arm to her. "It shouldn't take me long to go over the tactical planning concerning the search for Michael. Allow me to escort you to the library. My sister is there; she will be thrilled to have you in her company while I am detained."

It wasn't long before Levi returned, and he and Reece set off for Casititor. Their afternoon was exactly what they both needed. After a trip to the jeweler to have Reece's ring fitted, they enjoyed a private lunch at the Anders' restaurant, where they had dined together for the first time in privacy months before.

After a delightful lunch, they spent the remainder of the day touring more of the city and sites that Reece had never seen before. Upon their return to the palace that evening,

Levi informed Reece that he would likely be away from the palace for close to a week while he led the search mission for Michael. She was mildly disheartened that she wouldn't have the luxury of spending time with him; but she knew that finding the escaped perpetrator was imperative, and that she would be in excellent company with his mother and Elizabeth during his absence.

After Levi escorted her to her room and gave her a parting kiss, Reece walked in filled with gratefulness that they spent this entire day together. She stared down at her ring and smiled at the realization that soon she and Levi would be married, and she would be spending every night in his arms.

Chapter 2

After a long, relaxing bath, Reece ambled into the vanity room to meet Jasmeen. The young maiden, jubilant as usual, wasted no time in transforming Reece into a product of exquisiteness. Reece watched in humor as Jasmeen went through the extra efforts of pinning up her hair and placing tiny flowers sporadically throughout it.

"If I had to guess," Reece started, "I would think that Levi was back at the palace." She said while scrutinizing Jasmeen's face.

Reece's heart rate picked up as she noticed Jasmeen avoid her statement. It had been four days since she had seen him last, yet it seemed much longer. Without saying a word, Jasmeen walked over to Reece and smiled sweetly as she placed a blue velvet box in her hands.

Reece looked at Jasmeen in confusion. "What's this?"

Jasmeen smiled a knowing smile. "I was instructed to give this to you once you were prepared for the day."

Reece slowly opened the box. A shimmering silver arrow hung from a delicate chain, and sparkled brilliantly in the morning light. As she pulled the necklace off of the satin pillow it was arranged neatly on, she noted that it perfectly matched the bracelet Levi had given her when he first brought her to Casititor.

"Wow," she said in admiration.

"Allow me to help you put it on," Jasmeen offered politely.

Reece handed her the box. After the necklace was in place, Jasmeen handed Reece a folded card. "I will leave you to read this alone." She added kindly before exiting the room.

He is back! Reece thought, as she traced Levi's initials on the wax seal before sliding her thumb underneath it and unfolding the card. Her heart raced with anticipation as she began reading his perfectly penned note to her.

My Beloved Reece,

You, my only love, will forever hold my heart. We have been apart too long, and I must have this entire day alone with you. The day I have arranged for us will start with this small gift. I hope you are prepared to receive gifts today, as I have planned to present you with more than one. Once you are ready, I ask that you meet me in the courtyard.

Reece stood up. The idea of spending an entire day alone with Levi was exhilarating. Her excitement had her practically running through the palace out to where Levi was waiting for her.

When she arrived at the courtyard, she stopped at the top of the steps. She looked below to where four magnificent white stallions stood harnessed to a luxurious black carriage. Her eyes were drawn to the initials engraved in silver on the door. They were her and Levi's initials; the *L* and *R* were intertwined in a stylish script, and encircled by a bold silver and onyx letter *O*.

Her heart fluttered with excitement when Levi came around from the other side of the carriage. Her breath halted as she stood and admired his handsome appearance. Yes, it had definitely been too long since she had seen him last. He was dressed immaculately in a cream, high-collared shirt, navy waistcoat, cravat, and crisp, ivory trousers. "Well, if it isn't Prince Charming," she teased.

Levi stopped at the bottom of the steps and gave her an exaggerated bow. "At your service, madam!"

He displayed a brilliant smile as he leaped up the steps to where Reece waited. Full of excitement, she wrapped her arms tightly around his neck, stood on her toes, and gave him a quick kiss.

"Good morning, love," he said with laughter. "I have missed you."

"I think I've missed you more. I'm so thrilled you're back." She looked up into his vivid blue eyes. "Did you guys find Michael?"

Levi kissed her forehead and smiled lovingly into her eyes. "No; however, Harrison has taken over the search, giving us the opportunity to spend some time together."

"Lucky for me." she said, as she reached out and interlaced her fingers through Levi's. "Thank you for my necklace. It's beautiful."

Levi released one of her hands and caressed her cheek. "*You* are beautiful," he said, before bringing his attention to the silver arrow that rested against the center of her décolletage. His fingers brushed against her skin as he held the delicate charm and studied it. Her flesh burned in response to his gentle touch. "It lies perfectly over your heart, as I'd hoped it would. Not too short, not too long," he said with a wink. He drew her arm up into his. "Now, for your next gift," he started, as he led her down the steps. "I purchased this for you; it will serve as your personal transportation in Pemdas."

Reece leaned into him, squeezing his arm with delight. "Who would have ever imagined that I'd go from driving a car to getting around in a horse-drawn carriage?"

Levi laughed softly as he dismissed the footman and turned to help Reece into the carriage. The plush interior was fashioned out of an exquisite blue velvet material, with a dark mahogany wood trim. Levi settled in next to her, gave a quick rap to the top of the carriage, and they were off.

He stretched his long legs out, crossed them, and lazily reclined back into the plush seats. He put his arm around Reece, bringing her closer to him.

"This carriage is extraordinary," she said as she admired the elegance of it.

Levi's embrace tightened around her. "I'm glad it meets with your approval."

"Well, it's obvious that you're in the gift-giving spirit today, and it's got me thinking. What if I wanted to buy *you* something? I'm kind of stuck—I don't have any money here."

"Forgive me for not addressing this sooner; I believe I have been so busy lately that I haven't taken the time to go over these particular details. When we return to the palace this evening, I will bring you to Pasidian's vaults and introduce you to Mrs. Stridewell. She manages the vault, and will allow you access to the funds at any time. Currency is valued and used here in Pemdas very similarly as it is on Earth, and you should have no trouble getting used to it."

Reece twisted to face him. "A *vault*, huh? That's it?" She

teased. "Well," she exhaled dramatically, "I guess that'll do for now."

Levi's lips drew up into her favorite grin, and Reece was instantly entranced with the vividness of his humored, electric-blue eyes. "I have missed you." His expression grew more serious. "I must admit, not having been in your company has made this week somewhat trying on me."

He slid his hand around the back of her neck, eyes now fixed on her lips. Reece bit her lip with eagerness as he drew her face closer to his. She smiled faintly in response, and her mind became fuzzy as Levi softly kissed each corner of her mouth. He gazed intently into her eyes as his thumb traced along her bottom lip. "And all I desire now," he brought his lips to her chin, "is to indulge myself in the woman I love."

She smiled provocatively at him, and ran her fingers through his wavy hair. "Sounds like an excellent idea to me," she said, bringing his face closer to hers.

In that moment, Levi's lips claimed hers in a crushing kiss. His hand braced the back of her neck as he deepened his powerful kiss, and Reece sighed with satisfaction. He relaxed, reclining back into the seat, and placed his other arm firmly around her back as he molded her body against his. She responded wholeheartedly to him, and indulged herself in the savory kiss he offered her.

When he ended their ardent kiss with a soft kiss to Reece's nose, she was somewhat disorientated. She sat up, glanced out of the side window, and observed that the carriage was traveling down a tree-covered road. Dazzling blossoms in a variety of colors cascaded from their branches in the unique forest that surrounded them.

Reece gazed at Levi quizzically. "Where are we going? I haven't seen any of this before."

"You'll see." He straightened himself and gave a quick

tug to his waistcoat. "Now, in order for you to fully appreciate your next gift, I must ask that you close your eyes."

Reece happily acceded to his request. After a few moments, she sensed that the carriage was slowing, and heard the clattering of the horses' hooves silence soon thereafter.

She listened as the door opened, and heard Levi step out of the carriage. He helped to guide her out of the carriage, and swept her into his arms.

"Can I open my eyes yet?" she asked enthusiastically.

Levi placed her feet on the ground, and enclosed his arms around her waist. "Yes," he answered softly.

When Reece's eyes opened, she was speechless.

Levi pressed his cheek against hers. "Welcome to our new home," he whispered.

The enormous white house was a magnificent sight to behold. It was three-story home; complete with a large balcony, porch, and Greek-style columns that ran the entire façade, and continued on to wrap around the house. The broad steps that led up to the elaborate entryway doors gave this stately home an overwhelming sense of grandeur.

"Our home?" Reece's voice cracked as she fought back tears of overwhelming gratitude.

Levi stepped around her and took her hands into his. "Yes; this is where you and I will live when we are married. Do you approve?" He looked down at her, and brushed away a tear that slipped down her cheek.

She smiled at his beaming expression. "Approve? I love it!"

Reece took in the massive, park-like setting that surrounded them. The grand house sat impressively at the end of a circular, cobblestone driveway. To the left of the house was neatly trimmed, vivid-green grass with large trees scattered throughout, offering an abundance of shade. The lush grass grew all the way to the shoreline of a small, shimmering blue lake. Across the small body of water were more trees, and a tall mountain range that spanned the horizon behind the estate.

She looked back at Levi, who was watching her with amusement. "All of this is breathtaking, and it's more than I would have ever asked for."

He kissed her forehead. "I am thrilled that it agrees with you. I have been drawn to this house for as long as I can remember. I have ridden by it many times with the hope that someday I would share it with my wife and children. To have your approval means more to me than you will ever know."

"It's absolutely perfect."

Levi offered his arm. "Shall I escort you inside?"

Reece took his arm. "Why, Mr. Oxley, I thought you'd never ask."

As they entered through the impressive double doors at the front of the house, a massive atrium with a sweeping staircase greeted them. The house was empty, with no furniture to speak of, and still, it was a breathtaking sight.

A luxurious blue velvet carpet covered the center area of white marble steps that led up to the second level of their home. She gazed in wonder at the variety of circular patterns that had been intricately carved into the high, alabaster ceilings. An enormous chandelier hung over the entryway and dazzled in a rainbow of colors, reflecting the light peering in from the windows as a prism would.

Reece held tightly to Levi's hand as they toured the main floor of their home. The detail and craftsmanship that was brought into the structure was so elaborate that Reece remained silent, clearly overwhelmed by the rich atmosphere of this extravagant home. Fortunately, her excitement overruled any intimidation she might have had with such a lavish manor.

With each room they entered, she fell more in love with their new home. The first floor consisted of a library, two parlors, a music room, and a large dining hall, as well as various other rooms for guests. At the end of the large corridor on the south wing, two doors opened into an enormous room, with floor-to-ceiling windows lining three walls. Each wall had glass doors, giving access to the porch that wrapped around the home. When Reece questioned what the purpose of this particular room was, Levi teased her in response, letting her know that this ballroom was where Reece would be hosting many future celebrations for family and friends.

Once they finished touring most of the first level, they ascended the massive staircase that led to the second floor. Directly in front of them, more floor-to-ceiling windows offered spectacular views of the rolling hills that lined the horizon behind the manor.

Levi then led her down the hallways to their left. "This wing of the second floor consists primarily of private apartments for our close friends and family. There are more apartments on the northern wing of the home that will be for additional guests."

They toured the different rooms on the second floor, and she sighed and smiled as they approached a staircase that led up to another level of the home. "I have no idea how we're supposed to furnish all of this."

"We will meet with decorators that will help design the interior of the home with what brings you the most comfort. Now," he added with a mischievous grin, "our chambers will be up these stairs, on the third floor."

Reece felt a shiver of excitement course through her as she took Levi's extended hand. When they arrived at the landing, Levi pointed over to the hallways on their left. "Those rooms will be reserved for our children," he said, as he gazed adoringly into her eyes.

Reece looked down the long hallway and then back to Levi. "There must be over ten doors, and I can't even see to the end of the hall! Exactly how many kids are you planning on having, Mr. Oxley?"

Levi laughed and brought her hand to his lips for a kiss. "A man can never be *too* greedy, Miss Bryant."

"Um, in this case, I believe he most certainly can."

Levi's eyes dazzled with humor as he drew her arm up into his. He turned and led her down the hall to their right. "There are numerous rooms down this wing; a private sitting room, a parlor, offices and a private library." He turned to face two double doors on their left. "These will be our personal bedchambers, unless you decide otherwise." He reached for the two doors and opened them. "This area will serve as our sitting room." He informed her as they walked through the doors.

A large fireplace dominated the wall to her right; its marble mantle was glossy white with vibrant silver trim that highlighted the scroll patterns that were carved into it. The high ceilings were adorned in an architectural wonder, with rich mosaics of vines and other floral carvings that were defined with the same shimmering silver as the mantel of the fireplace. The bright marble floors had unique patterns, complementing those on the ceiling, etched in silver, and positioned in the center of room. To her left were two glass doors that led onto the balcony that faced the back of their home.

Levi strode across the room to where two more double doors stood and opened one. "Our private parlor is through here, and our bedchamber and dressing rooms are just beyond that."

They entered their sleeping chamber, where windows and two glass doors filled the wall to her left. Across the room and up on a marble platform was a large bay of windows that wrapped around the corner of the house. Marble columns framed the entrance of the platform area, and it was easy to see that this was an excellent location for their bed.

"No one will have access to these porches," Levi said, as he walked over to the glass doors and opened them. "They are only accessed by our room." He stepped up the four steps that led onto the elevated floor, and motioned for Reece to follow him.

Reece crossed the room to where Levi stood in front of the large windows that framed the magnificent views of a river that spilled into the lake off the side of their house. "This small river feeds our lake, and also continues through it to meet with the Pasidian River."

"I don't think I'll have a problem lying in our bed and staring out of the window, watching that river glow every night." She looked at Levi.

Levi smiled wryly. "I believe my attention will be distracted with something more stunning and desirable than that of a glowing river."

Reece arched her eyebrow and then turned, seeing the colossal fireplace on the wall to their left. "Hmm, well, I guess we have an excellent view of the fire from here as well." She teased.

Levi smirked as he pulled her into his arms. "The fire will definitely enhance the splendor of having you fall asleep in my arms every night." he said as he withdrew and took her hand. "Our dressing rooms are separate," he continued, as he led her toward another door in their room. They walked through a small hallway. "My valet will have access to my dressing room through those doors." He pointed to another door on their left. "And your maiden will have access to your private dressing room and bath right through here. The servants' passageways lead directly to them, and I will be sure to inform both the maiden and the valet of the rooms that will give them easiest access."

Reece marveled at the splendor of her bathroom after Levi led her into it. "You'd think I'd be used to having a bathroom like this by now." She turned and smiled at Levi. "I'm beyond impressed by all of this. I love this house, Levi."

Levi smiled. "Would you care to walk out on your private balcony and see the view it offers?"

"You mean the tour is already over?" Reece teased.

"Hardly; I believe I was only showing you the necessary rooms. We can tour the kitchens, the indoor pools, and the children's—"

"Levi—" Reece interrupted him, and then stood on her toes and gave him a quick kiss. "It was a joke," she said with a laugh. "Anyways, I need some fresh air to get my thoughts straight, and find the appropriate words of appreciation for all of this."

Levi led her from the room. "Fresh air it is, my lady."

Chapter 3

When they stepped onto the private balcony, Reece was ahead of Levi, and she stood in awe of the panoramic view the back of their house had to offer. Rolling hills and pastures disappeared into a forest of trees that lined the horizon. Directly below, a crystal-clear creek snaked its way around the neatly sculpted bushes that decorated the outdoor gardens. Out to her left, a stone wall led up to and surrounded two large structures. Reece cocked her head to the side, endeavoring to figure out what the buildings were for.

"Those are the horse stables and the carriage house," he said, as he came up behind her and wrapped his arms around her waist, pulling her back into him.

"I'm sure Arrow and Areion will be impressed with your

choice of a home for them."

"I'm sure they will." He said as he placed a soft kiss on the top of her head. "I should make you aware that Arrow's training is due to commence this week; you might be surprised by how much he has grown when he returns to the palace."

"Really? They grow that fast?"

"Guardians horses are unique in almost every quality they possess." He brushed his lips against her cheek. "So, yes, he will be nearly full grown when you encounter him again."

Reece sighed, "I shouldn't be surprised; they are remarkable animals." She exhaled in wonder as she took in more of the surrounding scenery. "These views are breathtaking." She rested her head back against his shoulder. "I love everything about it this place."

A low rumble in the distance announced the heavy, dark clouds that had appeared from behind the thick forest. Levi released his hold on her. "I believe my plans for an outdoor picnic must be changed," he said humorously. He glanced out at the threatening sky that was quickly darkening due to the incoming storm. "I'll be back in a moment. I need to retrieve some things from the carriage before the driver and footman seek shelter."

Reece remained on the balcony, absorbing the tranquility of the cool, brisk breeze that appeared from out of nowhere. The nearly black skies flickered, followed by another rumble of thunder. A curtain of rain shimmered like glitter falling to the ground out in the distance as the storm rapidly approached their location. *So beautiful!* Reece thought, as the last of the sun's rays disappeared behind the ominous clouds.

Reece was distracted by the sound of the horses rapidly bringing the carriage to shelter in the carriage house. A gust of ice-cold wind nearly blew her over, dropping the temperature in that moment drastically. As Reece turned to walk back into the house, a bright flash of light nearly blinded her, followed by an extremely loud crack of thunder. Reece was startled, and jumped backward. Luckily, Levi had just returned, and caught her before she stumbled to the ground.

"That was close," Reece said in a shaky voice.

Levi put an arm around her, guiding her back into the house. "Are you okay?" he asked with humor in his voice, attempting to lighten the tension of the moment.

Reece rubbed her arms, trying to warm up. "That came out of nowhere. I can't believe how cold it got all of a sudden."

"Springtime storms in Pemdas are relatively unpredictable and unexpected. After the storm passes, the temperature will warm again." He glanced at the glass doors where the rain was now pouring down. "This storm may be here for a while. Let us go downstairs; I have an area prepared in one of the sitting rooms, and will start a fire to help keep you warm."

Levi escorted her down to the first floor, where he had spread out a blanket in the living area with four plush pillows and a basket of food. "There are muffins and a variety of fruit in the basket, if you desire. Give me a moment to retrieve some wood from the shed outside."

Before Reece could say anything, he was out of the room. She strolled over and lowered herself onto the blanket amongst the pillows. Even though she was cold, she was completely relaxed as she watched the heavy rain pour down onto the front lawn. She curled her legs underneath herself, and crossed her arms in an effort to keep warm until Levi returned. The winds were howling and forcing the rain sideways, and the thunder was so loud that it practically shook the entire house.

As soon as she started to become concerned about Levi's whereabouts, he walked into the room carrying an armful of wood. His dark hair was soaking wet, and so were his clothes. Reece admired him_with satisfaction at | how devastatingly handsome he looked.

"Is there anything I can do to help?" She sat up as Levi strode briskly across the room.

He dumped the wood in the fireplace and knelt down. "No, just try to stay warm; I'll have your fire started in a moment," he answered her as he arranged the logs in the fireplace.

Reece reclined against the pillows again and watched as Levi brought a silver rod to the pile of wood, instantly sparking a flame. Within seconds, a healthy fire was crackling in the fireplace, and illuminating the previously darkened room with a warm, amber glow.

Levi poked and moved the logs around in the fireplace, allowing the flames to begin consuming the wood. When finished, he placed the poker to the side, stood up, and began to unravel the wet cravat around his neck. After it was removed, he laid it out on the mantle above the fireplace, and with casual ease, he started unbuttoning his waistcoat. *Looks like this storm was a blessing in disguise,* Reece thought, as she settled comfortably into the pillows. She was greatly appreciating the rain, the storm, and him having been out in it. Levi must have noticed her watching him, as he glanced over at her and grinned while he removed his waistcoat and hung it over the top of the iron poker next to the fire to dry.

Reece's chin dropped down and her eyes widened as Levi started removing his muslin shirt. After he casually draped his damp shirt in front of the fire, he turned and walked over to where she was. Reece remained quiet, fully appreciating the strong man in front of her. The tight-fitting, white undershirt he wore left nothing to her imagination. She saw the ridges of the hard muscles of his chest, and the tightness of his abdomen. It was obvious that Levi was well-built, but Reece was absolutely amazed witnessing such perfection with her own eyes.

When her eyes met Levi's, he smiled sympathetically. "I hope you won't be too upset about having to dine with a poorly dressed man," he said, as he smoothed his wet hair back and sat next to her.

Reece arched her eyebrow at him. "Poorly dressed? Not the phrase I would use." She ran her hands along his back. "This shirt's a little damp..." Levi glanced at her, and she used this opportunity to tease him with her eyes. "Are you sure you don't need to take it off, too?"

Levi smirked in response. "I don't want to make you too uncomfortable, love."

"Believe me, I'd be far from uncomfortable," she said playfully.

Levi laughed softly as he reached over to the basket, pulled out a plate, and placed muffins, along with different pieces of fruit on it. Once he finished arranging the food, he reclined back, and casually leaned against Reece.

He picked up a piece of fruit, which resembled the size and shape of a strawberry, and brought it to her lips. "You'll like these."

She accepted gladly, eager to try one of Pemdas' native fruits. Levi watched her as she began to chew it. It may have appeared to be a strawberry, but the taste was far from that. It was the lushest piece of fruit she had ever eaten. Flavors of vanilla, sweet cream, and a tiny zest of citrus erupted in her mouth. She swallowed and licked her lips, as she indulged herself in its sweetness.

"What is that?" she asked in amazement. "That was

delicious!"

Levi offered her another. "It's a special fruit that comes from a plant that grows underwater; they're only ripe for one month out of each year. They came into season a few days ago, and the villagers delivered them to the palace this morning."

"You know, I could probably get sick from eating these," she said, as she reached for another.

Levi nodded in agreement as he swallowed. "I agree. When we return to the palace, you will have to try the juice that Pasidian's staff makes from them."

As Reece sampled the variety of fruit that Levi offered her, she nestled in closer to his side and fully immersed herself in the cozy atmosphere of this indoor picnic. The darkened room, which was slowly being warmed by the fire Levi had built, was extremely relaxing. With the skies constantly flickering from the lightening flashing throughout them, the rain pouring down, and the comfort of being next to Levi, she was perfectly content. She instinctively brought one arm around his back, and used her other hand to caress the well-defined bicep of his seamlessly chiseled arm.

Levi glanced over at her in amusement, and she smiled brightly in response. "You're absolutely gorgeous, you know that?" she stated confidently, as she gazed proudly into his eyes.

Levi kissed her nose. "I believe it's a matter of perspective, but I am indeed grateful that *you* feel that way," he said with a wink.

Reece began tracing along his arm. "This is really nice, being here with you like this in our new home. I have to say, it has me very excited to be married."

"I feel the same way," he said, as he offered her a piece of muffin. "That reminds me; I wanted to talk to you about our wedding ceremony, and how they are performed in Pemdas."

Butterflies swarmed in Reece's stomach as she tried to keep a confident expression. "It's gonna be pretty big, isn't it?"

Levi placed the plate of food to the side and twisted to face her. "Quite the opposite, actually," he said with a sympathetic grin. "In Pemdas, after a man and woman decide to commit their lives to each other, there is no ceremony such as there would be on Earth. Their vows are honored simply by saying words of devotion in front of a few witnesses."

"Sounds *so* romantic," she teased. "So all we'd have to do is walk up in front of your parents, say a couple of words of love…and that's it, we're married?"

"In a way, yes. However, in Pemdas, we celebrate the couple's union after they return from their vacation, or rather, honeymoon. It is quite a celebration, to be sure." He reached for her hand. "So actually, we could walk in tonight and become a wedded couple." He sighed and gazed longingly into her eyes. "And believe me, it is tempting; but that is not how I would like to see our wedding performed." He raised her hand to his lips and softly kissed it. When his eyes once again met hers, they were piercing. "Reece, I wish to honor you and our marriage with a traditional wedding ceremony from Earth. I understand you are already sacrificing a lot simply by being required to live in Pemdas, and I want to do everything in my power to honor traditions from your culture as well."

"Levi," she smiled, as he tenderly rubbed the back of her hand. "I'm not sacrificing anything and I can't imagine anywhere else I'd rather be."

"It may feel that way now, but as you already are aware, Pemdas' culture and Earth's culture varies widely. I will tell you that I am astounded by how well you have adjusted already. However, you will have moments where you will find yourself missing the only traditions you have ever known." He smiled warmly at her. "This is why, in regard to our wedding, I want to give you everything that you, as a new bride, would expect to have on Earth." He smiled wryly. "Engagement parties and all!"

Reece stared intently into Levi's humorous eyes, "You're the most thoughtful man I've ever met." She said meaningfully, "And as tempting as it is to have a Pemdai ceremony and become your wife as soon as we get back to the palace, I think it would be wonderful to have a wedding ceremony to honor both of us. So," she lifted her chin and gazed knowingly into his eyes, "while you've been considering all of this, have you thought of a date, too?"

A brilliant smile stretched across Levi's face. "Of course," he said proudly. "Although, all of it will depend on what is most comfortable for you. As far as time periods go, I am confident that everything can be arranged for our ceremony to take place three months from now."

"Well, you are certainly not one for wasting time."

"When it comes to you becoming my wife? You are correct; I most definitely will not waste any time."

Reece laughed in disbelief. "Will we be able to plan all of this in that amount of time?"

"You will be surprised at how swiftly my mother will have everything arranged in three months. I hope you and I will be able to keep up with her." He smiled sympathetically. "And while we are on the subject of planning, I wanted to advise you about a celebration that we have been invited to attend."

"Celebration?"

Levi nodded. "There are numerous times throughout the year that my family vacations away from the palace for months at a time, giving my father the opportunity to go over business matters with those in leadership of the various kingdoms. As it turns out, we will be visiting the Sandari Kingdom, where my father's closest friend, King Hamilton, reigns. My family has an estate there, which I believe you will enjoy, given its proximity to the ocean shoreline."

"That sounds really nice. Is that where the celebration is going to be?"

"No, it will be hosted by the Hamiltons at their estate. King Hamilton has arranged a ball in order to honor the emperor and his success in recovering our men and keeping you safe from the Ciatron. This will be an interesting gathering, due to the fact that all of the kings and their families will be in attendance, not only to celebrate, but also to meet with their emperor to discuss the events that took place that day in the Council of Worlds." Levi's lips turned up into an admiring grin. "These kings and their families are highly anticipating making your acquaintance as well."

Reece was doing fine up until the last part. She swallowed hard. "Um…exactly how am I supposed to prepare for something like this?"

"All you need to do is walk into the room and they will all…"

He went to kiss her, but Reece held one finger over his lips and stopped him. "Any other time I would gladly listen to you over-exaggerate how wonderful I am, but let's get real for a minute; a ball?" She cleared her throat. "Do I need to do anything to prepare for this?"

Questions started lining up one by one in her head. She'd done pretty well in this land so far as she struggled to blend in with its culture, but wearing seventeenth-century clothes instead of t-shirts and jeans, or riding in a horse and carriage instead of driving in a car, wasn't the same as attending an extravagant ball with royal families.

Levi pressed his lips into her fingers for a soft kiss before taking her hand into his. "You've already admitted to Harrison, Elizabeth, and me that you've taken dancing lessons; am I not correct?" He laughed softly. "So it appears to me that the only thing you would need to prepare for is already resolved."

She narrowed her eyes at him. "Laugh it up, Mr. Oxley, because you're going to look like an idiot when your future wife busts into some square dancing moves on the ballroom floor."

Levi's eyes crinkled in humor. "Square dancing? That most certainly will be delightful to witness. I'll see to it that the emperor secures the first dance set with you."

Reece arched her eyebrow at his smug grin. "Or the two-step…" she taunted.

His eyebrows shot up as he softly laughed. "Ah, indeed, the two-step…now that I should love to see," he said, as he reached for a small piece of fruit. He tossed it in his mouth and leaned back. It was obvious that he had no concerns about bringing her to this ball, prepared or not. "I will say, that if this is your preference of dance at the celebration, Harrison will be extremely delighted to help you introduce this way of dancing to the Pemdai culture—preferably those in royalty." He laughed again.

Well, if he wasn't going to worry about it, then neither was she.

Reece shrugged her shoulders. "Forget it. You've been warned," she said with a smile.

Levi turned to face her. "Whatever style of dancing you should decide upon, I can assure you, I will not ever consider myself an *idiot* to be at your side." He ran his long fingers along her neckline and over her shoulder; his vivid blue eyes followed the fiery trail his fingers created on her skin. "However, if you should choose the Pemdai way of dancing, I will happily volunteer my services to help instruct you."

"The *Pemdai* way of dancing?" she repeated with confusion.

"It is similar to what those of Earth consider ballroom dancing," he absently answered her, while he slowly pulled her sleeve down, exposing her shoulder.

Well, that's not so bad, she thought, while having difficulty keeping her thoughts straight now. Levi's attention was solely on her bare shoulder as he tenderly caressed it with his thumb. "How long do we have until this ball?" she whispered. Her heart was now racing at seeing the hunger in his eyes.

"Two weeks; and I'm confident you will be proficient with your dancing skills long before then," he said in a lower, raspy voice before he placed a soft kiss on her shoulder. When Levi's eyes returned to hers they were dark with desire, instantly entrancing her.

His eyes pierced through her. "You are so incredibly beautiful," he said hoarsely.

Levi slowly lowered his face closer to hers, and his expression sent butterflies swarming in her stomach. When his lips were close to her neck, he closed his eyes and inhaled deeply. His mouth gently claimed the side of her neck. Reece reacted as if she had never been kissed by him before. She tilted her head back, offering more of her neckline to Levi, and he eagerly accepted her invitation. One of Levi's knees slid underneath her legs as he positioned himself to lean further into her, tenderly kissing the base of her throat and under her chin. Her eyes closed in utter satisfaction as his soft yet powerful lips lovingly caressed her hot flesh. She massaged her fingers through his damp hair, encouraging him for more.

As Levi pursued her collarbones with lingering kisses, Reece ran her hands under his shirt and up along is warm, muscular sides. Levi groaned softly and brought his eyes back to hers. The light of the fire flickered in his dark, smoldering irises as he gazed deeply into hers. She ran her hands up his back, seized his sturdy shoulders, and let her lips linger at the base of his throat. Levi's mouth parted slightly as he closed his eyes and moaned in response to Reece actively kissing and tasting of his intoxicating flesh.

With the warmth the fire had created in the room, and this being the first time Reece had ever tasted of his rich fragrance she loved so much, Reece became wild with desire for more. Levi remained perfectly still, only low groans escaping him, while she continued to pursue his tantalizing skin. She ran her hands along his sturdy back. "My love," she whispered, as her lips tenderly tugged at his earlobe.

"Reece—" he replied breathlessly, obviously as taken by this moment as she was.

She brought her mouth back to his, needing to feel his lips on hers. He kissed her with more passion than before. He ran his hands through her hair, gripping it tightly as he kissed down the center of her chest, and then ran a blazing trail of fire along the daring neckline of her dress. Reece closed her eyes, completely consumed by the pleasurable sensations of Levi avidly kissing her.

It was not long before his lips were hungrily on hers again, sending Reece's heart rate soaring. She moaned softly in response, and couldn't be more grateful for this sudden thunderstorm that gave her this moment with Levi. Time appeared to have stopped, and Reece had no idea how long they remained in this delicious kiss, before Levi slowly withdrew from her.

Reece sighed softly while Levi grinned at her. He kissed her tenderly on her lips. "You, Reece Bryant, are most fortunate that the rain has let up, or I would insist upon you becoming my wife tonight," he finished with a laugh.

Reece smiled as she caressed his cheek. "I wouldn't have a problem with that."

As Reece's better judgment slowly began to return, she sat up and glanced out the windows. The sun was shining brightly on the wet grass, making it appear as though thousands of diamonds had been thrown out into it. *Just when I thought this place couldn't get any more majestic.* She looked over at Levi, who was lounging on his side, running his fingertips along her arm. As tempting as it was to maneuver her way back into his arms, she realized that it would probably be a better idea to start preparing for this ball that was two weeks away.

She pulled her sleeve back over her shoulder and laughed when Levi frowned in response. "Unless we're going to be tap-dancing to "Mary had a Little Lamb" at this royal ball, you should probably get busy on giving me some dancing lessons."

Chapter 4

The days leading up to the Oxley's trip to Sandari Kingdom passed quickly. Reece, Allestaine, and Elizabeth met with the seamstress every morning to be fitted for the extravagant dresses that were to be made for their trip. Since this was Reece's first introduction into the royal society of Pemdas, all of her gowns were given the utmost attention, with not one detail unattended to. Allestaine was determined to present her future daughter-in-law in such a way that no one would question her as Levi's intended wife. Reece was to marry the future emperor, and Allestaine would leave no room for speculation about whether or not Reece was the perfect match for her son.

Despite everyone's reassurance, Reece had natural insecurities about meeting the royal families in this land.

She had no idea where to start with the etiquette that she knew would be expected of her amongst royalty. On Earth or in Pemdas, Reece was not accustomed to royal lifestyles or traditions. Knowing that Reece was somewhat nervous about the Hamilton's ball, Levi held to his word and spent a few hours each day teaching her the Pemdai style of dancing.

The dance lessons turned out to be Reece's favorite part of the preparations for the celebration. Levi was not only an impeccable dancer, but his way of leading her so properly in this ballroom-style of dancing was quite charming. When Reece teased him about his flawless dancing skills, he laughed and informed her that in Pemdas, it is expected that a young lady or gentleman achieve proper dancing abilities by the time they are of age to court.

All-in-all, by the time the week was over, Reece had learned the Pemdai way of dancing to the best of her ability, and she felt somewhat ready to step out formally as Levi's future wife.

The morning of their departure, Reece and Elizabeth walked out to the waiting carriages together. The maidens, butlers, and other staff had already departed in the carriages that carried their luggage. The previous evening, Reece learned that Levi wouldn't be along for the first part of the journey. Word had come to Samuel that Michael had been spotted in the dimension of Armedias, and Levi was asked to assist Samuel in learning more about this latest discovery. In a letter he penned to Reece before he left the palace, he expressed his apologies, but assured her that he would likely meet up with the convoy at their first stop on the way to Sandari.

They walked into the courtyard, which was filled with Pasidian Guards who patiently waited in perfect formation on their horses on front of two luxurious carriages.

Navarre led Allestaine to the first carriage before turning to see Reece and Elizabeth being ushered into the second carriage. The emperor gave a final word to one of the guards before he loaded into his carriage; and after a quick shout from the palace's guards, the massive convoy was on its way.

They traveled through an area of the countryside that Reece had never seen before, and the terrain that surrounded them was breathtaking. Flowers that were sprinkled throughout the meadows glistened in light of the brilliant sun, while an array of majestic birds flew in lazy circles throughout the cloudless sky. The subtle rocking of the carriage, the crisp, fresh air, and the majestic scenery they were traveling through, filled Reece with utter contentment. Even so, after nearly four hours of sitting in the carriage, she was starting to become weary. She glanced out the window of the carriage, wondering when they were to reach the first city that they would be spending the evening in. Her eyes widened in astonishment when she saw large boulders poking out of the grass, glistening like gemstones.

Large red rubies, yellow diamonds, and different formations of crystalline spears were scattered throughout the glistening meadows. The terrain was becoming plentiful with these stones as the carriages started their winding ascent up the mountainside. Reece was speechless; the polished mountains they were traveling through were transparent, and they illuminated a rainbow of different colors.

"Elizabeth," she finally managed. "Where are we? This is absolutely amazing!" she said with wonder.

Elizabeth beamed. "The Syskanah Highlands are glorious, are they not?" she said, as she glanced out of her window to admire the beauty as well. "There are many who travel great distances to view these sites."

"I can definitely see why." Reece answered, still awestruck.

The sounds of the horses' hooves clicking against the hard surface of the polished stone started to become muted, and soon after, the carriages halted completely. Elizabeth and Reece looked at each other in confusion, while it sounded like a mob of horses were aggressively approaching their location. Reece's eyes searched, but couldn't see anything but the gemstone mountains to her right, and a luminous forest of trees to her left. Deep voices of men subtly echoed, coming from the carriage in front of them. Reece glanced out of her side window, and her breath caught when she saw Levi standing amongst a group of men.

She pressed her lips together, trying to conceal her smile of excitement that he had already joined up with the convoy. "It's Levi, Harrison, and Samuel," she informed Elizabeth while she admired Levi, who was wearing his Guardian regalia. Areion, who stood patiently behind Levi, was also dressed in some type of black, shiny armor. To Reece's surprise, he had a round shield strapped to his saddle, while a long sword hung at Levi's side. She looked back at Elizabeth. "They look like they're getting ready to go to war," she said with a nervous laugh.

Elizabeth smiled faintly, and before another word was spoken, the door to their carriage opened. Levi propped one foot up on the step and reached for Reece's hand. His smile broadened as he raised it to his lips for a tender kiss. His eyes left hers for a brief moment to acknowledge Elizabeth. "Good afternoon, my ladies," Levi said with a smile. He looked at Reece. "I trust your journey has been uneventful thus far?" he asked with a wink.

Reece laughed as Levi guided her out of the carriage and

turned to assist his sister. The convoy had pulled into an open area, giving the horses a break, and giving the family some time to stretch their legs, and take in some fresh air. Levi drew Reece's arm up into his and led her over to where Samuel was relaying information about Michael Visor to Navarre.

"Is everything okay?" she whispered softly to Levi. "Why are you dressed like you're heading into a battle?"

"Protocol," he said with a soft laugh, "and yes, everything is perfectly fine. Whenever we enter another dimension with plans of confronting their leaders, we wear our Guardian attire." Levi led Reece to a more secluded area. "We believe Michael is in Armedias; however, their ruler, Lucas, will not comply with our requests to begin a search throughout his domain."

Reece stepped back and looked up at Levi. "Lucas—that name seems familiar."

"Yes, you may recall his obtuse comments toward my father in the council meeting on Earth."

Reece suddenly remembered that frightening day in Scotland, when Navarre presented her before all of the aliens in order to restore their trust in the Guardians to continue protecting their worlds and Earth. It was easy to remember who Lucas was; he was one of the few who looked human, and not like some frightening creature that she was sure would cause her nightmares.

"He was that young man who argued with your father, right?"

Levi nodded and smiled. "Correct."

"He's also an arrogant fool!" Harrison interjected, as he came up behind Reece. He looked down at her with his icy blue eyes and grinned. "It's been too long, Miss Bryant," he said, as he reached for her hand and bowed over it dramatically.

Reece laughed softly. "It's nice to see you again, Harrison. I have to admit, it's been pretty quiet around the palace without you there entertaining us all."

"This does not surprise me." Harrison responded with a wink as he clapped his hand on Levi's shoulder. "How'd this old man treat you while I was away? He has a tendency to become deeply depressed whenever I leave him behind to go on assignment. I can only imagine what you must have gone through."

Levi rolled his eyes while Reece smiled in response. "I have no idea how he did it, but he found a way to manage."

Harrison smiled and turned to greet Elizabeth, who was standing next to Reece. "It is always a delight, sweet one," he said, as he bowed properly over Elizabeth's hand.

"Harrison, it is always good to have you amongst us," she answered.

"Well, gentlemen, we have at least thirty more minutes until we arrive at our destination for the evening. I know our ladies must be famished, so we can convene this discussion later," Navarre said, and before turning to escort Allestaine toward the carriages. With that, the rest of the group followed behind. Levi, however, hesitated and used the opportunity to steal a quick kiss from Reece.

The next two days of travel to the Oxley's oceanfront estate went fairly quickly. Levi and Harrison followed close by the convoy on their horses, giving Reece plenty of time to admire him along the way. They traveled through numerous villages, stopping only to eat, before they were soon on their way again. The terrain they traveled through began changing on the third day. Glistening-white sandy hills replaced the vivid green pastures, and it became obvious they were nearing the ocean. Reece was eagerly anticipating what an ocean in Pemdas would look like, given the beauty of everything else in this world.

When the ocean came into view, it was absolutely breathtaking as she imagined it would be. Aquamarines, turquoises, silvers, and a brilliant jade color sparkled brightly off of the surface. The white foam of the waves rushing toward the shoreline appeared as if someone had thrown silver glitter into the water, and it shimmered brightly as the waves surged toward the seashore. It was like a whole new world inside of Pemdas was opened up to her. There were people walking arm in arm, using umbrellas to shade themselves from the sun. The trees were similar to palm trees, except their leaves were an iridescent green, and their trunks were shimmering white. The glittery sand gave Reece the overwhelming desire to ask if they could stop, so they could walk barefoot through it.

Seeing the coastline again made memories from her life in San Diego come rushing back to her. A strange pain stabbed in her heart as thoughts of her father returned to her. She hadn't thought about him much lately. Levi had filled the void that his death left her with; but for the first time since she had been in Pemdas, she saw a landscape that reminded her of being home with her father. She fixed her eyes on the surf rolling in as memories of her father flooded over her, accompanied by the grief of losing him. She inhaled deeply, and forced back the tears. *I miss you, Dad,* she said to him in her thoughts, as the carriage stopped unexpectedly.

Reece snapped out of her daze to find Elizabeth watching her with concern. She had been so absorbed with remembering her father that she hadn't noticed her cheeks were wet from tears that had been streaming down her face.

"Is everything okay?" Elizabeth asked, as she handed Reece a handkerchief to dry her eyes.

Reece sniffed, while blotting her wet cheeks. "Yes, of course. I'm sorry, it's very beautiful here. I grew up at the beach as a child—" Her words caught in her throat. She managed a confident grin, took a deep breath, and tried to speak with casual ease. "I guess all of my memories are coming back and hitting me all at once." She shrugged, but the uneasy pain in her heart was still there.

Elizabeth smiled and reached out, placing a caring hand over Reece's. "Do not apologize, Reece."

The door to the carriage opened. "We'll see you then, Harrison!" Levi called out, and then brought his attention to the ladies in the carriage. He glanced at Reece with an expression of sympathy and concern. He looked at Elizabeth, "I believe I will take this time to introduce Reece to the beauty of Pemdas' shorelines," his promising eyes returned to Reece's as he extended his hand to her. "We will see all of you at the estate this evening."

Reece accepted Levi's hand and let the beauty of his brilliant eyes ease her heartache. Having him in her life was so comforting, especially at a time like this. Before Reece could question what Levi was doing, he kindly guided her away from the carriage. The convoy was soon continuing its journey on the cobblestone roads, leaving Levi and Reece alone. Reece felt mildly embarrassed, wondering if she had caused a scene by becoming emotional in the carriage.

Levi turned to face her, and tenderly brushed his thumb under her eye, capturing a stray tear. "Care to join me on a stroll along the shoreline?" he asked softly.

This was exactly what she needed, and her heart swelled with love for this man. "I would like that, thank you."

Levi drew her arm up into his, and they strolled through the sandy banks and down toward the water. Reece, still somewhat frazzled by her unexpected emotions, remained quiet. She inhaled deeply of the salty air, enjoying the familiar fragrances of the beach. The warm breeze rushed through her hair and soothed her spirits even more. She leaned into Levi, absorbing everything she loved about this environment. "I haven't gone back to the beach since my dad died." Her eyes began burning again as she fought back the tears. "I was too afraid. There were too many memories of him there," she said, as she glanced away from Levi and studied the glittery foam of the waves rushing into the shoreline.

"You and your father were particularly close," he said in his low, smooth voice. "I learned that very early when I was assigned as your Guardian."

Reece nodded, but couldn't respond. Never once did she think that seeing a beach in Pemdas would resurrect these memories of her father. Now, here she was, an emotional wreck, and Levi was about to witness her having a total breakdown.

They strolled silently together through the thick, powdery sand before Levi stopped and pulled Reece into a sturdy embrace. "I remember the first time we were assigned to guard you." He placed a kiss on her forehead. "You had recently graduated high school, and I believe you were the first woman from Earth I had ever encountered who was distressed about the idea of leaving her home for college." He laughed softly. "You and your father walked along the oceanfront, and he seemed to be the one begging you to leave and follow your dreams."

"That was one of the only arguments my dad and I ever got into." Reece said as she looked up at Levi. "You were following me then?" she asked, intrigued by the idea that Levi was around at that time.

"Yes," he said, as he ran his hands along her back. "I thought it was admirable that your father encouraged you to pursue your goals, even though the last thing he wanted was your absence."

Tears formed in Reece's eyes again. "I turned down that university—I couldn't leave him, Levi." Her eyes began throbbing and burning as she forcefully fought back her tears. "I might've been a baby, but I was all he had for family after my mother died." She frowned, and then clung to Levi tighter, finding security in him. "So I decided to stay in San Diego for him; and how did he thank me?" She stepped back and stared intently out at the ocean. She crossed her arms and faced this memory as if she were looking her father in the eyes. "He left me," she said coldly. A shiver of guilt coursed through her as she tried to work through her emotions of anger. She sighed softly, and looked up at Levi. His handsome face displayed nothing but love and concern for her.

Levi traced his fingers along her forehead, and his gentle touch calmed her further.

Reece sighed again. "I'm really sorry about this. I truly thought I had made peace his death. How can I possibly be angry at someone for dying?" She sighed in defeat. "Even when I went to settle out the last of his estate before I was brought to Pemdas, I felt so much better about letting him go and moving on."

"My love, you mustn't fault yourself for having these emotions." He embraced her again. "Those who survive the death of a loved one are left with emotions that manifest themselves in many ways. The best thing to do is to embrace them, and know that it is your way of working through your loss. There is no right or wrong emotion, but how you react to them can either benefit you, or harm you." He affectionately brought his lips to her forehead. "You are never wrong to express them, as the more you do, you're releasing them and becoming that much closer to healing. That is not weakness; it is the single bravest act a person can do." He tilted her chin up so her eyes would meet his. "He will always be a part of your life, if only through your memories now."

Reece studied Levi's expression. "He would have definitely approved of you."

Levi flashed a tiny grin. "Is that so?" he said, with an arch of his brow. "A man from another world?" he teased. He caressed her cheek. "I will promise you this, my love; I will spend every day of my life ensuring that you are loved beyond measure, and that whether or not I have your father's consent of marriage, he will not be displeased with my care of his daughter."

Levi knelt down and removed the straps of her left shoe. Reece's heart skipped several beats as he tenderly caressed her ankle. He ran his fingers along the flesh of her calf muscle as he slowly removed the strap of her heel. After her shoes were removed, he interlaced the straps into his long fingers and rose up.

"Now, from what I recall, the woman I fell helplessly in love with has always enjoyed walking through the surf," He kissed her lips briefly, "and feeling the warm sand beneath her bare feet."

"I love you so much." Reece said as she wrapped her arms tightly around him. She dug her toes into the warm sand, absorbing the velvety texture against the bottoms of her feet. "Will you be joining me?"

Levi gazed at her for a moment before answering. "I believe I will be most fortunate to have the opportunity of admiring you strolling through the water from a distance."

Reece glanced down at Levi's polished, black shoes. "What a pity. I would've thought a Guardian would be much more adventuresome."

Levi arched his eyebrow, and smiled in response to her

challenging statement. "Well, if you must put it that way, Miss Bryant." he said, as he bent down and began removing his shoes and cuffing his slacks, "It would be my greatest pleasure to join you on an adventurous stroll along the shore."

They spent the next hour or so enjoying the solitude of the beach together. They walked through the shallow waves, holding hands and laughing when the unexpected larger waves caught them by surprise. On more than one occasion, Levi seized her firmly around her waist and drew her body tightly against his, kissing her ardently. It was more than enjoyable sharing these moments with him and Reece was content in every way.

When Reece was ready to move on, Levi helped her onto Areion, and used the vast, empty beach to his advantage. To Reece's greatest delight, they rode along the sands of the beach almost the entire way to the Oxley's beachfront estate. The sun had slid below the horizon on the ocean as they left the beach and began riding down cobblestone streets, passing various estates along the way. A large gate opened as soon as Areion approached the secluded road that led to the Oxley's estate.

They followed along the drive, which was lit by dozens of lanterns. Reece leaned back into Levi's sturdy chest as Areion cantered at a brisk pace down the road. She admired the illuminating foliage above them, watching multi-colored, glowing insects dart through the iridescent leaves. Areion's hooves clicking on the cobblestone surface, the sounds of the ocean waves crashing in the distance, and the harmonious sounds of the night creatures cast a spell of tranquility upon Reece.

They rode under a large, stone archway that opened up into a magnificent courtyard. A servant promptly retrieved Areion's reins as Levi helped Reece from the massive stallion's back. "Miss Bryant," Levi winked, as he offered his arm. "Welcome to Stavesworth Hall."

Chapter 5

Servants greeted them at the front doors, and behind them was a magnificent foyer. The estate paled in comparison to Pasidian Palace, but the décor was equally as splendid. The same Queen Anne-style furniture was placed throughout the foyer, giving an air of elegance. Reece covered a yawn as Levi led her to the alabaster staircase that curved up along the wall, leading to the second floor. A long day of traveling, coupled with her emotional upset from earlier, had left her quite exhausted by the time they arrived at Stavesworth Hall.

"Once you have freshened up, I will arrange to have

your dinner sent up to your room," Levi said in a humorous tone.

"Do I really seem that..." she paused for another yawn that escaped her. Reece shook her head. "Forget it; I don't think I have enough strength for Jasmeen to dress me up for dinner tonight." She looked up at him. "Would you care to join me?" she asked.

Levi brought his arm around her. "It would be my pleasure."

They turned down a long corridor and stopped in front of a richly carved entryway. Levi leaned over and opened her door, guiding her in. "This will be your room; I hope you find it agreeable."

Reece walked in, and serenity and comfort immediately engulfed her. The fragrance of lavender and vanilla filled the room. A beige silk fabric covered the walls, and was accented with alabaster carved trim and capped with an elaborately carved alabaster ceiling. Large French-style doors at the front of the room were separated by a white ornamental framed fireplace with a healthy fire glowing within it. Sheer white curtains danced in the breeze, blowing in and out of the front of her room.

"This is perfect," Reece said, feeling rejuvenated by every passing second standing in the room.

Levi brushed his lips over her cheek. "I will send for Jasmeen, and return within the hour when you are ready for dinner."

With that, he turned and left the room. Her bedchamber was located through the door to Reece's right. The mahogany four-poster bed sat in between two matching end tables holding dimmed porcelain lamps. The fluffy cream comforter and numerous pillows were so inviting, Reece had to resist the urge to climb onto the bed and sprawl out. Instead, she closed the door and finished locating the various chambers within her room. A bath was already drawn, and Jasmeen was laying out all of the supplies to prepare Reece for the evening.

After a rejuvenating bath, Reece dismissed Jasmeen for the evening, letting her know that she and Levi would be having their dinner on the terrace outside of her room. Before leaving, Jasmeen located a simple cotton gown for Reece to lounge in. Reece had finished tying the sash on her robe when Levi had returned to her room. The staff, carrying tablecloths and trays filled with silver-covered dishes and a tea set, walked purposefully out onto the terrace and began setting up an intimate dining atmosphere for the couple.

Levi's eyes roamed over Reece's lounging clothes, and his smile halted her breath for a moment. He said nothing, waiting for the staff to finish setting up their dining area. After the staff left the room, Levi brought Reece into a tight embrace.

"This may have been an unwise idea," he said in a low voice. "You are positively stunning this evening."

Reece smirked and stepped back. "You are biased. Believe me; the last thing I am right now is *stunning*. No makeup, no detailed hairstyle, no bells and whistles…just plain ol' Reece," she teased.

"*Plain* is not the proper term, my love." He swept her hair over her shoulder and drew his face in closer to her neck. "Natural beauty would best describe your utterly desirable appearance." He said as he placed a soft kiss against her skin.

Reece shuddered at the sensation of his warm breath against her neck, unable think straight.

Levi inhaled deeply. "I never would have believed that the aromas of vanilla and lavender could intoxicate one's mind in such a way," he said with a laugh.

Reece slowly opened her eyes to find him staring at her in amusement. She smiled at him lazily, recovering her senses. "I must keep that in mind in case Jasmeen decides to switch up my bathing products for some reason."

Levi grinned, took her hand and led her out onto the terrace. He walked over to their private, candlelit table and pulled out her chair. "Your chair, madam?" he offered politely.

The rest of the evening passed delightfully. Their private dinner was romantic and altogether enchanting. Reece's room overlooked the back side of the estate, giving her an excellent view of the ocean that was beyond the private gardens beneath the balcony. Glimmering insects darted throughout the tall trees and the star-filled, iridescent sky. The ocean reflected the majesty of the white, glistening moon high above it. The glassy waters sparkled in an array of silver, blue, and magenta colors, all of which formed swirling patterns beneath the seawater's surface.

When Reece expressed her desire to spend the remainder of their evening wrapped in his arms and to stare out at the glistening ocean, Levi happily accommodated her wish. He carried a chaise from her room and situated it out on the balcony to offer the best view. Reece lazily and contentedly reclined into Levi's embrace, asking him various questions about their home here.

His low, smooth voice was starting to have an effect on her emotions, and she twisted in his arms to secure a passionate kiss, cutting him off mid-sentence. Levi didn't seem to mind, as he softly laughed against her hungry kiss before his strong hands grasped along her waist and up her back. Everything was perfect, and this moment was making Levi irresistible to her wild emotions. She slowly withdrew and whispered in between placing kisses along his jaw, "I love you."

Levi's breathing had picked up, but before he could respond, a loud knock hammered against Reece's door. Reece glanced at Levi, somewhat startled by the interruption, only to find him biting his bottom lip as he closed his eyes. He exhaled frustration before opening his eyes and looking at Reece. "I can only imagine who that would be," he said, as Reece sat up.

Levi stood up. "Give me a moment," he said as he tugged on his waistcoat, straightening it.

Reece leaned back, her mind still dizzy from her emotions taking a rapid turn on her.

"An evening on the balcony sounds marvelous!" Reece heard Harrison proclaim loudly.

Reece stifled a laugh, as she heard the shuffling sounds of feet walking toward the terrace. Harrison stepped out and glanced at Reece with a knowing grin before turning to walk to the edge of her balcony. He placed both his hands on the rail. "Reece's room certainly captures the best view of the Sandarin Sea. Would you not agree, Lizzy?"

At that moment, Elizabeth and Levi walked onto the balcony. Elizabeth wore an apologetic expression, while Levi seemed utterly annoyed by the blatant intrusion. "Good evening, Reece," she said, smiling.

Harrison spun around and propped his elbows up on the banister behind him. He crossed one leg over the other, and stared down at Reece in reproach. "Is there any particular reason you and Levi over there have chosen to avoid sweet Lizzy and me tonight?"

"Harrison, calm down," Levi interjected while bringing out two plush chairs for Elizabeth and Harrison to join them.

Reece shrugged. "Sorry; the view from the room must have gotten the best of my manners."

"I'll say." Harrison nodded toward Levi. "You both

should know that I intend to keep all rumors at rest while we are here for the week." He teased.

Levi sat next to Reece and put his arm around her. "I'm fairly confident that you will be the one who, as usual, is the topic of discussion throughout the week's festivities."

"Those days are over, my friend," Harrison said smugly. "I'm certain the uproar at these particular festivities shall be caused by the fact that you are engaged to be married."

"Regardless of what is said," Elizabeth interjected, "I'm thrilled that Reece will be meeting some of our closest friends, and I'm confident they will all adore her," she finished with a reassuring smile.

"Confident or not, sweet one, this shall be Reece and Levi's first experience amongst royals as a couple."

Reece stared at Harrison with confusion. "Is it really going to be that bad?" she asked, feeling a little intimidated.

"Harrison is simply searching for conversation now that he's realized he's ruined our time alone."

"Mark my words; these young women will sing praises to your face, and as soon as your back has turned, their words will turn into venom."

"Harrison!" Levi interjected. "Are you aiming to make Reece uncomfortable at her first ball?"

"I'm fine," Reece retorted. She lifted her chin. "I think if I can handle Simone single-handedly trying to get me killed, then I can handle a group of gossiping women."

Elizabeth giggled as Harrison grinned and ran a hand through his dark blonde hair. "And now that you are prepared, let the festivities begin!" he said with a laugh.

The next evening, Reece was dressed impeccably for the Hamilton's ball. She, Levi, Harrison, and Elizabeth spent most of the day exploring the shorelines and caves that surrounded the Oxley's ocean-front estate. The day passed quickly, and Reece didn't want to admit it, but she was nervous about the Hamilton's ball.

One last glance in the mirror should have given her enough confidence to formally step out as Levi's future wife, but she struggled to remove the nervous emotions. Her emerald-green gown was exquisite in every way. Tiny white diamonds sparkled throughout the velvet material. It was the first gown Reece had worn that required four full underskirts, and it was somewhat uncomfortable. *How am I supposed to get around in this dress?* she thought nervously. She lowered her eyes, pressed down on the voluminous skirt and tried to imagine how she would fit in the carriage.

"You, my love, are unquestionably enchanting," Levi announced, as he entered Reece's dressing room.

Reece spun around. "Well, this is a pleasant surprise!" she said with a laugh.

"Jasmeen informed me that you were dressed and waiting for her to retrieve your jewelry for the evening."

Levi was perfectly polished, wearing all black aside from his green velvet waistcoat and silk cravat. He stepped toward her and slowly spun her around to face the tall mirror before her. "Something's missing."

Reece watched him speculatively. "I have to argue with you on that." She fanned her hands over her gown. "You see, this dress has four skirts, and—"

She nearly choked on her words when Levi held an open rectangular box in front of her. A large emerald stone glistened underneath the bright lights of her dressing room. It hung on a diamond string, and a slender emerald bracelet lay neatly in the middle. On the top side, two golden hoops with emerald drops dangled from the velvet material they were attached to. She reached out and brushed her fingers over the surface of the brilliant, polished stone. "Oh my goodness," she whispered. "These are extraordinary."

Levi pulled the necklace from the box and clasped it

around her neck. "Just another heirloom that your beauty surpasses, of course."

Reece let out a breath, clearly overwhelmed. "It's absolutely stunning." She turned to embrace him, yet he caught her hand, stopping her.

He glanced at the white satin gloves that she held. "These gloves are the only problem I have with your wardrobe this evening—," he started to say, as he removed the gloves from her hand and brought his lips to the inside of her wrist. He closed his eyes and inhaled deeply while pressing his lips tenderly against her skin. "This fragrance..." he said, "is it new?" His eyes reopened.

Reece managed to steady her emotions in response to the effect Levi was currently having on her. His jewel-like blue eyes were not helping as they bore into hers. "I was playing around with some of the perfumes Jasmeen made available, and I liked the smell of this one." She brought her wrist to her nose and inhaled. "It smells like a mixture of jasmine, and some kind of sweet fruit. I was hoping the oils weren't too strong, though."

"Quite the opposite; this fragrance is extremely pleasant, and now I am struggling with foregoing this evening's extravaganza and instead take you in my arms at this very moment."

Reece laughed and playfully tugged at his elaborately tied cravat. "Sounds quite enticing, Levi." She inhaled dramatically. "But I'm pretty sure if we skip out Harrison will more than likely come barging into the room and ruin everything."

Levi shrugged. "That is true."

"Now, if it helps," Reece started pulling on her elbow-length gloves, "I will keep these on."

He smiled, and clasped the emerald bracelet around her wrist. One more kiss to her gloved hand, and he drew her arm up into his. "Shall we go introduce the royals to their future empress?"

Chapter 6

The emperor's convoy arrived at the Hamilton's large estate about thirty minutes after departing Stavesworth Hall. As the carriages crept up to the entrance of the estate, Levi placed a reassuring hand over Reece's. He could sense her trepidation as the large number of people before them ascended the stairs into the manor.

Levi leaned into her. "I'm confident that you will steal all of their hearts with your energetic personality, as you did mine."

Reece laughed nervously as she stared out of the window. "I'm not used to being in the spotlight like this."

She exhaled. "Cross your fingers that I don't embarrass your entire family by foregoing some important Pemdai custom."

"Lucky for you, you're with the emperor and his family; and since we make all of the customs around here, we'll make sure you get away with it." He winked.

"Even if I use the wrong fork at dinner?"

"I wouldn't care if you licked your fingers." He smiled wryly.

"In that case, I'll be sure to take my gloves off before I eat."

Levi and Reece laughed in unison as the carriages halted. Levi put his top hat on, adjusted it, and gave Reece a confident smile. Her eyes glistened as she studied him. "You look extremely handsome in that hat."

"Enjoy it while you have the opportunity." Levi said dryly.

Their conversation was interrupted when the carriage door was opened by a servant. Levi stepped out and dismissed the man in order to assist Reece personally. Upon descending from the carriage, he drew her arm into his. He glanced down, and the pride he felt having her at his side was indescribable.

Together they followed Navarre, Allestaine, and Elizabeth into the Hamilton's home. Once in the grand foyer, the emperor and his family were greeted by King and Queen Hamilton, the hosts of the evening. King Hamilton, with his usual wit, managed to engage them all in a short, humorous conversation before the group was escorted into the large reception area. After numerous formal introductions to many different kings and their queens, Allestaine brought Reece and Elizabeth off alone and began introducing Reece to some of her closest friends.

Levi and Harrison stood in conversation with their

fathers while the guests awaited the announcement for dinner. From where he stood, Levi had an excellent view of the entire room. His eyes focused intently on Reece, watching in humor the numerous expressions that crossed her face. His heart swelled with love for her as he watched her animated personality radiate from across the room. The different women that she was being introduced to seemed impressed by her, and Levi understood why. There was something extremely unique about Reece's outgoing personality; she could make any stranger feel comfortable in her presence. Her kind heart, high-spirited nature, and friendly personality drew people to her; not only on Earth, but also here in this room of royals. For the first time in his life, he found himself enjoying one of these ostentatious celebrations.

"I'll say," King Hamilton said as he came up from behind Levi and clapped him on his shoulder, "I do not believe I have ever witnessed Levi appear so..." His eyebrows knit together as he studied Levi's face in humor, "so bright-eyed at a ball before." He finished with a teasing grin.

"That, my lord, is because Miss Bryant has never been in attendance," Harrison said with a laugh.

Levi pursed his lips in humor. "True."

King Hamilton grinned and addressed Harrison. "Surely the next surprise to be heard throughout all of Pemdas shall be when *you* settle down with a lovely lady of your own."

Harrison rolled his eyes as King Nathaniel, and Navarre laughed in unison. "The odds of you capturing a three-headed dragon are better than you seeing Harry settle down." Nathaniel teased.

"Not the analogy I would use, father, but I believe your point is well-taken."

Levi remained quiet and watched Reece discretely while the men continued to tease Harrison about his prejudices towards relationships. Dinner was announced, and the multitude of guests began filtering into the dining hall. Levi quickly made his way to Reece, and they followed behind the emperor and empress into the large room.

Levi noted the glint in her eyes and her bright expression. "You appear to be enjoying yourself, Miss Bryant."

"Indeed, I am, Your Imperial Highness." Reece teased as she smiled up at his amused expression.

Levi laughed and subtly rolled his eyes at her formality. He brought his hand up to cover the hand she had on his arm. "It appears as though we need to get you out of here before all of these Pemdai formalities start to take over."

Seating had been pre-arranged by the evening's hosts, situating the guests sporadically amongst each other. This was a common practice at social affairs in Pemdas, the intent being to encourage the guests to make new acquaintances.

Levi dutifully escorted Reece to a seat that was across the table and adjacent to where he would be sitting. He cringed when he saw the young man whose seat was next to hers. *How could Prather have possibly been invited to this event?* His lips tightened, but fortunately, he concealed his expression of irritation when Reece glanced up at him. He offered her a reassuring smile, and then strode over to his seat. After King Hamilton gave a quick greeting to the evening's guests, they were all seated, and the staff began bringing out an abundance of food.

As Levi ate, he politely interacted with the two young women seated on either side of him; but he was also keenly aware of Mark Prather's persistent conversation with Reece. The young man was disrespectful in every way. Of all the people Reece could be seated next to at her first social event, it had to be him.

As the meal slowly progressed, Levi felt his frustration rising. Each time Reece would attempt to take a bite of her food, the man would ask her a pointless question.

"Mr. Prather, I appreciate your fervent concern about how I feel living in Pemdas, but I would love the opportunity to enjoy this delicious meal, too," Reece said in a low voice.

"Miss Bryant, the food is quite delicious," Mr. Prather replied. "Do you find any differences in dining on Earth as to that of dining in Pemdas?"

The expression on Reece's face in response to Mr. Prather having ignored her statement was enough for Levi to finally intervene on her behalf. As Levi began to interject, King Hamilton abruptly spoke out.

"Mark Prather!" King Hamilton announced from the head of the table. "Tell me, how is your uncle these days?" He swallowed a sip of his wine. "You must know I was astounded to see you standing in for him this evening."

Levi sat back and watched intently as the young man's faced displayed frustration for King Hamilton's blatant interruption. Then, as the table grew silent waiting for the young man to reply, Mr. Prather's face turned to that of embarrassment. He glanced over at Levi, only to see Levi's disapproving expression, which was waiting for the man's response.

"Forgive me, my lord," Mark answered, after he brought a napkin to his lips. "What was your question?"

Maybe if you closed your mouth for once this evening, you would hear what people said when they spoke to you, Levi thought.

King Hamilton's eyes narrowed as he smiled cynically at Mr. Prather. "I do believe this is the first time I have ever been asked to repeat myself." He laughed as he looked at

Navarre sitting to his right.

Navarre studied the young man silently. Ever since issues with Simone and Michael Visor endeavoring to harm Reece had arisen, the emperor had a heightened awareness of those he didn't necessarily trust being in her presence.

"I believe the good king was inquiring as to why you are so fortunate to be in our presence tonight," Harrison interjected loudly from the opposite end of the table.

Mr. Prather glared at Harrison and cleared his throat. "Forgive me, King Hamilton; I thought you received the missive." he sighed as his expression turned to sorrow. "My uncle is still unwell."

"Unwell?" Navarre interjected with a stern expression. "This is certainly news to me. When did he become ill?"

"Your Majesty, please have no concern. My uncle seems to be recovering, although he did not wish to make the long journey to Sandari. He expressed his apologies in the missive." Mr. Prather took a sip of his wine, and Levi could see that the young man was seeking to avoid any more talk about his uncle's situation. "The kingdom is well, and I can tell you this from personally standing in place of King Prather while he has been ill."

Levi and Harrison exchanged knowing glances.

Navarre sipped his wine. "Mr. Prather, I am deeply interested in continuing the conversation after dinner." He looked at King Hamilton. "Perhaps we can retire to a more private area after we have finished dining."

King Hamilton nodded. "Of course."

"As I just mentioned, your Imperial Majesty," Mr. Prather spoke out boldly, "It is nothing of concern. Please do not relinquish your enjoyment of the evening's festivities over a simple illness."

Navarre's features darkened. "I will do as I please, Mr. Prather," he said in a low, commanding voice. "And right now, your uncle's health is of concern to me, be it your concern or not."

Mark nodded. "If it does please Your Majesty, the kingdom is quite well."

"As I said, we will continue this conversation in a more private setting." Navarre answered.

Levi exhaled at the blatant absurdity of the man. Fortunately, King Hamilton quickly spoke out, attempting to end the conversation until Navarre could speak with the man in private.

"Now, I wish for nothing more than my guests to be happily filled with their meal this evening; and it seems as though Miss Bryant might be the only one in attendance who may indeed leave hungry due to your incessant chattering at her. Perhaps you'll allow her a reprieve in order for her to take a bite?" The king said as he brushed his hand over his well-trimmed beard.

Mr. Prather's face instantly matched the color of his fiery-red hair. Levi smiled at Reece, who was refraining from laughter as she stared at the food on her plate. Navarre and Levi exchanged subtle glances, knowing that only King Hamilton would outwardly embarrass a guest in such a way. Even though it was brazen and may have offended some attendees, Levi didn't care, and once again found himself admiring the king for his bold personality. Although the mood at the table seemed to calm, Navarre seemed notably disturbed by his conversation with Mr. Prather.

The remainder of dinner was uneventful. Reece was finally able to enjoy her meal in peace, as Mr. Prather remained silent and unengaged from the entire dinner party. The guests were soon finishing their desserts, and Levi wasted no time dismissing himself and Reece from the others so that they could share a moment alone. They sauntered out to the balcony, both enjoying the crisp, salty air blowing in from the oceanfront. Levi used this opportunity to apologize to Reece for Mr. Prather's rudeness, and that she had to suffer through his interruptions at dinner.

Reece and Levi's solitude was soon interrupted by other guests slowly filtering out onto the balcony. The sounds of the orchestra tuning their instruments alerted Levi that the dancing would soon commence.

"Miss Bryant," he said with a grin. "I believe your first dance is spoken for by a gentleman who is significantly spellbound by your beauty. Shall we rejoin the guests in the ballroom?"

Reece lifted her chin and accepted his offered arm. "Yes, we shall."

The guests were lined up facing their dancing partners, waiting for the music to begin. Levi watched in humor as Reece stared down at his feet. He cupped her chin and raised her eyes up to meet his. "Nervous?" he asked softly.

Reece narrowed her eyes some. "I think *you* should be the one who's nervous."

The music began, and Levi took her right hand into his left, and placed his other on her slender waist. Despite Reece's nervousness about dancing, her performance was impeccable, and Levi was quite impressed. Once the dance was over, Levi led Reece to the refreshment table.

"This will be the most trying part of the evening for me," Levi said, as he offered Reece her flute of sparkling wine.

Reece took a sip. "So this is where we have to split up?" She smiled at him playfully. "Now, it would be an insult to the evening's hosts if I were to turn down a request from a man to dance with me, right?"

"If you are uncomfortable in any way, feel free to

dismiss yourself. You are not obligated to dance with everyone in the room."

Reece gulped the last of her wine, handed Levi the glass and said, "Don't even trip, I've got this." She smiled brightly. "You worry too much; I'll be fine."

Levi choked on his laughter, knowing very well he had nothing to worry about with Reece. He reached for her hand and brought it to his lips. "So it seems." He said with a laugh as Elizabeth and her closest friend, Angeline Hamilton, approached them.

"Ladies," Levi acknowledged them with a proud grin.

As Levi assisted the two young women with their drinks, King Hamilton approached from behind and requested a dance with Reece. Levi used this opportunity to admire his future wife from a distance. He also took notice that there were more men than women at this gathering, and it would be quite easy for him to avoid dancing with any partners other than his sister and his mother.

After a few dance sets with his mother, sister, and her friend Angeline, Levi spent the remainder of the evening in conversation with his father, King Hamilton, King Nathanial, and some of the other men. The night was playing out extremely well. Reece appeared to be extremely happy, and every now and then she would smile at him with a flirtatious grin. The only unfortunate part of the evening was that it wasn't passing fast enough, or so he thought. His selfish worry about wanting Reece all to himself was rapidly replaced with concern when she reentered the ballroom with Elizabeth and Angeline.

When they returned from what Levi believed was a trip to the ladies powder room, Reece's face was pale and expressionless. She made eye contact with Levi, and then quickly diverted her eyes and disappeared into the crowd of women standing near the refreshment table.

Levi dismissed himself from the group of young men he was in conversation with to find Reece. He wasn't sure what could have happened, but her lively appearance from moments before was non-existent. As he walked through the group of women, he was approached by Isabelle Hamilton.

"Levi." She curtseyed and gazed up into his eyes. "I haven't had the opportunity to speak with you this evening. Forgive my rudeness."

Levi acknowledged her politely while he continued to study his surroundings, looking for Reece. Given his current concern about his future wife, the last person he wanted to encounter was the woman he had formerly courted. Even though he was annoyed by the interruption, Levi had shown nothing but the proper respect for King Hamilton's oldest daughter. "Miss Hamilton, there is no need to apologize. There are many in attendance, and I am sure you have been detained by your guests. Think nothing of it."

"I was fortunate to make the acquaintance of Miss Bryant; she is a lovely woman." Isabelle looked longingly up into Levi's eyes, forcing an awkward moment for him. "She must be remarkable in every way, to have stolen your heart."

Oh, give me a break! Levi thought in irritation. "I am thrilled that you have met her." Levi said as he caught a glimpse of Reece exiting out to the balcony. "Excuse me, Miss Hamilton; there is something I must attend to," he said, abruptly ending their conversation. He knew it was rude of him; however, he was more concerned about Reece than Isabelle Hamilton's discomfort from his behavior.

Levi strode briskly across the room, but was interrupted by numerous people along the way. By the time he made it to where Reece was, she had accepted a young man's dance request. Levi discerned her discomfort and forced smile; but as the young man led her to the dance floor, she seemed as though she would cry at any moment.

Someone must have insulted her in some way, but what could they have said? She had dealt with all of Simone, Lillian, and Catherine's hatefulness amazingly well; and those three women were insulting and unwelcoming in every way towards her.

"A few more dances, my man, and you will have your lovely lady all to yourself again," Harrison announced, as he came up from behind him.

Levi continued to study Reece's expressionless face as she and her dance partner waited for the music to start. "Something's not right with her, Harrison," Levi said in a low voice.

Harrison scanned the room and found Reece. "I think any woman would have the same expression on her face, if that young man desired to dance with them." Harrison clapped Levi's shoulder. "Give me a moment; I'll go rescue her."

"Harrison!" Levi blurted out, but he was too late; his cousin was already on the dance floor, and about to do one of the most offensive things that could be done at one of these events.

Levi knew Harrison well enough to know that he didn't have a problem with breaching propriety in a situation like this. Inwardly, he was grateful for Harrison's boldness, and the scene it would create for Harrison to barge in and replace Reece's dancing partner did not concern him. He watched his cousin tap the man's shoulder, and smoothly step in his place. He then began to lead Reece to the music, ignoring any scene he may have created. Even Harrison's good humor did not change the expression on her face. Levi watched intently as Reece pointedly ignored Harrison, and appeared to force herself to get through the dance.

When the song ended, Harrison drew Reece's arm possessively into his, and with a subtle nod to Levi, led her out of the room. Levi followed, and caught up to them in the corridors.

"Really, Harrison, I'm fine." She acknowledged Levi with a smile when he approached. "I'm fine." She said reassuringly as she reached for his hand.

Levi felt the trepidation in her grip. Something wasn't right, but he wasn't going to make matters worse by forcing answers from her. Luckily, the evening was coming to a close, and Navarre and Allestaine began making their final farewells to the guests. Levi and Reece followed the emperor and empress in bidding everyone goodnight, and soon after, they were in the carriage on their way back to Stavesworth Hall. Levi's concern was growing by the second as she remained silent and leaned into his embrace.

"Sweetheart," Levi spoke softly, while brushing his hand along her arm. "Please talk to me; what has happened?"

"Really, it's nothing," she responded absently.

Levi pressed his lips into her temple, absorbing the rich fragrance that always assaulted his senses. "I would happily believe that, if your expression had not changed to one of absolute distress when you returned to the ballroom."

"I think I got a little overwhelmed by everything tonight." She looked up at him. "I'm feeling much better being alone with you now."

She wasn't being entirely honest with him, and Levi knew it. Levi brushed his hand over her cheek, seeing the troubled expression that she was trying to mask with a smile. "I love you," he said, with concern in his voice.

At the moment he said it, he caught a glimpse of tears filling her eyes before she quickly turned her head away.

"Reece..."

"Levi, don't…please." She sniffed.

Levi refrained from asking any more questions. Instead, he gently massaged her arm, as he contemplated how to get her open up about what had upset her so badly. By the time they arrived at Stavesworth Hall, Reece insisted on going straight to her room. Levi didn't have much time to argue, as his father requested a short meeting with him.

He led Reece up to her room and before departing, pulled her into a tight embrace. "Once I've finished speaking with my father, I will return to check on you."

Reece stepped back and looked up into his eyes. "And if I'm already asleep?" she teased.

Levi nearly sighed in relief when he saw the humor in her eyes.

Levi reached for her hand. "Then I will ensure that you are properly tucked in." He raised it to his lips. "Go freshen up, my love. Jasmeen can mix up a relaxing tea remedy for you."

Her smile was brighter now. "I love you."

Levi smiled, absolutely taken by her beauty. She raised her hand up to his lips, her fingertips delicately tracing them. "I so love this smile," she whispered, with a look of sadness.

Levi started to respond, but she turned to walk into her room. As he stood there, confused and struggling to make out what was going on, she turned back to him and smiled. "I'll see you when you get back."

Levi nodded, and then quickly turned to leave. As he made his way to his father's study, he desperately hoped that this meeting would pass quickly.

Chapter 7

Reece leaned against the balcony railing, observing the ocean waves as they slowly rolled into the shoreline. She watched as the waves crept up and swept over the glittery sand, drawing it back out to sea again.

"Miss Bryant, your tea," Jasmeen said, as she stepped out onto the terrace.

She turned around and smiled. "Thanks, Jasmeen."

"Is there anything else I can get you?"

"This is perfect, thanks."

Jasmeen turned to leave, giving Reece her privacy. Reece slowly sipped the tea, letting the unique flavor of it soothe her. She gazed out onto the surface of the water, watching the many brilliant shades of blue glisten. This time she wasn't able to appreciate the majestic beauty of Pemdas the way she usually did.

"This view has never appeared more enchanting," a low voice spoke from behind.

Reece glanced over her shoulder to see Levi leaning up against the doorframe. "It's really beautiful tonight."

Levi came up from behind her and wrapped his arms around her waist. He molded his body around hers while kissing her softly on her cheek. "You appear to be feeling somewhat better." He caressed her cheek. "I have something I want to show you; would you be up for a walk?"

Reece looked down at her cotton pants and navy blue top. "Hopefully the walk consists of staying inside my room, because I really don't want to put another gown on."

Levi's forehead creased, and then he laughed. "The route we will be taking will not require that you dress in a gown. You will be perfectly fine." He lightly ran his long fingers under the thin straps on her shoulder. "I will say, I am exceedingly grateful you chose to bring some of your clothes from Earth."

Reece sighed, feeling goose bumps cover her shoulder. "You find yoga pants and tank tops attractive?"

Levi's eyes grew somewhat mysterious as he smiled at her. "It reminds me of the way you dressed on Earth, and I find it extremely attractive." His lips twisted while he studied her. "It is also probably the reason we should leave your room quickly."

Reece smiled as she brushed passed him and walked over to her sofa. She picked up her light cotton jacket, pulled it on and exhaled. When she was ready, Levi approached her, clutched her hand, and led her to a door in her room she hadn't previously noticed. "These are the servants' passageways," he advised her as he led her through the dimly lit hallway. "Harrison and I used to play in all of these hidden passages as young boys," he added, with humor in his voice. "Those wooden doors over there were where we convinced his sister, Lillian to hide one time." He laughed out loud. "I thought we were merely going to lock her in the room; however, little did I know, Harrison had a mouse in his pocket that he threw in the room as I was closing the door. I do not believe I have ever seen our parents so upset with Harrison and me, after Lillian told them what we had done to her."

Reece laughed, but didn't feel sorry for the woman. Her opinion of her hadn't changed, as she recalled how Lillian had treated her when she first arrived in Pemdas. "Well, now I know why she grew up to be such a bi—" Reece stopped herself, prompting Levi to glance back with a wide smile.

"Yes?" he questioned in an encouraging voice.

"A real piece of work," she finished with a smug grin.

Levi smiled and brought his arm around her. "You could have used the other term, love. I will admit, it wouldn't be the first time anyone as referred to her or Simone in such a way."

"And you?"

"I've been known to agree with Harrison on more than one occasion about those women."

The stairs ended on a stone floor, and the fragrances of fresh herbs filled the area. She looked around, and saw that this was the area where the kitchen staff brought in the fresh produce and food for the Oxley family. Levi guided her through two doors, which led to an outdoor garden.

The herb fragrances became more potent as Levi led Reece past numerous, vividly glowing plant life. Lime-greens, yellows, and reds colored the leaves all around them. They stopped at the end of the long pathway, and Reece stood in wonder at the numerous vibrant blue rose blooms climbing archways that lined the entire length of the garden. They sparkled and glistened unlike any other bloom she had seen in Pemdas thus far.

The aroma of the unique blue roses was like a rich gardenia flower, and its color shimmered like a blue sapphire reflecting the light of the sun.

"If there is anything that could be comparable to the beauty of your eyes, it would be these roses," Levi said, as he plucked a bloom from the vine and handed it to her. "These roses only grow near the seaside; I thought you would like them."

"This shade of blue is so fascinating." Reece brought it to her nose and smiled as she looked into his radiant eyes. "But I have to argue with you, I've actually witnessed your eyes glow like this."

Levi smiled faintly. "That's simply a little quirk that I have when I am reading someone's thoughts."

Reece was reminded about her concerns from earlier. She quickly diverted her attention from Levi, and stepped toward the flowering bushes. She sighed softly, knowing she needed to talk about this with him, but not knowing where to start. "Reece," Levi said in a low voice. He reached for her arm, turning her to face him. "What happened tonight?"

Reece gazed past him, striving to gather her thoughts.

"Reece," he persisted.

Just come out and say it! she ordered herself. She mirrored his somber expression. "I know that you and I have already talked about the," she inhaled, *"complications* of our relationship."

Levi tilted his head to the side. "Yes, and?"

"Levi, I don't know how to say any of this, because I know you're already aware of what people might say—"

"I am," Levi simply stated. "Reece, I care nothing of what they think. All I care about now is who offended you outside of my presence."

She tucked a piece of hair behind her ear nervously. "I wasn't offended; I was actually enlightened."

"What happened? Please, be straightforward with me."

"I overheard Mr. Prather and a group of men talking in one of the sitting rooms while I was waiting for Angeline and Elizabeth to leave the powder room. I was in the hall, looking at the artwork on the wall when I heard a group of men speaking about how a foreigner from Earth would never be accepted as their empress. That you and your father have disgraced Pemdas by allowing such an abomination to take place."

Levi encircled her with his arms. "I do hope you will trust me when I tell you that those men's opinions are of absolutely no consequence, and you shouldn't let them affect your opinions about our relationship."

"Mr. Prather—"

"Mr. Prather has put himself in quite the complicated position with his emperor tonight."

Reece stepped back and looked up into a grave face. "What are you talking about?"

Levi's expression recovered some. "It appears as though Mr. Prather is quite the power hungry individual these days. My father believes he is part of a plot to destroy his uncle, King Prather, and has been trying to manipulate his way into reigning over Brunack Kingdom. Without going into detail that will only bore you, I can safely say that after my father has finished visiting the kingdom, Mr. Prather and his friends will never be a concern to anyone." He stared at her purposefully.

Reece turned away from him. "Levi, this isn't right. These men may not be a problem; but what about everyone else? What made me so ignorant to think I could take up residence in your world and think everyone would be perfectly fine with some foreigner marrying the intended emperor?"

"Foreigner?" Levi said with humor in his voice. "Reece, look at me."

She turned. "We could go on and on about this, Levi, but it doesn't change the fact that not only will people disagree with me as your wife, it could ruin the peace you have in Pemdas."

"Peace?" Levi looked at Reece as if she'd lost her mind. "Reece, my father is dispatching a group to investigate the fact that one of his kings is most likely being slowly murdered by a group of men, and you believe that there is harmony in Pemdas? Hardly; and without burdening you with what my father deals with on a continual basis, I will say that he is constantly involved with localized governments, ensuring that Pemdas will not encounter any unnecessary uproars."

She shook her head. "Has he considered what could happen if the majority of Pemdas opposes my marrying you?"

Levi inhaled deeply and took her hand. "Come with me," he said in a low voice, while reaching for her hand. When they were out of the garden area, Levi led her on a path that followed a stone fence line. The path led up a small hill, where three large buildings stood, detached and isolated from the main house.

"Where are we going?" Reece asked; a little confused as to where Levi was dragging her off to. She was slightly hesitant, given the outfit she was wearing.

"We're going to answer your question," was all he said in response.

Horse stables? she thought, as they walked in through a side door. They walked down the wooden floors in between the stables where the horses were being held. Some horses took notice of them, holding their heads over their stable door and watching in silence as Levi and Reece passed them. A deep whinny from their left alerted Reece to Areion, who seemed interested that they were in the stable building. Areion began nodding his head up and down, and softly pawed the ground.

"Areion, settle," Levi said, as he took the horse's reins off a hook. "Give me a moment," he told Reece, as he walked into Areion's stall.

As soon as Levi entered the stall, Areion began stamping his feet impatiently. "Settle," Levi firmly ordered the horse again as he brought a navy-blue, padded blanket over Areion's back.

Levi took the reins he held over his shoulder and brought them up over his head. She watched with apprehension as Levi's fingers encouraged the bit into Areion's mouth, and cringed when Areion bit down hard on the mouthpiece. Levi had the horse saddled and ready to ride within minutes of entering the stable. He tossed the reins up and over Areion's head, gripped the loose ends under the horse's chin, and led him out of the stall.

As Levi approached Reece, he reached out for her hand and walked toward the back exit of the stables. He said nothing, and neither did Reece; the only sound was the clicking of Areion's heavy hooves against the hard wood surface of the building. Once outside, they made their way along another path that led down toward the shore.

"Seriously, Levi," Reece finally spoke out. "What are you

doing?"

"You're about to find out."

Reece pressed her lips together, wondering how a horseback ride was going to solve any of their problems. Maybe this was Levi's therapy, but it was hardly hers. Even if they had an excellent ride, they would still end up where they started, facing a serious issue in their relationship.

The moonlight glistened on the water's surface, and the white sand illuminated like glitter. The view of the ocean from where they stood was absolutely astounding. A soft breeze blew the salty air onto her face and through her hair, and Reece's irritability started to fade away.

Levi softly called out to Areion, halting him. He turned to Reece and smiled warmly at her. "You questioned whether or not our relationship would bring problems however, after this night, you should be assured that our marriage will be accepted in Pemdas."

Reece's eyebrows knit together in absolute confusion. "Sorry, Levi, but you lost me somewhere between ending our conversation in the garden, and showing up at the horse stables." She laughed in disbelief at how their serious conversation somehow became a moonlit horseback ride on the beach. "I don't think riding the horse is going to help solve anything."

Areion grunted, and Levi smiled in response. "Do you remember what I told you about this particular breed of horse in Pemdas?"

"They're the only horses that can cross the protective barriers of this dimension," she answered.

Levi nodded. "And they have a unique way of reading whether or not anyone will bring us trouble."

She looked over at Areion, whose golden eyes seemed to bore through her.

"Areion can decipher emotions and people's mental

states very easily. This breed will not allow anyone or anything upon his back that would cause his land or master," he paused and grinned, "*complications*," he said slowly, using her word from earlier. "I trust this horse completely when it comes to his intuitive abilities."

Reece looked at him in confusion, "What are you trying to say?"

"You're going to ride my horse." He stated. "Now, if you'll allow me." He firmly gripped her waist and hoisted her effortlessly up into the saddle. "Swing your leg over the other side," he said, as he adjusted the stirrup to match her height.

"Levi! NO!" she said in a panicky voice, resulting in Areion grunting and shifting his weight from underneath her. "Please. We'll figure this out some other way."

Levi looked up at Reece with a smug grin. "No, we can't; now, relax," he said in a firm voice, and then observed Areion, who seemed as agitated as Reece was about this. "Areion, settle."

"I'm not riding this horse by myself." Reece said in a firm voice.

Levi didn't respond. Instead, he mounted the horse and sat behind her, alleviating Reece's fears. Areion seemed to calm down in the same moment she did. Levi reached around her and grabbed the reins that were hanging loosely around Areion's neck.

He carefully pried Reece's hands from where she held tightly to the saddle. "Take the reins," he said.

"Levi—" she said through clenched teeth.

"You have no reason to fear. Areion has already accepted that *you* will master him. Now, he is feeling every emotion you are experiencing. He senses your fears, and therefore, will not budge until you are prepared to ride. Your anxiousness is making him uneasy as well, which is why he is fighting you some."

Reece let out her breath, fighting to calm down and trust that Areion wasn't going to run wildly out of control. She may not have been around this horse much, but she had witnessed his personality enough to understand that he was a fierce horse, and she still couldn't understand how Levi mastered his high spirit so effortlessly. Areion began stamping his feet, and Reece shivered at the raw power coming to life beneath her.

"Settle," Levi ordered the horse. "Clear your thoughts, and encourage him to go," Levi said with a laugh.

Fine! She bit her bottom lip. "Let's go, boy," she said nervously.

Areion stepped out and began trotting down the beach. Reece tightened the reins, thinking that Areion was going to explode into his usual speed at any second. He didn't. Instead, his nose was pulled tightly into his chest as Reece fought to stay in the saddle and not bounce off his back.

"Give him his head," Levi instructed.

"What?" Reece responded in frustration, while pulling in hard on the reins.

"Loosen the reins, love."

She did, and Areion sprang into a gentle gallop. It took her a moment to adjust to the magnificent feeling of the powerful horse beneath her. Areion galloped gallantly along the oceanfront, and the liberation Reece felt was inexplicable. Levi's hands latched onto her waist as Reece began imagining the excitement of Areion moving at a faster speed. In the moment she desired it, the horse responded, gaining even more speed as he dug heavy hooves into the wet sands of the shore.

Reece squealed in delight, and then guided Areion toward the shallow waves rolling into the shore. The horse responded, spraying water up with every lift of his hooves.

Levi buried his face in her neck, trying to avoid getting wet. Areion kept at a steady pace through the water, soaking them. Finally, she guided him out of the water, and pulled back on the reins. Areion halted, and Levi dismounted before pulling Reece down with him. He gently kissed her forehead and pulled her close.

"Did you enjoy yourself?" he teased.

Reece looked up into his brilliant eyes, dancing with humor. Levi was completely soaked; his dark, wavy hair dripping wet. She reached up, ran her hands through his thick hair, and smiled in relief.

"Sorry I got you wet," she said with a laugh. "But you look adorable."

Levi arched an eyebrow as he clasped her waist and lowered her to the ground beneath him. Reece laughed in amusement as the dry sand of the beach coated her wet clothes. She giggled at her sudden discomfort, yet became entrapped by Levi's humored expression. Before she could say anything, his lips nuzzled her chin while he framed her face with his hands. "I believe the last time someone referred to me as *adorable* was when I was five years of age."

"Well, you looked adorable. And now," Reece squinted at him, "I have sand all over my back." She tried to squirm out from underneath him, but it was pointless.

"You're not going anywhere, Miss Bryant," he said in a lower voice. His eyes roamed over her face, and then he brought his lips down onto hers.

The discomfort of the sand clinging to her skin and her clothes faded as she wholeheartedly accepted his affectionate kiss. Everything disappeared; her concerns, her discomforts, and all of her anxieties. All that mattered was savoring Levi's always-tasteful kiss and passionate touch. She shivered with the knowledge of how safe she felt with him, how his love and affection made her feel complete, regardless of what anyone thought about their relationship. Her fears subsided, and her emotions became more powerful in response. She gripped his shoulders, rolling Levi onto his back. He moaned softly as his hands grazed her sides and rubbed along her hips. Her kiss became more possessive and fierce with desire for him.

They stayed this way for a long while, taking time to appreciate their strong love for each other. The waves crashed into the shore, while the leaves in the trees rustled in the soft breeze. As awkward as a moment like this was, both coated in sand in their wet clothes, it was also surprisingly pleasurable.

Reece slowly withdrew from him and stared deeply into his eyes. Levi smiled sluggishly, his brilliant eyes glazed. She smiled when she saw the clumps of sand in his hair, and traces of it throughout his face.

She started picking it out of his hair. "You're a mess," she teased.

Levi tilted his head to the side, running his hands through her matted hair. "You're beautiful."

Reece sighed, while continuing to pluck sand from his onyx hair. "What am I going to do with you?"

Levi grabbed her hand, and raised it to his lips. "Do you realize how fascinating it was to watch that horse respond to you as he did?"

She kissed his nose. "That was really incredible."

Levi sat up, bringing her to sit in front of him, facing the ocean. He wrapped his arms around her, and she happily relaxed back into his chest. "Reece, you are the only other person that horse has ever allowed to master him in such a way. Areion is extremely particular of anyone, and at times, he will even fight *my* will." He kissed her on the side of her face. "But tonight, he happily adhered to your riding him. If you cannot trust my word that our love will not cause our lands problems, trust the stubborn horse you recently rode. His intuition goes farther than you might understand."

Reece ran her fingers over his hands at her waist. "I'm not trying to insult Areion here, but how can a horse know if Pemdas will have problems because of you marrying a woman from outside of your world?" She twisted in his arms to face him. "How can he know if half of your world, or your entire world, will or will not rebel over my becoming your wife?"

Levi looked over at Areion. "Simple. He senses your spirit, your heart, and your enthusiasm."

"Levi?" Reece interrupted him. "I'm serious."

Levi became serious as his eyes intently stared into hers. "I am serious, too. However, it would bring Pemdas greater trouble if I were to renounce my leadership as their emperor."

"You wouldn't…would you?"

"What did I tell you the day I professed my love to you?" Levi gazed out toward the ocean. "Reece, if the kingdoms went to the extreme of voicing their disapproval of my choice in a wife, I would not hesitate for a moment to abdicate my throne." He laughed softly. "Believe me, they would not desire me as their emperor should I lose the only woman I could ever love over their ignorant opinions of you."

"You can't do that," she firmly ordered him.

"I will do just that, my love." He said resolutely. "When I courted Isabelle Hamilton I realized I would not be able to tolerate a marriage out of duty. After I ended that relationship, and before I fell in love with you, I was certain I would be a lonely man for the rest of my life."

"I met her tonight," Reece said, brushing sand off his taupe sleeve. "She's seems pretty nice."

Levi's eyes were unreadable when they locked onto hers. "Miss Hamilton is an amiable woman. However, she's not the woman I envisioned myself marrying. She is everything Pemdas expects as their empress, and frankly, it is all she has ever known. Growing up with the burden of being an entire world's next emperor isn't as charming as one would believe," he said with a laugh of disgust, "To have parents eyeing you skeptically, watching you and studying you in hopes that you would consider taking their child as a wife. To have every woman you encounter stare up into your eyes, longing for your attention, and seeing their strong desire to be the wife of an emperor is utterly repulsive to me." Levi ran his hand along her arm. "You never looked at me in such a way." He smiled. "Not only did you have a vibrant, strong personality, but you never changed how you interacted with me once you realized my status."

Reece smiled and reached for his hand. "I still have difficulty seeing you that way." She shrugged. "I think that's why all of this hit me so hard tonight. I keep forgetting about your position in this world."

Levi stood up and extended his hand down to her. Reece accepted, and when she was on her feet, he embraced her. "We will get through all of this together." He stepped back and caressed her cheek. "I am grateful that you told me this, as my father must be made aware of what you overheard as well so that he can determine if these men will act upon their words." His eyes were piercing as they stared into hers. "Your safety goes beyond that of being my intended wife. We will not be taken off guard again, as we were with Simone and Michael."

Reece nodded. "I just don't want our relationship to be the cause of any problems here."

"Do not concern yourself over that. As I mentioned before, I am prepared for it."

Reece smiled weakly. "If you're confident it won't be a problem, then I trust whatever you say. I honestly didn't want to make a selfish decision with our relationship.

"Of course I'm confident; I never doubted it for a second." Levi kissed her forehead. "And you feel that *I* worry too much?" He called for Areion and smiled at her. "Let us go. Tomorrow I shall take you into a town that is roughly an hour away; and if you like, you can start picking out items to furnish our new home."

"That sounds exciting." She said as she wrapped her arms around his neck, "I'm looking forward to seeing more of this kingdom we're in. I love you," she said as she stood on her toes and kissed him enthusiastically.

Chapter 8

The rest of the week in Sandari passed too quickly. Levi and Reece spent the majority of their time touring shops and picking out items of furniture to be delivered to their home. For the first time in his twenty-seven years, Levi found the usual bore of a shopping excursion quite enjoyable. Watching the expressions on her face as she contemplated what furnishings they should chose for their home was entertaining to say the least. It was obvious the process of furnishing a stately house was a daunting task. To Reece's relief, Navarre, Allestaine, and

Elizabeth joined in on a shopping excursion later in the week. With Allestaine and Elizabeth's assistance, Reece appeared more confident with the decisions she was making.

The morning of Levi's departure from Sandari, he patiently waited in Reece's sitting room while her maiden attended to her. With the implications of their relationship behind her, Levi felt confident that she would enjoy the rest of her stay before she returned to the palace. Navarre had been made fully aware of the conversation Reece overheard at the ball and had made arrangements to investigate the matter further. Relieved as he might be that Reece would be in no danger outside of his presence, he wasn't looking forward to leaving her so soon; if it were up to him, he would opt out of instructing the new Guardian recruits with Harrison, and spend the next two weeks enjoying Reece's company.

"Master Levi," Jasmeen greeted him as she returned to Reece's sitting room.

Levi stood. "Yes?"

"Reece will be out shortly," she informed him.

"Thank you, Jasmeen."

After a cordial nod, the maiden disappeared through the side door. Levi sat on the sofa and continued to patiently wait for Reece. Reece entered the room moments later, and Levi found himself, once again, enraptured by her radiance.

"I hope I'm not going to make you and Harrison late," she said with a humorous smile.

Levi stood and walked over to her. "Whether we are late or not, I can assure you I have no problem with it." He reached for her hand and brought it to his lips for a tender kiss. As he rose up, his eyes took in the beauty of her creamy skin, highlighted by the blue silk gown she wore. Her daring neckline was tempting beyond all measure, and

Levi was now desperately searching for an excuse to get out of training the new recruits. "You look absolutely stunning, and I believe Harrison may be making this journey on his own."

Reece encircled her arms around his waist. "You and I both know that you're not getting out of this."

Levi smiled wryly. "Well, in that case," he said took her into his arms and brought his lips down onto hers. Her fingers traced through his hair, as he deepened their kiss. A soft laugh from Reece ended their fervent kiss much sooner than Levi would have liked.

"We should probably get going," she said, with a smile in her voice. "You're already late, and now I'm having second thoughts about you leaving."

Levi stepped back, tenderly kissed her forehead, and then offered his arm. "If you insist."

"So I've been thinking," Reece said, as they walked out into the corridor. "I can't get it out of my mind how exciting it was to ride Areion. It seemed so much easier than having to ride sidesaddle, and I was wondering if I could look into getting a riding outfit, something different than riding in a dress."

Levi glanced down at Reece. "The future Empress of Pemdas riding a horse in a man's riding suit?" he teased. "I dare say, you will definitely give the Pemdai people cause for concern."

Reece laughed. "True."

They made their way out onto the landing, where the groom was waiting with Saracen. Before Levi could respond to Reece, he heard his stallion whinny loudly as he was being led into the courtyard. *What's his problem?* Levi thought, wondering why his horse appeared so agitated.

"It appears Areion is as upset about leaving you as I am," he said, as he removed Reece's arm from his. "Let me see what his problem is."

Levi strode toward where the groom was fighting to hold onto his horse.

"Your Imperial Highness, I have examined him thoroughly, and am unable to determine what is distressing him."

Levi ran his hand along Areion's neck and walked along the horse, watching any movement the horse made in response to his firm touch. When he glanced down, he observed that Areion's right hoof hardly touched the stone walkway. Levi ran both hands slowly down the horse's hind leg, feeling for any swelling. Areion grunted and tried to jerk his leg out of Levi's grip when Levi lifted his hoof to examine underneath it.

"Settle," he ordered the horse, while keeping a secure grip on Areion's leg. Levi bent over and studied the horse's shoe for a moment before he found the problem. He pressed his finger against the edge of the silver shoe and found that Areion's hoof was not trimmed properly to fit over it. For any other horse, this would not be a problem; however, this was Areion, and his stallion was known for his particularities. Levi exhaled softly, annoyed about his horse's spoiled nature. *Areion, I should retire you to the pastures! Javian spoils you far too much.*

Areion audibly protested the thoughts he read in Levi's mind, and tried to jerk his foot away.

"Is he okay?" Reece called out from the steps.

Levi unbuttoned his waistcoat and pulled out his concealed dagger from its sheath. "He's perfectly fine." He glanced over at the two groomsmen that were intently watching him. "It appears that the farrier didn't get a proper fit for this shoe."

"I will arrange for the farrier to have him shod properly, Your Imperial Highness," the man responded hastily.

Levi pulled Areion's hind leg up and grasped it with his knees. "There is no need for that; I can fix the problem," he said while he began trimming Areion's hoof to fit flush on top of his shoe.

When Levi finished, he rose up and dismissed the two groomsmen, thanking them for their service. He gave Areion a final going-over as he put his dagger away. "Next time, I'll just remove the entire hoof," he taunted.

He gave Areion a sturdy pat on his rump, and turned to walk back to Reece. When he approached, she arched her right eyebrow sharply. "Just when I thought I couldn't possibly find you any more attractive, you do something like that."

Levi's eyes followed hers, back to where Areion stood. "I didn't realize that a man dealing with a highly obstinate horse could be attractive." He said as he finished buttoning his waistcoat.

To his surprise, Reece wrapped her arms around him and stared seductively into his eyes. "I'm really going to miss you over the next couple of weeks."

Levi happily welcomed her gesture. He buried his hand in her golden hair, and indulged himself in the pleasure of her offered lips. His other hand tightened around her waist, drawing her closer, and made sure this kiss would last until she was in his arms again.

"I think both of you should probably consider the Pemdai wedding ceremony," Harrison proclaimed boldly from behind them.

Reece jerked and tried to pry her lips from Levi's. He was amused by her reaction; however, felt no sympathy for Harrison's discomfort at finding them in such a passionate state. He withdrew slowly and glanced over at his cousin who was standing proudly on the top step. Levi brought his arm around Reece as he acknowledged Harrison.

"You're late!" Levi said. "And I was simply making the best of the inconvenience your tardiness has caused me."

Harrison grinned mischievously. "Yes, indeed. Nevertheless, I am only late because I decided to have the staff prepare me breakfast after I learned that you were waiting for Reece to walk you out." He glanced down at Reece. "It appears that my predictions were correct, and I still haven't given you both enough time for farewells."

"You're lucky I'm not demanding he stay here with me." Reece teased.

Harrison rolled his eyes and hopped down the steps to Saracen. "Such possession is not in your nature, Reece." He stepped a foot into his stirrup and hoisted himself up onto his stallion's back. "It never has been."

Levi laughed as Reece folded her arms and tightened her lips as she stared at Harrison. Levi leaned down and whispered. "It's best to let him have this argument, love." He embraced her before turning to leave. "Enjoy shopping, and I will see you when you return to the palace."

"I love you," she muttered against his chest.

Levi kissed her forehead. "And I love you."

He reached for her hand, raised it to his lips, and turned to walk down the stairs toward Areion. Once on his mount, he gripped the reins and winked up at Reece.

"Don't spend too much money, Reece!" Harrison called out.

Reece returned Harrison's smug grin and then offered Levi a brilliant smile. Levi nodded and smiled warmly at her before guiding Areion out of the courtyard.

Levi and Harrison were halfway down the estate's long drive when Harrison observed Areion fighting the reins for a faster speed.

"Might as well make up some time," he said with a laugh. "Want to race?"

Levi studied Harrison for a moment. "In truth, why were you late?"

"As I mentioned before, I opted to give you and Reece—"

Levi laughed aloud and shook his head in disbelief. "Did you actually walk away without some poor woman slapping you across your arrogant face?" he said with laughter.

Harrison shrugged. "You know me too well, my friend!"

"The only time you ever offer to race these horses is when you have a false sense of confidence."

"A false sense of confidence, now is it?" Harrison huffed. "I do believe I may keep this lovely lady around for a while."

Levi's eyebrow's shot up in humor. "Oh? How gentleman-like of you," he replied in a mocking tone. "May I ask who this lovely woman is who has achieved the impossible?"

"You may not," Harrison responded smugly.

"I didn't think so." Levi answered and eyed Harrison's cheek. "It is red; but fortunately, this one didn't leave a sweltering bruise on your face."

Harrison smirked. "I moved quickly. I couldn't risk the new recruits seeing their instructor in such a pathetic way."

"Of course not," Levi replied in humor.

Instructing the new recruits helped the week to pass quickly. Since the palace was offering tours during the emperor and his family's absence, Levi and Harrison spent their evenings either in the command center with Samuel, or dining in Casititor with the other Guardian instructors.

Two nights before Reece's intended arrival at the palace, Samuel notified Levi and Harrison that they were to return to Earth for an assignment. Levi would have argued, but understood he was fortunate to have had this long of a reprieve from guarding Earth, given the Guardians were being kept continually busy.

Levi penned a quick letter to be delivered to Reece upon her arrival, letting her know that he would most likely be on Earth until Samuel ordered their return.

As he made his way down to the stable, he noticed something strange about his horse's demeanor. Levi called out to him stridently, but the horse would not respond to his command. He was attentively focused on another Guardian horse, and was keeping it separated from the rest of the herd.

Levi watched Areion charge out of the herd, throwing his front hooves into the other stallion. His brows furrowed as he tried to understand what issue Areion had with the other horse.

He watched every move the rivaling horses made. As Levi approached closer, he noticed it was Michael Visor's horse. *Why is that horse free from his stable?* he thought in disbelief.

"Are we to gaze upon horses all day and dream of our bride-to-be nestled in our arms?" Harrison called out, as he came up behind him.

Levi turned toward his cousin. "Why is Michael's horse out with the herd?"

Harrison scanned the field where the horses were. "That is an excellent question. Areion seems as upset about the situation as you are."

It remained a mystery that a trained Guardian horse would transport someone with evil intentions across Pemdas' barriers. Somehow, Michael was able to manipulate his horse to carry him and Simone across the vortex with the intention of betraying Pemdas. This horse was a danger to Pemdas, making Michael, if he had possession of this horse, a danger as well.

Levi shook his head, extremely annoyed by the

negligence that produced the hostile situation between the rivaling horses. He turned toward the stables to question the stable master, Javian. As he and Harrison strode briskly into the building, Javian approached him with the same look of distress.

"Master Levi, we are aware of the situation, and I have my men tending to it now," Javian informed him.

"How is it that Michael's horse is free from his stall?" Levi demanded.

Javian swallowed hard. "Master Levi, there is no excuse. I am as shocked as you are. I found him only moments before you arrived for Areion. We have questioned Christian, the stable man who was in charge of him, and he has no answer as well. We are unsure at the moment if someone intentionally turned him loose, or if a young stable man mistakenly did so. I will arrange to have the horse put down; it is my only option."

"You will not put the horse down. We will have him retrained and looked after. If I must, I will work with him myself when I return from Earth. For now, retrieve him and find a better way to secure him. It would be best if you reinforced new locks on his stall gates, in case this was not an accident. Until Michael has been found, we will not take chances with this horse. Also, inform the emperor of what has taken place; he must be made aware of this."

"We will do so immediately," Javian answered. He cleared his throat, "Forgive me for not having prepared Areion. I was distracted by trying to assemble a group to attend to the soured horse."

"I will prepare Areion myself. Just remove that horse and lock him away. I will make it a priority to work with him upon my return."

After the morning's delay, Harrison and Levi were finally en route to Earth. Levi and Harrison raced their horses toward the protective barriers that led to the outer boundaries of Pemdas. Saracen remained in the lead; but it was when they made it to the empty void that Areion found his next burst of speed. As the horses landed gracefully on the other side of the great divide, Areion charged through the forest. Levi glanced back and saw Harrison's look of defeat as they arrived at the gates.

Both men dismounted and ordered the horses to return to the stable yard.

Levi glanced at Harrison. "You already know Areion enjoys defeating you and Saracen in such a way," Levi said, as he clapped his cousin on the shoulder.

Harrison laughed and plucked a vibrant red leaf off of a low-hanging tree branch. "I will never be able to understand how your horse has such energy. Enjoy the victory once again, my friend," he said, as they walked into the stone structure where their car was.

Harrison found his usual place in the driver's seat. "I must say, I'm glad to be returning to Earth."

"I agree," Levi answered, as Harrison pulled the car out of the structure. "It's good to be back into somewhat of a routine again."

"Indeed it is." Harrison said as he sped down the road toward the vortex that was designated to bring them to their assigned location; a small town in Wyoming, which was home to a possible impending abduction.

As Levi and Harrison came through the vortex, they traveled down the highway which would lead them to their destination. Levi was too preoccupied retrieving their assignment information from his communication device to notice Harrison traveling at a high rate of speed. It was when he heard a siren alarm, and he saw the blue lights out of his side mirror, that he exhaled in annoyance.

"Nice one, Harrison! You know how these small towns

are. Their law officials only remain out on these roads in the hopes that someone would speed past them."

As Harrison tried to find a place to pull the car over, he glanced at Levi. "Are you already turning into an old, married man on me? You should thank me for adding a little flavor to our exciting Wyoming trip," Harrison said, as he brought the car to a stop on the side of the road.

"Well, I certainly won't be thanking you if I end up spending my night in a jail cell."

Before Harrison could answer, the officer approached the vehicle.

"Sir, I'm gonna need to see your license and registration. Do you know how fast you were going when you passed me?"

Harrison cleared his throat. "I'm sorry, Officer. I thought I was driving the speed limit." He looked at the officer, feigning innocence.

The officer bent down to study both men in the car. "You believe that ninety miles per hour is the speed limit? Where are you two gentlemen headed this afternoon?"

"Officer, we are headed to Laramie, on our way to a business conference."

"Where are you coming from? I see your vehicle's plates are from New Mexico."

Harrison smiled as he handed the officer his license. "Yes, sir. Roswell, New Mexico."

The officer narrowed his eyes at Harrison. "Roswell? And you chose to drive instead of fly? That is quite a long drive for a business conference."

"You're telling me! You see, my friend here is terrified of flying, so we must travel by car. I apologize for my speeding; I believe I've been so anxious for this trip to be over that I didn't recognize how careless I was being." Harrison sighed as he leaned his head against the headrest.

"And now, it would seem that I not only have the pleasure of driving the entire way, but it looks like I get to pay the speeding ticket as well."

The officer stared at Harrison suspiciously. "I'm glad you're willing to accept that, sir. Please give me a moment."

As the officer walked back to his car, Levi ran his hand through his hair in agitation. "Harrison, find a way to end this quickly. Roswell? Really?"

"Levi," Harrison answered in annoyance. "You need to relax. Where is your sense of adventure?"

Levi laughed. "My adventure awaits in the town of Laramie, if we ever arrive there. This is a waste of our time. I am sorry that my idea of adventure doesn't include getting a speeding ticket and playing games with law enforcement."

The officer soon returned and handed Harrison his citation. When he finished his reprimand of Harrison's reckless driving, he sent them on their way.

As Harrison eased the car back onto the road, Levi looked over at his amused cousin.

"Well, congratulations on your speeding ticket. Your heart must be on the verge of bursting from all of the adrenaline coursing through your veins," Levi quipped.

Harrison shrugged. "Well, I tried. It is not my fault the officer was in the same dull mood you are currently in."

They arrived in Laramie an hour later, where they were instructed to wait for their person of interest to make their appearance. They spent the next three days going through their usual routine of making preparations for the assignment.

Late in the afternoon on their third day in Laramie, Samuel confirmed to the men that there was a plan of abduction set to occur that night. Reports from other Guardians came back that it was planned to take place at a small bar on the edge of town. Levi and Harrison dressed themselves appropriately to blend in with the townspeople, and made their way to the bar. Upon their arrival, they discretely secured a secluded seat at a small table in the back corner of the room.

"It is strange that the Armedites keep choosing to abduct people from Earth. They've never had any interest in this planet before," Harrison contemplated softly, as he studied the patrons in the bar.

Levi sipped his water. "I believe Lucas was offended by the outcome of the council meeting far worse than we assumed."

"Either way, it's his problem since the Guardians enjoy the constant action."

As Harrison finished his sentence, their person of interest walked into the room. Harrison grinned as the attractive woman glanced over at the table where the men sat. She offered him a flirtatious smile in return, and turned to exit the bar. Unsure of her plans, they stood immediately to follow her out.

"This is interesting," said Levi, as he glanced at Harrison. "I was unable to read her thoughts."

"Since when do Armedites have protected minds? Whatever Lucas is up to now, whether he's striving to distract us with beautiful women or send us on wild goose chases, he's accomplishing nothing."

As the men exited the bar, they found the woman walking toward their car.

She traced her fingers along the polished surface of the vehicle as she slowly walked the length of it. "It appears that I didn't give the Pemdai Guardians enough credit," she said, as she stopped and turned around to face them. She smiled seductively, "It seems as though you already knew I was planning to take a human with me tonight. So what happens now? Is this where you take me prisoner?"

Harrison smiled charmingly at the striking woman. "I beg your pardon, madam, but the action has not taken place; therefore, we have no problem with you."

Levi examined the woman's long red dress, and questioned what her true motives were. It was frustrating that he couldn't read her mind and get this over with. "Tell me, what are your intentions on Earth? By the way you're dressed, I would not believe you were prepared to take a human from Earth into Armedias."

The woman gazed into Levi's eyes. "You are Levi Oxley, are you not? Emperor Navarre's only son?"

"Who I am is none of your business, madam. I believe I was the one asking the questions."

She smiled adoringly. "So, Levi Oxley, it was especially intriguing to hear the news of your engagement. I believe this will be a first for Pemdas; an empress from Earth?"

"How would you know that?" Levi snapped.

The woman smiled. "Well, you have fallen in love with the one person every world seeks." She gazed speculatively at him. "May I inquire; do you really love this mundane creature? Or is this how you plan to find your importance with your father?"

"My personal affairs are none of your business. Tell me now, how do you know any of this?" Levi demanded.

"We have a new resident in Armedias, and Emperor Lucas, could not be more thrilled. You see, Michael Visor has given our emperor more than enough information about Pemdas."

"So Michael *is* in Armedias." Levi answered as he glanced at Harrison. "Inform Samuel that we will be escorting this woman to Pemdas for further questioning."

The woman giggled. "I look forward to it. I cannot wait to meet the future Empress of Pemdas."

Levi's expression grew dark as he glared the woman. "It

would be wise of you to not concern yourself with her."

"My concerns are not what you should be worried about. Emperor Lucas and Michael have their own plans for the Key!" she sneered.

Without warning, Levi seized the woman's arms tightly. "Those plans shall be the last they ever make," he growled.

At that moment the woman's expression went blank, and a painful jolt of energy radiated through Levi's body. Instantly, he released his powerful hold on her and mentally conquered the pain.

The woman stumbled backwards, eyes wide as she pointed at Levi. "Levi Alexander Oxley...*you* know where the stone is!"

Chapter 9

The carriages arrived at Pasidian Palace as the sun was slipping below the horizon. Reece was completely exhausted, and wanted nothing more than to go straight to her room and collapse on her bed. Even though the journey home was tiring, she did, however, thoroughly enjoy her time with Allestaine and Elizabeth while Navarre handled the issues regarding King Prather.

Navarre's investigators uncovered a plot that a group of men had put in motion to take over the Brunack kingdom. Medical personnel had confirmed that King Prather had been slowly being poisoned over the previous month, but with proper treatment he was making a full recovery. Upon conducting many interviews at the king's palace, the group of men were implicated, imprisoned, and awaiting trial. Mark Prather could not be directly linked to the men, but after hearing Reece's report about Mark's opinions of her, the emperor requested Mark Prather stay under close guard while Reece remained in Sandari. The imperial guards were assigned to follow the man discreetly to ensure that there would be no plots formed or carried out against Reece.

While Navarre spent the remainder of their visit tending to business, Allestaine took Reece and Elizabeth to various shops, purchasing an abundance of items for Levi and Reece's engagement celebration. Reece was astounded by Allestaine's stamina; and toward the end of their stay in Sandari, Reece had finally grown weary of shopping and wedding planning. She laughed inwardly at the fact that she no longer had any clue as to what they had purchased or why they had purchased it.

After dinner that night, Reece's wishes were granted. The entire family retired early, and she was able to fall into a much-needed slumber earlier than she anticipated. Even though it was strange to be back at the palace without Levi, Reece knew that she would be so preoccupied helping Allestaine to prepare the palace for the engagement celebration that she wouldn't have much of a chance to miss him.

The next morning she woke up well rested and ready for the day. Allestaine had planned to start going over the details of decorating with the palace's staff after their lunch. Because it was their first day back at the palace, everyone had matters of business to attend to, leaving Reece with some free time on her hands.

In the letter Levi had delivered to her while she was away, he let her know that Arrow had returned from his training, and she could go visit him at her leisure.

As soon as Reece was prepared for the day, she grabbed some apples from the palace kitchen and walked out toward the stables. When she approached the field where the Guardian horses were grazing, she leaned against the fence and searched for Arrow. It wasn't but a few seconds later that a horse stopped grazing and directed his attention toward her.

There is no way he grew that fast! she thought as he trotted over to her briskly. The young colt was now practically fully grown.

She handed him one of the apples and ran her hands through is long, silky mane. "Look how big you've gotten, boy!" she said, as she patted his strong, muscular side. "Levi was right; you have grown up."

While Arrow indulged himself with the juicy apple, Reece was surprised to see Areion trotting boldly over to them. When he arrived, he stood tall and magnificent before her. Areion glanced over at Arrow, who was finishing the last of his apple, and then back to Reece. When he pawed the ground with his hoof and grunted, Reece laughed in response, knowing the massive stallion was expecting her to give him an apple as well.

She reached out and carefully raised her hand to pet the side of his face. "Hey there, Areion!" she said enthusiastically. "I would love give you an apple, but I'm not sure Levi will be okay with that."

"Good morning, Miss Bryant," Javian said, as he approached her. "Are you surprised by how much your young colt has grown?"

"To say the least," she said with a laugh. "He looks like he's old enough to be ridden already!"

Javian chuckled. "In about a month he'll be ready for the saddle." He patted the colt on the shoulder. "I must say, it is intriguing to watch these horses take to you the way they have. I do not believe I have ever seen Areion approach anyone out of his own volition, except for Master Levi, of course."

Reece smiled. "He's only here for an apple. I'm pretty sure he watched me give Arrow one."

Javian laughed. "I would agree with you, ma'am; but if these horses were that easily persuaded, you would have hundreds of them patiently waiting alongside Areion."

Areion brought his head over the fence and lightly nudged Reece's arm with his nose.

Javian chuckled. "I believe he is waiting for his apple."

"I'm not sure Levi would be okay with that," she said, while petting Areion down the center of his face. "He gives me a hard enough time about spoiling Arrow. I wouldn't want him to think I'm ruining *his* horse now," she said with a laugh.

"Areion will be fine. He tends to be on edge when Master Levi is away, and since he will be gone until next week, I am sure having a treat will help to ease Areion's angst."

"Next week? Is everything okay?"

"Everything is perfectly fine. I was recently informed that Samuel has requested Master Levi and Master Harrison stay on Earth for another assignment after they have finished their current one."

"Sounds like it's pretty crazy on Earth right now," she said, as she petted Arrow, who was nudging her for more attention.

"Indeed, it is; we have never had so many Guardians dispatched at one time," Javian said, as he softly chuckled at Arrow attempting to reach for the basket in Reece's hand. "Master Levi wanted me to inform you that if you wish to bring Arrow on your afternoon walks with you, he might help pass the time if you get a bit restless."

Reece smiled in return. "That sounds like it would be fun. Maybe after Elizabeth is finished with her studies, we'll get Arrow out on a walk."

"Very well," Javian answered. "If you'll excuse me, I must be returning to the stables."

Reece searched into the basket and retrieved two more apples for the patiently waiting horses. She watched in amusement as the horses devoured their treats enthusiastically. Without notice, both horses startled and snapped her out of her daze. Areion whinnied loudly, and Arrow fled swiftly back to the herd.

Reece stepped back, mildly frightened by Areion's spontaneous aggression. She was perplexed; nothing seemed to have transpired to startle either horse. She looked around for Javian, but he was nowhere to be found. Areion reared back, and began pacing hostilely along the fence line in front of her. It didn't take long before she decided it would be best for her to leave and allow the horse to calm down.

Reece turned around and was stunned when she saw Simone approaching her. She was so shocked at the woman standing before her that she didn't hear Javian call for Areion and Saracen, to prepare them for Harrison and Levi's return.

"Good morning, Reece," Simone softly spoke, "Please forgive me for startling you."

Reece's body tensed. *You've got to be kidding me!* If there was ever a person she wished she would never have to see again, it was Simone.

"Simone," she answered in a low voice. "What are you doing here?"

Simone smiled pleasantly at Reece. "Since my sister has joined Lillian in traveling abroad, and my father is rarely home these days, it was growing quite lonely around our estate. I thought it best to join him here until Catherine returns."

"Oh, well, I was heading back inside. I guess I'll see you around," Reece said dismissively, as she started to walk past her.

As Reece walked past Simone, the woman called after her. "Reece?"

Reece stopped, closed her eyes, and exhaled. She turned around to see Simone manage an uncertain smile.

"What do you want, Simone?" She crossed her arms and stared darkly at the woman.

Simone stepped toward Reece. "Before you leave, please hear me out. The main reason I decided to visit the palace was so I could offer you my sincerest apologies and to ask for your forgiveness."

"Forgiveness?" Reece answered in a high voice of disbelief. "Simone, whether or not you choose to apologize to me now, I will never trust you *or* your motives."

Simone swallowed hard. "I understand that. I know I judged you prematurely, and believed that you didn't belong in Pemdas. After I learned that my plans to have you traded to the Ciatron would have resulted in your death, well, I slowly became aware of the horrific monster I had become." She diverted her eyes to the ground. "*I* am the one who is unworthy to live in Pemdas," she said, as her voice cracked.

You deserve to live in a padded cell! Reece thought in annoyance.

Simone looked at Reece with tears now filling her eyes. "Reece, I want to take this opportunity to make you aware of my earnest remorse about everything I did to you and our land. I have lost all of my friends, and my sister and father do not even treat me the same. I hope that, one day, they will all understand how I have changed. You may never forgive me, and I will understand if you don't; I believe that I am getting what I deserve. Even so, I have acknowledged how wickedly I have behaved and I feel compelled to convey my deepest apologies to you."

Reece felt somewhat bad for the woman. Simone's malicious actions had cost her everything, and now Reece commended her for having the courage to apologize to her. Even though she could easily hate Simone for the rest of her life, Reece was a better person than that.

"I understand what it must've taken for you to be able to apologize to me, so thank you for that." She managed a smile.

"Thank you for your forgiveness, Reece."

Chapter 10

The woman turned to run as soon as she proclaimed that Levi knew where the stone was. She ran briskly out of the parking lot and into a large field. She was overpowered when Levi grabbed her arm fiercely and forced her to the ground. Before she could defend herself, Levi was straddling her and holding the side of his sharp blade to her neck.

After he realized she was able to have read into his mind, Levi was no longer thinking rationally, but was more intent on his own self-preservation. He had to protect himself. She had to be destroyed.

Harrison calmly approached where the woman lay

underneath Levi, her eyes wide and peering into his. "Levi, don't do this," Harrison ordered.

"She knows where the stone is!" Levi growled, as he pressed the side of the blade firmly against the woman's throat. "How are you able to read my thoughts, Armedite?" he demanded.

Harrison advanced toward Levi from the side. "Levi, step away. Whether she knows or not, this is not your decision to make. I will deal with the woman."

Levi ignored him. "How did you read my mind?" he insisted.

The woman closed her eyes and remained silent, infuriating Levi even more.

"Levi!" Harrison yelled.

Levi didn't respond.

Harrison gripped his cousin's shoulder. "You must remove yourself from her now. It is essential you leave; she is reading your mind, even now."

Levi's breathing relaxed, and Harrison's grip loosened, knowing he had gotten through to him. Levi shouted angrily as he withdrew from the woman.

Once Levi was off of her, as the woman tried to flee, Harrison restrained her with locking devices around her ankles and arms.

Levi sank his dagger aggressively back into its sheath. His jaw clenched as he stared down at the woman sinisterly. It was repulsive to him that she could read his thoughts. Never in his life had he felt so vulnerable.

Rage and fury reignited within him when the woman smiled mockingly at him in return. He did not want this woman imprisoned in Pemdas. Her strong interest and threats about Reece gave him an overwhelming desire to end her life, whether or not Harrison agreed with him. After the thought of Reece entered his mind, he came back to his senses. He inhaled deeply and unclenched his fists, regaining control over his emotions.

The woman's eyes widened as she continued to watch him. "*You* truly love this human." she said as her eyes became mysterious. "Your love for her is more powerful than—"

"How are you reading my mind?" Levi roared.

"Leave us!" Harrison ordered him sternly. "I will take care of this from here. Contact the command center immediately, and tell them to send two men from Pemdas to retrieve her. I will await their arrival."

Levi didn't respond; he waited for the woman to answer.

"Levi! You must inform Samuel of this situation, now! You can no longer stay here; you are a risk. She is actively reading your thoughts, you must leave!" Harrison shouted out to him.

When Levi brought his attention to Harrison, his cousin exhaled in relief. Levi quickly nodded, and turned swiftly to remove himself from the Armedite woman's presence.

Levi marched briskly through the field toward the parking lot and back to their car. Once inside, he contacted Samuel and notified him of the encounter and the new information about Michael. Samuel confirmed that he would have men dispatched to their location at once.

The Guardians who were assigned to retrieve the woman arrived within the hour, and left with her almost immediately thereafter. As soon as Harrison was seated in the passenger's seat, Levi put the car in gear and sped quickly out of the parking lot.

"Was that woman able to see the location of the stone in my mind?" Levi asked.

"I am unsure; she hasn't spoken a word since you left us. But I believe all she saw was that you have knowledge of the stone's whereabouts."

"Why would you assume that?" Levi asked, while staring intently at the road.

"Because it's what I saw as well."

Levi glanced over at his cousin, perplexed by what he had said. "My mind wasn't open to you at that time."

Harrison rested his elbow on his knee and twisted to face Levi. "That's the strange part. I wasn't trying to read your thoughts. I was still amazed by what that woman was revealing to you at the time. Then, one moment you grab her angrily, and the next thing I know your mind is projecting thoughts into mine. It was why you had to leave. When she validated your love for Reece, I realized that your mind was projecting thoughts into hers as well."

Levi glanced over at Harrison in disbelief. How had his mind become weakened? What exactly had taken place when he gained this imprint from Reece? *This is absurd! My mind is projecting its thoughts? Impossible!* he thought as he stared out of the front windshield.

"This is odd," Levi said softly. "This is exactly what happened when I first saw the location of the stone. Reece's mind projected the images into mine. Queen Galleta mentioned that I now carry an imprint of the map." He rubbed his forehead in utter confusion as to what was going on within him. "I have to speak to the queen about this when we return."

"Very well. Queen Galleta also needs to be summoned for this woman," Harrison replied. "Our devices were unsuccessful in removing her memories of this encounter. We need to see if the queen can alter her memory in some way."

Levi gripped the steering wheel tightly. "Isn't this just delightful?" he said with disgust. "Hopefully she possesses the talent to do such a thing; otherwise, this woman can never leave Pemdas. Having this information makes her too great of a risk."

"Did you notify Samuel of Michael's whereabouts?"

"Of course. My father has ordered him to dispatch a troop to Armedias, demanding they turn Michael over to us," he said, as he maneuvered the car around a vehicle that was going half their speed. "It was only a few moments before you arrived at the car that Samuel had informed me that Armedias will not deliver Michael to us unless we release the woman."

Harrison laughed. "Well, that's not going to happen anytime soon." He scratched his head. "I do wonder why she would offer such interesting information about Lucas and Michael."

"Oh yes, their *plans* for Reece?" Levi grimaced. "Lucas is a young, arrogant fool, and he should know that with or without Michael's help, he's never going to get to Reece."

Harrison smirked, "It would be interesting to watch them try; wouldn't you agree?"

Levi's eyebrow arched. "Provoke war with Pemdas? Not going to happen. Lucas' armies could never stand a chance against ours. Lucas is obtuse, but I believe him to be somewhat smarter than that," he said, as he directed the car toward the cliff where the vortex to Pemdas was. "That's why none of that is really my concern at the moment."

As the car traveled on the road in the outer boundaries of Pemdas, Levi audibly called for the car to connect to the command center. As he pulled into the stone structure and parked the car, the front windshield projected Samuel in the command center alongside a group of Guardians holding the woman in restraints. Samuel stepped into his office, and informed both men that the emperor had already requested that they bring the woman to Queen Galleta for interrogation.

Levi and Harrison arrived at Queen Galleta's home

shortly after Samuel and the Guardians left with the woman from Armedias. They followed a servant into a small sitting room, where Galleta waited for them. When they entered, the queen gestured for them to make themselves comfortable on the sofas.

"Levi. Harrison," she announced, as she sat in a chair across from the two men. "I have just concluded my interview with the priestess. She is currently being escorted into a chamber of isolation, given that I still need more time with her."

"A priestess—from Armedias?" Levi asked, stunned at the reference to the woman. "Since when do the Armedites have such beings?"

"Nearly five years ago, she and her four sisters sought residence in the dimension of Armedias. After they demonstrated their exceptional abilities to Lucas, he appointed them as his chief advisors. These beings are unique, and I am still in the process of learning more about their kind. For now, all I have learned about their history from this particular woman is that Lucas refers to them as his priestesses."

"Tell me, your Excellency; this priestess read my mind," Levi interjected. "Did you learn how she was able to do this? Do you believe she was able to see where the stone is?"

"As I informed the emperor and Samuel, I need more time with this woman. Her mind is strong, and I must break down her mental barriers to get through to the information she is withholding from me. I advised the emperor that due to this woman's secrecy, I believe she may have seen the location of the stone. She is impressively guarded, but I believe in time, I will have an effect on her. For now, I feel it is best to assume she knows where the stone is, and act accordingly." Galleta sighed and regarded

Levi with some sympathy. "Levi, it appears she has achieved the impossible with your mind. She has found a way to break down your natural protective barriers, and I can now see that your thoughts can be read by any individual who has the talent to do so."

Isn't this perfect? Levi's stomach cinched into a knot. "How could something like this happen? This woman— how could she do such a thing? The only one who has been able to read my mind at will is Harrison, and that is because we were trained in such a way."

"When I tried to use my mental persuasion and remove the memory the priestess had of her encounter with you, I was able to see exactly how she was able to..." Galleta's lips twisted, while she seemed to search for the proper words. "I was able to see how she was able to damage your protective mental barrier," she finished, sitting back and watching Levi in response.

"Damage? How?" Levi said in a tone of disgust. "What are you talking about?"

"She was probing into your mind, and that is why she was provoking you. She was using your anger as weakness; and in the end, when you made contact with the woman, you gave her enough physical power to not only destroy your mental barriers, but also project your thoughts into her mind as well."

"That's where that energy jolt came from." Levi muttered to himself, recalling the strange sensation he experienced when he held the woman's arms tightly in his grip.

"It makes perfect sense," said Harrison in astonishment. "It explains why Levi's thoughts were forced into mine for no reason."

"I'm not sure it makes any sense at all," Levi said in sheer annoyance. "This is absurd!"

"Whether you wish to acknowledge it or not, this is how she was able to achieve what we believed to be impossible; reading the mind of a Pemdai warrior," Galleta said.

Before Levi could say anything, Harrison spoke up. "Will there be any success in removing her memories?"

"I am confident that with more time, I will be able to remove her memory, and learn more about her and her kind."

Levi leaned forward and placed an elbow on each knee. "Why? Why did this woman seek us out? It was obvious she was not there to abduct a human."

"Yes," answered Galleta, "and from the minimal information I have learned, the priestess was sent exclusively to meet with you and Harrison. Lucas has formed a great interest in Reece. With Michael making him aware of the fact that you and Harrison served to protect the Key, he believed that if he sent his priestess, she would give him more information about her. He was convinced that the woman's strong mind could read your thoughts and he could see for himself whether Emperor Navarre was speaking the truth in the council. He wanted to know if the Pemdai brought Reece here for protection, or to use her to locate the stone." Galleta cleared her throat. "It appears she was successful in that matter, and now she must remain in Pemdas until the information is removed from her mind."

"I still do not understand why Lucas seeks to trouble himself with all of this. Why he would cause dissention between Pemdas and Armedias." Levi shifted uncomfortably in his seat as he weighed the situation. "I agree, she must remain imprisoned...I suspect that if the Council of Worlds learns that I have knowledge of where the stone is, it would cause another misconception amongst us and the other worlds. It would give them all an excellent excuse to disregard the Pemdai's honor and duty in protecting their worlds and ours. I don't believe anyone would ever believe how I was able to see the stone's location."

"Very true," said Galleta. "Apart from your current weakened state of mind, I believe that everything, in time, will work itself out regarding this woman."

"So now that my mind is able to be read, this means I am no longer qualified to serve as Guardian on Earth." Levi said in irritation.

Galleta nodded, as Harrison sat there expressionless. This was definitely more than he could process. Before Galleta could respond, Levi stood and turned away from both them. He brought his tightened fist to his mouth and closed his eyes. *This can't be happening.* Never in his life had he felt so inadequate.

"There has to be something you can do, your Excellency," Harrison said.

"If Levi is willing, I believe there may be a way we can work together to fix this. It will take some time, and he must isolate himself from everyone and everything."

Levi turned back to her. "I am prepared to do anything."

Galleta smiled reassuringly at Levi. "There are mental exercises we will do to help strengthen your mind for protection again. I will inform Samuel of this situation. Once I am assured you have successfully strengthened your mind, you will be able to resume your duties on Earth."

Levi relaxed some. "I am ready to start this as soon as possible."

Galleta nodded. "I will inform Samuel of the process, and we will arrange the training."

The men thanked the queen politely for her counsel, and walked out to their horses. Despite Galleta's encouraging words that Levi may be able to overcome this new vulnerability, he was growing more upset by the minute. He was revolted at the thought that this woman had the ability to weaken him. The idea of him not being qualified to guard on Earth was not an easy thing for him to accept.

He grabbed the reins, stepped his foot hard into his stirrup, and hoisted himself onto Areion's back. The stallion instantly sensed Levi's aggressive tension and began stamping his feet forcefully onto the ground. Levi glanced over to find Harrison smiling broadly at him. "It looks like we'll be traveling the high road home," he said, knowing that they would be taking a more challenging route to the palace. "After you, my friend."

Without hesitation, Levi directed Areion away from Galleta's home, and out toward a steep mountain range. A fierce ride on Areion always helped to ease his nerves. He pushed the horse hard, and the noble steed greatly welcomed it. As Areion charged up the steep mountain ridge, Levi's nerves began unwinding, and a sense of calmness washed over him.

As he and Harrison continued at a rapid pace back to the palace, Levi's troubled thoughts were replaced by his anticipation of seeing Reece again. Being a Guardian was what Levi had always been passionate about; since he was a young boy, it was all he ever desired. But it wasn't until he admitted his love for Reece that he saw everything so differently. Of course, serving on Earth was always his greatest desire, but it wasn't what defined who Levi was anymore. Sharing a life with Reece, having her love...*that* was what defined the man he was now. His love for this woman was far superior to anything he had ever known, particularly his own needs and desires. So why would he be so upset if he no longer had the qualifications to serve as Guardian in the other worlds? It all seemed so trivial to him now. He already promised Reece on the day that he proclaimed his love to her that he would give everything up, if only she gave him her heart. So why would he hesitate to give up guarding the humans on Earth?

Adrenaline surged through his veins as Areion began the descent down the steep mountainside, knowing they were not far from the palace. It had been too long since he had seen Reece, and he longed to be in her presence more than anything now. He needed to see her eyes fill with eagerness as they always did when she stared into his. He needed to hear her laugh, and most of all, he needed to feel her closeness. As the grounds behind the palace came into his sight, Areion found his next burst of speed, sending Levi to where he knew Reece was waiting for him.

Areion had barely halted when Levi dismounted and turned him over to a stable man. Without hesitation, Levi spun and strode briskly up to the palace as Harrison followed closely at his side. "When you report to the command center, let Samuel know that I will discuss my current situation with him later this evening." He stopped before entering the palace. "Right now, I am finished concerning myself with what happened with the priestess."

Harrison grinned and clapped Levi on his shoulder. "Enjoy your afternoon with Reece. I'll see you this evening."

With that, they parted ways, and Levi sought out the closest servant. "Do you know of Miss Bryant's whereabouts?"

"Master Levi, she is taking her tea in one of the sitting rooms with—"

"Very well," Levi said, interrupting the man. "Notify the kitchen staff that I will need an area set up, and a basket of food delivered to it. Miss Bryant and I will be leaving the palace for the afternoon."

"Yes, sir. I will have the staff arrange everything. Is there anything else, sir?"

"That is all, thank you," Levi answered, and turned to walk briskly up to the third floor where his room was.

As he walked in, his valet met him in the entryway. "Henry, have any packages been delivered to the room in my absence?"

"Two gift boxes arrived early yesterday morning."

Levi grinned subtly. "Excellent." He made his way toward his desk and quickly wrote a note to be delivered with the packages. When he was finished, he sealed it and placed it in Henry's hand. "Have this and the packages delivered to Miss Bryant's room."

With that, Levi turned and strode quickly toward his shower. His eagerness to see Reece, and spend the rest of the afternoon alone in her presence, faded any and all stress about the encounter with the priestess. All he wanted now was to have Reece in his arms.

Chapter 11

Upon returning to the palace, Reece and Simone entered one of the sitting rooms where the servants had tea prepared. *Just my luck I run into Simone on the one day everybody else has something to do,* Reece thought as she pondered excuses to dismiss herself.

"I have not been in this room since the afternoon Levi came back, hostilely upset with me," Simone said, as she poured the tea. She handed Reece a cup and sat down. "That was such a dreadful experience, and I have never been more frightened of Levi."

Reece took a sip of her tea and glanced out toward the valley, wishing by some miracle Levi would ride up the hill and rescue her from having to be in the company of Simone.

Simone continued, "Even though my father and Emperor Navarre were in the room, I truly believed he would harm me."

Reece restrained herself from rolling her eyes when she looked at Simone. "I think we were all in shock by what took place."

Simone managed a faint smile. "I deserved his wrath, I am aware of that now." She cleared her throat and sipped her tea delicately. "I can't forgive myself for the danger I put him and all of the Guardians through." Simone clutched her teacup tightly as she stared at the fireplace. "It wasn't supposed to happen in such a way. None of it." Her features darkened as she looked back at Reece. "Michael only made things worse…I've heard he is missing. I wish there was something I could do to help locate him."

Yeah, I'll bet you do, Reece thought as she struggled to believe anything Simone was saying. She took a sip of her tea and inhaled deeply. "Emperor Navarre is confident they will find him, it's just going to take time. You of all people should know that since your father is the Guardians' commander."

"My relationship with my father has become increasingly nonexistent. He will hardly look at me anymore; I don't know what to do to make things right with him again."

Before Reece could respond, a sharp pain jolted between her eyes. She gripped the bridge of her nose to ease the pain. As suddenly as the pain came over her, it left, along with the tension that had been building in her.

"Are you okay, Reece?" Simone asked with concern.

Reece exhaled and glanced over at the concerned expression on Simone's face. With her tension now subsiding, she felt more relaxed in the woman's presence. "I'm fine," she said with a smile. "I'm sure everything with your father will work itself out in time. For now, let's just move forward."

"I would like that very much." Simone brushed her ebony hair over her shoulder and smiled warmly, "Please tell me; how is the celebration planning coming along?" Simone asked with excitement. "I have heard that this celebration will be traditional wedding ceremony from Earth and will be Pemdas' biggest event yet. Everyone is talking about it."

Reece smiled in return. "I'm having a wonderful time making the plans with Allestaine and Elizabeth. It's a little intimidating when I think about how many people will be here for it though."

"Do not fear," Simone said with a giggle. "You will be marvelous, I have no doubt."

For the next hour or so, the two women found enjoyment in each other's company. Reece was amazingly relaxed in Simone's presence, and could see the woman's genuine excitement for her and Levi's engagement. Simone offered her ideas, and her willingness to help with the engagement party. Reece's discomfort of the woman had vanished entirely, and she found herself enjoying Simone's visit immensely.

Knowing it was close to the time to meet Allestaine for lunch, they stood and made their way from the room. Upon their exit, a servant met them at the doorway.

"Miss Bryant, I have been sent to notify you that Empress Allestaine has been delayed a while longer. She has asked to postpone lunch for an hour from now, if that is agreeable to you."

Reece smiled. "That's fine, thank you."

"Have you been to the palace's flower gardens yet to pick the flowers you will be using for the table centerpieces?" Simone asked, as the servant left. "It will give us something to do before lunch is served."

"That sounds nice," Reece responded cheerfully.

The ladies walked out of the palace and down to the garden. They strolled leisurely through the garden, discussing more about the engagement party. After perusing the many different varieties of flowers the gardens had to offer, the women decided they should head back for lunch. Before they turned to leave, Simone stopped Reece.

"Reece, wait here; there is one more particular flower I wish you to see. Allow me to find out if it has bloomed yet. I will return in a moment."

Reece smiled in return and nodded. She and Simone had picked a variety of flowers, and Reece held the bunch of fresh blooms in her hands, studying the uniqueness of their appearance. She brought the bouquet up to inhale the rich fragrance of the blossoms. While absorbing the delightful scents, her heart stopped when she was scooped up into strong arms.

She had only a moment to acknowledge that it was Levi before his mouth claimed hers in an enthusiastic kiss. Reece ran her fingers through his hair, welcoming the eager and powerful kiss.

"Oh!" Simone said, with surprise in her voice.

Seemingly annoyed with the interruption, Levi slowly withdrew his lips from Reece's, and placed her feet back on the ground. Reece glanced up and saw Levi standing rigidly, staring ominously at Simone. She gently held his stiff arm, hoping that it would calm him.

"Simone," he acknowledged her.

Simone's cheeks turned crimson. "Levi, please forgive me for interrupting you two. If I may be so bold, I am surprised to see you here," Simone stammered.

"I believe you have stolen the very words right out of my mouth, madam. May I inquire as to what business you could possibly have at our home?"

"Since my father is here, I decided to use the opportunity to express my deepest apologies to Reece for my despicable actions last month. I also wanted to congratulate her properly on your engagement," Simone pleasantly responded, as she approached where Levi and Reece stood.

Reece looked up at Levi for his response; all she found was his tight-set jaw, and his darkened eyes staring down at Simone speculatively.

"I am afraid your business must wait. I have plans to steal my intended wife away for the afternoon. I have not had the pleasure of her company for quite some time." He looked down at Reece. "If that is agreeable to you?"

"It sounds wonderful. Although, I think your mother and sister are waiting for us to have lunch with them," Reece replied with a smile.

"I have already met with my mother, and she is aware of my plans." He brought his attention back to Simone. "If you'll excuse us."

"Yes, of course," Simone answered him with a faint smile. "Have a delightful afternoon together. I shall see you both at dinner tonight."

"Very well, then," Levi responded, dismissing her with a quick nod.

Simone gave Reece one last encouraging smile, and quickly strode toward the palace.

Levi exhaled and turned to look at Reece. He wound his

arms around her waist and pulled her closer into him.

"This is a nice surprise!" Reece said as she embraced him. "Javian told me earlier that you wouldn't be back for at least a week." She squeezed him tighter, "It's so good to have you home."

Levi rested his chin on top of her head. "I am grateful to have you in my arms again; I have missed you." He sighed softly. "It appears I have returned in excellent time. I had no idea that woman had come back to the palace."

"It's fine. She arrived this morning, and I really think she is a changed woman."

Levi withdrew from Reece so that he could study her. "A changed woman?" Both of his eyebrows shot up in shock.

Reece looked adoringly into his eyes. "Levi, she's apologized to me more than once, and I figured it would be best to make peace with her. Your parents forgave her; don't you think it's time we do the same?"

His expression softened in response, and he smiled. "Whether or not you or anyone else forgives her, my opinion of that woman will not change. I do not trust her." He brushed the back of his fingers along her cheek. "And I do not trust her alone with you."

"I understand, but—"

"Reece," Levi interrupted her, with some reproach in his tone. "I have no issue with you forgiving her; truly you are a better person than I. I also will not try to dissuade you from your opinions; I only ask that you be cautious in her presence." He softly let out his breath. "For now, I wish to speak no more of Simone."

Should she have expected a different reaction from him? Strangely, she didn't really know what came over her to forgive Simone so easily. Maybe it was the excitement of planning their engagement party; she was unsure. She wouldn't argue with Levi on this issue though; he had every right to feel the way he did.

"Let's change the subject then. So," she tilted her head up and kissed him tenderly on his chin, "you were saying something about spending the day out with your intended wife?"

Levi's vibrant blue eyes glistened as they stared down into hers. He clasped both her hands in his. "You are correct. But before we leave, I must ask you to return to your room and change."

"What exactly do you have planned?" Reece asked.

Levi laughed at her response as he offered his arm. "You will find out soon enough. Come, there are a few additional arrangements that must be made while I await your return."

Levi escorted Reece back to her room. "When you are finished, I will be waiting for you in the courtyard." A tiny smile drew up in one corner of his mouth as he winked and turned to walk away.

Reece walked into her room and toward the sofa, where she came across two large white boxes wrapped elaborately with red velvet bows. With no sign of Jasmeen, she approached the boxes and saw that they had been addressed to her from Levi.

She picked up the folded card that lay on one of the boxes and slid her finger under the red wax seal. Her heart raced with anticipation as she read Levi's penned note.

Upon your request, I arranged to have this outfit tailored for you. I hope it will meet with your expectations.

Reece reached into the box and pulled out an English-style riding jacket. She held it up and examined it. The jacket was crimson in color, with silver trim, along with silver buttons that had tiny arrows engraved on them.

Reece was reminded of their conversation when she had asked him for a riding outfit like this the morning he left Stavesworth Hall. Given his reaction and response, she assumed that she would have to get used to riding in long dresses living in Pemdas. *Should have known he was giving me a hard time,* she thought with a grin.

She explored further and found taupe riding pants to complete the ensemble. Without hesitation, she opened the second box and found tall, black leather riding boots. Reece was overjoyed, and scooped up her new riding outfit and made her way toward the closet to change into it, and get back to Levi. She nearly ran into Jasmeen as the maiden was walking out of her wardrobe closet.

Jasmeen smiled. "I must say, I was skeptical when Master Levi approached me for your measurements; however, I couldn't bring myself to dissuade him. I have never known the young master to be so excited about anything. Now," she held out her hands for the outfit, "let's get you ready," she said with a smile.

——→

Reece stared at her reflection in the mirror and giggled with excitement. She looked like a perfectly polished equestrienne. The outfit was impeccable. Jasmeen finished making sure her lapel was straight, and with a quick tug on the tails of the coat, she confirmed to Reece that she was prepared to leave. "Now, is there anything more that you require?" Jasmeen asked.

"I'm ready to go. Thank you, Jasmeen," she answered, and swiftly left the room to meet Levi.

As Reece walked out into the courtyard, she smiled widely at the scene before her. She stood in silence, admiring Levi as he adjusted the straps on Areion's saddle. He was so impossibly handsome, and she was so thankful he was home. Her heart responded gleefully when she saw Arrow standing at Levi's side. As Levi turned to his left to adjust the halter on the colt, he noticed Reece, quietly watching him from the top step.

Without hesitation, he marched up the steps to her, and pulled her into a tightened embrace. He withdrew from her leisurely, and glanced down at her in her riding outfit. "Do you approve of the riding attire? I must say, it agrees with you perfectly."

"I love it! Thank you. I really believed that you were against my riding a horse in an outfit like this."

Levi chuckled as he led her down to where the horses waited. "I would never deny you anything that you desire; especially if that desire happens to be in regard to one of my greatest enjoyments."

Levi escorted her down to the horses, where she noticed a new halter on Arrow. It was crimson with a silver plate, engraved with Arrow's name.

"This is beautiful," she said, as she traced her fingers along the letters.

"I disagree; it is a horse's halter, and therefore, it is hardly beautiful." He bent down to kiss her. "You are beautiful." He gave Arrow a sturdy clap on his shoulder. "I deemed it was necessary. Your new outfit should match your horse in some manner. Since Arrow still has a few more weeks until he is ready for the saddle, I decided upon having this custom halter made for him instead." His brilliant eyes sparkled as he grinned at her.

Reece reached her arms up around his neck, and he welcomed the embrace. "Thank you, Levi." She turned to pet Arrow. "Looks like we match now, boy. When Levi and I get back, we'll take our walk together," she promised.

Levi brought his attention back to Areion, and tightened his bridle. "That will not be necessary, love. Arrow will be accompanying us on our outing today." He turned back to Reece. "Ready?"

"Absolutely," she answered.

Once they were on Areion, Levi reached down and unfastened the rope that was tied to Arrow's halter.

"Don't you need that rope so that he'll stay with us?" Reece asked with concern.

"Arrow will follow closely along our side; Areion will make sure of it. The colt will be fine," he said as they turned to leave.

Reece squeezed tightly around Levi's waist, thrilled to be with him again. Once they were out of the courtyard, Areion sprang forward and into a faster gallop, carrying them away from the palace.

Chapter 12

Levi directed Areion toward an area that he knew Reece had never seen before. His plans were to enjoy a long horseback ride together before returning to their estate, where the palace's staff would arrange the outdoor picnic he requested.

The horses galloped at a steady pace through a meadow that was blanketed with vibrant flowers. Levi directed Areion toward a steep and rugged mountain. He felt Reece's arms clench around his waist as the horse began to ascend. Once they reached the top of the ridge, Levi halted Areion so that Reece could take in the astounding view that surrounded them.

"Nice job, Arrow!" Reece shouted enthusiastically. She squeezed Levi's waist. "Did you see how well he kept up with us?" she asked proudly.

Levi twisted in the saddle, strongly desiring to see the expression on her face. Her stunning blue eyes were bright with excitement, her smile enticing, and he couldn't resist the urge to bring his lips down onto hers at that very moment.

"I've missed you." He said.

Reece smiled, "I've missed you too." she said, before turning her attention to the valley below them. "It is absolutely gorgeous up here. Where are we, anyway?"

Levi shifted forward in the saddle. "We are on the outer boundaries of our property." He pointed to the horizon in front of them. "Over there we will ride alongside the river that will take us to the backside of our estate." He glanced back at her. "This part of the journey may seem frightening, but I do believe you'll appreciate the scenery."

Reece's grip tightened around his waist as Levi guided Areion over to the steep ledge carved into the granite mountainside. The narrow rocky ledge forced Arrow to follow behind them, as both horses slowly stepped down the rugged surface of the mountain. When Reece's grip tightened around him even more, he could sense her fear. He placed a hand reassuringly over her clenched hands, which were digging into his abdomen.

"Areion's not going to slip, is he?" Reece asked, her voice muffled with her head buried into his back.

"Areion will be fine," he answered in a reassuring voice. Reece embraced him even tighter, and he chuckled softly. "I would have never taken this route with you if I wasn't confident that we would be safe. You're missing out on the spectacular view of your property."

"That's fine; just let me know when we make it to the bottom," she stammered.

"Open your eyes, love," he said in humor. "Do you not trust me?"

The clicking of Areion and Arrow's steady hooves on the smooth surface of the rock echoed in the large canyon they were traveling through. The steadiness of the horse's making their descent down the mountainside seemed to encourage Reece to relax some. He felt her grip loosen as she removed her face from his back. "This is breathtaking! The lavender leaves on the trees are incredible!"

As the horses continued their descent along the narrow mountain ridge, Reece seemed exhilarated by the scenery. The glistening aqua-colored river to their left, along with the rocky cliffs covered with the lavender trees all along the banks of the river, astounded her most.

"This is on our property?" she asked as the horses came upon the vibrant pink mossy pathway that followed alongside the river.

"It is," Levi answered. "We are about five miles away from our home."

Levi loosened the reins on Areion, and the massive stallion responded eagerly. As they came out of the canyon, they continued to follow along the banks of the river that snaked through lush green meadows. In the distance, their estate came into view; but instead of riding directly to it, Levi guided Areion over a stone bridge to where the staff had been instructed to arrange their outdoor lunch on the meadow, across the lake from their home.

As they approached the location where a large blanket was laid out underneath a canopy of trees, Levi smiled with satisfaction. The staff had done an excellent job on such short notice, and they had exceeded all of Levi's expectations.

A bouquet of freshly cut flowers was arranged neatly next to a large basket overflowing with food from the palace's kitchen. Levi halted Areion a few feet from their picnic area, and his heart beat erratically when Reece squeezed him tightly and unexpectedly placed her soft lips on the back of his neck.

"You will never cease to amaze me!" she said cheerfully.

"I was sure that this would be a perfect day to make up for the picnic that I had planned when I first brought you to our home."

After Levi dismounted, he turned to help Reece off of the horse. When she was on the ground, she gazed up into his eyes. "It's perfect!" she said with a beaming smile.

Levi grinned. "Give me a few moments to unsaddle Areion."

Levi turned to remove Areion's bridle and saddle, while Reece walked over to where Arrow had busied himself grazing on the lush, green grass. He watched discretely as the young colt happily welcomed Reece's attention; it still astounded him how the young Guardian horse had taken to her in such a way.

After the tack was removed from the horse, Levi strolled over to the picnic blanket and dropped the saddle next to it. As he knelt down and reached for the basket of food, he was instantly enraptured by the scene in front of him.

It was an exquisite portrait of serenity, and Levi would never allow the images of this particular moment to leave his mind. Their future together was laid out before his eyes; their home across the small lake was set magnificently in the background, and the woman he would spend the rest of his life with was standing right before his eyes.

When Reece turned around to walk over to where Levi

sat, she was unbuttoning her riding coat. Once she had unfastened the last button, she glanced up and laughed softly when she became aware that Levi had been watching her every move. He grinned when her demeanor changed, and at that moment, she smiled at him provocatively. She strolled over to him slowly, gradually removing her coat in a playful, yet seductive manner. Levi dropped his chin and arched his eyebrow as she slowly shrugged off the coat, revealing her ivory silk shirt tucked neatly into her fitted riding pants. He watched with absolute pleasure as she continued to tease him while gracefully running her fingers through her long, golden hair.

Reece gently laid her riding jacket on the blanket; and before she could say a word, Levi gripped her waist and pulled her onto his lap, facing him. He ran his hands along her firm thighs, and gazed into her brilliant blue eyes. "You probably shouldn't tease me like that," he said in a low voice.

"Tease you?" she said with laughter. "All I was doing was taking off my jacket." She lightly kissed his nose. "I was starting to get hot."

Levi placed a soft kiss to her lips. "Is that so?" he answered, while he brought his hand up to the silk cravat that concealed her neck. "Well, we must not have you uncomfortable in any way. We should probably remove this as well."

Levi loosened the cravat, exposing her delicate neck to him, he relaxed against the saddle, and traced his fingers down her enticing skin. "Would you care for lunch?" he asked softly, as he twisted his fingers in the silk cravat that now hung loosely around her neck.

Reece bit her bottom lip as her eyes roamed over his face. A rush of energy jolted through him as he saw the hunger in her eyes. He grinned in satisfaction, knowing what her answer would be.

"I think lunch can wait, don't you?" she answered with a lively grin.

"Indeed it can." was all Levi said before the couple lost themselves in a passionate kiss.

After some time, and with great effort, they both withdrew. As Reece sat across from him, Levi began setting out the food prepared for their lunch.

After placing three small sandwich squares, a variety of fruit, and fresh vegetables in an orderly fashion on her plate, Levi handed it to her. As he started preparing his own plate, he watched Reece subtly as she picked through the food on her plate. When Levi instructed the kitchen staff on the foods he desired for their picnic, he specifically requested a particular fruit, wanting to see Reece's reaction when she tasted it for the first time.

Reece examined the unique fruit; and without questioning Levi about it, she popped it in her mouth. Levi's lips tightened as he restrained himself from laughter while he watched her try to keep her composure. After a violent shiver, her brow furrowed and her nose crinkled, as she forced herself to chew on the fruit.

She glared over at Levi with the most adorable look of disgust he had ever seen. "What is this?" she muttered through her teeth. She took the fruit out of her mouth, and placed it a cloth napkin. "I'm sorry, but that was the most disgusting thing I have ever eaten," she said with another shiver, as she bit into her sandwich, endeavoring to erase the flavor of the fruit from her mouth.

Levi laughed aloud, took the wadded-up napkin from her, and set it aside while he continued to watch her in amusement. "That was a helion fruit; they are quite a delicacy in Pemdas," he answered, while pouring her a glass of wine.

Reece accepted the glass he offered, and gulped down a large mouthful. "Delicacy?" she said with disbelief. "There are people who like to eat that?"

Levi placed his plate on the blanket in front of him and lazily reclined on his side, facing her. He grinned widely. "I believe you have to develop a taste for them. I'm quite fond of its flavor."

Reece's eyebrows rose up. "I don't think it's possible to develop a taste for something like that." She picked up the other helion fruit on her plate and brought it to his lips. "Here you go, crazy guy. I don't understand how you could like something that sour."

Levi accepted the fruit she placed in his mouth and gently pressed his lips against her delicate fingers in appreciation. He laughed while Reece watched him with a look of disgust as he chewed and swallowed the small piece of fruit.

"So," Levi started, as he reached for a sandwich square on his plate. "Did you enjoy the rest of your visit in Sandari?"

Reece's expression brightened. "I did," she said with excitement. "I met with the seamstress that will be designing my wedding dress."

"And will you be holding to the traditions of Earth and keeping the gown concealed from me until our wedding day?" Levi teased.

Reece nodded, "Of course!" she playfully added. "By the way, your mother has all of the decorations picked out for the engagement party. She's absolutely unstoppable when it comes to planning stuff like that."

Levi laughed. "I am not surprised."

As Levi continued to eat, Reece proceeded to inform him about all of the details of their intended engagement party. Her many expressions had him laughing and greatly intrigued by the information she was giving him.

"So now I guess we'll be spending the next few weeks decorating the palace," she concluded.

"Sounds intriguing," Levi answered with a laugh.

Reece smirked playfully. "You can help, you know."

Levi sipped his wine. "I think I'll pass." He gently took her hand in his. "It sounds like you ladies had an excellent time. Now all we have to do is get this engagement party out of the way so that we can focus on a more important event." He brought her hand to his lips. "And that is, the day you become Mrs. Reece Oxley," he said proudly.

The smile on her face ignited every nerve in his body. "I like the sound of that." She angled herself to face the lake in front of them. She quietly gazed at their home, bringing Levi to do the same. Areion and Arrow were peacefully grazing, and the harmonic sounds of the birds flying throughout the sky added to the serenity of the moment.

She sighed softly. "I love everything about this place. I wish we didn't have to leave."

Levi sat up and pulled her into his arms. She reclined back into his embrace, and continued to stare out at their house. Levi brushed his lips on her cheek. "I hadn't planned on returning to the palace anytime soon. I understand exactly how you feel; I look at this home and all of the surroundings, and can't help but to envision our future here together. This place gives me more peace than I ever imagined it would."

Reece stroked the back of his hand. "I hadn't thought about this until now, but when you go to Earth, that big house is going to get lonely."

Levi inhaled deeply as the thought of not being able to serve on Earth again came rushing back to him.

"Well, I might be able to ease your concerns about that," he said reassuringly to her. "There is a possibility that I may not be guarding on Earth anymore."

Reece twisted in his arms. "What?"

Levi smiled at her concerned expression. "A strange event took place on our assignment. We encountered a woman who seemed very interested in you. She not only revealed to us that Michael is living in Armedias, but she found a way to read my thoughts." Levi shuddered absently at the memory of what the woman had done to him.

Her forehead crinkled in disillusionment. "I didn't think anyone could read your mind unless you allowed them to."

"You are correct; however, something strange occurred with this woman, and not only was she able to read into my thoughts, she found a way to debilitate the way my mind naturally remains guarded from those who can read minds."

Levi proceeded to inform Reece about the events that took place on Earth. Understanding his passion for guarding on Earth, she encouraged him to do the training with Queen Galleta. To have her support and reassurance meant more to Levi than she could ever understand.

As their conversation shifted back to talking about their future together, Reece grabbed the picnic basket and smiled mischievously at him.

Levi laughed in response. "I had the kitchen staff pack a few apples, as I know they're Arrow's favorite treat."

Reece gave him a quick kiss, and then jumped to her feet. "I'll be back in a minute."

Levi reclined against the saddle. "Take your time."

When Reece approached Arrow, Levi laughed when Areion's head darted up and he promptly trotted over to her. Levi's forehead crinkled in disbelief as Areion rudely nudged Reece's arm that held the basket. *Really, Areion?* he thought, while Reece tried to ignore his horse and discreetly give Arrow an apple. She glanced back at Levi and smiled innocently at him. It was obvious she wanted to give Areion a treat, but most likely out of fear for what Levi would think, she tried to ignore his horse's begging. Instead of giving Areion an apple, she tried to appease him with a sturdy pat on his neck. Levi watched the entire scene with amusement. Areion would glance over at Arrow, and then bring his attention back to Reece, obviously devastated that she wouldn't offer him a treat as well.

"It appears that Areion's feelings are hurt by your lack of interest in him."

Reece turned back to Levi and smiled innocently again. "I'm petting him; he's fine."

Levi chuckled. "I believe he would appreciate an apple also."

A broad smile stretched across her face. "You won't give me a hard time about it?"

"I will always give you a hard time about spoiling those creatures; however, at least Areion will be appreciative."

Reece turned to the stallion, and handed him an apple. As Reece continued to appease the two horses, Levi let the serenity of the moment relax every nerve in his body. He sank back against the saddle, crossed his long, outstretched legs, and let his eyes slip closed.

$$\longrightarrow$$

After the horses lost interest in Reece, she turned back and saw that Levi had drifted off to sleep. She smiled at how handsome he was as he slept peacefully. After everything he had explained to her, she was surprised he'd had the energy to venture out with her today.

She strolled leisurely along the bank of the lake, admiring the beautiful surroundings that would soon be their home, before she returned to where he lay on the blanket. She slowly crawled onto the blanket and nestled into his side.

She gazed contentedly out where Areion and Arrow were grazing along the banks of the pond. She snuggled in closer to Levi's side, and watched the wind whip through the long grass as the colorful birds lazily circled above their heads in the vibrant blue skies.

She had no idea how long she had lain there staring at everything, soothed by the rhythmic breathing of Levi resting at her side. The afternoon seemed to have passed rapidly, and Reece thought she should probably try waking Levi. They had been out for the entire afternoon, and she believed that preparations for dinner would soon be underway.

She reached up and lightly brushed the side of his face, and he moaned quietly in return. She carefully twisted out of his arm, which he had absently wrapped around her in his sleep, and positioned herself to place light kisses all over his face. As she did, his eyes remained closed, but she could tell he was starting to rouse when she saw his lips turn up slightly. She brought her mouth to his, and before she could calculate what had taken place, she was on her back, and Levi was pinning her down aggressively beneath him.

She gasped when she felt a sharp object pressing against her throat. She could hardly take a breath, and therefore, couldn't call out to him. His eyes were dark and perilous, and her heart hammered against her chest as Levi glared viciously down at her. She tried to swallow, but the pain at her throat would not allow it. She feared for her life as she stared into Levi's desolate eyes.

"How could you do this to me?" he growled.

She couldn't answer. She couldn't think. She closed her eyes, hoping he would snap out of whatever had come over him.

"Answer me, now!" Levi snarled.

In the darkness of her mind, with her eyes closed, Reece knew she had to remain calm and find a way out of this dangerous situation.

She was grateful when she was able to answer him in a whisper.

"Levi...it's me. It's Reece. Please...don't." She pleaded with him.

Instantly, Levi was gone. Her eyes flew open and as she sat up, she was shocked at her surroundings.

The day hadn't passed as quickly as she had presumed. The radiant sun was still high in the sky over them. Perplexed, she looked over to where Levi had been lying next to her, and discovered he was no longer there. Panic started to grip her as she tried to figure out what just happened. *It was a dream.*

She looked out toward the horses, and saw Levi saddling Areion. Arrow was next to him, and Levi seemed to be perfectly fine. The basket from their lunch had been packed up, and it was obvious Levi had been awake for a while, making preparations for them to leave.

She exhaled with relief, but was frightened about her dream. She called softly for Levi, and he turned quickly. He had a brilliant smile on his face as he walked back over to her. As he approached her, his expression changed to one of concern. "Are you okay?"

He knelt down next to where she sat, trying to pull herself together.

"Yeah, I'm fine," she said, rubbing her mildly aching forehead. Still trying to come to her senses, she recalled what Levi said to her in the strange dream. "This woman who read your mind; you don't think it's because of what happened between you and me? You know, how my mind transferred the imprint of the map to the stone into yours?"

Levi ran his fingers tenderly through her hair. "No, this

woman has very strong abilities. Do not worry over this; I will find a way around it. Why would you consider such a thing?" he said, as he gazed somberly into her eyes.

She didn't want to tell him about this dream; she had a feeling he would feel guilty about telling her what had happened to him on earth. She decided to dismiss the question with a light-hearted laugh. "Who knows…maybe just trying to over-analyze what happened. I feel pretty bad this has happened to you."

She slowly stretched her arms out and stood to her feet, with Levi following her. "This afternoon was really nice, we'll have to find a way to do this more often."

"I couldn't agree more." Levi said as he escorted her over to the horses.

Chapter 13

eece and Levi were back at the palace with a few
hours to spare before dinner. After leaving the
horses in Javian's care, they made their way up to the
palace. As they walked through the corridors that led to her
room, Reece felt a sudden wave of exhaustion come over
her.

"Ugh," she softly groaned in frustration, forcing Levi to
glance down at her.

He wrapped his arm around her shoulders. "Are you that upset that we left our home?" he asked in humor.

Reece laughed softly. "Sorry, I'm suddenly feeling really exhausted and irritable. I don't know where that came from."

Levi's grip on her shoulder tightened. "We've been out most of the day. You'll feel much better after you have freshened up."

Let's hope so, Reece thought. Her eyes were burning, and it was becoming increasingly difficult to keep them open. Her head was pounding, and Levi's arm around her was starting to annoy her. She discreetly tried to shrug it off, hoping he wouldn't take offense.

Fortunately, Levi removed his arm from her shoulders, and took her hand instead. Reece felt compelled to get to her room; a nice, hot bath sounded so enticing. She clasped Levi's hand tightly, forcing them into a faster pace up the steps to her room. Once at her doors, she turned to face Levi, hoping to make this farewell quick.

"Reece?" he said, as he brushed his thumb underneath her eyes. "You look exhausted. Maybe you should take this time to lie down."

Her heavy lids closed with the soothing feeling of him tenderly caressing underneath her eyes. "That feels nice," she said with a smile. When her eyes reopened, Levi was still watching her with concern. "I'll be fine."

Levi's expression softened. "There is a tea that Jasmeen can make for you; it will help to rejuvenate you."

"That sounds great."

Levi bent to kiss her. "I probably won't be at dinner this evening," he said, as he ran a hand through her hair. "I have much to discuss with Samuel and my father about the events that occurred on Earth."

She rubbed her forehead, as the lingering headache

started throbbing again. "That's fine."

"Go freshen up; I'll be sure to check on you before I retire for the night."

After a quick hug, Reece walked into her room and called for Jasmeen. The maiden responded promptly, and quickly prepared the tea Levi mentioned. Once the hot bath was drawn, Reece entered the bathroom, and her skin tingled in its soothing environment. The room was dimmed, lit only by candles, and filled with the aroma of lavender and vanilla. Reece's throbbing headache eased with every step she took toward the bath.

She sank into the tub up to her neck, letting the warm water relax every exhausted nerve in her body. As her exhaustion slipped away, she let her mind roam back to the wonderful day she'd spent with Levi. It was great to have him home, and she couldn't wait to be back in his arms again.

That evening, the ladies had their dinner in the palace gardens. Allestaine discussed in more detail her plans for the engagement party. Reece was perfectly content during their meal, so she couldn't understand why her head began aching again. Listening to Allestaine talk about the décor for the party wasn't helping; everything was starting to weigh on her and Reece couldn't determine why she was feeling this way. She was never so thankful as she was when dinner was finally over, and the women went back into the palace.

Elizabeth mentioned that she had been working with the palace's orchestra, and had written her own music for Reece and Levi's wedding ceremony. She asked Reece if she would join her in the music chambers in order to hear some of the pieces. Reece wanted nothing more than to return to her bedroom, slip into something comfortable, and curl up in bed; but for fear of hurting Elizabeth's feelings, she pressed on.

Reece sat on the sofa with Simone at her side as Elizabeth began to play her compositions. The music was relaxing, but it didn't take long before her headache returned. She nearly let out a growl of frustration when Elizabeth had finished her performance and Levi and Harrison entered the room. *Will this night ever end?* she thought, while she forced a smile on her face.

Levi promptly strode over to where Elizabeth had joined Reece and Simone on the sofa while Harrison busied himself pouring a glass of wine.

"Good evening, ladies." Levi said as he leaned over to give Reece a kiss on the forehead.

Harrison came over and sat next to Levi on the sofa across from the women. Out of nowhere, Reece started to feel panicky. *What is wrong with me?* she thought, as she tried to fan herself discreetly.

"Reece is there anything I can get you? Perhaps some wine?" Levi asked, aware that she seemed uncomfortable.

"That sound nice, thank you." Reece said with a forced smile.

When Levi returned with a glass of wine, she sipped it in hopes it would relax her nerves.

Harrison relaxed into the sofa and gazed speculatively at Simone, who sat between Reece and Elizabeth. "Well, isn't this a lovely portrait?" He looked at Levi. "A venomous thorn sitting in the midst of two roses."

Levi's lips tightened as he restrained himself from laughter.

"Don't you think that was a little uncalled for, Harrison?" Reece snapped impulsively in utter annoyance.

"Absolutely not," Harrison said with a laugh. He took another sip of his wine, and his scrutinizing gaze was back on Simone. "Your sudden return to the palace has me

curious as to what you may have in store for us this time."
He looked at Levi. "I mean, she couldn't successfully finish
all of us off the last time, so she must have a better plan
now."

Simone cleared her throat. "I know you may find it
difficult to believe, but I came back to apologize to Reece
for everything I did to her." She smiled at Reece.
"Fortunately, she has forgiven me. It is my hope that you
will learn to forgive me in time as well."

Harrison took a large gulp of his wine, and offered
Simone a smug grin. "I've known you for a long time,
Simone; don't hold your breath waiting for my forgiveness.
I think for now you should just delight yourself with the
fact that Reece has forgiven you."

"Exactly what are you trying to say?" Reece blurted out.
"Am I wrong to forgive her?"

Reece had no idea why she was being so confrontational
with him, but she couldn't help it. Her head was throbbing
and everything was irritating. Harrison had every right to
feel the way he did. Simone put his life in jeopardy, along
with Levi's.

"Of course not; I'm sure it's completely natural to
forgive someone who threatened your life," Harrison
replied, obviously aiming to make some form of a point.
Reece rolled her eyes and looked at Levi, hoping his
expression would calm her. It didn't. He sat there with his
usual noble posture, watching her intently. *Gee, thanks for
getting my back.* Reece's lips tightened in frustration and she
gazed out of the windows.

"Reece," Simone said softly, forcing Reece to look at
her. "Please don't be upset with Harrison. I created all of
this myself," she said, as she reached for Reece's hand.

Reece jerked her hand away from Simone. Her emotions
seemed like they were on a roller coaster; what was really

wrong with her? She took a gulp of her wine, begging the drink to calm her.

Luckily, Elizabeth helped to change the subject, and brought up the engagement party planning. Her soft voice and kind spirit seemed to relax the sudden tension that filled the room. Reece continued to sip her wine, but the bizarre headache was not subsiding, and every time she spoke, she was curt and rude with her response.

"So, Reece, are you looking forward to dancing for hours on end at this engagement party?" Harrison said with laughter. "I believe this celebration will outdo the Hamilton's—"

"What makes you think we'll be having dancing at the engagement party?" she cut him off abruptly.

Her head was pounding, her eyes burning and her mood entirely out of control. She had to leave this room before she made a bigger spectacle of herself than she already had. She stood abruptly. "I'm sorry about that, Harrison." Before anyone could respond, Reece rapidly fled the room.

She wasn't far from her room when Levi caught her gently by the arm. Reece stopped and exhaled, frustrated. She wanted to be alone and exhaustion was now weighing heavily on her.

"Is everything okay?" Levi questioned softly.

Reece glanced up and for the first time since being with him earlier that day, she was entrapped by his vivid blue eyes. "I don't know what's wrong with me. I don't feel good, and my head is killing me."

Levi tenderly caressed her cheek. "Let's get you back to your room. I'll send for a remedy that will help with your headache."

As Reece reached for his offered arm, she stumbled, and her legs gave out. Before she collapsed, she was cradled in Levi's arms, as he walked rapidly to her room. She laid her head against his shoulder, and his rich, masculine scent soothed her. She reached up and gently caressed his face. It was amazing how much better she felt having him holding her securely. "I'm actually feeling a little better now. Maybe I just needed to be close to you." She said with a soft laugh.

"I'm relieved to hear that." He gently kissed her forehead. "A quiet evening alone with you does sound quite enticing and this gives us an excuse to do just that."

Once they were in her room, Levi went directly into her bedchamber and placed her on the bed. "Let me send for your maiden and the remedy, and I'll return after you have changed and are settled into your bed."

After Jasmeen helped Reece into a long, silky gown, she snuggled under the covers and reclined against the overstuffed pillows that were set up for her. She sipped the medicine tea that Levi had sent for her, and gazed out of the windows that offered a perfect view of the illuminating grounds outside.

Her headache was starting to subside. *I'd better not be getting sick!* she thought, taking another sip of her tea. She laid her head against the pillows, and her heart skipped a beat when Levi walked into her room, smiling with the smile he held only for her.

"You are unquestionably beautiful," he said, as he approached her bed.

She motioned for him to sit next to her, and without hesitation, he did.

"Has the remedy helped?" Levi asked, as he brought his arm around her.

"I'm definitely feeling more relaxed; I hope I'm not getting sick." She snuggled into his sturdy side. "It's really nice to have you here with me."

Levi kissed her softly on her head. "Soon, we will spend every evening in this manner. I long for the day I wake up with you by my side."

Reece placed her arm sluggishly over his chest. "Me, too," she answered softly. "I forgot to ask; how did the meetings go with Samuel and your father?"

"Well, it appears that the exercises I will be going through in order to strengthen my mind will require that I leave the palace for a couple of weeks."

"Why do you have to leave?" she said with a yawn.

"I will not be far. Queen Galleta's residence is only about an hour north of the palace. Apparently, it will take a gratuitous amount of concentration; therefore, I must isolate myself. I cannot have any distractions."

"I think you're trying to get out of engagement party planning," she teased.

She felt Levi laugh as he ran his fingers through her hair. "I might be."

"So when do you have to leave for your training?" She said covering a yawn.

"I planned to leave before first light tomorrow morning; if all goes as planned, I should be back within a week or so."

As Levi continued to inform Reece about the process of his training, his soothing voice was making it hard for her to stay awake. Reece felt him kiss her gently on her forehead, and heard him mumble something. It was the last thing she remembered before falling asleep in his sturdy arms.

$$\longrightarrow$$

Levi sat for a few quiet moments, savoring the contentment he felt with Reece asleep at his side. He tilted his head so that he could have a better view of her sleeping soundly. His movement roused her somewhat, and she turned away from him and curled up on her side. Levi smiled; she was so beautiful, and it was going to be difficult to leave her.

While walking back to his room, he encountered Simone walking through the dimly lit hallways.

"Levi, is everything okay with Reece?" Simone asked.

Levi stared intently at the woman, annoyed by her concern. "Reece will be fine," he replied. "Simone, tell me; exactly how long do you plan to stay with us at the palace?"

A hint of red touched her cheeks. "I had planned to leave tomorrow, but Reece asked me to stay and help with the engagement celebration planning." She inhaled deeply and stared down at her fidgeting hands. "I misjudged her from the beginning. I'm amazed that Reece has forgiven me after what I did," she said with a smile, as she looked at Levi. "She's really a wonderful person. I'm thankful she's accepting me as her friend. I don't deserve it."

Levi felt the blood boiling beneath the surface of his skin. "Simone, I've never loved anyone more than I love her. I will forever protect her with my life," he spoke with warning, and continued when he was assured Simone understood. "In regard to her befriending you after what you put her through—you are indeed correct, madam; you do not deserve the privilege of her even acknowledging your presence. I will only caution you once; if you do anything to take advantage of her forgiveness, you will answer to me personally for it," he stated firmly.

Simone nodded, and the sad expression on her face only encouraged Levi further.

"If she so much as suggests to me that you have upset her for *any* reason, I will see to it that you are removed from my home." His eyes narrowed as he stared at her pathetic expression. "I will be honest, Simone; I am not as forgiving as Reece. Your pathetic apology has only served to upset me further over everything you have done.

However, I will not argue with Reece about her opinion of you. I will also not allow my opinion of you to cause a quarrel between us, either. Now, if you will excuse me."

Unable to stare into her mournful eyes and watch the tears well up in them, Levi quickly left her presence.

Before light had made its way onto the land, Levi departed the palace. He hoped that this training would be successful and would be over quickly.

Chapter 14

eece was startled awake by the sound of voices in her sitting room. She overheard Levi speaking angrily at someone. From what she could tell, he was ordering this person to stay away from her, and demanding they leave the palace. *What is he still doing here?*

She noticed that a chair had been pulled next to her bed. *What's going on?* she thought, as she heard a woman crying in the sitting room.

Confused, she got out of bed, and pulled on her robe. She was lightheaded, but she felt much better than she had the previous night. As she went into the next room, she saw Simone sitting on the couch with her head in her hands, sobbing. Levi was irate, and staring intently at the hysterical woman.

"Levi?" she questioned in shock at the scene before her. "What happened?"

Levi turned his darkened gaze to where she stood. "Reece, what are you doing out of bed? Why did you not call for Jasmeen?" His voice was deep and commanding.

"Excuse me?" she said in a high-pitched voice. "Last I remember, I didn't need anyone's permission to get out of bed. What's going on out here? And why are you so angry?"

Levi looked at her in frustration. "Reece, you must return to your bed now; you are unwell. We have someone on their way to evaluate your condition."

"I am perfectly fine. Now, tell me what's going on out here? Why are you yelling at Simone?"

Levi stalked over to Reece and without warning, reached out and grabbed her upper arm. He swiftly spun her around and escorted her back to her bedchamber. Reece became enraged by his hostile approach. She jerked her arm out of his grip and gazed severely into his darkened eyes.

"Don't you dare grab me like that." she snapped. "What's your problem? Why are you still here, and why are you yelling at Simone?"

Levi turned to stare out the window and exhaled. "You have been unconscious for over two days. None of us can figure out why, and I've been with you this entire time."

"Unconscious?" She said disbelievingly.

"Yes," Levi responded as he looked back at her. "And that is why I was questioning Simone. It's strange that she returns to the palace, and then you fall ill that very same day."

"Why would you jump to a conclusion like that? Simone hasn't done anything."

Levi turned his livid gaze upon her. "You are being

imprudent and foolish by accepting her as your friend. I forbid you to be in the presence of that woman."

Reece felt her cheeks burning with anger. "Forbid me? Who do you think you are to speak to me like this?"

"Yes, Reece, I forbid you. I know what is best, and you will abide by my decision. I do not trust Simone; therefore, I will not permit you to be in her company."

"You don't have to be so demanding with me." She retorted.

Levi's expression darkened. "I can be any way I want. You will find your place at my side, Reece. Your speaking to me with such disrespect is inexcusable."

Reece didn't respond to him; instead, she slowly stepped back in absolute disgust of the man standing in front of her.

"I will not have a wife who questions me, am I clear?"

Who are you? Reece's heart was pounding in her chest. She experienced an array of emotions; anger, frustration, shock, disbelief and most of all, heartbreak. She continued to stare at him as tears started to well up in her eyes.

Levi approached her, and his strong hands clenched tightly around her upper arms. She flinched in pain, but he didn't seem to care.

"Answer me," he growled.

"No!" she snapped. "Get out of my room, now!"

Unexpectedly, Levi's entire demeanor changed. He released his tightened grip. "Reece," he said, in a softer voice. "I do not wish to frighten you." He offered her a subtle grin, and reached for her face. "I love you."

Reece abruptly jerked her head away. "I said, leave my room," she said through clenched teeth.

Levi's expression grew black with rage again. He snatched her arms and aggressively pulled her close to him.

Reece gasped in pain. "Levi! Stop!" She tried to wrench

away, but his bruising grip prevented it. "Stop! You're hurting me!" she demanded.

Levi ignored her and instead, brought his lips onto hers forcefully. Reece was fighting for air, and she tried to push him away. As hard as she tried to fight him, he only grew stronger against her resistance.

Tears streamed from her eyes, and when Reece believed she couldn't take anymore, Levi was gone. Her eyes flew open, and she was in her bed. Reece gripped her forehead. "It was a dream," she said softly.

Even though she was relieved that it was only a nightmare, she was quite disturbed by it. The dream seemed so real that she couldn't help but to feel a little disgusted by Levi at the moment. She had to get up, get going, and get rid of these awful images in her head.

Reece managed to dismiss the dream and go through the entire day feeling more like herself; however, that night would only send another nightmare. The next morning she woke up crying, and she realized her night clothes were drenched in sweat from the horrible dream. She couldn't figure out why the nightmares were occurring, and why her subconscious would portray Levi in such an abusive manner.

She chose not to tell anyone about the dreams. Throughout the day, the bad feelings about Levi would subside; but at night, the nightmares would always return. After three nights of these tormenting dreams, she began to make efforts to stay awake. Even though she tried, she would inevitably fail and end up face-to-face with the hostile Levi again.

After she woke up from another nightmare, she cried in desperation. *Why is this happening to me?* She thought in anguish. Half-awake and terrified to go back to sleep, she got out of bed and was startled when a dark shadow was framed in the entrance of her bedchambers. Her heart raced; it was Levi. He was home? Why was he in her room?

She didn't think twice; she needed him desperately. She ran toward the entrance and embraced him tightly.

"Levi, I'm so relieved you're home." Then she sighed. "I've had the craziest dreams since you left."

His hand ran tenderly through her hair. "We can't have that now, can we?"

His voice was chilling. She glanced out of the windows at the dark, illuminating land. "What time is it, anyway?"

"It's three o'clock in the morning."

"Three?" She stepped back and looked up at him. "Why are you here?"

Levi's eyes were dark as they gazed into hers. "Is it wrong that I check on you if I am concerned?"

Reece inhaled deeply; she was still dreaming. This was the possessive, hostile Levi, the unpredictable man she was growing more terrified of with every dream she had.

Wake up, Reece! she thought, as Levi stared darkly at her. "Levi, leave," she confidently told him.

He approached her, and Reece was frozen. His hand ran through her hair, and then he clenched it tightly, pulling so hard it caused Reece to cry out in pain. "Please, Levi," she said in tears.

Levi's lips seized her neck, and his other arm forced her body tightly against his. "You'll learn soon enough not to question me," he said in a hoarse voice.

Reece's body trembled with fear. "Please, don't."

Without warning, Levi withdrew and stood tall and rigid in front of her. He clenched her chin in his strong hands, and she gulped as her eyes widened in fear. Dream or not, the pain was real. Levi felt real, and she wasn't waking up from it.

"I'm sorry," she said through sobbing tears.

Levi's lips turned up slightly as he withdrew his crushing grip. "I love you, Reece," he said, as he tenderly embraced her and gazed hungrily at her mouth. Reece became nauseated as he brought his lips to hers, securing another possessive kiss. Finally, he pulled away, and stepped toward the exit of her room. He looked back and smiled with what seemed to be satisfaction. "You were wise to offer me an apology." He smirked. "You're learning," he said in a mocking tone, and then he left.

She heard the door in the other room shut, and her eyes flew open to the sun peeking through the curtains in her room. She ran both of her hands through her hair, gripping her head tightly. "Why is this happening?" she said through tears of frustration. How could she conquer this? Running in the morning seemed to be the only thing to pull her back into reality, but she had no energy to do that this morning.

"Reece?" Jasmeen called softly from the other room. "Are you okay?"

Reece quickly wiped the tears away before Jasmeen entered the room. She sat up in bed and forced a pathetic smile on her face. "I'm just missing Levi," she lied.

Jasmeen walked over to open the windows, allowing a cool, fresh breeze to enter the room. "I have your running attire prepared for your morning jog; that seems to always lift your spirits." she said, as she moved toward the doorway.

Reece got out of bed. "I don't think I'm up for a run this morning," she replied, as she slipped on her robe. "Will you get me a cup of hot tea instead?" That didn't even sound refreshing. Nothing did.

"Absolutely," Jasmeen answered in surprise. "Are you sure you're feeling alright?"

"I'm fine," Reece said, as she followed Jasmeen into the sitting room. "I think I'd rather start in on the decorations for the engagement celebration instead. Do you know where the wedding planner journal is that Elizabeth bought for me?"

"Yes, it's in your desk," Jasmeen said, as she walked over to Reece's writing desk. "Let me get it for you."

Reece had an idea. She would document these horrific dreams, from the very first one she'd had, and every one after that, and maybe it would be therapeutic. Something had to be causing this. After Jasmeen gave her the journal, Reece began writing about the bizarre dreams. She wrote in detail about the day she'd dozed off at Levi's side, and he'd held a knife to her throat. She shuddered at the memory of that dream, and that she could still recall it as if she had just woken up from it.

It had been two weeks since Reece's night terrors had begun. During this time, her appetite had diminished, and because of her sleep deprivation and lack of nourishment, she began to feel herself losing her grip on reality.

She became obsessed with writing in her journal, and believed that this book was the only thing that she could rely on to help her cope. Her dreams not only included Levi threatening her in some way, but they also consisted of the terrifying beings that she had seen in Scotland at the Council of Worlds.

She couldn't remember the last time she drank anything, or ate an entire meal; all she did was pick at the food on her plate. She was sick to her stomach from lack of sleep and fear of everyone around her. The only thing that served to help her now was planning the engagement celebration with Allestaine, Elizabeth, and Simone. She spotted more than one concerned expression, but managed to make light of her exhaustion and current despair. She couldn't tell them about what was going on; they would insist she rest, and she couldn't do that.

Because she had not been eating, and not sleeping well, she struggled to get through each day. She sat down on the edge of her bed and strained to keep her eyes open.

Stop it, Reece! If anyone catches on, they will make you sleep! Pull it together! she told herself. She laughed softly as she stood. *You've officially gone insane, Reece! Who knows? This is probably a dream, too!*

As soon as she considered herself presentable, she walked out to have Jasmeen help her get ready for the day. She sat in the makeup chair, and watched as Jasmeen displayed a look of sympathy toward her. "Is there something wrong?" she snapped at the maiden.

"Reece, you appear unwell," she said softly.

"Oh, give me a break!" Reece huffed.

The maiden remained quiet as Reece stared at the reflection of herself in the mirror. She looked pitiful; her eyes hollow, no color in her complexion, and no fullness in her face. It was a horrific sight, and most likely an image of herself from another horrifying dream. Fortunately, Jasmeen remained quiet while she went to work on Reece's hair and makeup. But it didn't matter how hard Jasmeen tried to cover her pathetic appearance; her face was worn. A wave of anxiety washed over Reece, knowing that the family would eventually question her about this, and then force her to rest.

Jasmeen poured Reece a hot cup of tea and gave her breakfast. "I had the staff prepare a tray of food for you this morning. I do hope you will eat." she said, as Reece took the plate.

Reece eyed the maiden, wondering what she was really thinking. *Eat the food, and she probably won't say anything.* Reece forced herself to take a small sip of her tea, and nibble on the muffin until the maiden left the room.

After Jasmeen left, Reece waited a few minutes before

joining Jasmeen in the dressing room. Jasmeen looked at her pitifully, provoking Reece's irritation. "Quit looking at me like that. Please, just help me get ready so I can get on with this day." Reece ordered her.

Jasmeen's expression didn't change as she studied Reece.

"Jasmeen!" Reece snapped. "Stop staring at me like that! I'm fine. I'm only depressed because I miss Levi. Now, please help me get ready," she said, hoping Jasmeen believed the lie.

After Jasmeen silently conceded to Reece's request, she went through extra efforts of altering the dress to fit her, having to take it in a bit more than usual due to Reece's weight loss. Once ready, Reece set off to the grand ballroom, where she and Allestaine had been working on preparations for the engagement party.

After she had been in the room alone for close to an hour not knowing where to start or what to do next, Allestaine, Elizabeth and Simone arrived.

"Reece, sweetheart? We expected you this morning for breakfast. Did you heed my advice and rest?" Allestaine asked.

Reece brushed her hair away from her face, and stared at the three impeccably dressed women. They appeared so energized, and Reece was bitterly jealous that they weren't experiencing the same torment as she was.

It's probably another dream anyways, she thought, as she gazed at Allestaine's perfection. "Oh! Well, forgive me for not heeding your advice!" she said abrasively. "I skipped breakfast because I want to make sure everything is getting done for the engagement party." She glared at the women. "Apparently it's only important to me these days," she snapped.

Reece turned her back on the women, not able to look at them for another second. She proceeded to go through the many boxes of décor, and then she heard Allestaine quietly dismiss Simone and Elizabeth from the room.

Allestaine gently placed her hand on Reece's arm, and turned her to face her. Reece exhaled in annoyance and pulled her arm from Allestaine's gentle grip. She glared at the empress, waiting for the lecture to begin.

Allestaine's expression didn't falter. "Reece, I take great offense to your assumption. I do not know what is happening with you, but I will not abide being spoken to in such a manner."

"Forgive me, your majesty." She mocked.

Reece's hands started shaking, and her legs became weak. She wanted to scream, she wanted to rip her hair out; why couldn't she escape this?

"Reece, you will return to your room until you've been examined by a physician."

"I'm not going anywhere." She responded firmly.

Allestaine stepped closer to Reece, "You can go on your own," she said in authoritative tone. "Or I will have someone escort you there."

"Please, don't," Reece whispered. "I'll go." Her heart began racing and she tried desperately to take in air but couldn't. She wanted to run away from this sudden feeling of panic, but where? How could she get rid of it? The more she panicked the worse it became. Her palms started sweating, her entire body became weak and she started sweating profusely. She needed to leave the presence of this woman at once.

Reece fled the room before Allestaine could respond. As she stumbled through the corridors and back to her room, she had a strange feeling this wasn't a dream. She had completely made an irrational fool out of herself with Allestaine, and there was no turning back now. But that wasn't what she was worried about. If she went to that room, she would fall asleep. With what sanity she had left, she knew she needed help. But she couldn't wait for the doctor in the room where the nightmares were waiting to torment her again.

She had to stay awake; she had to get outside. She stormed out to the gardens and sat on a bench facing away from the palace. She stared into the flowering bushes, and forced her tired eyes to stay open.

Chapter 15

Levi had successfully finished his training, and he couldn't be more relieved to leave Queen Galleta's estate and return to the palace. Finally, the palace came into view, and Levi's anticipation to be home with Reece was stronger than ever. He halted Areion abruptly when he saw his mother standing at the top of the steps in the courtyard. He dismounted quickly when he discerned the look of distress on her face.

"What has happened? Why are you out here?" he asked as he bounded up the steps to where she stood.

"I was awaiting the physician in the sitting room when I

noticed your return to the palace. I wanted to speak with you before you reported to the command center. I am so thankful you are home; Reece is ill."

"She's ill? How so? What's going on?" he demanded.

"She hasn't been eating or sleeping—"

"Where is she?" he interrupted.

"She is resting in her room."

Before his mother could say another word, Levi charged past her and headed toward Reece's room. When he arrived at the room, Jasmeen informed him that she hadn't seen Reece since she had left for breakfast that morning. Levi left the room swiftly, in search of where Reece may have gone.

He maintained a calm demeanor as he searched the areas where he believed she may have gone. As he strode through the halls, he encountered a servant. "Miss Talinger, do you know the whereabouts of Miss Bryant?"

The servant offered him a proper curtsy. "Master Levi, I have not seen her, sir."

Before she rose up, Levi had already thanked her and continued down the hallway. *Where could she have gone?* he thought in concern. He realized that he was wasting his time searching for her in the palace. Reece always found her solace outdoors, and that must be where he would find her. He promptly made his way toward the doors that exited out to the back garden of the palace.

As he stepped onto the balcony, he gazed out toward the pastures to see if she might be with Arrow. She wasn't there, so he briskly strode down the steps. He was almost out of the garden when he spied Reece sitting on a bench, facing away from him. He sighed in relief as he walked over to her. On his approach, his heart nearly stopped when she looked up at him with seemingly lifeless eyes.

———————▶

Reece stared up into Levi's darkened expression, and feared that this was yet another nightmare.

"My love?" He spoke softly, as he knelt in front of her.

She smiled at him, hoping he would not scold her as he always did in these terrifying dreams.

He carefully took her hands into his, and she trembled at his soft touch; she couldn't remember a time when she'd encountered a dream in which his strong hands were not gripping hers painfully. Tears began to fill her eyes as she took comfort in the sight of his hands tenderly holding hers; but if this was a dream, she knew at any moment they would tighten their embrace. They were so beautiful; everything about Levi was beautiful—or at least, it used to be.

"Reece? I need you to look at me."

His voice was becoming stern. She inhaled, waiting for him to lash out at her. She couldn't look at him; she was too afraid to take her eyes off of the peaceful sight of his hands gently holding hers.

He placed his index finger under her chin and brought her eyes up to meet his. The gesture startled her. She flinched, frightened of what would happen next. She stood abruptly and tried to flee from him, but he effortlessly prevented her escape. Levi stood in front of her and embraced her. *No, please…please don't hurt me,* she thought, as he held her close. She did everything in her power to free herself from him, but as always, she was powerless.

"Reece, I beg of you. Please stop fighting me. You are unwell, and I need you to communicate with me so I can help you."

Help me? You caused this! Reece thought angrily. She was at her limit with these nightmares of Levi controlling her. "I am fine, Levi! Why can't anyone see that? Leave me alone," she snarled in a weak voice.

"You are not okay, Reece," he answered. "Something is severely wrong. You must return to your room so the physician can evaluate your condition."

Reece closed her eyes. There was no way out of this; he would eventually force her to do his will. "Are you ordering me to my room, Levi?" she said with disgust.

Levi's expression was unreadable, and Reece cringed in fear.

"A physician should arrive at any time now. You must be examined."

"Fine! Get out of my way!"

She tried to walk past him, but he clutched her arm to prevent her passing.

"I will not get out of your way," he said in a stern voice. "You are in no condition to walk alone."

She jerked her arm away from him. Strangely, she was successful, unlike in her nightmares. She turned to leave, but her weak legs gave out on her. The next thing she knew she was cradled in Levi's arms.

With the last of her energy depleted, she laid her head against Levi's shoulder; she then experienced something that she never noticed in her horrific dreams, the fragrance she loved so much about him was present. *Is this the real Levi?* she thought as his rich, masculine scent soothed her entirely.

It really is him! This isn't a nightmare! She tried to reach up and touch his face to be sure this wasn't a nightmare, but her arms were too heavy. *No! No! Don't go to sleep, Reece.* She couldn't keep her eyes open, and her mind was fading. In a panic, she tried to scream his name so that he wouldn't let her fall asleep. Nothing came out. She used every last bit of energy she had to open her eyes. It was only for a brief moment, and then everything went black.

———————▶

Levi carried Reece directly to her bed. Jasmeen met him at the entrance to her room, while still preparing for the doctor's arrival. His heart was pounding in his chest because of what was taking place; but as much as it disturbed him to see Reece in this condition, he would not let emotion cloud his ability to ensure that she was properly cared for, and that her health was restored.

As soon as Reece was safely on her bed, he ordered the maiden to bring a tray of food and water. When Jasmeen reentered the room, Levi turned to Reece; as much as he wanted her to rest, it was painfully obvious that she needed nourishment and hydration more. He carefully brushed the back of his hand over her pale face to awaken her. His heart twisted in pain, because even as she slept, she flinched away from his touch.

"I need you to wake, love," he said softly.

Her eyes snapped open, and she stared at Levi fearfully. He instantly reacted to her expression, to assure her that he would not hurt her. *What has happened to you?* he thought as he went to embrace her. If he would have known the reaction it would cause, he would have never considered the gesture.

As he reached out to her, her eyes became wild with anger. "Get away from me! Get out of my room!" she snarled.

Levi's heart was breaking; he couldn't imagine what was causing her irrational behavior. The physician needed to arrive, and soon. He reached for the tray of food, and placed it on her bed in front of her.

"Tell me what happened, Reece." He asked with

concern.

"I said leave my room."

"Very well, if you are not going to tell me what's wrong, then you must at least eat something."

"I'm not hungry, Levi!" she snapped.

"Your body desperately requires nourishment, and I will stay here with you until I am confident that you will eat."

Reece looked at him with disgust as she reached for a morsel on her plate. "How much do I need to eat before you will leave?"

As much as Levi wanted to appease her and leave, he wouldn't. Reece depended on him to help her, whether she wanted him to or not. Her feeble appearance gave him even more strength to fight this appalling situation head on. He stared at Reece as he called for Jasmeen.

The maiden entered the bedchamber promptly.

"Find out where the physician is." He commanded.

He watched as Reece timidly placed small crumbs of food in her mouth. Levi pulled the chair to her bed, settled himself into it, and waited.

He studied Reece's condition. It appeared that she had not eaten or slept since he had been away. He started to wonder if she was struggling with a severe form of depression, brought on by being forced to live in Pemdas. She had dark circles around her sunken eyes, and it was quite obvious that she had lost a significant amount of weight.

He wanted so badly to lean forward and drop his head into his hands, but he maintained his composure. A few more minutes passed, and finally, Allestaine and the doctor were admitted into the room.

Levi dismissed himself, leaving Reece in his mother's care so that the doctor could examine her.

As he walked into Reece's sitting room, he encountered

his father. Navarre held a confident expression, and Levi was grateful for it.

"How is she? We had trusted that when she saw you again, it would have helped her. Is she any better?" Navarre asked.

Levi shook his head.

"Son, your mother and I are perplexed by this as well. She never mentioned she was unwell. I must say, she has done an excellent job of concealing everything from us this entire time."

Levi walked over and sat numbly on the sofa. He stared into the flames of the healthy fire in the fireplace. Something about the way they danced and flickered calmed his mind.

"Has anybody said that she's been acting strange?" Levi asked.

"Your mother only noticed the severity of her condition this morning." Navarre said as he sat on the sofa.

Levi looked at his father. "This doesn't make sense; why would she stop eating?"

"We will find out as soon as Doctor Fletcher finishes his examination."

"You're right. Has Harrison returned to Pemdas?" He asked, changing the subject.

"No, I have not seen him in over a week." Navarre said with a laugh. "It appears he threw himself into assignments on Earth until you returned to the palace. He mentioned more than once that he was not about to spend his days lounging around a house full of women chattering about an engagement party."

Levi laughed faintly, and brought his attention back to the flames in the fireplace.

He ran both of his hands through his hair, and exhaled. "I wish I hadn't been gone for so long."

Before they could say anything more, the doctor appeared. Levi and Navarre stood to greet the man.

"She is resting now," Doctor Fletcher said. "She was severely deprived of nourishment, and critically in need of rest. Her hydration levels were low as well. I have given her a remedy to replenish her health, and the effects are already starting to take effect."

"Did you discover anything that would have caused her lack of appetite and rest? Did she mention anything to you?" Levi asked.

The doctor shook his head. "I found no underlying causes; she's in excellent health. I believe that stress may have been a factor in all of this. I understand that she was heavily involved in planning the engagement party. Also, you should consider that she is from Earth, and not a natural resident of Pemdas. That is a monumental transition for anyone to be required to make."

"What are your orders for us to help her recover?" Navarre asked.

"I have already advised her that I do not want her out of bed for at least a day or two. She may not remember our conversation when she wakes up, so she needs to be reminded of that. She must rest. The remedy I concocted for her promotes this, so she will be asleep until morning. When she has recovered, she must be careful not to overexert herself in any way. Other than that, she will be feeling renewed by morning. Simply make sure she is cautious with her activities over the next few weeks."

After giving further instructions to them, the doctor was escorted out. When Allestaine stepped into the sitting room, she explained to Levi that she agreed with Doctor Fletcher's assessment and suggested to Levi that they postpone the engagement celebration.

Levi agreed somewhat, but he couldn't remove the idea

from his mind that Reece could be having a hard time living in Pemdas. He understood exactly what the doctor implied about her not easily adjusting to Pemdas; he had considered that himself. *Is she missing her home on Earth? This must be why she was so upset with me earlier.* Levi thought.

After Navarre and Allestaine left Levi to stay with Reece, he walked back into her bedchamber. He stared at her peaceful expression, and it alleviated his distress. He approached the side of her bed, and caressed her cheek. He bent over and kissed her tenderly on her forehead.

He sat in the chair next to her bed, and pulled her hand into his; as he sunk into the chair, overwhelmed with grief. Levi had no idea how long he sat deep in thought, when Jasmeen entered the room.

"Master Harrison has arrived."

"Send him in."

Her expression was that of concern. "Sir, may I advise you to join him for dinner? I will stay with Reece and watch over her in your absence. If there is any problem, I will have you notified at once."

Levi stood. "That will not be necessary, Jasmeen. I thank you for your concern, but I will not leave Reece's side for any reason at this time. Please arrange to have a tray sent up, and I will take my dinner here."

Jasmeen nodded and left the room.

Levi moved toward a more secluded area in Reece's room, where two chairs were positioned around a small table along the wall. He could view Reece from where he sat, yet he and Harrison could have a quiet conversation without disturbing her rest.

Harrison entered the room and glanced at Reece as he walked over to where Levi sat. "I am curious. Are they sure that Reece was the one in need of the doctor? I believe it is *you* who looks to be on the verge of death." He gave Levi a quick pat on his shoulder, and then sat across the small table from him. "It is good to see you again, my friend."

Levi smiled briefly. "Likewise, Harrison."

"Samuel informed me that your training was successful with Galleta!" Harrison smiled proudly at Levi. "Excellent work! I must admit, serving on Earth is not the same without you."

Levi chuckled. "The other men couldn't put up with your nonsense, I assume?"

"*Keep* up!" Harrison corrected. "*Keep* up with my amazing talents, of course." he laughed, and then looked over at Reece. "I heard she's going to come out of this okay."

"I do not know what has happened to her. I cannot tell you how long I've been sitting here struggling to understand what caused this. I can only conclude that it is a result of her being forced to live in Pemdas." He looked at Harrison.

"Was she really that bad?"

"I can't describe to you how she looked when I first came upon her. It was horrid. The worst part was that she was extremely frightened of me. The repulsion she held for me in her eyes…" He trailed off, unable to finish.

"Levi, you need to pull yourself together. She'll be fine now. This is most likely a result of her trying to keep up with all of the engagement planning." He stretched out his long legs and crossed them. "I encountered her for a few moments before I left for Earth, and she appeared quite frantic about it all, even then."

"What do you mean?"

"I passed her in the downstairs corridor walking with Simone the other day. She was carrying linens, her hair falling out of its pins, and she seemed like she was in a hurry to get somewhere." He softly laughed. "Of course, I teased her, and asked if Jasmeen had taken the week off."

Harrison looked over at Reece. "I guess I should have read into it more, especially after the colorful words she paid me in response to my teasing her."

"All of this is inexplicable to me. Maybe she was overdoing it with the planning?" Levi added.

"That's possibly why I didn't read any more into her frazzled demeanor. She only reinforced why I was returning to my duties, and why I advised you to avoid a traditional ceremony from Earth." He leaned back and crossed his arms. "There was no way I was about to stay here and listen to the voices of stressed-out women planning parties, and all the other nonsense that is included with these celebrations."

Levi leaned forward and rested his elbows on his knees. "Well, apparently she managed to hide it all rather well from everyone." He exhaled. "She wasn't feeling well the night before I left; I wonder if that was the start of all of this. But why would Reece overexert herself like that?"

"If you spend your time obsessing over how you and everyone should have seen this coming, you will go mad. Reece will recover; and when she does, I highly suggest that we kick Simone out of the house, and then cancel the ostentatious engagement party."

Levi's eyes widened in revelation at what Harrison had said, but before he could say anything, Jasmeen entered with Levi's tray of food.

"Jasmeen, I must say, I am offended!" Harrison said with a smug grin. "Are you not concerned for my well-being also?"

Jasmeen laughed softly. "Forgive me, Master Harrison. Will you be taking your dinner here as well?"

"Well, I am not necessarily going anywhere for a while. I believe it is my duty to make sure Levi doesn't fall apart on you," he said with a wink.

"Give me a moment," she said, and left the room.

Levi remained focused on Reece, ignoring the food that was brought up to him. He ran both hands through his hair as he contemplated what Harrison had said.

"You should probably eat; staring at Reece is not going to solve anything right now," Harrison added. "And quit running your hands through your hair every time you become bothered by something or you will soon have none left!" he said with a laugh.

Levi looked back at his cousin. "I believe you may be on to something."

"Of course I am; now eat, before you go bald and are forced to stay in your bed as well."

Levi rolled his eyes. "I am talking about Reece." He eyed Harrison. "Do you suppose Simone could have had something to do with this?"

Harrison smiled at Levi mischievously. "There's only one way to find out," he answered.

Levi's darkened expression didn't change as he nodded in agreement.

Chapter 16

Levi awoke early the next morning, somewhat stiff from sleeping in the chair next to Reece's bed all night. Any discomfort was replaced when he noted Reece's improved appearance as she continued to sleep. The natural, healthy glow of her complexion had returned, and that meant her health had improved drastically.

Soon enough she would be awake, and he would have the satisfaction of staring into her healthy, blue eyes. He looked forward to discussing with her the events that had transpired during his absence.

He stood and cautiously made his way over to where she lay in bed. He gently brushed her hair from her forehead and leaned over to place a tender kiss on it. "I love you," he whispered.

He pulled his waistcoat on, and had begun the process of tying his cravat, when Jasmeen entered the bedchamber. The expression on her face was that of distress.

"Jasmeen?" he said, as he finished tying his cravat. "Is something wrong?"

"Forgive the intrusion, sir, but Simone is here to call on Reece."

What is she doing here? Levi thought in annoyance. He was irritated by her visitation, but this gave him the perfect opportunity to question what had happened in his absence.

"Have her wait in the sitting room; I'll be out in a moment." He said.

After Jasmeen left, Levi took a few moments of silence to calm himself and gather his senses. He couldn't approach this with the anger that he constantly felt toward the woman. He needed to deal with Simone rationally. It was only an assumption, but after Simone proved her initial hatred toward Reece, Levi would never be able to trust the woman's motives. With one last glance at Reece, he exited the bed chamber.

$\longrightarrow$

Reece's eyes snapped open after fighting for her life in yet another terrorizing dream, but something was different this time. She felt a little weak, but her thoughts weren't so scrambled. For the first time in a long time, she could validate that she had woken up from a dream.

Without hesitation, she reached for her journal, and quickly jotted down this particular nightmare. This one was about Movac, and the other aliens in the council, fighting to get the map to the stone from her mind. She shuddered at the memory of the excruciating pain she'd felt in her head.

As she recalled that particular part of her dream, her head began to throb. She sat up to call for Jasmeen, but before she got out of bed, she froze when she heard voices out in the sitting room. Her heart started racing when she noticed the chair that was pulled up next to her bed. *That looks strangely familiar,* she thought, as she realized this exact situation took place in one of her very first nightmares about Levi.

She swallowed hard when she recognized that both of the voices in her sitting room belonged to Levi and Simone. *Am I having premonitions now?* she thought. It was definitely strange and frightening that a dream could have predicted the future.

She grabbed her journal and flipped to the pages of the nightmare she'd had about this exact moment. "No," she softly whispered. "It can't be." she said to herself, as this scenario was identical to the previous dream. She would have to change it, then. Her entire approach to Levi had to be different, and she had to find a way to get him out of her room. She carefully slid the journal back in its hiding spot and pulled on her robe. Her head was pounding with this awful headache, and she was struggling to walk toward the exit of her bedchamber.

She stopped at the entrance, using the door frame to hold herself up. She noticed that Levi and Simone were in the exact same places she remembered in her dream. Levi was staring solemnly down at Simone, while Simone cried into her hands.

She glanced at Levi, and was instantly repulsed by the expression on his face. How many times had he looked at her like that in her nightmares?

"Levi!" she called out to him sternly.

Levi's head snapped up and his eyes were wide with amazement. "Reece, why did you not call for Jasmeen?" Levi approached her, and she instinctively avoided him by quickly walking over to sit by Simone on the couch. If that nightmare was a premonition, there was no way she would give Levi an opportunity to hurt her.

"Tell me what's going on out here, Levi!" She looked up to find him standing in the middle of the room, staring at her with a look of total confusion.

Levi's brow furrowed in question. "Forgive me if I woke you, it was not my intention. Simone and I were—"

Reece let out an exaggerated exhale. "Levi! Just stop. It's obvious that you are out here blaming Simone for something."

"I have not blamed Simone for anything," he said in disillusionment. "She sits here distraught, concerned for you."

Reece studied Levi's bewildered expression, and even though this was no longer playing out like her dream had, she could hardly look at him without feeling absolutely disgusted by his presence. *Have these nightmares destroyed my love for him?*

Simone interrupted her thoughts. "Reece, Levi has been nothing but kind since I entered the room. Of course he had his fears of me harming you, but I understand why he would feel that way."

Reece's eyes narrowed as she stared at Levi. "I think you should leave," she said flatly.

"Leave?" he responded.

"Yes, leave my room. I don't need you in here lecturing Simone and jumping to conclusions about her hurting me."

Levi's posture stiffened, and his expression was

unreadable. "Reece, the doctor has requested you rest for at least a day in bed. Before I leave, I must be assured that you will remain in bed until your health is restored," he finally responded.

"I don't need you giving me orders!" she answered, as she stood and brushed past him toward her room. She gazed up into his dark expression. "But I will get in bed so you'll leave."

"Reece, please." His eyes were pleading as they stared into hers. "After returning to find you so ill yesterday, I was hoping we could talk—"

"Later," she interrupted him. "For now, just go."

Reece's head was throbbing, and she had no idea why she was being so rude to him.

"Very well," he answered, before turning to leave the room. As Simone proceeded to follow him, Reece called out.

"Simone, please stay," she said, forcing Levi and Simone both to stare at her in disbelief. "I want to talk to you."

Levi watched Simone speculatively as she walked over to where Reece stood. One last glance at Reece, and he was out of the room.

Once he was gone, Reece felt a sudden wave of emotion and the need to have Levi back in the room again. *Ugh! My head is killing me!* she thought, as she massaged her forehead. *Why am I acting like this? All I want is him out of my sight, and now all I want is him back with me?* She wanted to scream at how psychotic she was behaving. She was absolutely disgusted with herself for treating Levi the way she did.

"Is everything okay?" Simone asked.

"I don't know," Reece answered honestly. "I need something to get rid of this headache." She looked at Simone. "I have to apologize to Levi for that; I feel horrible."

Simone gently guided Reece back toward her bed. "Once you are feeling better, I'll have Jasmeen send for him."

For the next hour or so, Simone brought Reece up to speed about how she'd been acting over the last week when she'd stopped eating and sleeping. Unable to remember much of anything, Reece was mortified by her behavior, and she wondered how she would be able to face everyone again. After Simone had left, Reece sat in her bed contemplating how she would apologize to everyone.

That evening, food was sent up to Reece, and even though Elizabeth and Allestaine visited her, Levi never returned. Elizabeth and Allestaine forgave Reece's irrational behavior, thankful she was feeling better. Now there was only one person left to apologize to, and she wondered if Levi would check on her before he retired for the night. She was desperately missing him, and most of all, she had to apologize to him. She sat there, tracing the pattern of the quilt on her bed, wondering if she should have Jasmeen send for him. She went to call for Jasmeen, and her heart nearly stopped when she heard Levi's voice out in her sitting room.

She wanted to jump from the bed and into his arms; however, she had no idea how to act around him. She was unforgettably rude, and she deserved Levi being upset with her.

Jasmeen entered her bedchamber. "Reece, Master Levi is here."

"Please, tell him to come in," she said.

As soon as Levi entered the room, Reece smiled warmly at him.

"You appear to be feeling much better," he said, as he walked in and stood at the foot of her bed.

"I'm so sorry about this morning." She started to get out of bed.

Before she could get up, Levi was there, stopping her. "Don't get up." he said.

"Will you sit with me?" she asked, as she stared up at him.

Levi's solemn expression faded. "Of course."

She moved over and gestured for him to join her on the bed. When he did, Reece embraced him, and couldn't fight her uncontrollable sobs if she wanted to. She didn't understand why a few seconds ago all she wanted was him to hold her, and the moment he did, she felt repulsed by his closeness.

Don't push him away, she commanded herself.

Levi ran his hand over her hair. "My love, please tell me what is wrong."

Reece choked back the tears, and Levi gently pulled her up to face him. "Let me help you," he said purposefully.

Reece forced a smile. "Nothing's wrong." Her eyes locked onto his. "You're already helping me, just by being here." She hoped he believed her lie.

He reached for her face, and Reece resisted the urge to pull away from his touch. As he tenderly rubbed her cheek, her teeth clenched together, wishing he would stop touching her. She focused on his eyes, which were dark with desire, and Reece was nauseated by the fact that he may kiss her.

Why am I feeling like this? she thought in absolute frustration as her head began pounding.

"I love you so much," he said in a low voice.

"I love you," she managed to answer him.

His vivid eyes continued to stare into hers as he brought his hand up to cradle her head, and then his lips were on hers. Reece pressed her lips together tightly, absolutely repulsed by him. Levi withdrew, "Forgive me." He said in a soft voice.

Reece didn't know what to think, say, or do. The sorrow apparent on his face was heartbreaking to look at. She had to make this right somehow.

She brought her lips back to his and ignored her feelings. She deepened their kiss, striving with all that she was to find her passion for him again. It seemed to help, but it wasn't enough. Levi made her feelings of repulsion increase as he withdrew from her mouth and began kissing along her jaw and her neck. Her fingers dug into his back as she restrained herself from shoving him away.

This wasn't fair. *All because of these nightmares?* she thought in frustration. *Will I ever love him again?* She started crying in utter defeat, and Levi withdrew from her instantaneously. She couldn't look into his eyes, so she embraced him.

Levi's arms tightened around her. "Talk to me, Reece," he said, concerned. "What happened while I was gone?"

She couldn't talk to him; and right now, she needed him to leave. She had to find a way to ask him to go without being as harsh as she was earlier.

"If you don't mind, can we talk about it tomorrow?" she said, as she withdrew from his embrace.

"Of course." He reached for her cheek, but she reflexively shied away.

"Please," she begged, "just let me rest; I'm not feeling well again. This annoying headache is killing me." She said as she started rubbing her temples.

"I'll have Jasmeen send for another remedy. Would you like me to stay until the pain subsides?"

"No," she blurted out. She managed to recover her rudeness with a forced smile. "I'll be fine." She got under her covers, and relaxed back into her pillows. "That remedy will help, and I think going back to sleep might help too." she said.

Levi stood up, "I will let Jasmeen know, and will be back

to check on you in the morning." He offered a faint smile. "Rest well." He said as he turned to leave her bedchamber.

As the next two weeks passed, her feelings of repulsion toward Levi drove her further away from him. The terrorizing nightmares had started to diminish, and she was able to eat and stay nourished. The help of a soothing tea provided her with the ability to sleep well. A stronger remedy was concocted for her headaches, and it eased her pain somewhat. It was no longer the lack of food or rest causing her irrational behavior; there was no explanation now.

She was in torment, fighting the feelings she was having for Levi. He had tried numerous times to bring her off somewhere alone with him, but she would make Simone or Elizabeth join them. She had no desire to be alone with him anymore.

She did her best to make him believe that she still loved him, but it was difficult. On the rare occasion that he did try to kiss her, she always turned her face away from his. Levi was very hesitant with her now, but she could sense his patience with her irrational behavior toward him as well. Reece knew she needed more time; a lot of her irritability toward Levi and his family seemed to stem from her relentless and unexpected headaches. Doctor Fletcher returned to the palace, but had no answers for them. Reece's examinations proved she was perfectly healthy; the only cause for her pain must be stress.

Reece figured that if this was all due to stress, then she should deal with it the best way she knew how. She decided to start her morning off with a jog and planned to get back into her normal routine again. The day was playing out well, and so she decided to resume planning for the engagement party.

She went directly to the grand ballroom and started

going through the decorating books. "Can I help you find something, Reece?" Allestaine asked politely as she walked up from behind.

Reece turned and smiled. "No, I was just going through the planning books again. I promise I won't go crazy like I did last time," she said with a laugh.

Allestaine smiled sympathetically at her. "Reece, sweetheart, forgive me for not telling you earlier, but we have cancelled the engagement celebration—"

Reece didn't hear anything else Allestaine said. Her headache returned in full force. She stared at Allestaine in repulsion as she gritted her teeth angrily. She had no doubt that this must have been Levi's idea. The last time it was discussed with her, the engagement party was postponed; now it was cancelled? The unexplainable hatred she felt toward Levi came flooding through her again. She shook her head in disgust. *Who does he think he is?* Her head was pounding, but her repulsion toward Levi helped her ignore the excruciating pain.

"Well, don't I look like an idiot?" She nearly growled.

"Reece, it was for your own good. If you want to proceed with having the celebration, we can arrange it. It was just that Levi thought it best to cancel it until further notice—"

"So he *did* cancel it," she said, with utter disgust in her voice. "I knew it!"

"Reece, darling, it is not what you are thinking," Allestaine replied.

"Don't call me darling!" Reece snapped as she gripped her aching forehead. She stared sternly at Allestaine. "Does it matter what I think, anyway? Obviously it didn't to Levi, because he never discussed any of his plans to cancel it with me!" She laughed in disbelief. "Well, I guess this is the first step toward the perfect marriage, right?"

Allestaine's eyes filled with tears, and Reece couldn't help but feel badly for what she'd said. *Reece! What is wrong with you?* She thought as she struggled to pull herself together.

"I'm sorry, that was uncalled for. I'm just really confused about everything these days." She sensed her own tears starting to surface.

"I am confident you and Levi will find your way through all of this. You are correct; he should have discussed his plans to cancel the party with you. I was under the impression he had done so already, or I would have never approached you in this manner."

"If he returns early, will you let him know I need to talk with him?"

"Of course. Would you care to join Elizabeth and me on a trip down to the village within the hour?"

Reece could sense herself becoming unwell again and couldn't trust herself around anyone. Given the fact that she had just snapped at Allestaine, she felt it would be best to spend the afternoon alone relaxing in her room.

"I'm really tired all of the sudden; I think I'll go lie down." Reece answered.

"Very well then, we will not be gone for long." She embraced Reece. "It's all going to be okay."

Reece returned to her room and rested for the next hour or so. She had taken a small nap, and felt revitalized. When she woke, she thought of Levi cancelling their engagement party. She inquired of Jasmeen to see if he had returned, and the maiden let her know that he wasn't expected until later that evening. Reece spent the rest of the afternoon in her room, not prepared to be in the company of anyone until dinner. She relaxed in a chair by her fireplace with a blanket and a book.

When Reece was prepared for dinner, she made her way

to the dining hall. She hoped to walk in and see Levi already at the dining table, but he wasn't. She found her usual seat, and forced herself to be patient. He would return from guarding on Earth tonight, and then she would question him about cancelling their engagement celebration. She sipped her wine, letting it calm her anxious nerves; the more she thought about what he had done, the angrier she became.

Chapter 17

Levi didn't know how to feel or what to believe about Reece anymore. It was clear; she wanted nothing to do with him any longer. She was still recovering from her illness, and he needed to be patient with her. He would not allow himself to consider that she no longer loved him. He did wonder that, aside from her recovering from being sick, perhaps things could have moved too fast in their relationship.

Levi understood very well that he handled his love for her a lot differently than how most men on Earth would. Maybe it would have been better that he waited to ask for her hand in marriage. *I should have courted her longer and given her more time with me.* He thought as he ran a hand through his hair. His thoughts shifted to the one underlying issue that he assumed Reece now despised him for; the fact that she was forced to live in his world.

How was it that he and his kind had, for their entire existence, served to protect the humans on Earth from harm, and yet the one human woman he loved the most was suffering because of his world and their cause? What could he do to make her smile, to see her laugh, and want to be in his presence again?

"Levi!" Harrison called loudly, and by the frustration in his voice, it wasn't the first time he'd called his name.

Levi snapped out of his daze. He looked at Harrison darkly while he gripped his communication device angrily. "What?"

Harrison returned Levi's glare, "What are Samuel's orders? Have they overheard anything more on the local police scanners?" Harrison demanded while speeding down the dark road.

Harrison ripped the communication device from Levi's hand and conversed with Samuel. It was obvious that Harrison's irritation with Levi was growing swiftly, but Levi didn't care anymore.

As soon as Harrison was done receiving the information from Samuel, he tossed the device back over to Levi in frustration.

"You are driving me insane," he said, as he spun the car around. He glared at him firmly. "We passed the turn-off thirty miles ago. With any luck, the family that the Plerityons are planning to terrorize won't already be abducted by the time we get there." He shook his head. "You seriously need to pull yourself together."

Levi glared at his cousin. "Harrison, just drive the car.

All we have is a UFO sighting from local law enforcement and the neighboring communities. That's all we've had from these creatures for the last three days. They are playing games like they always do. You know how they are. They can't shape-shift into human form, and therefore it is very rare—"

"Levi!" Harrison called out, interrupting him. "They are on the ground! The latest police report said that there were four or five green individuals spotted walking around this innocent family's farm house." He stared at Levi in utter annoyance. "But how would you know that? You haven't listened to a word Samuel's said to you."

Levi looked back at his cousin in defeat. "Harrison, forgive me—"

Harrison turned onto a private dirt road, and increased their speed. "I'll forgive you later, let's just handle this business and get home."

$$\longrightarrow$$

As dinner progressed, Reece grew more impatient. *Are they ever going to get back tonight?* She thought as she grit her teeth.

"Is everything okay, Reece?" Allestaine spoke with concern from across the table.

Reece looked down and noticed her tightly clenched fists. She relaxed her hands and forced a smile; but before she could respond, the doors to the dining area opened, admitting Levi and Harrison into the room.

"Good evening, all. It is truly wonderful to be home again. Have you missed us?" Harrison announced, while smiling mischievously at Reece.

Levi took his usual seat next to Reece and greeted her. "Good evening, Reece. You look lovely this evening."

Reece shuddered. She thought she was in a bad mood a few minutes ago? Now it was heightened by Levi's presence. "Why are you guys so late?" she asked bitterly.

Harrison laughed aloud as he took a sip of wine. "And so it begins; the lovely lady questioning her man about where he's been."

Reece's eyes narrowed. *This guy can be so annoying.* She was so infuriated by Harrison's interjection that she restrained herself from responding. She looked to Levi, and waited for his answer.

"Our last assignment went longer than planned," he answered, while a servant placed his plate of food in front of him.

The way he seemed to brush her off fueled Reece's agitation.

"Yes," Harrison said. "But, I have to admit, if it wasn't for Levi, we wouldn't have had the opportunity to charge into a spacecraft today."

"Wow, how exciting," Reece said in a mocking tone.

"Indeed, it was." Harrison grew more serious as he locked his gaze on Reece. "Whenever we are successful in saving those on Earth from being terrorized by other entities, there is a great sense of excitement that follows."

Reece's lips tightened as she restrained herself from countering back at him. She inhaled deeply and took a sip of her wine. It served to calm her some, and fortunately, Samuel started asking questions about the assignment. Reece remained silent throughout the rest of dinner. She wanted so desperately to get out of this horrible mood, but no matter what she did, she was irritated.

After dinner, the family retired to one of the sitting rooms. Reece planned to take this opportunity to question Levi about cancelling their engagement party. She sat next to Simone on the sofa, and the men took up seating across from them. She knew it wasn't the best time to bring the issue up, but she didn't care. And so, without regard to anyone present, she did it anyway.

"Levi? I found out some interesting news today," she said, with excitement in her voice.

Levi's eyes widened and he smiled in response to her cheerful tone. "What is that, Reece?" he answered.

Her eyes narrowed as she smiled at him. "Well, apparently our engagement party is cancelled. Could you imagine how surprised I was when I got the news?"

Harrison stifled a laugh, and Levi sat there expressionless.

"I believed it would be best," he responded.

"Really! Best for whom, Levi? You?"

"Reece, this is not the place to discuss this matter. Allow me to escort you on a walk, and I can explain myself in a more private setting."

"No, I think this is the perfect place to discuss it. I'm sure that everyone here is already aware of the decision you made. From the expression on everyone's faces sitting around us right now, it's obvious that I was the only one you decided *not* to tell about your bright idea."

"Reece, please—"

"No, Levi!" She faced Simone. "Simone, tell me; were you aware of this brilliant decision before now?"

Simone looked at Levi, and before she could answer her, Reece already knew the answer. "Never mind, I think it's obvious." Reece ignored Elizabeth sitting at her other side and looked directly at Harrison. "And you, Harrison?"

Harrison smiled in return. "Of course I knew of it; however, I feel you are being quite harsh on Levi, as it was *my* idea in the first place."

Reece rolled her eyes. "Why am I not surprised? Maybe you should stay out of our business, Harrison."

"Reece, please…Levi only considered cancelling it for fear of it causing you any unneeded stress. He was concerned for your health," Elizabeth said softly.

"Really? So not only did everyone know about this – except for me, of course – but you all also knew *why* he would do it?" She glared at Levi. "Wow, Levi, I don't even know what to say."

"Forgive me, Reece. You must understand, it wasn't my intention to upset you like this. I am sorry I didn't discuss it with you first. If it is your desire to have the celebration, I will arrange for the preparations to resume at once," Levi replied.

Harrison exhaled, rolled his eyes, and slouched back, watching Reece intently.

Reece stared at Levi warningly. "Obviously we aren't in very good place right now. As a matter of fact, I think I need to get away from this palace."

She stood up, and looked down at Simone. "Simone, is there any chance you will be returning to your home soon?"

Simone swallowed hard as she looked at Levi, and then Reece. "I wasn't planning on it, but—"

"I don't want to impose," Reece interrupted her, "but if by chance you decide to leave, can I go with you?"

"Reece, what are you doing? This is absurd. All over an engagement party being cancelled? Like I said; blame me, not Levi. I encouraged him to cancel it. Don't you think you're overreacting just a little bit?" Harrison cut in.

"No, Harrison, I don't!" she snapped harshly. She looked down at Simone. "Simone, would you mind?"

"Yes, of course you are welcome to stay at my home. But I really think it would be best if—"

"Then it's settled. When can we leave?" Reece cut her off again.

Levi stood up. "I can have your carriage arranged for tomorrow. Jasmeen will accompany you as well, if that is your wish," he replied flatly.

Reece's heart beat rapidly as he stood there, tall and imposing, staring down at her. It startled her for a moment, and then she recalled how many times he looked at her like this in her nightmares. She shuddered internally, wondering if he would grab her arm harshly and force her out of the room with him.

Unexpectedly, his expression softened. "If or when you should decide to return, your personal guards will arrange for your transportation back to the palace."

"Guards?" Reece said, annoyed. "I don't need people following me around, Levi."

"Unfortunately, you don't have an option on that one, Reece," Harrison spoke out. "That little map in your mind mandates that you be guarded at all times."

"This is so ridiculous!" She glared at Levi. "I don't need anybody following me around." She ordered him.

Levi stared at her commandingly. "They are there for your safety. I'll have everything prepared for you first thing tomorrow," he said, before turning to briskly leave the room.

How dare he walk out on me? she thought in her rising anger. She became distracted when Harrison stood and stared at her in confusion.

"What, Harrison?" she bitterly demanded.

"Don't you think you're going a little overboard, Reece?" Harrison asked.

"Harrison, this isn't your problem!"

Harrison smiled but it didn't reach his piercing icy blue eyes. "*You* have no idea how much this is about to become my problem!"

The smile on his face was fueling her rage. "Whatever."

Harrison's expression changed. He grew more solemn. "Reece," he said deeply. "Perhaps you and Levi need to talk about this in private. You don't need to leave the palace in order to prove your point that you are upset with him."

"I agree with Harrison, Reece." Simone reached for Reece's hand.

Reece jerked away. "You're taking their side on this?" She snorted. "Are you going to help me or not?" she asked Simone.

Elizabeth remained silent as she watched Reece lash out at everyone around her. Harrison's gaze was almost threatening as he stared at Simone, waiting for her response.

Simone sighed. "Yes, we can leave tomorrow."

Reece smiled with satisfaction at Harrison's concerned expression. "Then it's settled."

Before either could respond, Reece quickly fled the room. She wasn't done with Levi yet, and she needed to find out where he went. She turned down the corridor, and encountered a servant.

"Sir?" She startled him with her brazen tone.

He bowed. "Miss Bryant, how may I be of assistance to you?"

"Where's Levi?" she demanded.

"Miss Bryant, Master Levi has retired to his chambers for the evening. May I call on him for you?"

Hiding out in your room and feeling sorry for yourself, huh? she thought with disgust. "No! Take me to his room."

The confusion in the servant's eyes told Reece this was highly improper, but she didn't care; her argument with Levi was not over.

"Sir!" she snapped. "Take me to his room!" she ordered again.

The servant nodded, and with some hesitation, turned and led Reece up to the third floor of the palace. She had never explored these floors before, but understood that this was the Oxley's private living area.

At the end of the long hallway were two large double doors. The servant knocked on them softly. The hesitation the servant was displaying was aggravating, and she stepped forward abruptly. "Thank you." She arched her eyebrow, and dismissed him with her reproachful gaze.

The door opened, and when Levi's valet saw her, he stared at her in utter astonishment. She let out a quick breath; all of this propriety was making her irritation worse, and validating why she wanted to leave this pretentious place.

She crossed her arms. "I need to speak with Levi." She spoke loudly, hoping Levi would hear her.

"Who is it, Henry?" Levi called out distantly.

Before the servant answered him, Reece shoved the other door open and stormed into the room. Levi stood in front of the large windows at the front of his room. He turned at the sound of Reece entering his room.

Her eyes were drawn to the paintings that lined the burgundy walls of his room. The pictures were magnificently set into rich mahogany frames, and displayed beautiful images of scenery and Guardian horses. Levi's room was exceptionally warm and inviting. The décor, in Reece's opinion, spoke of his personality very well. She walked past a large mahogany desk toward charcoal-colored sofas situated around the fireplace. Various books lined the elaborate, mahogany mantel that lavishly framed the large fireplace.

Levi was watching her in suspicion. "Reece?"

"We need to talk!" she demanded.

Levi addressed his butler. "That will be all for this

evening; thank you, Henry." When he brought his attention back to Reece, his expression was somber. "I trust you have said everything you needed to say to me tonight."

"No, and that's because you ran out of the room before I was finished!"

Levi ran a hand through his hair and exhaled. "I'm listening."

"First of all, for a man who seems to be so *proper* all of the time, I'm trying to figure out why you were so rude to me tonight. How dare you walk out on me! And then you come up to sulk in your room?"

Levi's expression was unreadable, and she went on. "I don't know what's going on between us, but right now, I don't know what to think anymore! Tell me why you think that it's okay to go running around and making decisions behind my back!"

His expression changed to that of regret, and it repulsed her. He reached for her arm. "Reece," he said softly.

Reece shook his hand off of her. "Don't, Levi! I simply came up here to tell you that I can take care of myself! I don't need anyone telling me what I can and can't do! Or what I should or shouldn't be doing. Maybe that's how it works in the royal family, but that's not how it's going to work for me."

Levi didn't answer her; instead, his countenance grew dark as he studied her. She started to demand a response from him but before she could, her emotions took a wild turn again. At first her head felt as if it would explode, and then almost as quickly as the pain hit her, it left, and she found herself overwhelmed by Levi's presence.

What is wrong with me? She thought as she battled her emotions. It felt as though something were controlling her. No matter how hard she fought she couldn't resist it. A strong desire came over her to have him kiss her deeply and powerfully; then other thoughts began consuming her. They were so great that she couldn't think about anything but wanting him.

Levi stared at her indifferently as she sauntered over to where he stood. She reached up, bringing both arms around his neck, drawing his face down onto hers. He didn't embrace her in response, and when his lips touched hers, they were motionless. She had to get him to give in, so she must apologize.

She stepped back and allowed tears to fill her eyes. "Levi, I'm so sorry. I'm such a horrible person."

"Reece, you should rest. We can work this out tomorrow. I'll have Henry escort you to your room."

Tears ran down her cheeks, "Right now I have to be with you." She said as she reached for his face.

Levi's eyes closed as he inhaled deeply.

"Kiss me, Levi," she said in a seductive tone.

Levi opened his eyes and stared down into hers. He wasn't saying no, so once again she wrapped her arms around him, pressing her body tightly into his. Levi didn't fight her, and he fulfilled her aching desire by placing his lips lightly on hers. Without hesitation, she deepened their kiss, and Levi accepted.

She hungered for more as though she had never kissed him before. She ran her hands along his sturdy sides. *He's unimaginably perfect.* A strange voice sounded in her head. Reece sensed the awkwardness of the situation, but she was powerless against the force taking over her. So lost was she in the sensations of everything she was feeling and wanting, she couldn't understand why Levi's hands gripped hers firmly and he stepped away from her.

Reece grew infuriated, but resisted the urge to laugh when he brought his fingers to his bottom lip to examine the trace of blood on it.

Did I just bite his lip? she thought in humor. "Looks like the brave Pemdai warrior isn't so tough after all, eh?" she said with a dark laugh.

Her humor was replaced when Levi stared at her in disbelief. "I think you should go." Levi's eyes were fierce. "I have no idea what is happening with you, Reece. Something is not right; you are not acting like yourself."

She cocked her head to the side. "You know what, Levi? It doesn't matter anymore, anyway. Forget it. I'm trying to make things work out between us, and apparently kissing you was a bad idea." She whirled around and stomped to the door.

She opened it and turned back to him before walking out. "Make sure you have the carriage ready for me to leave tomorrow."

With that she spun on her heel in a fury, and stormed through the corridor and down the steps to her room.

Chapter 18

Levi was motionless, and his eyes were fixed on the door that Reece slammed on her way out of his room. After weeks of enduring her aggressive mood swings and her constant irritation with him, Levi had finally reached his breaking point.

He began unbuttoning his shirt as he walked into his closet. He shrugged the shirt off, gathered it up, and threw it forcefully against the wall. It was obvious that he needed to unwind. He quickly changed into a pair of shorts, pulled on a dark robe, and left his room. He strode briskly through the servants' passageways down to one of the large pool rooms in the palace.

He wasted no time removing his robe and plunging head first into the crisp water. His chest barely grazed the bottom of the pool before he swam back up to the surface. Once above water, he swam vigorously through the crystal clear water, letting each lap he made calm his tense nerves.

What was happening between him and Reece? How did it come to this? No matter how aggressively he swam through the water, it could not erase the strange feelings of the last kiss they shared. For the first time ever in Reece's presence, Levi had no desire to kiss her. This was not the woman he fell in love with. Something had changed drastically, and Levi was losing her.

With these thoughts resurfacing, Levi felt all of his energy draining. He finished a final lap, and held onto the side of the pool. He placed both elbows upon the stone surface, and smoothed his hair back with his hands. The thought of losing Reece sent a violent pain through him. Regardless of her behavior, he loved her so greatly, and he couldn't imagine his life without her in it. What had he done to cause her such bitterness? After all of the years he guarded her on Earth, she had never acted like this toward anyone. Maybe honoring her request and giving her this time away would bring her back to him somehow.

The next morning, Levi reported to the training facility as part of his morning routine. His agitation was still present, but not as intense as the previous evening. The men began their rigorous drills, and Levi let it serve as therapy. After finally pinning Harrison to the ground, Harrison laughed when Levi let him up. Levi's eyes widened has Harrison brushed the blood away from his cheek.

"That was excellent!" Harrison said, as he clapped Levi on his shoulder.

Levi sighed. "Forgive me; I didn't intend to make contact

with you." Levi was disillusioned that he'd injured Harrison in their training. Yes, the Guardians' training was extremely aggressive, but the men were skilled enough to not cause each other injury.

Harrison grinned. "It was nothing, and you will teach me that new move!" He arched his eyebrow at Levi. "I think Reece needs to irritate you a little more often."

Levi rolled his eyes. "I am not upset with her; I am merely confused by her behavior."

"Well, what do you expect? It appears her new best friend is Simone, it's pretty obvious—"

"Harrison!" Levi snapped, cutting him off. "Do not compare Reece to that woman." He reached down for his towel, and wiped the sweat from his face. "You've known Reece long enough to understand this is not like her. Something else is wrong."

Harrison sighed. "She'll get over it soon enough."

"I do hope you are correct."

They turned to follow the other Guardians out of the training unit. "Samuel has a pretty complicated assignment for us today; are you up for it?" Harrison said enthusiastically.

"Pennsylvania again?" Levi said with a soft laugh. "Let Samuel know that once I've seen Reece off, we'll leave for Earth."

$$\longrightarrow$$

It was nearing daybreak when Levi headed to the courtyard to arrange Reece and Simone's transportation to Samuel's estate. On his way through the dimly lit corridors, he encountered Jasmeen.

"Master Levi, Reece is still asleep. Forgive me if I'm out of line by saying this, but I am concerned for her being alone in Simone's company."

"She will hardly be alone, and Reece may be aggravated about this, but the Imperial Guards have been instructed not to let her out of their sight. They will be guarding her heavily, and Samuel is returning to the estate to ensure her safety as well."

"That is relieving to hear," she replied.

"If you'll excuse me, I must finish making my preparations for her departure."

"Very well, sir," Jasmeen said, and offered him a short curtsy.

With a nod, Levi turned and walked through the corridor, down to the courtyard where he encountered Samuel as he was preparing to leave.

Levi walked over and shook his commanding officer's hand, "Sir, I am indebted to you for returning to your estate in order to ensure Reece's safety."

Samuel nodded, "Think nothing of it, Levi. I regret to admit that I do not trust my own daughter alone with Miss Bryant." He hoisted himself up onto his horse and looked down at Levi, "Vincent will be in charge and will be reporting to me in my absence."

"Very well, sir." Levi answered as Samuel directed his horse to leave the courtyard.

By late morning, Reece and Simone made their way out to where Levi was finalizing their transportation arrangements with the guards at her carriage. Levi looked up and noticed Reece. Seeing her prepared to leave the palace sent a wave of despair through him. All he wanted was to have her in his arms, to see her smile at him again, and to hear her laugh. He was dismayed that she was leaving, but he wouldn't interfere with her wishes.

As soon as the women descended the steps into the courtyard, Levi dismissed the footman in order to have one last opportunity to feel the softness of Reece's delicate hand in his. Simone led the way, and Levi managed to repress his hatred of the woman long enough to offer his hand to help her into the carriage. He avoided any eye contact with her, and once Simone was seated, he turned with some anxiety to offer his hand to Reece.

Surprisingly, she didn't decline his hand, but instead placed it carefully into his. Her tender touch burned against his skin, and his heart beat erratically as he assisted her. He resisted the urge to grip his hand tightly around hers and beg her not to leave him, but he had to let her go. When she accepted his help into the carriage, she never smiled or made eye contact with him.

Levi was distraught as he stared at Reece in the carriage. He exhaled in defeat when the driver called out to the horses. Levi stood and watched as the carriage left rapidly. He ran his hand through his hair, straining to keep his thoughts straight. *Just give her time,* he told himself.

"I give her two days at most before she comes screaming back to the palace," Harrison called out, as he hopped down the steps to where Levi stood.

"Only time will tell."

Harrison clapped Levi on the shoulder. "Javian has our horses ready, and I am ready to get out of here."

Levi nodded. "I couldn't agree more."

Levi did his best to throw himself fully into assignments on Earth, but it wasn't helping. Even with Harrison's light-hearted personality, Levi found no reprieve. There was no word of Reece wishing to return to the palace, and he began to turn numb to everything around him.

After a few short days serving on Earth, Levi requested leave. He was unable to be effective in his duties in such a distracted state of mind. It had been a week since Reece's departure, and Levi became increasingly despondent. He isolated himself from everyone, wishing to be left alone. He sat in a chair, staring out of his window and recalling the cherished times he shared with Reece.

"Upon my word, cousin, you look frightful. Is this what it has all come to?" Harrison said as he entered Levi's sitting room unexpectedly.

"I do not understand what you are trying to imply." Levi answered curtly.

"Oh, I believe you know exactly what my implications are. First you demand a leave of absence, and then you fail to attend the meeting Samuel returned to the palace for this morning? I believed you would have been interested to know about the progress Queen Galleta has made with the Armedite priestess. Apparently nothing interests you these days."

Levi looked up at him. "I had forgotten about the meeting, forgive me. Well, what kind of progress has Galleta made?"

Harrison sat in a chair across from Levi. "I must say I am impressed that I have your attention. Unfortunately, there has been no progress because the priestess will not cooperate with Galleta at all. Galleta seems to believe there is more to this woman than she's letting on. She's certainly unlike any individual we've encountered."

The memory of Levi's encounter with the Armedite priestess and how she altered his mind resurfaced, and it irritated him more. "Whether or not Galleta reaches her mind, she's not a threat so long as she remains imprisoned here in Pemdas." He sat up some. "And if this woman chooses not to cooperate, she is deciding her own fate, and that is not my problem."

"True." Harrison answered with a smile. "Oh! You'll appreciate this new information; Samuel has been informed that Michael is Lucas' new commanding officer," he said with a laugh. "Imagine that! Michael leading the Armedite's army."

Levi inhaled, annoyed. "Harrison, forgive me, but I am in no mood to talk about any of this. I really do not care what happens with the priestess, Michael, or anyone else for that matter. Please, leave me be; I need to be alone."

Harrison leaned back and chuckled. "I wish I could comply with your demands; however, I am not inclined to do so at the present moment."

"I am in no mood for this. Why have you come? To lecture me on my negligence for missing Samuel's meeting? Or to engage in simple conversation? I will tell you again, now is not the time," Levi responded sternly.

"Well, since we are listing things we are not in the mood for," Harrison said sarcastically, "let me go on record and say that the number one thing on my list is seeing you like this."

Levi closed his eyes, and ran his fingers through his hair.

"You need to pull it together and find a solution, or move on. Sitting alone in your room sulking is accomplishing absolutely nothing."

Levi glared at Harrison. "I do not sit here and *sulk* because Reece and I have quarreled. I have done something to upset her severely; something has forced her to see me differently. Before she decided to leave, she would not allow me to so much as touch her. I only sit here withdrawn because all I *want* to do is ride to Samuel's estate, retrieve her, and bring her back."

"And you do not…because?"

Levi let out his breath. "It is not what she wants. Why would I force her to live in my presence when she has proven to me that it is the last place she desires to be?" He gazed at the glass he held. "I believe she blames me for being forced to live in Pemdas."

Harrison sighed in annoyance. "I am sorry, but I will no

longer sit and watch you wallow in self-pity." He stood. "However, I am also not going to watch you drown your sorrows away," he looked down at the glass Levi held, "in your glass of water, either. Would it interest you to know, I believe I have an excellent idea to fix all of this?"

"Please, Harrison, you are wasting your time."

"That is true. There are plenty of other things I'd much rather be doing. Nevertheless, I can no longer stand by and watch you suffer like this. This is all gotten way out of hand; therefore, it is time we fix it, and remove Reece from Simone's presence."

Levi eyed Harrison blandly. "What is it you suggest? I am curious. I believe I have thought of everything already."

A broad smile stretched across Harrison's face. "Have you now? Well, you may have thought of everything except fixing the very problem you believe is causing Reece's discontentment."

Harrison smiled when light seemed to reappear in Levi's eyes.

"After I tell you of my ingenious plans, you can thank Samuel for approving them."

Levi stood. "You have my attention," he said somewhat annoyed, knowing Harrison wouldn't let up until he agreed to his arrangements. "What is it that you have planned?"

Harrison clapped his arm onto Levi's shoulder and smiled. "First of all, you will clean yourself up and shave. You must look like the handsome and appealing man Reece will have remembered falling in love with. After that, I will happily divulge my plans to you."

Levi's eyes narrowed as he studied Harrison's smug grin. "I'm not promising you I will agree to your plans. I will not put Reece in an awkward situation merely because I want her back."

Harrison turned to leave the room. "Just go get cleaned up,

and I'll meet you at the command center."

Chapter 19

Reece exited the shower, forcing herself to go through the motions of another day staying with Simone. She was haunted by the memories of what had happened to bring her to this point. She continually struggled to figure out why she acted out in the manner that she did at the palace. Never in her life had she been so overcome with such powerful, negative emotions. She couldn't understand why, no matter how hard she tried, she couldn't control herself or her reactions.

Thinking back to how hateful she was toward Levi was nauseating. How could she act the way she did with him?

She began to wonder what had taken over her because there was no other logical reason for her to behave so hatefully toward everyone, especially Levi.

The strangest part was that everything changed the moment she stormed out of Levi's room the night before she left. When she walked into her room, for the first time in weeks, Reece could think clearly again. It was like a weight had been lifted, and she had control over her thoughts and actions. That was when Reece realized she had destroyed her and Levi's relationship, and in the process, insulted everyone in the palace. How could they forgive her for what she did when she couldn't forgive herself?

The morning she left, she could hardly look Levi in the eye when he helped her into the carriage; the expression on his face validated the fact she could never go back to the palace and face any of them again.

She hadn't had any bizarre outbursts since arriving at Simone's house, and all she could think about was Levi and how much she loved him. Her heart ached to be with him again, and the realization that it wasn't going to happen overwhelmed her with grief. Levi had every right not to forgive her, and frankly, she didn't expect him to.

She sat and stared at her reflection in the mirror as the tears ran down her cheeks.

"Reece, it has been a week now. I do not believe there has been one day in which you have not shed tears in my presence. If you wish to return to Pasidian Palace, I will arrange for it immediately."

Reece sniffed and blotted her tears with the handkerchief Jasmeen handed her. "I'll be okay Jasmeen. After what I did, I don't think I will ever be welcomed back in the Oxley's home again. I can't blame them, either. I don't know what I was thinking."

"I believe that if you were to return, the reception would be far from what you assume."

"No, Jasmeen, I can't. Not right now, anyway. I don't think I can face any of them yet; not after what I did." She lowered her head, fighting to restrain tears. "I can't even imagine what they all must think about me now," she said remorsefully.

"But Master Levi—"

Reece shook her head. "Please, Jasmeen, I was worse to him than anyone."

Reece stood and turned to face the young maiden. "I know I was probably difficult for *you* to deal with at the palace, too; and for whatever it's worth, I'm sorry for being so rude to you."

"No apology is necessary." Jasmeen smiled sympathetically. "We understood you to be ill; that is all. It appears that you have recovered completely, and I suggest you consider going home."

"I can't," Reece said in torment.

Jasmeen gazed at her somberly. "Yes, you can, Reece. That is your home; this is not."

Reece sighed in frustration. "I don't know what was wrong with me. Whatever it was, I ruined everything I loved because of it. Sick or not, now I'm here; and I'll be honest, if all these guards weren't here with us, I'd be scared to be in this place alone with Simone."

Jasmeen stared at Reece's sorrowful expression.

"I don't know how to make all of this right again."

"We start by returning home, back to Pasidian Palace."

Reece sniffed. "I know, but give me some time to build up the confidence to face them again," she smiled faintly, "then we'll make our plans to leave this place."

Jasmeen gave Reece an encouraging hug and their conversation was ended, when Simone arrived early to escort Reece to breakfast.

"I will never understand the relationship you have with that girl," Simone said, as they made their way to the breakfast room. "It is bizarre that you would befriend your maiden in such a way."

I find it bizarre that I would befriend you, Reece thought, as she managed to refrain from snapping back at Simone's rude comment. In Reece's opinion, she had done plenty of lashing out at everyone these days, and it was best if she kept quiet; but it wasn't easy, Simone's friendly personality toward Reece had started to change a few days ago. Simone persistently suggested to Reece they return to the palace; when Reece didn't agree, Simone seemed to become more agitated. With the stress of coming to grips with what she had done to the Oxleys, and now Simone's usual pernicious attitude, Reece was barely able to tolerate being in the presence of the woman.

Simone sipped her tea. "Reece, dearest, if you're ever going to work things out with Levi, you need to get back to the palace," Simone said, as they sat alone at the dining table.

Where is Samuel? Reece thought nervously. Simone's father had been in constant company with them, until now. She glanced back and let the four Imperial Guards standing protectively in the doorways give her a sense of security.

"Where's your father?" Reece asked.

Simone swallowed a bite of her muffin. "He left early for Pasidian Palace." She rolled her eyes. "And apparently, more Guardians have shown up to protect you from me in his absence."

"Simone, I know that may annoy you, but you can't blame anyone for being a little concerned about—"

"I know exactly the world I have created for myself, Reece," she snapped with a fiery gaze, forcing Reece's body to become tense. "Forgive me for that," she said, as her expression softened. "Reece, look around you. This is my life; my sister and Lillian will not speak to me," she sniffed. "And I miss them dearly."

Reece felt no sympathy for the woman and was in no mood to listen to her sad story, whether it was true or not. She tried to focus on eating her breakfast, and nearly jumped when Simone rested her hand over hers. "I'm sorry I am in a disagreeable mood this morning. You seem to have been the only one to forgive me, Reece, and I will not ruin our friendship."

How did I let this happen? Reece thought, absolutely miserable with the idea that her only friends in Pemdas now were Simone and Jasmeen.

"It's fine, Simone," she said dryly.

"No, it's not fine." Her grip tightened on Reece's hand, forcing Reece to look up at her. "We must return to Pasidian," she smiled brightly. "As your friend, I will do everything to help you gain confidence with Levi again. We will fix this, Reece."

Reece jerked her hand away from Simone. To listen to Simone talk to her like this was more than Reece could deal with right now.

"Simone, please just drop it. I'll deal with Levi when I'm ready," she said angrily.

For the last week, Reece was able to control her irritability with Simone, but she was finally reaching her limit. Having to stomach sitting in a room and listening to Simone try and console her was more than she could handle.

"Reece," Simone said, her eyes wide with shock as she glanced at the doorway behind Reece.

"No!" Reece stood up and tossed her napkin on the table. "I'm done with this conversation. Right now, I don't know what I'm going to do about anything anymore. When and if I choose to talk to Levi again, I will decide that, not you!"

When Reece turned to leave the room, she nearly tripped over her feet in absolute shock to see Levi standing in the doorway. *Of all the times he could show up! This can't be happening. What did he hear?* She knew exactly what he had heard, and what he saw; Reece treating Simone the exact same way she had treated him. She knew she sounded like the psychotic, hateful woman she was at the palace. She was far from that woman now, but how could Levi know the difference after her outburst? *Think he'll believe you when you say you're sorry now, Reece? Not a chance.*

Reece stared at the stunning man in defeat; how could she ever forget how undeniably handsome he was? What a sickening reminder of what she'd lost. How could she make such a fool of herself in front of him like she did? Could she ever find the confidence to apologize to such a noble and dignified man? She noticed that he was wearing one of his pristine suits, the ones he wore when serving on Earth. She swallowed hard at the serene expression he wore on his face. *Is he taking me back to Earth?*

"Levi, this is indeed a surprise!" Simone said in a voice of excitement, forcing Levi and Reece both to bring their attention to her.

"Simone, if you'll pardon my interruption, I am here to speak with Miss Bryant." He looked at Reece. "Miss Bryant, if you would be so kind as to join me on a short walk?" he requested formally.

This is it. He was either here to work things out, or he was taking her back to Earth. The Ciatron were no longer pursuing her, and she believed they could easily send her back to Earth to live under heavy guard. Of course, that was a bit extreme; but with the expression on Levi's face,

Reece understood very well there was nothing positive about his visit. Should she have expected it to be positive, especially after he witnessed her recent outburst with Simone?

Reece went over to him, her heart racing. She tried to think of something to say, but nothing came to her. This could be her only chance to apologize, and she was too mortified to speak a word.

As they left the room, Levi clasped his hands behind his back while walking nobly at her side. "The reasons for my visit today are to inquire about your health, and to see if you are well enough to travel." Reece closed her eyes, afraid of where they would be traveling to. She had no idea how to ask him what his plans were; it was so frustrating that she was too embarrassed to speak to him now.

She stared up into dark eyes. "I'm feeling fine, thank you. When did you want me to go?"

His eyes studied hers intently before he responded. "Immediately, if that agrees with you."

"What about Jasmeen?" she asked nervously.

"Arrangements have been made for her to return to Pasidian Palace."

"Can I tell her goodbye?"

Levi's brow furrowed in response. "Of course, you may do whatever you wish. Jasmeen will also be preparing you for your departure. I will inform Simone of your leaving with me, and I will be waiting for you in the front courtyard."

She stared past Levi; should she tell him she was sorry now? Should she say anything to him? She had to admit it; she didn't have the courage to make all of this right again. Her embarrassment was too great, and it was obvious he wasn't here to work anything out. "I won't be long," she finally answered, and then quickly walked back to the room she was residing in.

When Reece entered the room, Jasmeen was there, ready to help her change for her departure with Levi. She stared at the clothes in Jasmeen's hands, and swallowed hard. *My Earth clothes? Guess I know where I'm going.* Reece thought sadly.

Jasmeen said something, but Reece didn't hear it. She gave the maiden her best smile, and before another exchange was made, she snatched the clothes out of Jasmeen's hands and went into the other room to change.

Tears poured out of Reece's eyes as she fought the corset dress, struggling to take it off. She couldn't believe this was happening. She really was leaving Pemdas, and worse than that, she was leaving Levi.

Jasmeen knocked on the door, "Reece, please allow me to assist you in—"

Before Jasmeen could finish her sentence, Reece had already changed and had opened the door. She smiled at her, gave her a farewell hug, and fled the room.

When she walked out to where Levi awaited her, any hope that she may have had that he might bring her back to Pasidian Palace had vanished. Instead of a carriage waiting for her, it was Levi and Areion.

He stood formally, and his expression was unreadable, making Reece somewhat intimidated to be in his presence.

For the entire time since she had known him, he'd never looked at her in this manner. She recognized that there was no reason left to hope that he would forgive her. Not even now, when it would probably be the last time she ever saw him.

Heartbroken, she couldn't bring herself to smile at him. She had no idea why it was Levi and not Harrison who would take her back to Earth. He must have been forced to do it, because right now, he seemed as though he wished he could be anywhere else. With all of these insecure thoughts running through her head, her stomach twisted in pain at the realization that it was over. A love that could never be replaced in her heart had ended and she struggled to accept how she would go on without him. How she would deal with such a dramatic and painful change in her life. Her love for Levi was endless and her comfort of living in the captivating domain of Pemdas could never be replaced. How could she ever move on in her life after she returned to Earth?

Levi went through his usual motions of helping her onto Areion, and they were soon swiftly leaving Simone's home. She wrapped her arms tightly around Levi's waist, certain that this would be the last time she would have this closeness with him. She closed her eyes and leaned her head against him, savoring these final moments. His fragrance filled her senses, soothing her as it always did. She loved this man with all that she was and now she would never have the joy of spending the rest of her life with him.

She kept her eyes closed throughout the entire ride, savoring the final moments of being near him. When Levi called back to prepare her for crossing over the Pemdas barriers, she opened her eyes and was confused by her surroundings. She had never traveled this way back to Earth before. *This isn't the way we traveled through the vortex out of Philadelphia.* She inwardly thought.

The red-leaved trees were nowhere to be found; instead, there were tall cliffs surrounding them. If she had not witnessed Areion leap over the barrier, she wouldn't have believed they were on their way out of the dimension of Pemdas.

They approached a short stone wall, and on the other side of it, a black Pemdai vehicle awaited them. Once they dismounted, Levi commanded Areion to return to the palace stables, and she questioned where on Earth he was taking her. She looked up at him, hoping to see that his expression had changed. It hadn't, and she was left to question what was going on. As they approached the Pemdai vehicle, she watched in disbelief as Harrison stepped out of the driver's side.

She was comforted when he smiled widely at her. "And now…it is finally us three again!" he shouted.

"I guess it is." Reece answered softly.

Levi guided Reece to the passenger seat of the car, and sat in the back behind her. Feeling uncomfortable, she remained silent the entire time. It didn't help her discomfort that, as they sped down the road, and everyone else sat in silence as well.

Reece found solace in staring out the front windshield, wishing they would hurry and get to where the men were planning to bring her. None of this was normal, and she couldn't help but think it was about to end badly for her.

Her wishes were quickly granted when they made it through the vortex. Now they were on Earth; but, she had no idea where. They sped through winding roads in the countryside somewhere. As they approached a private airport, Reece looked at Harrison curiously.

He smirked, "You will be thanking me later for this, I assure you."

She gazed out of the front windshield again and noticed that Harrison was pulling up to a large black helicopter. *Thanking him? For what, a helicopter ride?* Reece didn't know what to think. She didn't know where they were, but the land that they traveled through was absolutely beautiful.

Once they were parked, Harrison quickly got out of the car and opened her door.

"Welcome to Greece, my friend," he proclaimed, as he

helped her out of the car.

Reece looked at Harrison in surprise. She finally gained the courage to question him. "Greece? Why are we back on Earth? Is it safe?"

Harrison took her arm gracefully and placed it into his while guiding her toward the helicopter.

"Reece, if it was unsafe, we would have not returned. Now, do not be mistaken; since you are the most sought-out individual in every domain, you will be heavily guarded by Pemdai warriors. Nevertheless, have no fear, as you will not even notice the Guardians amongst you on this visit."

"You're not bringing me back to live here?" she inquired, still confused about everything that was occurring.

"Of course we are not returning you to Earth to live here." He looked down at her, shocked at her remark. "Reece, we are bringing you back for a little vacation. We figured you missing your life on Earth may be the cause for your irritability lately, so we sought out a wonderful area for you to return to."

She had definitely done more than cause a scene between only her and Levi. It was sickening, but at least Harrison was in decent spirits about having to do this. Levi, on the other hand, was acting quite the opposite. He went directly from the car to the pilot's door of the helicopter without saying a single word. She realized then that this would probably be an uncomfortable vacation with him acting this way. The last thing she wanted was to see that he had no desire to do this or to be around her.

Harrison led Reece to the passenger side of the luxurious helicopter, and she looked at him in amazement. "You guys have a helicopter, too?"

Harrison smiled sympathetically down at her. "Reece, as I told you that day in Scotland on our aircraft; you would be surprised at how we get around protecting Earth."

Once she was in the helicopter seat, Harrison fastened her safety harness. He reached for a headset, and handed it to her. "Levi will communicate with you through these during the flight."

"You're not coming with us?"

"Someone has to get the car to the location where we'll be staying." He glanced over at Levi, and then back at Reece. "And Levi's favorite vehicle to operate is a helicopter, so being the kind man that I am, I let him have his way."

Reece glanced over at Levi, only to find him glaring at Harrison before abruptly bringing his attention back to the gauges in front of him. *Yeah, Levi seems absolutely thrilled to be flying the psycho ex-girlfriend around.*

"Now, enjoy yourselves. I will see you both later this evening," Harrison said with a friendly wink, as he closed the door.

She put her headset on, and quietly stared out of the front window while Levi finished going through his pre-flight check of the helicopter. He slipped the log book between the seat and the instrument panel, and started flipping numerous switches that were all around them in the cabin.

Her adrenaline picked up as the helicopter engines suddenly roared with a high-pitched sound. The sound grew louder, and then the main rotor above them started slowly moving. She looked up, out through the front window, intrigued as the loud engines started propelling the two blades so fast that it seemed like they were spinning in slow motion.

Reece remained quiet, but was filled with excitement as Levi communicated with the tower. Then, slowly, the helicopter lifted from the ground. They hovered over the ground for a few minutes before the nose dipped down some, and they glided forward.

It was an incredible and peaceful feeling, floating through the air like this. The helicopter stalked the Pemdai car traveling rapidly down the road beneath them, and then suddenly they banked left toward an ocean that seemed to appear from out of nowhere.

She glanced at Levi more than once, only to see that he was focused intently on the instrument gauges in front of him. As thrilling as this was, her heart sank when she saw his somber expression. It brought her back to the reality of their situation; this was such a remarkable experience, and she couldn't share it with him even though he was sitting right next to her. She felt strangely alone, but tried to focus on the sights they flew over, letting the incredible views surrounding them give her some comfort.

She listened as Levi communicated with someone who was giving him flight information and updating him on the wind patterns over the headset. It was quite intriguing, being a part of the whole flight process. As they flew over the ocean, Levi announced that they were flying over the Aegean Sea.

They toured the coastline for a little over an hour before they came to their final destination. Levi landed the helicopter faultlessly, and as he began to shut the engines down, two men exited from a Pemdai car and approached them. The two gentlemen helped Reece from her seat, and once she was out, Levi was at her side. After speaking briefly with the two men, he led Reece to the car.

"We have reserved five villas in this area for your safety while you are here. You will have no need to fear being on Earth; as Harrison mentioned to you earlier, you will be heavily guarded. Currently, there is no threat to you in this location, and you should be able to freely enjoy your time here."

Reece glanced at him. "Okay, thank you. You guys didn't have to do all of this for me," she responded softly.

"It was nothing. Harrison believed it would help if we brought you back to your world, to prevent the possibility of your feeling as though you were confined to living in Pemdas."

He had said it himself; this was Harrison's idea. She sighed in defeat, knowing that she and Levi would never be the same again. She stared down at the ring on her finger, and was embarrassed that she still wore it. *This really couldn't be any more awkward,* she thought.

Levi escorted her into the villa, and if Reece hadn't lived at Pasidian Palace or visited Stavesworth Hall, along with her living in the beautiful lands of Pemdas, she would be awed by the villa they were staying in.

In the center of the room, cream sofas were positioned to face the glass doors that displayed a pool that gave the illusion of it ending in the aquamarine ocean behind it. It was something she had only seen in movies and magazines. She couldn't fathom how much a room like this would cost for a night. She followed Levi as he gave her a tour throughout the large villa. He showed her the rooms that he and Harrison would each occupy, and then hers, which was essentially a honeymoon suite.

She tried to gain enough courage to look up at Levi and thank him, but she couldn't. Every time she looked at him, she felt more insecure. She had to find a way to get past this, and to find her confidence again.

"With the help of an assistant at the hotel, we have taken the liberty to have clothes purchased for you, which will suit Earth's fashions while you are here. They are prepared for you in your closet. If the attire does not meet with your approval, other arrangements can easily be made to replace them. We will depart for dinner as soon as you are ready,"

Levi informed her formally.

She gazed up at him in amazement of what they had done for her. She didn't know what to say. It made her feel all the more horrible for what she had done. She had obviously displayed to them that she was miserable with her life in Pemdas, and now they were going completely out of their way to placate her.

"Thank you. Will Harrison be joining us soon?" she asked, knowing his personality would alleviate the tension between her and Levi.

"If that is your wish, I will see to it that he joins us. Now, if you will excuse me, I will return within the hour when you are ready for dinner."

Before she could reply, Levi left room.

Chapter 20

Upon being informed by two of the Guardians that were positioned at the front entrance of the villa that Harrison was in the main hotel lobby, Levi walked quickly there in search of him.

He was trying to remain optimistic about all of this, but he really didn't know how to approach Reece anymore. Her confrontation with Simone proved that she must be reaching her limit with not only him, but her entire life in Pemdas. It also validated that Harrison's plan may work to

SL MORGAN

give her happiness again.

Talking to her about why she was so upset lately was not an option anymore, in his mind. After so many failed attempts, and now her current demeanor, there was no way Levi would force conversation with her. It was obvious that she didn't want to be alone with him; why else would she request Harrison join them? He was fairly certain that things wouldn't be the same between them again; now it was up to him to find a way to let the only woman he could ever love, go.

He walked into the hotel lounge, and rolled his eyes when he found Harrison engaged in a lively conversation with a waitress standing next to him at the bar counter. *Can't he wait at least five minutes before he seeks out the first eligible woman?*

Levi acknowledged the young woman respectfully before requesting a private conversation with his cousin. Harrison followed him reluctantly to a secluded area in the lounge.

Harrison sat down and narrowed his eyes at Levi sitting across the table from him. "Where's Reece? I figured you both would be madly in love again, on your way out to dine under the stars."

Levi exhaled. "Harrison, I already informed you that this may not work. She will hardly even glance in my direction. She has changed somewhat, but she seems extremely uncomfortable in my presence."

"Is this a joke? She was unimpressed with your piloting her on a helicopter ride? I thought that would've definitely done the trick!"

Levi ignored the comment and replied, "She is requesting that you join us this evening."

"Are you out of your mind? Absolutely not! You should know, I intend to enjoy myself fully on this little getaway as well. I am not here to babysit you two!"

Levi leaned over the table and gazed sternly into his cousin's irritated eyes. He spoke in a low, authoritative voice. "This was your idea, my friend. I will not have Reece uncomfortable in my presence. I have already told you as much when I agreed to go through with this. If things do not work out between us, I will have to accept it." He leaned back and relaxed some. "So you will join us until she requests otherwise."

Harrison's lips tightened as he glared out of the windows behind Levi. After a moment, he sighed in utter annoyance, and glanced back at Levi, who was patiently waiting for him to respond.

"This is preposterous!" Harrison said in a raised voice. "You better start making more of an effort!" He mirrored Levi's stern gaze. "And you may want to try smiling every once in a while; that constant look on your face is even making *me* feel weird." He stood and exhaled in utter annoyance. "Well, shall we then?" He held out his arm dramatically toward the exit. "I believe a table with a prearranged romantic serenade awaits all three of us. This is absurd."

Levi laughed with disbelief. "You arranged to have us serenaded at our dinner tonight?"

As they strolled out of the lounge, Harrison answered him, "You will be surprised at what I have arranged. Unfortunately, I didn't believe I would be subjected to any of it at the time I made the arrangements!" He spoke in a loud voice out of frustration.

Levi glanced over at him. "Harrison, quit yelling. As I said—"

"I'm not yelling!" he shouted. His features softened as he grinned at Levi. "I'm unnecessarily raising my voice." He stated smugly.

Levi laughed in response. He understood his cousin's

frustration; however, Reece's well-being was his only priority on this trip.

They walked in silence the rest of the way back to the villa. Before they entered, Harrison grasped Levi by his arm.

He eyed him sternly. "I expect you will make your best effort to make Reece comfortable around you again. I will not spend our entire week here, going on the prearranged romantic adventures that I have planned for you. I am serious; you need to find your confidence with her again. I will grant you this favor tonight only. The rest is up to you to figure out."

If Harrison knew that he would be spending the next three days helping to make Reece and Levi comfortable in each other's presence, he would have reconsidered making these plans.

$$\longrightarrow$$

It was the third day in Greece, and Harrison, yet again, was required to join Reece and Levi on a prearranged helicopter journey to Venice, Italy. Harrison appeared to be reaching his limit, but Levi didn't care. Reece seemed to be happier and more relaxed in Harrison's presence; therefore, Levi would not budge on his demand that Harrison accompany them.

The apparent lack of interest that Reece had been displaying towards Levi over the past few days seemed to validate to him that she no longer loved him. It was difficult for him to accept this reality, but at least he could finally admit it to himself. Returning her to Earth was definitely what she needed. She was smiling and laughing like she used to. She was happy again, and that's all he cared about. There was no way he would confront her about her feelings toward him; it would only force an awkward situation, and he would not interrupt her newly found happiness.

Even though Harrison was relentlessly vocalizing every ounce of his frustration about having to go on these excursions, it was his usual sarcasm that seemed to keep Reece energetic when she teased him playfully in return. Levi wanted to be more interactive with them, but she displayed no sign that she wished for him to do so. When they did return to Pemdas, Levi had resolved to pull her aside and relieve her of their relationship. Hopefully, that would help her to be more comfortable while living in Pemdas.

While in Venice, they spent the day touring many unique parts of the city before they arrived at the location where Harrison had arranged a romantic gondola ride for Levi and Reece. He had spared no detail with his planning; the boat was decorated with flowers and chiffon, along with two hired musicians who were waiting to board the gondola with them.

As they boarded, Levi observed Harrison's highly annoyed expression. Up until now, his cousin had managed to conceal his exasperation with everything he had been subjected to; but now, Levi understood that he was beyond his limit.

Levi did his best to ignore Harrison's demeanor, but this time he failed. Levi was forced to restrain his laughter from the torment he was putting his cousin through, and he was struggling to maintain his composure. As soon as everyone was seated, and the musicians joined them, one glance at Harrison had Levi fighting back laughter. He brought his fist to his mouth to conceal his smile from everyone, and looked away from everyone in the boat as he fought to get a grip on himself. The last thing he needed was Reece seeing him acting like a childish fool.

They were soon moving through the grand canals, and when Levi regained his equanimity, he brought his attention back to everyone in the boat. Harrison sat at the front, facing Reece and Levi, while the musicians serenaded them from the middle of the boat, singing every romantic song Italy had to offer. Harrison was leaning back, legs crossed, resting on one elbow, and clearly annoyed. When he was not looking up into the cloudless sky trying to refrain from making a comment about how ridiculous this was, he would look at Levi, threatening him with his glare.

You don't know how close I am to throwing the musicians off of this boat so I can reach across and slap that grin off your both of your faces, Harrison told Levi telepathically.

Levi's lips tightened in humor. *I must say, I am impressed with your romantic side, Harrison. In all my life, I would have never guessed you had it in you.*

Harrison's eyes narrowed. *I am at my limit with all of this.*

That's your problem. You planned it, so you get to deal with it until Reece says she doesn't want you around, Levi ordered.

Harrison gave Levi a harsh expression before glaring up at the innocent musicians, and then pointedly ignoring Levi and Reece by staring out at the water they were gliding through.

$\longrightarrow$

This entire five-star vacation was, no doubt, all of Harrison's planning. Reece caught on to that after all of these wonderful romantic outings they had been on thus far. She still hadn't found the courage to look in Levi's direction. He was so somber that she really didn't know how to approach him anymore. She'd hoped that if he saw her acting normally again, he would start to interact with her again.

She tried to move past the way she'd treated him and his family in order to gain the confidence to apologize; but Levi's unremitting stolid demeanor reminded her of how horrible she was to him. She wasn't giving up; she was simply waiting for an open opportunity. Harrison served as an excellent way to relieve the tension, and until Reece knew how she'd approach Levi, he was excellent entertainment for all the tours they'd been on.

It was at dinner that night in Venice, that she became overwhelmed with the fact that things would never be the same with her and Levi again. They dined in a restaurant on an outdoor terrace. It was beautiful and perfect, and she longed to spend this time alone with Levi.

It would have been amazing to have had her arm in his as they toured through the popular sites in Athens, but it didn't happen. She observed Levi as he engaged Harrison in conversation at their dining table. She watched every expression play out on his face; he was so unbearably handsome. She missed him so painfully that she could hardly stand to be separated from him any longer. *What are you going to do about it, Reece? Should I just tell him I love him and deal with whatever reaction I get?* she thought, as she searched for confidence to talk to him again. She ran her moist palms over the cloth draped across her lap and softly exhaled. She had to get over her insecurities and uneasiness about approaching Levi. She was a stronger woman than this.

She was so distracted by Levi, that she didn't notice Harrison had been watching her. She was startled when, for no reason, Harrison stood and extended his arm to her.

"Reece, would you mind joining me for a dance?"

Reece looked around. All that surrounded them were couples dining quietly at their candlelit tables. A string quartet played in the corner, and there was a large open area in front of them. It was obvious patrons could dance out on the terrace if they wished; however, no one was doing so.

When she caught a glimpse of Levi, she realized that he didn't know what his cousin was up to either. Her heart nearly stopped when her eyes locked with Levi's; she saw that his brilliant eyes were radiant with humor, and for the first time in too long, they were directed toward her.

She eyed Harrison warily. "That would be fine, but no one is dancing. I don't want to interrupt anyone's dinner."

Harrison came around, smoothly pulled her chair back, and kindly took her by the arm. He placed her hand in the bend of his arm as he gracefully led her to the open area. He held her in an elegant dancing frame, and began to lead perfectly to the rhythm of the slow, romantic music.

"Don't you think this is a little awkward, Harrison? Nobody is—"

"Reece," he interrupted her, "do not tell me that you worry about what others think. You see, in all my time serving as Guardian on Earth, I have learned that those of Earth instinctively follow others. This dance floor will be full in no time."

She smiled at him as other couples slowly began making their way to the dance floor.

"So, Reece, I must know; have you fallen madly in love with me?"

Reece nearly choked with disbelief at what Harrison asked her. "Of course not, Harrison. What are you talking about?"

He grinned. "Well, it is obvious that you no longer care for poor Levi over there, so the only other obvious choice is that you have fallen in love with me. Why else are you demanding that I come along on all of these romantic escapades with you two?" He arched his eyebrow in reproach at her.

Reece stared earnestly at him. "I love Levi more than anything," She looked down, "but I don't know how to approach him anymore after everything I've done. I can't believe how hatefully I treated him."

Harrison chuckled. "It is all in the past now, Reece; however, Levi feels as though you will never love him again."

Reece looked up at him in astonishment. "He still loves me?"

Harrison exhaled. "You two need to work on your communication skills! Of course he still loves you; he's only keeping his distance since he is unsure of your feelings. For the reason that you two can't manage to talk to each other, I'm stuck playing middle man." He clasped her hand. "Please know, this goes against everything I am."

Reece laughed. "I understand. I'm glad you told me. I'll take it from here. I caused all of this, and I'll fix it."

"Finally! So does this mean I will no longer have to follow you two from here on out?" He winked at her.

"No, you've outlived your usefulness," she teased, "Although, you could have told me this earlier and saved yourself a few romantic escapades."

He shook his head. "I would have, but Levi had standing orders that I was not to make you uncomfortable in any way. I did very well, I might say; but that gondola ride was the last straw."

Reece smiled widely at him. "Well, I think watching you ride on that had to be the most amusing part of this entire trip." She laughed.

"I'm glad I could accommodate you, since this is also my way of making up for forcing Levi to cancel your engagement celebration."

Reece looked up at him sincerely. "I really don't know

what possessed me to be so furious about the cancellation. I need to apologize to you for my outburst that night; it was completely uncalled for. The strangest part is that when I left the palace, I felt completely normal for the first time in more than a month. While I was there, my emotions seemed uncontrollable; it was like something was driving me to hate everyone around me, especially Levi."

Harrison cocked his head to the side as he stared down at her. "That is interesting. Perhaps it was all the wedding excitement that overwhelmed you more than we all expected; that coupled with the fact that you decided not to eat or sleep for a solid week."

Reece sighed. "I guess so." She then lifted her chin. "Well, it's all over now, and I need to make this right with Levi again."

Harrison ended their dance. "Then, let us go. The helicopter awaits. I've planned for you and Levi to have a lovely day at sea tomorrow; I suspect that you and he will have a lot of catching up to do."

Chapter 21

Reece woke up from a dreamless sleep, hoping it was nearing sunrise. She had fallen asleep on the ride back from Venice, and the last thing she remembered was closing her eyes, trying to plan how she'd approach Levi the next morning. She wanted to talk to him on the journey back to the villa, but with Harrison and four other Guardians riding in the helicopter with them, she knew she would have to wait.

She lay there wide awake, and unable to return to sleep. All of the thoughts she had about Levi, since she spoke with Harrison, started running through her mind again.

The room was illuminated somewhat by the moon's light, and it was obvious that it was not nearing daybreak yet. She glanced over at the clock and discovered it was only two in the morning. She leaned back against the pillows and closed her eyes. She didn't know if she had the patience to wait until dawn to make everything right with Levi again. She so desperately wished for all of this to be over, and for him to hold her in his arms again.

Her entire body ached with longing for him. As she rolled onto her side, she re-opened her eyes; her heart quickened by the sight of Levi, sound asleep in an oversized chair at the foot of her bed. She had no idea why he was in her room, or why he slept in the chair. She knew him well enough to know that he would not have stayed unless she asked him to. *What could I have said in my sleep to make him stay with me like this?*

Her heart pounded in her chest as she tried to decide what to do next. *Just go over to him, Reece.* She quietly got out of her bed, and walked over to where he was asleep. His long legs were stretched out on the floor before him, attempting to seek comfort in the chair. He had fallen asleep with his head resting against his propped-up arm, staring in the direction of where she was.

She studied his face as he slumbered. Even as he slept, she saw the lines of distress apparent on it. This was the expression he had worn ever since he had approached her at Simone's estate. Until now, she believed it was a look of disdain for her. However, it was not; instead, it was a look displaying his agony.

She delicately traced the creased lines of his brow, distraught that she had caused him such pain. She ran her fingers gently through his hair, and in that instant, two brilliant sapphire-blue eyes were staring up at her. She caressed his face with her hands, and sat on his lap gently.

———▶

"Reece?" Levi questioned.

She nodded, and smiled brilliantly at him. Her eyes sparkled radiantly as the moonlight peering through her open doors reflected in them. *You will never know how much I love you,* he thought, as the pain of losing her vanished the moment she smiled at him. Levi stared silently at her beautiful face, and memorized its image, unsure of how long it would last.

The next thing he knew, her soft lips were at his ear. He shivered at her warm breath against his skin. The sweet aroma of Reece assaulted every cell in his body. He wrapped his arms around her, bringing her closer to him.

"My love," she whispered breathlessly.

Levi couldn't respond.

Her urgent lips found his. He accepted her kiss gradually, but was unsure of her intentions. After the kiss they shared in his room, he wasn't sure if he could trust her motives; but it seemed different now, and she seemed different now. This was *his* Reece, kissing him slowly and persuasively. He sensed the true love and passion within her loving kiss that he'd always felt before he'd lost her.

Levi returned her kiss with more eagerness than he ever thought himself to be capable of. Lost in the desire of what he had so desperately missed, and never assumed he would have again, his kiss became more powerful than it had ever been.

He noticed that Reece didn't let his impulsive and demanding kiss overwhelm her; instead, she responded to him with the same hunger and urgency. Without breaking his fervent kiss, he cradled Reece into his arms, stood effortlessly, and moved toward the bed. Her fingers continued to massage through his hair, reminding him of all the passionate times he had kissed her before. By some miracle, the woman he loved had come back to him.

He laid her down gently, and covered her body with his own. All sense of control and propriety was rapidly slipping away, and Levi didn't care. He willingly gave himself over to his emotions, letting the passion and desire he felt so deeply for Reece control him.

Reece's hands firmly pressed into his back, drawing his body closer into hers. "I need you, Levi," she whispered breathlessly, before bringing her lips to the base of his neckline.

Reece determinedly kissed along his jaw and down the center of his throat, while she steadily started to remove his white undershirt. It was obvious that she wanted him; and as driven as Levi was to renew their love, he also knew there was a possibility that Reece would regret this sudden impulse of emotion.

After she successfully removed his shirt, Levi used his mental strength to maintain his focus. He gently raised his hands to each side of her face, bringing her eyes up to meet his. Her usual bright-blue eyes were wild with desire, and he was instantly transfixed by the beauty of her gaze.

He exhaled slowly, calming himself. "Are you sure this is what you desire?" he asked quietly.

"All I want is you."

Before Levi could say any more, her hands massaged along his lower back, and her soft lips were on his chest. A low groan escaped him as her fingertips ran up his back, and she gripped his shoulders. "Please," she pleaded as she stared into his eyes.

Levi brought his lips down onto hers, attempting to hold back the intense energy that was threatening to take control of the situation. It was when she moaned in satisfaction while gripping his arms that Levi thought of nothing more than answering her pleas. He clasped her wrists with his hands and stretched her arms up into the pillows above her head. As he interlaced his fingers into hers, his conquering kiss became wildly possessive.

When Reece withdrew, gasping for air, Levi began pursuing her tantalizing body further. After three weeks of being in torment, wondering if Reece would ever love him again, he became more aggressive with tasting her delicate body than ever before.

His mouth possessively ran down the center of her chest as he placed one hand under her thin top, feeling for the first time the soft skin of her firm abdomen. She was flawless, and Levi yearned for more.

Reece's hands massaged through his hair as Levi's hand slowly grazed her sides while proceeding to remove her top.

Before he could go any further, Reece called out to him breathlessly, "I'm sorry for what I did to you."

His lips froze against her hot flesh, and his hand absently slipped out from beneath her camisole. He let out a slow breath, calming himself, and when his eyes reopened, he saw a tear slip from the corner of her eye.

What am I thinking? he inwardly scolded himself. He loved Reece, and all he wanted was to prove every ounce of his love to her tonight; but this wasn't right. She smiled sympathetically at him; however, Levi would never take advantage of her like this while she was begging his forgiveness. He had to find a way to end this, without hurting her. It wasn't easy, as he had already withdrawn and collapsed onto the bed at her side. Directly after, Reece positioned herself on top of him, aggressively pursuing him for more.

Levi gasped as he gently cupped the sides of her face with both hands. His heart nearly stopped when she smiled widely at him. He didn't know how he was able to speak the words, but he managed.

"Reece...please, we cannot do this. Not like this."

His heart twisted in pain when he saw the remorse and embarrassment in her eyes. She had no idea the strength that he required at this moment not to appease her in this manner. He closed his eyes, fighting back the strong impulse to ignore the difference between what was wrong, and what was right.

He inhaled deeply, his mind still spinning, as Reece curled up to his side, crying uncontrollably. He tried to console her, but she would not allow it. She only pleaded with him to hold her instead, and that is what he did. She laid her head on his chest and cried into the blanket until she fell asleep.

Levi had no idea what the next day would bring; but by now, he was ready for anything, be it good or bad.

Chapter 22

The sun shone brightly through the open doors of the balcony into Reece's room. Reece was awakened by the gentle sounds of the ocean waves rolling into the shoreline just beyond their villa. Finally, and for the first time in weeks, Reece felt peaceful. Knowing Levi still loved her had changed her outlook completely.

Upon discovering that Levi was no longer in her bed, she began to wonder how he felt about her actions the previous evening. Hopefully Levi didn't pass this all off as the erratic Reece he had been encountering over the past few weeks. Even if he did, today was the day she would put an end to any insecurity he might have in regard to her. She was determined to restore their relationship to the way it was before.

She got out of bed, feeling more rested and rejuvenated than she had in a long time. Excitement coursed through her as she recalled what Harrison had planned for her and Levi today. With that, she went directly to the shower, and began the process of preparing to leave with Levi on a boat for the entire day.

After her shower, she walked over to a dresser and searched for a swimsuit. Not wanting to waste any more time, she reached for a bikini, found the matching strapless dress to wear over it, and dressed for the day. Once she finished, she grabbed a pair of sandals, and quickly left the room.

She stepped out of her room and saw Levi and Harrison in quiet conversation, standing in front of the large windows that overlooked the pool. Their conversation halted, and both men turned when she entered the room. Levi's eyes widened when he first noticed her, and he smiled warmly at her.

Harrison stared at her speculatively. She restrained her laughter. *I bet I've given them a lot to talk about this morning!*

"Good morning, gentlemen," she greeted them cheerfully.

Harrison's expression softened and he exhaled in relief, while Levi addressed her formally. "Good morning, Reece." He glanced down at her outfit before his eyes met hers. "It appears Harrison has already informed you that we will be spending the day out at sea. Would you care for some breakfast before we depart?"

Reece could tell he was unsure of how to take the entire situation with her. It all encouraged her to tease him more. "Breakfast sounds great!" She looked at Harrison. "I hope you've made other plans today, because I'd like to spend the day alone with Levi."

A broad grin stretched across Harrison's face. He clapped Levi on his stiff shoulder, startling him as he stood there speechless.

"Reece, I believe I have three days of vacation plans I need to catch up on." Harrison said as he nodded to his cousin. "You two have a marvelous time!" Harrison walked toward the door. "Wear plenty of sunscreen," he called out as he left the villa.

Reece laughed softly, and then brought her attention back to Levi, who was still frozen in place.

She arched her brow at him. "I was told I needed a swimsuit for the day; please tell me you plan on getting in the water as well?" She crossed her arms and eyed his clothes. "Or do the Pemdai warriors swim in button-down shirts and slacks?"

A faint smile turned up in the corner of Levi's mouth. It was easy to see that he was questioning her mood. "Give me a few moments to change. I will have breakfast sent up, and then we can leave after that."

Reece smiled. "Hurry, I'm starved."

She could see the excitement in Levi, but she also saw his hesitation as well. She could tell that he was guarding himself from her, in case her emotions took another irrational turn. She didn't mind; she'd created these insecurities in him, and now she must correct them.

They strolled down to the dock where a luxurious yacht awaited them. He helped her aboard, and then gave her a quick tour of the inside, showing her where everything was. Once the enormous boat was secured to leave, Levi started the engines.

Reece was flooded with excitement as they headed out of the bay and the massive boat raced across the crystal-blue waters of the Aegean Sea. They sped across the ocean for quite some time before Levi directed the yacht toward an isolated island. Enormous rock cliffs surrounded the location, and she was awed by all of the extraordinary surroundings. She sat in silence as the boat idled into the private bay. The turquoise-blue water was crystal-clear, and an astonishing sight for anyone to behold.

As Levi set anchor, she disappeared into the enclosed bow of the boat to prepare herself. She took off her cover-up dress, and inhaled deeply to calm her nerves. She let her hair out of its ponytail, and quickly brushed through the tangles the wind had created. She glanced in the mirror to do a final check. *A spray tan certainly wouldn't have hurt anything,* she thought with a nervous laugh.

As soon as she was prepared, she left the stateroom, and made her way toward the exit. She opened the door and smiled when she saw Levi at the stern of the boat preparing diving gear.

He looked up as soon as he became aware of her. After a brief smile he brought his attention back to the gear before him. *Such a gentleman,* Reece thought mischievously, as she gracefully walked to where he was.

When she approached him, she brought her finger to his chin, bringing his eyes up to hers. "Will you be ignoring me on this entire trip?" she asked.

Levi stood and gazed down at her, seemingly at a loss for words. She moved closer to him, never once taking her eyes from his. She grasped his shirt gently and proceeded to remove it.

"You won't need this for the plans I have made for you," she said with a flirtatious grin.

Levi smiled faintly, "I disagree, I will need it," he stammered.

After his shirt was removed, she slowly slid her fingertips along his muscular sides. His skin was so warm, strong, and perfect. Levi's eyes closed, and he exhaled.

"Open your eyes, my love," she murmured.

He did.

"Reece…" he managed.

She smiled provocatively at him. "Are you afraid?" she taunted.

Both of his eyebrows shot up, and his eyes glistened as he stared intently into hers. "Terrified," he said with a smile.

She giggled. "You should be." She stepped back and admired Levi for the first time without his shirt on. *They certainly broke the mold when they made you.* She thought as she fought to maintain her composure. She stood on her toes and kissed him on the tiny cleft in his chin before she brushed past him.

Levi looked around in confusion, watching as Reece stood up on the edge of the boat and playfully twirled his shirt in her hands. She lifted her chin. "Well, if you do really need this shirt…" She grinned. "Then, you'd better come and get it."

With that, she winked, turned, and dove over the side of the boat into the crisp ocean water. As soon as she came up from under the water, she looked back, and her heart raced with anticipation when she saw Levi quickly diving into the water after her. She radiated with excitement as she swam quickly away from him toward the back of the boat. Levi caught her as she tried to climb out of the water; and with one arm holding onto the platform of the boat, and the other securing her tightly in his arms, he covered her mouth in a zealous kiss.

Reece wrapped her arms around his neck as she accepted this overwhelming kiss. They remained lost within each other's ardent kiss for a few moments before Levi slowly withdrew from her. She watched as his eyes roamed over her face. She smiled brightly at his expression, and relief flooded through her when his smile showed her that he was no longer questioning if she would hurt him again or not.

Reece held onto the back of the boat as she studied his face. "Levi?" she asked, wondering what he could be thinking about.

He remained silent as looked at her. He brought his hand up to caress her face, and his solemn expression broke her heart. *Oh, Levi, I'm so sorry!* she thought as she wondered if she could ever make up for everything that she'd put him through.

His head tilted to the side. "I love you," he said softly.

Relief washed over her, "I never thought it was possible to love anything as much as I love you." She said as her voice cracked and she smiled at him lovingly.

Levi's eyes were drawn to her mouth as his thumb gently brushed over her bottom lip. He sighed. "I have so desperately missed this smile." He gazed into her eyes, and his vividly blue eyes were so striking that they pierced through her. "I have longed to see you staring at me like this again." His thumb absently stroked her cheekbone, and he frowned as he tightened his lips. "I have missed you— so greatly—my love. Is this really happening?"

"Yes, it's really happening. I love you so much." Tears filled Reece's eyes, as she understood that the unbearable separation between both of them had finally come to an end. Levi's expression was so sincere, that she could only wrap her arms around him in response. She pulled him close to her and closed her eyes, fighting to calm her emotions.

"It's over, Levi, I promise. You have to know that I can't imagine my life without you." She withdrew from him and stared purposefully into his eyes. "I am so sorry for everything I've done to hurt you."

Levi gently brushed her tears away. "Let us put it all behind us. I have you in my arms again, and that's all I've longed for." After a reassuring kiss, he smiled quizzically at her. "Now, would you care to go snorkeling, or did you have other plans?"

Reece splashed him with water. "Snorkeling was exactly what I had planned this entire time. Why else would you need to take your shirt off?"

Levi smiled the smile that always took her breath away. Then he reached out, grasped her with one arm, and brought her closer into him. "I have missed you."

Reece gave him a quick kiss. "Let's go so see some fish." she said as she turned and climbed the ladder to the boat to where their snorkeling gear awaited them.

When their gear was ready, they dove back into the water and swam away from the boat. They held hands while they explored the breathtaking sea life in the water beneath them. Vibrantly colored fish and other sea creatures swam through various rock formations deep in the water below. Reece was captivated by everything she saw, and she could sense Levi's amusement as she pointed out different types of fish to him. Then, without warning, Levi broke free and dove down, swimming deep into the water beneath her.

She stared into the crystal-clear water in awe of how deep he was in the water. *Is he trying to set a new record for holding your breath under water?* She thought nervously. As Levi explored the rocky ocean floor, he reached for something, and swam gracefully back up to her.

She raised her face up out of the water, took the snorkel out of her mouth and pulled her mask up onto her forehead. By that time, Levi had done the same thing, and swam over to her.

She stared at him in amazement. "How were you able to hold your breath for that long?"

Levi laughed and handed her an exquisite, multi-colored seashell. "I've got something for you; a little souvenir." He brought his hand up to her face and stole a quick kiss.

She smiled. "It's beautiful."

He took his mask off his forehead, and brought the strap through her arm. "Wait here—"

She grabbed him before he could get away. "Seriously, how are you able to hold your breath for so long?"

Levi's expression was filled with more excitement than she'd ever seen.

He smiled brightly at her. "Remember how I told you before that the Pemdai have control over their minds, unlike humans."

"Oh the super-human stuff again?" She teased.

"No, more like Super-Pemdai." He said with a smile. "My mind simply tells my body it doesn't require oxygen; therefore, I have no desire to breathe."

"Well, aren't you impressive?" She said as she rolled her eyes.

Levi's eyes crinkled in humor. "Oh! You're not impressed?" he laughed, "Would you care to try it for yourself? We could have a little contest."

Reece splashed him with water, "Just go get me another sea shell."

Levi winked, and then dove down toward the ocean floor. Reece floated above as he swam deep in the water beneath her. It wasn't long before he reached into a rock, pulled something out, and swam up to her. Once at the surface, Levi smoothed his wet hair back, and swam over to her with another seashell in his hand. Reece nearly screamed when she saw the legs of a crab retreat back into the beautiful shell Levi held.

Reece held a hand over her heart. "Get that thing away from me!" she shouted as she turned and swam to the back of the boat and climbed up the ladder. She sat on the swim platform, letting her legs dangle in the water.

Levi laughed as he came around the side of the boat and saw Reece's reproachful expression. "It won't harm you, sweetheart." He said as he reached for her hand.

Reece jerked away. "Not a chance! I'm not holding that thing!"

Levi chuckled. "Here, hold your palm flat." He cupped her hand under his, and turned her palm up. "Trust me." He kissed the center of her tense palm. "You know very well that I will not allow anything to harm you. Now, relax."

"You're crazy; I saw the claws on that thing!"

Levi's lips quirked up as he placed the tiny crab shell in the palm of her hand.

Reece closed her eyes tightly. "I swear, if this thing pinches me…" she trailed off.

"Relax."

She felt nothing but the smooth shell in the palm of her hand. She slowly opened one eye and stared apprehensively at the beautiful seashell. She looked over at Levi; his face was radiant with excitement as he stared intently at the shell in her hand. She glanced back at the shell, and then all of a sudden, something tickled her hand.

She startled and laughed. "See, it's not so bad, is it?" he said proudly as he looked up at her.

Reece smiled at his smug grin. "No, it's not that bad," she answered.

"I told you." Levi said as he took the crab from her hand and placed in the water. He brought his sturdy arm around Reece, lifted her off of the platform, and brought her back into the water with him. He embraced her and kissed her lips softly. "Would you care for some lunch?"

Reece ran her hands through his wet hair, and locked her legs around his waist. "Yes, but right now," she kissed his chin, "I'd like to enjoy the fact that I'm finally in your arms again."

One of Levi's hands gripped the swim platform of the boat, while he used his other hand to bring her body tightly against his. "I couldn't agree with you more." he said, as his lips captured hers.

Everything disappeared around Reece as she fully indulged herself in Levi's sensual kiss. It was quite some time before she slowly withdrew from his soft lips and smiled at him. She ran her fingers across Levi's forehead and smiled up into his sapphire eyes, "So what's for lunch?"

Levi grinned, and before she could do anything, he hoisted her up onto the boat platform.

He quickly boarded from behind her. "There has been a meal prepared that I believe you will enjoy. He grabbed a towel that had been warming in the sun and wrapped it around her. After a hug and a kiss to her cheek, Levi guided her over to a table where they were to eat their lunch and lounge in the rays of the warm sun.

"Give me a moment, and I will return with our food." he said as he walked toward the cabin of the boat.

Throughout the course of their meal, they spent their time appreciating that their painful separation was over. Levi never once addressed her behavior toward him in Pemdas, and Reece was grateful. It was all in the past, and they were happy to move forward.

When another large boat pulled into their location, Levi decided they would move on. He mentioned that there was an additional island with caves along the shore that Reece might enjoy exploring. Reece happily agreed, eager to explore more locations in the fascinating Aegean Sea.

Levi walked up to the helm and prepared the vessel to leave. Reece watched absorbedly as Levi focused on the control panel of the boat, pulling anchor and starting the engines. When he engaged the boat to idle slowly out of the cove, Reece decided to join him. She stepped up onto the platform where he stood and softly rubbed along his arm. "Can I drive?"

Levi smiled admiringly, and guided her to stand in front of him. "I don't see why not."

He kissed her shoulder as she gripped the boat's wheel tightly. Even though Levi was standing behind her, it was quite intimidating to be the one that was controlling such an enormous vessel. Levi softly caressed her right hand, and gently took it off the wheel. He placed her hand onto the twin throttle levers. He kissed the side of her neck, "Relax," he said in a low voice.

With his strong hand on hers, he slowly pushed the throttle levers down further, gradually giving the boat more power. As the yacht gained speed, the bow leveled out, and sent them cruising smoothly over the choppy, white capped waves of the ocean. Reece relaxed some, as the boat effortlessly dominated the waves as if they weren't even there. It was euphoric, driving the colossal boat, feeling the wind rushing through her hair and gliding across the aquamarine waters of the sea.

When Levi wasn't distracting her by tenderly running his hands along her sides, or across her abdomen, he would place a hand over hers on the wheel to help navigate the boat. Normally she would become weak with desire from what he was doing to her, but right now, all he was doing was making her nervous with the distraction.

"Levi, I'm going to crash this boat if you keep doing that!" she said as he kissed her shoulder.

Levi's fingertips traced along her side. "You are doing perfectly fine, my love," he said in a soft voice.

Reece shook her head after Levi brought his lips to her neck. "Levi, stop! You're going to get us killed." She clenched the wheel tighter. "I should've put my cover-up back on."

"You're probably right," Levi said as he ran his hand down the center of her back, "although, I'm particularly grateful that you did not."

"I'm sure you are." She said with a laugh.

They continued traveling for a while across the open sea before Levi pointed out a rock formation he wanted her to guide the yacht toward. As soon as they were in the private cove, Levi went through the necessary actions to set anchor. They spent the rest of the afternoon exploring the caves, and enjoying their day alone together. Reece was speechless as they explored the caverns and she saw the pools of clear water in them.

After a beautiful day together exploring the ocean, caves, and renewing their love for one another, they decided to go back to the villa before dark. When they arrived, they went to their separate rooms to freshen up and prepare for dinner.

Chapter 23

Once Levi was ready for dinner, he stepped out onto the terrace and waited patiently for Reece to finish preparing herself for their evening together. It would seem that his assumptions were correct that Reece being forced to live in Pemdas had something to do with her previous angry outbursts. When they returned to Pemdas he planned to do whatever was necessary to ensure that she still had her freedom, even though she needed to live in his land for her protection.

He folded his arms and smiled at the lit water of the

aquamarine pool as he recalled how unsure he was of Reece before Harrison stepped in. He owed his cousin a debt of gratitude for everything he had done to help bring Reece back to him.

"Um, Levi?" Reece called out hesitantly.

Levi turned, and was instantaneously spellbound by her beauty as she stood in her doorway wearing a vibrant red dress. The silky dress outlined her flawless figure, and brought out the liveliness of her light-blue eyes. After a few moments of admiring her, he restrained himself from laughter when he noticed the troubled expression on her face. She held both hands behind her back, and her lips were twisted into a particular frown that Levi couldn't discern. He walked back into the villa. "What is it you need, love?" he asked with a grin.

She sighed. "As much as I love that smile of yours, right now I'm not really in a position to fully appreciate it." She tilted her head to the side. "I'm gonna need your help."

She looked up at him, forcing Levi to laugh at the many expressions of helplessness crossing over her face. "What's wrong?" he asked, struggling to keep his composure.

She eyed him warily. "I need you to cut my hair."

Levi stared at her incredulously. "What are you talking about?"

Reece slowly turned around and Levi immediately brought a fist to his mouth, restraining himself from laughing aloud. He swallowed hard and cleared his throat. "How did you manage this?"

"That's a really good question, and I'm still trying to figure it out." she said in annoyance.

Levi examined the back of her dress, and was baffled that she had caught her hair in her zipper, given that it only came up to the middle of her back.

He gently guided her back into her room. "We are not

cutting your hair, love. I will find a way to fix this," he said, as he knelt down on one knee and began to study how he would carefully remove her tangled hair.

"Is it really bad?" she asked nervously.

Levi softly chuckled. "It's not going to be easy, but I believe I can fix this. I am still trying to figure out how you managed this," he said, as he slowly began to try and maneuver her hair out of the zipper. "Don't tell me that after only a few of months of having Jasmeen—"

"Levi! Stop! Trust me, I already thought about that myself." She shook her head. "OW!"

Levi bit his bottom lip, struggling not to laugh. "You need to hold still."

"This is so embarrassing!" she said in an annoyed voice.

He stood up and unknotted the straps of her dress at the back of her neck to allow him more slack so that he could work with the zipper without pulling her hair. "Allow me to make something perfectly clear to you," he said, as he placed the untied straps into her hands. "You should never be embarrassed of anything while in my presence." He kissed her shoulder. "Now, hold still so I can fix this without causing you pain."

He knelt down and started to work on freeing her hair.

"Well, embarrassed or not, this is ridiculous."

"Reece, it's fine; but out of curiosity, how did this happen?" he said, finding the situation amusing.

Reece sighed. "I think it was a mixture of thinking about our day out together, and rushing to get ready to leave tonight. I leaned my head back as I was zipping the dress up, and now you're dealing with the result of that."

"Actually, I believe I'm working on the result of your attempting to fix this situation on your own." He laughed again. "It probably would have been easier if you'd called me when you first got into this situation."

"You're not making this any easier on me, Levi!" she grumbled.

Finally, the majority of her hair that was caught and tangled was removed. He was able to unzip the zipper slowly and free the last of her captive hair. "Got it!" he said triumphantly.

Reece gathered her hair with her hand and brought it over one shoulder. "Thank goodness. Thank you," she said, as she waited for him to zip up her dress for her.

Levi barely heard her as his eyes were drawn to the newly exposed skin of her lower back. Her body was so enticing, and he couldn't resist the desire to place his lips on the small of her back. Carefully and affectionately, he brought his lips to her soft skin and kissed her indulgently. He kissed up the center of her back leisurely, while he zipped up her dress.

Reece's breathing had picked up, yet she said nothing. Levi rose up and took the two straps out of her paralyzed hands. "I must say," he said, as he pursued her exposed shoulder delicately with his lips, "I am quite taken with your choice of dress this evening." Reece moaned and he grinned, knowing very well what he was doing to her.

Once he finished tying her straps, he kissed the top of her head. He let his lips linger there while he absorbed the sweet aroma of her silky-soft hair. He gently placed his hands over each of her shoulders, "I am also grateful we didn't need to go to the extreme of cutting your hair, either." He felt her body shudder as he slowly traced her collarbones with his fingers, and gathered her blond tresses into his hands, bringing her hair to fall freely down her back.

When he turned her to face him, her eyes were glazed as they stared up into his. Then her expression changed to that of her feigning reproach with him, and Levi laughed in response.

"If you keep kissing me like that," her eyes stared intently at his mouth before she brought her stern gaze up to meet his playful one, "you'll be lucky if we make it to dinner tonight."

"Oh, is that so?" He ran the back of his fingers up the center of her chest and along her neck. The V-shaped pattern of the deep-red halter dress perfectly displayed and complemented the glowing tone of her healthy skin. "Abandoning our dinner plans sounds like an excellent idea to me."

Reece's eyes narrowed at him as she playfully batted his hand away. "If we weren't sharing the villa with your cousin, I would happily agree with you." She glanced over at her bed, and then back at him. "We really need to go!"

"As you wish, my love," Levi answered as Reece brushed quickly past him and out of the room.

When they were in the car, Reece placed her hand in his. He raised her hand to his lips, inhaling deeply of the intoxicating aroma of her skin. "I haven't had the opportunity to tell you how stunning you look this evening." He smiled at the hint of red that touched her cheeks.

As he exited the parking structure, he looked over at her. "So, my love…" he brought the back of her hand to his lips again. After a small kiss, he looked over at her and smiled wryly. "Do I need to find a place where they serve hamburgers tonight?"

Reece laughed and squeezed his hand. "What am I going to do with you? I really don't care where we eat, but I'm sure Harrison already has our destination for dinner laid out for us."

"He has, and I believe you will enjoy it."

"I'm sure I will. I have enjoyed all of his little romantic

ideas so far. Who would've ever thought that Harrison had a romantic bone in his body," Reece teased.

"I don't know about romantic, but he certainly knows how to charm the ladies," Levi said with a laugh.

He pulled into the parking lot of a restaurant; after parking, he exited the vehicle quickly in order to open Reece's door for her. When they entered the elegant dining hall, the hostess led them to a table in the middle of the room. Levi glanced around, looking for a more isolated area for them to dine. "Excuse me, but if it is not too much of a burden, I would prefer being seated in a more isolated area." he said politely.

The young woman's face tinted red as she turned and locked eyes with Levi. "Oh!" She swallowed hard, "Absolutely, sir. I'm sorry, I was—" she stammered.

"It's not a problem," Levi smoothly cut her off with a kind smile.

He felt Reece laugh softly at his side as the woman struggled to maintain her composure. She turned to face the candlelit room, which was filled with patrons. When she looked back she avoided eye contact with Levi. "There is a secluded table in the front, if you'd like. Or I can have the—"

"A table in the front will be fine, thank you."

As soon as they approached the table, Levi pulled Reece's chair out for her. As Levi sat in his seat, the hostess handed Reece and Levi their menus. Levi requested their finest wine, and brought his attention to the menu before him as the waitress left.

"So," Reece narrowed her eyes at him. "It appears that the Pemdai are not the only people star-struck by you." She laughed. She stared intently into his eyes. "I can't say that I blame her, though; those sapphire-blue eyes of yours got the best of me, too," she said, as she placed her napkin in her lap. "Why do we have to sit in a secluded part of the room, anyway?"

Levi grinned. "Well, from this location," he glanced over his shoulder at the large glass windows that displayed the view of the glistening ocean behind him, "you have the best view of the Aegean Sea."

"And?" she asked.

Levi laughed softly. "And I prefer a location where I can better judge the room."

Reece's eyes widened with excitement as she leaned over the table. "So," she whispered, "are there any aliens in the restaurant?"

Levi chuckled pulled his menu open. "As a matter of fact, there are two." He dropped his menu down and smiled at her awed expression. "It's nothing to be concerned about, of course, or I wouldn't have brought you in here." He looked at her hands, which were clenched to her menu tightly. "Reece, would you care to decide upon what you want to eat this evening so that I may order for you."

She sat back in her chair and squinted at him. "We'll finish this conversation in a minute." She pulled her menu open and looked at it for a moment before she closed it. She sat back and took a sip of her wine. "I can't understand any of this." she said, "Feel free to order for me; you know what I like to eat."

"Very well, then." he said, as he brought his attention back to the menu.

Levi didn't fail to notice that since they'd arrived in Greece, Reece had hardly eaten anything. So tonight, he planned to order various delicacies for Reece to sample.

Once the waitress took their order and left, Reece crossed her arms and leaned into the table. "So there are really two aliens in here with us?" she asked discreetly.

Levi sipped his wine and nodded. He leaned forward, keeping his voice low. "They mean no harm; they are from a dimension known as Torlief. They are a species of beings that are very intrigued with how humans interact and so forth."

Reece lifted her chin. "Do they know that you're a Guardian?"

"Yes. They also know that there are four other Guardians among them in the room as well."

Reece smiled. "So this is the way it's always been? The people of Earth are just walking around with aliens among them all the time?"

Levi nodded. "Sort of. The ones who walk amongst humans are the ones who have the ability to shape-shift into human form."

"Are there a lot of those types out there?"

"Yes."

She stared at him in admiration. "And the Guardians keep all of them in line, huh?"

"That's what we do." He winked playfully at her. "As long as they pose no threat to any human, we allow them to enjoy their visit to the planet."

Their food arrived at the table; however, Reece had shown no interest in the plate of food before her. She reached for her goblet of wine and sipped it, her thoughts obviously elsewhere.

"Reece, please eat. I can see the questions lining up one by one in your head."

She stared at him with concern. "Reece, I didn't mean to frighten you. You will be fine—they have no intention of harming you. These particular beings have no knowledge that you are the Key."

Her eyes widened. "I just thought of something!" She placed her wineglass on the table, and then took a bite of her food, still deep in thought.

Levi sat there, clueless as to what could be going on in her mind. "Well? Are you going to leave me to guess about this revelation? What is it that you have thought of?"

After she swallowed her food, she stared somberly at him. "I didn't want to say anything about this, because I didn't want anyone to think I was crazy. Also, I didn't want to bring all of it back up again; but now, I think all of it makes perfect sense."

"What makes perfect sense?" Levi asked as he gazed into Reece's perplexed eyes.

"Reece, whatever it is, I will not think you are crazy."

Her expression softened. "You know when I stopped eating and then I got really sick? And then after that I was so mean to everyone?"

"Yes."

"I think I know why I was having those terrifying dreams now."

What? he thought in concern. "Terrifying dreams?" he asked in bewilderment.

She ignored Levi's concerned response, nodded and went on. "Maybe being at Castle Ruin somehow affected me subconsciously." She said, mainly talking to herself. "Especially when we walked into that room and I saw all those terrifying aliens—" She stared over at the wine in her glass. "That has to be the reason for those dreams." She spoke in a low voice, and then finally raised her eyes up meet Levi's.

Levi gazed at her, still trying to follow her. "I wish you would have mentioned something to me about these dreams."

Her eyes brightened. "I really think that's why I had those dreams, because of those creatures in the council." Her lips twisted, "I do understand that there are other dimensions out there. I know that you are not human." She smiled. "And even though I'm aware of it all, it's like I forget how scary it really is to me. It's a little unnerving to know that there are other beings not from Earth or Pemdas in this room with us. I keep forgetting that all that crazy stuff that people have always speculated about is real. That's what freaked me out so bad in the council! I witnessed it with my own eyes; weird creatures that I would never have believed existed, and it was definitely a frightening experience."

He reached for her hand that was resting on the table. "Reece, I am deeply regretful that you had to suffer through the council, but I wish you would have told one of us that your dreams were tormenting you; we could have helped you."

She stared down at her plate. "I couldn't. I would wake up from the dreams and be completely disoriented and scared. I decided to write them down instead to see if I could make sense of the dreams." She looked up at him. "I didn't tell anyone because I thought that they'd go away."

"Did documenting the dreams help you in any way?"

"Yes, but after I started writing them down, I would read what I wrote and then become sickened for dreaming such horrible things." She stared at Levi remorsefully. "They were mostly dreams about you being violent." She inhaled and brushed her thumb over the back of his hand. "I hated those dreams I had about you." She said through her teeth. "That's why I forced myself to stay awake, so I wouldn't have them. Then I completely lost my appetite, I couldn't eat or drink anything. That's where I got into trouble," she stared out of the windows behind him, "and couldn't tell the difference between dreams and reality."

"This is why you were so frightened of me." Levi replied, now understanding why Reece was so hesitant and defensive around him.

"I'm sorry. I'm sorry for everything."

"Don't apologize, I am glad you told me."

He gently rubbed his thumb over her hand. "Next time, you must let me know if you are suffering in such a way. It distresses me to know that you had to deal with this alone."

Reece smiled at him. "Well, it's all in the past now, and I'm sorry I brought it all up again." She shrugged. "The thought came to me when I got the eerie feeling that there are other aliens in the room with us." She raised her eyebrows at him. "But I promise you, no matter how weird the dream, I will tell you next time, because I'm not going through all those emotional outbursts again—ever!"

Levi smiled in relief as she brought her attention back to her food. "As I said, you have nothing to apologize for; and yes, you must tell me of these dreams if they return."

After dinner, Reece suggested spending the rest of the evening walking along the shoreline outside of the restaurant. There were couples walking about; however, it wasn't too busy, leaving Reece and Levi in perfect solitude as they took their shoes off and strolled along the shore.

Levi stopped, turned, and embraced her. "Remind me to thank Harrison for his excellent wardrobe planning with the hotel staff. I believe this is my new favorite dress; you look unquestionably ravishing in this particular shade of red."

Reece smiled and wrapped her arms around his neck. "We'll have to let Jasmeen know that then, won't we?"

Levi bent down and placed a tender kiss on her forehead. "Indeed." He kissed her nose. "We shall." Reece tilted her head up and offered her enticing lips to him, and he gladly accepted.

"There you two are!" a familiar voice called out.

Levi groaned softly as he ended their kiss and stared

over Reece's head. "Harrison," he informed her in a low, annoyed voice.

Reece laughed, squeezed him tightly, and kissed his chin. "Looks like you can thank your cousin for his wardrobe planning now—instead of later."

"All my gratitude for him left a moment ago." He reached down for her hand and smiled. "Come—let's go see what he needs."

As Harrison strode briskly toward them, he held both his hands out and smiled widely. "And so everything is as it should be." He stopped in front of them and grinned at Reece. "You two had nearly driven me mad over these last few days."

Reece chuckled softly. "Thanks for putting up with us."

"You are very welcome, and it appears that you did need to return to Earth for a while. I'm glad it helped," Harrison responded.

"It really did." Reece said.

"Now that everything is cleared up, and you two are happily in love again, some of the men and I were about to go exploring the wonderful nightlife in Greece. You're welcome to join us."

"Harrison, it's bad enough that I have to deal with this nonsense alone on Earth with you on our missions; why should I allow you to drag Reece into the middle of your crazy adventures as well?" Levi said.

Reece wrapped her arms around Levi's waist, "I think we'll pass on your offer, the three of us have spent enough time together already."

Harrison laughed, "Very true," he turned to leave, "you two enjoy the rest of your evening."

After Harrison left, Levi and Reece continued to walk along the shoreline. "This really has been a wonderful day." Reece said as she held Levi's hand.

Levi leaned over and kissed her on her temple, "I couldn't agree more."

Chapter 24

Reece was up early the next morning preparing for the day to be spent with Levi. As she left her room, she saw that the door to Levi's room across the way was open, and his bed was neatly made. The aroma of coffee filled her senses, enhancing her excitement for the day ahead of them.

As she walked past Levi's room, she noticed him standing out on his balcony. He was leaning against the railing, holding a cup of coffee, and quietly staring out at the ocean. Reece came up from behind him, and wrapped her arms around his waist tightly.

"Good morning," she said, as she kissed the back of his shoulder.

Levi rose up and brought his arm around her. "Good morning. You are up early. Did you rest well?"

"I did." She glanced over at the coffee he held in his hand. "You know, I think this is the first time I've seen you drink coffee," she said with a laugh. "And come to think of it, I haven't had a cup of coffee in a long time."

Levi offered her a sip. "Try it first; Harrison tends to make it stronger than most would like."

She did, and she shivered at the bitter flavor. Levi laughed softly as he raised the coffee mug to his lips.

"How in the world can you drink that?"

"I'm used to it," he answered with a grin.

Levi's expression changed unexpectedly, and the humor left his face. He stared somberly into the dark coffee and sighed.

"Levi?" Reece ran her hand across his back encouragingly. "Is everything okay?"

He exhaled. "Everything will be fine; however, we are being forced to return to Pemdas today. As of now, we remain unaware of all the details. Samuel contacted me late last night, and it appears that Armedias has formed an army outside of the vortex that connects Armedias to Pemdas."

Reece stared up at him, bewildered. "An army? Why? They can't come into Pemdas, can they?"

"No, they can't cross the barriers without our horses. That is why we are unsure about what it is they are planning. We will know more after we return. As of now, my father and Samuel are uncomfortable with you being on Earth, and we must return you to the safety of Pemdas." He looked at her with a tormented expression.

"Is Armedias the dimension that Michael Visor is in?"

"Yes, and he is leading their army."

"Why do you think they're doing this?"

Levi set his coffee mug on the railing and reached for her hand. "We knew something like this would likely happen when we took their priestess into captivity. When we encountered her on Earth, she was very interested in your residing in Pemdas."

Reece stared out at the ocean. "So they want me?" she looked back at Levi, "Because I'm the Key." She said dryly.

Levi nodded. "It is why we must return you to Pemdas as soon as possible. We need to come to some form of agreement with Lucas, Armedias' ruler, as well."

"So when do we leave?"

"Harrison is in the process of arranging our departure by noon, maybe earlier, now that you are awake." Levi stared intently at her, and appeared to be troubled by more than he was telling her.

Reece raised her hand gently to his face. "This isn't what is really upsetting you, is it?"

Levi turned and pulled her into an embrace. "I am concerned for you. It appears that you are happiest on Earth. I fear that everything we went through these past weeks was due to a form of depression from you being forced to reside in Pemdas. I believe the nightmares you were having were a result of that as well. You should be able to have your freedom to return to the world you are most comfortable living in; however, you cannot." He kissed her softly on her forehead. "You are unable to enjoy an entire week on Earth, and now it is perfectly clear to me that I cannot give you that happiness and freedom if you wanted it. It bothers me greatly."

She withdrew and smiled at him. "If you must know," she stood on her toes and kissed him. "I'm excited to go home; and my home is in Pemdas, whether you think I'm comfortable there or not. I really don't have any desire to live on Earth. Sure, yesterday was wonderful, but only because I was with you. I'm happiest wherever you are, Levi. You have to believe me."

Levi smiled faintly in return. "It delights me to hear you speak that way. Although, you must promise me something before we depart."

"Anything."

He brought his hand to her face, and his eyes were set with purpose. "You need to notify me at once if the dreams return or you start feeling distressed. I know you believe your nightmares were from your experience in the council meeting, but I'm not convinced of that fact." He exhaled and went on. "The physician that treated you made an excellent assumption in regard to your not eating or resting well. You are not a natural resident of Pemdas, and the fact that you are being forced to reside—"

"Levi, please," Reece firmly interrupted. "I love Pemdas, and more than that, I love you. Like I told you last night, I promise that I will let you know if the horrible dreams resume, or if I get any weird feelings again. Now, let's enjoy our last few moments alone before we go."

Levi brought his chin to rest on top of her head. "I can't bear to lose you again. More than that, I can't accept the idea of you suffering."

Reece ran her hands along his back, "That's why I'll tell you if I start to experience anything abnormal. So stop worrying."

Within the hour, they were in the helicopter on their way to the cars that would take them through the vortex to

Pemdas. It was not long before they were on Areion, and riding swiftly up the hill to Pasidian Palace. As the imposing structure came into sight, Reece's heart raced with anticipation. She squeezed Levi around his waist tightly, and he brought his hand to cover hers as the stallion trotted over the stone bridge and into the courtyard.

As wonderful as it was to see the palace again, Reece was slightly worried about seeing everyone that she had behaved so rudely towards. She wanted to be sure that each person knew that she was regretful for the way she treated them, and hoped they would accept her apology as Levi had. She planned to make amends with Levi's family upon their arrival.

Unfortunately, she was unable to do as she had intended. As soon as they arrived at Pasidian Palace, she became sick with a headache so great that she could hardly speak. It overpowered her so quickly that she released her hold on Levi, and fell from Areion when he halted. Fortunately, Harrison had already dismounted, and caught her before she fell to the ground.

⟶

The doctor was summoned, and gave Reece a remedy to take the painful effects away. Levi would not leave her side until his mother was present. When Allestaine walked into Reece's bed chamber, Levi guided her out into Reece's sitting room.

"How is she feeling?" Allestaine asked with concern.

"She is resting, the physician as given her a remedy that appeared to help the pain subside." Levi gazed at his mother somberly, "As you know, I am to report to Samuel immediately because of the situation that has arisen with Armedias."

"Rest assured, I will not leave her side."

Levi rubbed his forehead, "I have a bad feeling about all of this. She was fine when she was on Earth and as soon as we return to the palace she becomes ill again?"

"Do not worry, we will get to the bottom of this. Go to your meeting, and if she isn't feeling well when she wakes up, I will send for you."

"Thank you, mother." Levi said as he turned and left the room.

After Levi departed, Reece faintly heard Allestaine request for Jasmeen to send for tea. She walked into Reece's bed chamber just as Reece was starting to sit up.

Allestaine approached her, "How are you feeling darling?"

Reece smiled warmly at her, "Much better, thank you." She leaned back against her pillows, "I need to apologize for how rude I was toward you and everyone here before I left."

Allestaine sat on the side of the bed and held her hand, "Do not concern yourself over that, I am thankful you are feeling better."

Reece glanced around them room, "Where's Levi?"

"He's in a meeting with Samuel. If you feel strange in anyway, you must let me know, and we will send for him."

Jasmeen walked into the bedchamber, "Lady Allestaine, the tea is here, would you care to take it in here or in the sitting room."

Reece stretched out her arms, "Actually, I'd like to get out of bed."

Allestaine looked over at Jasmeen, "We'll take it in the sitting room, thank you."

As the ladies sat on the sofa drinking their tea, Reece

began to tell Allestaine about their vacation in Greece. During their conversation, Reece felt a flood of negative emotions wash over her. *This can't be happening again!* Her heart started to race, feeling as though something were taking over her rational thoughts, like before. She began to panic, and abruptly stood up. "I need to see Levi right away! Where is he?" she demanded.

"He's in Navarre's office," Allestaine stood, "Please, sit, and I'll send for him at once."

Reece started rubbing her temples; her headache was returning with a vengeance. "There is no time for that. I have to get to him quickly," she answered, and fled the room before Allestaine could stop her.

Chapter 25

ucas is an absolute fool if he thinks that lining up an army of men on the borders of Armedias is going to force us to turn over their priestess!" Harrison said in annoyance. He looked at Samuel. "Is she working with Galleta at all? She does realize that we'd be more than happy to kick her out of Pemdas after she allows us into her mind to see if she knows where the stone is?" Harrison leaned back and crossed his arms. "This is absurd! Well, what are our plans? Do we just go to war and get this over with?"

"Lucas will not agree to a meeting with the emperor. They have no desire to work any of this out," Samuel added.

"Gentlemen, let us not be too concerned with it all. For now, I want the necessary precautions taken. Reece cannot leave Pemdas until these matters are settled." Navarre stated.

The men were then interrupted when Reece was announced at the door. Levi stood and as he approached her he noticed a look of rage in her eyes.

"What has happened?" Levi asked.

Reece reached out to him. "I need to speak with you this instant!"

Her tone was firm and direct, and Levi would not argue. He looked back at the men, and they nodded in acceptance of his early dismissal. He turned and led Reece from the room.

"Is everything okay? Why did my mother not send for me?"

Reece ignored his question, "Levi, you have to get me out of here!" she said fearfully, "It's happening again, and this time I don't know how much longer I can control it. I have to get outside or something."

Reece clenched his hand as she walked out of the palace at a rapid pace. She sat down on a bench in the gardens, and tightly pressed her hands to each side of her head.

"Is your head bothering you again?" Levi sat next to her and brought his hand to her forehead, but she flinched away.

"It's happening again," she growled.

"What's happening, Reece?" he reached for her hand and she jerked violently away. "You need to talk to me, love. Have the dreams returned?"

She started sobbing. "No!" she snapped. "I'm having the same feelings that I had before I went to Simone's house. Is she here? Could she have something to do with this? I don't want this to happen again, and this time I recognize it. We were wrong, it wasn't the dreams—it's not depression—it's something else!" She looked up at him with fear in her eyes. "Levi, I don't know how much longer I have until it completely takes over my mind again!"

Levi stared at her, struggling to make sense of everything she was trying to tell him.

"Simone is not here; however, she will be by nightfall. Samuel has sent for her, as he will not return home until the Armedites retreat."

"Then why is this happening to me? Levi, please help me." she groaned.

Levi's heart pounded against his chest. Reece's demeanor appeared to be changing by the minute. He had no idea how to fix this, or where to begin to help her.

"Levi! Answer me!" Reece shouted.

"We must send for Galleta, hopefully she can read into your mind and figure out what's causing this. It's the only way I know to help you."

Reece rubbed her face in agitation. "Then call for her, now!" she snarled.

Levi escorted her back to her room quickly, and sent for Queen Galleta. Reece had become seemingly agitated by Levi's presence, so he suggested she take something to settle her nerves. It was not long after Reece took the remedy that she fell asleep.

Galleta arrived within the hour and met Levi in Reece's bedchamber.

Levi stood from the chair by her bed, "Should I wake her?" he asked.

Queen Galleta studied Reece for a moment. Levi observed the queen's expression change to that of disbelief. She looked at him somberly. "No, allow her to rest. I will speak with you in the other room."

As they made their way back into Reece's sitting room, Navarre, Allestaine, Elizabeth, and Harrison were already there, quietly waiting. Navarre and Harrison stood as Galleta and Levi entered the room. Galleta sat on the sofa. "Something has changed within her mind since I last met with her. I do not know what is causing this. What is strange is that I am seeing into her mind, but her thoughts don't appear to be her own. Her mind was projecting dark emotions and thoughts into mine. I've never encountered such a thing."

Levi ran a hand through his hair as he turned to stare out of the windows. "Then why was she not this way when we were on Earth?" He looked at Galleta. "She was perfectly fine there."

"That is interesting to know; but, you need to understand, Reece's mind is blocking me. Her mind will only reveal certain things. When I try and read past this, all I see is darkness. You must allow me some time to decipher what is happening. Unfortunately, I cannot make any conclusions at the moment."

"We may not have enough time!" Levi said in a raised voice. "I will not allow Reece to be in agony like this again!"

Navarre stood. "Galleta, take the time you need." He looked purposefully at Levi. "We will figure this out, but we will not pressure Galleta."

Levi mirrored his father's authoritative expression. "I will not allow her to suffer like this."

Harrison laughed softly, cutting through the tension of the moment. "Levi, if this is all about to go down the way it did before we brought Reece to Earth, then you know very well that we will be the ones who suffer the most. You are just going to have to get a grip on your emotions now. As you are well aware, she will despise you the greatest."

"Harrison is correct. Please, be patient as I go over all of this. I will work as quickly as I can."

Galleta stood and prepared to leave the room. Navarre, Allestaine, and Elizabeth escorted her out, leaving Levi and Harrison alone in the sitting room.

Levi sat on the sofa, leaned forward, and dropped his head into his hands. He exhaled, troubled by the lack of answers from Queen Galleta.

"I am unsure if I can endure this again. I cannot describe the distress it brings me knowing that I cannot help her." He shook his head. "Harrison, if she was not feeling this on Earth, then the only answer is to bring her back. I would find a way for us to live there safely. However, because of the current situation in Armedias, I cannot do that for her."

"Don't let your emotions overrule your common sense. The answers are before you already. You understand that Reece loves you, and that is all that should matter. Until we find a way to fix this, you're going to have to endure it."

"You're right."

Harrison grinned. "I know. You must realize that Reece is unique, Levi. What happened with you inheriting the imprint of the map from her was quite phenomenal, so we shouldn't be that shocked that it had some sort of effect on her. We'll find a way to help her, you must have patience."

Levi nodded in agreement.

Harrison stood, and Levi did as well. "Until then, let us return to our meetings. Unless, of course, you want to be here when she wakes and despises you once again?"

"I will stay with her. If Samuel needs me, send for me."

"Very well. I wish you luck, my friend." Harrison

clapped Levi on the shoulder. "In time, it will all be okay," he said, before turning to leave.

When Levi walked back into Reece's room, he was startled when he saw the expression on her face. She was sitting up in bed, staring at nothing. When she noticed him in the doorway, her expression darkened with hatred.

Her eyes were black with anger; however, she managed to smile at him. She fidgeted with her hands wildly, and appeared to be in distress.

"How are you feeling?" he inquired softly, unsure of how he should approach her.

She stared at him for a moment. "I'm better than before, I think. My mood is shifting constantly, though. One minute I feel normal, and then out of nowhere, I am anxious and angry."

"And now?" he asked apprehensively.

She tried to calm her fidgeting hands. "Scared to death."

Levi approached her hesitantly; but when she opened her arms to receive him, he joined her on the bed.

"Please sit with me. I don't want to get out of bed. I don't want to see anyone. I really don't want you to see me like this, but I need you. I don't want to be alone with this darkness in my mind."

"Darkness in your mind?" Levi questioned in confusion.

"Don't ask me to explain it. Please, just stay with me." She said anxiously.

"Is there anything I can get you to make you more comfortable?" he offered, unsure of what could help her at this point.

"No." Her face was fraught with desperation. "I only want you with me."

Levi brought his arm around her and she leaned into him closely. Levi could feel the tension in her as she held him tightly. Her arms were rigid as her fingers clenched his sides; he massaged his hand along her arm, hoping it would help her relax.

"Levi—you would never hurt me, would you?"

"What?" he said as he glanced down at her in shock. "Reece, no! Why would—"

"You wouldn't?" She asked as her voice trembled.

"I would never consider such behavior toward you. Why is it that you would think that I would ever harm you?"

Her grip tightened and entire body shuddered. "I had another dream about you."

"You have to understand, I would never hurt you, my love." He said, holding her closer. "Are these the dreams that you spoke of?"

"Yes," she said quietly. "They don't seem as scary this time though. What's strange is that I have an irrational sense of lingering fear. I'm terrified, but I don't know why." She rubbed her forehead. "I need you to help me."

Reece began to cry, and Levi ran his hand over her hair. "Tell me what you need me to do. I'll do anything."

She sniffed. "I don't know how much longer I can handle being this close to you," she said in a shaky voice. Her fingers dug into his side and she moaned. "You can't leave me. I need you to help me. I'm so scared."

Reece suddenly jerked away from him and pressed her fingertips into her forehead so tightly that they turned white. "Oh—my head; it's killing me."

"Let me get you different remedy for that."

He moved to get off the bed, and she grabbed him in a panic. "NO! You can't leave me. It'll go away. Promise you won't leave me."

"I am not leaving you, my love," Levi answered, and then called for Jasmeen to get Reece a remedy for her pain.

After Jasmeen returned, Reece stared at the bottle she held as if it would harm her. "Reece, it's a salve that will help with the pain." Levi said as he took the offered bottle from Jasmeen.

She shied away from it and pushed Levi's arm away. "Please, don't. I don't want anything," she said, as she looked at him fearfully. "Levi, I'm so scared."

What is happening to her? Levi thought in absolute confusion, wondering if somehow she was truly losing her mind. As distressed as he was seeing her in torment like this, he forced himself to ignore his emotions. The only way to help her was to try and get answers from her, and see if he could figure out what was going on.

"Tell me what it is you are afraid of." he asked.

She leaned back into Levi's embrace. "It's so strange. It's like all of this is hitting me in waves. Before, I didn't recognize what was going on, but now I can tell when it's going to happen."

"When *what* is going to happen?"

"I will be terrified of you, I will hate you, and I will hate myself for hating you. I will want nothing more than to be away from you and this place. When those emotions hit me, I have to fight them. That's what I'm doing right now, and I don't know if I can keep fighting this." She rubbed her head. "My head feels like it's going to explode when I fight these dark emotions."

Levi was at a loss, and before he could speak, she jerked away from him abruptly. He watched as she crawled on her hands and knees to the middle of the bed. She cradled her knees to her stomach and started to rock back and forth. She began to moan as tears streamed down her face.

Levi couldn't bare the image of her torment. "Reece—" he said, as he reached out to her.

"Don't!" she snapped. "Don't touch me." Her eyes were black with fury.

Levi lost track of time as he watched her rock back and

forth, moaning in torment. He sat in silence and listened as she quietly mumbled to herself. He tried to discern what she was saying but was unable to.

Suddenly, Reece collapsed back onto her pillows, and her expression was now peaceful.

She reached her arm out toward him weakly, "I love you," she said breathlessly.

Levi's brow creased. "And I love you."

She crawled back into his arms. "I am feeling so much better now. I think I may have fought it away."

Levi ran his fingers gently through her hair, something still wasn't right about her demeanor. "That *is* good to hear. Is there anything I can get you?"

"No, stay with me. Talk to me, in case it happens again."

Levi looked down into her eyes and noticed the blankness in them.

"Levi, talk about something, please," she said desperately.

"I wish we were still in Greece," he answered. "Oh!" he said as he reached into his pocket. "Here's your souvenir." He laughed as he handed her the shell he retrieved from the ocean floor.

Reece looked at the shell and smiled faintly. "Thank you, will you place it on the table for me?"

Levi set the shell on the table, fairly surprised that she showed no interest in it.

Reece looked up at him, "So have they decided what is going on with that other world?"

"No. We still cannot decipher why they would wish to gather an army, as if we were planning to invade them."

"If the Guardians chose to battle them, how would you fight them? How much better are the Pemdai warriors than theirs? Would you win?"

"Currently, we would not. Until Samuel calls in all the

Guardians, we are outnumbered against their army. It is why we would never invade their lands at the present moment."

"If you weren't outnumbered, how would you fight them?"

"Armedias is similar in their lifestyle to the Pemdai. We would battle with swords and bows."

"So you will fight with swords and bows?"

Levi became concerned by all the unnecessary questions Reece was asking of him, but still proceeded to answer her.

"We would mainly fight by the sword, if we had to. We are trained on the bow; however, it is not our preference."

Reece laughed. "So you are not well trained in that skill?"

Levi pulled away and looked down at her. It almost seemed as though he were talking to someone else, and not Reece. "Why are you so overly concerned with the way we would battle Armedias? The Pemdai have no desire to battle, and we will not. I do not wish to frighten you with all of these unnecessary details. Is there something else we can talk about?"

Reece's eyes were like flint when she jerked away violently and glared at him. "I think you should leave!"

"Reece you are no condition to be left alone." he said sternly.

"I'm fine, I want to rest." she answered.

Before Levi could respond, Jasmeen entered the bed chamber. "Simone is here to call on Reece."

Levi stood from the bed, "Reece desires to rest—"

"Send her in!" Reece blurted out.

Levi looked at Reece in confusion as she smiled smugly at him. "You can leave now."

Levi turned and exited the room without another word to Reece. When he encountered Simone in the sitting room, he looked at her darkly. "Reece desires your company." he said flatly. "However, she is unwell, so I ask you to make your visit as brief as possible." he commanded.

Simone nodded, "Of course."

Levi studied Simone for a moment, "I'll be in my father's office if she needs me." He said as he turned to leave.

Chapter 26

elief washed over Reece after Levi left, and Simone walked into her room.

"Simone!" she said with eagerness as she got out of her bed. She gripped both of Simone's shoulders in desperation. "I need your help. I need to leave Pemdas."

Simone smiled. "I have a horse waiting for you." she reached for Reece's hand, and led her away from the doorway. "In an hour, set out for an evening walk. I will meet you out in the forest where the creeks divide, the location where you always take your walks."

"An evening walk?" Reece asked. "This isn't a game Simone, I have to leave, now!"

"Reece, the palace staff will notice you leaving. You must not arouse suspicion." She wound her arm through

Reece's and walked slowly back to the door. "Now, simply set out for an evening stroll, as you've been known to do, and I will handle the rest from there." Before Simone left, she instructed Reece wait ten minutes before following after her.

Reece spent her time waiting, writing in her journal. Ten minutes had passed before she left her room discreetly. No one was around, and she strolled out to the forest without being questioned.

As promised, Simone was waiting with a young man about Reece's age, and a Guardian horse. Simone abruptly approached her. "If you still plan to leave, then you must not waste another second." She looked at the man. "Make haste, Mr. Prather." Simone said with a smile.

Reece gazed up into the man's eyes, realizing it was Mark Prather from the Hamilton's ball. "Mr. Prather, thank you so much for helping me!" she said desperately.

"Reece!" Simone snapped. "We waste time! Both of you must leave now!"

Mark Prather quickly mounted the horse, and offered his hand to help Reece. Once Reece was settled on the horse, Mark heeled the stallion, and they galloped rapidly through the forest.

It wasn't long after they left that Reece felt the negative hold that had taken over her vanish. As the oppressive feeling left, her rational thoughts returned. *What am I doing?* she thought as they rode further away from the palace. She feared for her life, and had to get back to the palace somehow. She considered jumping from the horse, but they were moving too fast. Her body trembled with fear, knowing that she was in imminent danger. Her only chance was to jump from the horse. She released her grip on Mark, but gasped in pain when he clenched down hard on her wrists, pulling her tightly against him.

"Hold on, we are crossing over the barriers."

"Where are you taking me?" she yelled.

Mark ignored her and then a bright light flashed, nearly blinding her. When her eyes readjusted, she realized that her surroundings had completely changed. "Where are we?" she demanded.

Without the glowing nature of Pemdas, she could hardly see anything. She started fighting Mark's hold on her, but was unsuccessful. *Think, Reece. Don't panic!*

"Well—well—well!" she heard a raspy voice call out loudly, as the horse slowed to a walk.

"The plans were executed flawlessly, My Lord Visor, sir." Mark proclaimed as the horse stopped. "You will be extremely proud of Lady Simone as well."

Lord Visor? Michael Visor? She looked around and noticed they were surrounded by an army of men. *I'm in Armedias!* she thought, as her heart started pounding. She screamed when she was jerked from the horse's back, and her arm was twisted in a tightened grip.

She looked up as Michael leered at her darkly. "It's been too long, hasn't it?" He glanced up at Mark. "What are you waiting for? Go! Get Simone out of there before someone realizes the little Pemdai princess is gone."

At Michael's orders, Mark turned and rode away briskly. Reece pried her wrist out from Michael's sturdy hold, and ran as quickly as she could. She had no idea where she was going, but she had to get away. She wasn't far before a strong hand seized the back of her neck and forced her to stop.

"Not so fast, little princess," the man said with a laugh.

He held her neck tightly, paralyzing her where she stood. "You're Michael Visor?" she managed.

"The one and only."

"Get your hands off of me," she demanded.

He gripped her hair, and yanked her head back. "Or what? Your boyfriend won't be helping you this time. As a matter of fact, our armies are already prepared for the arrogant Pemdai to come get their little Key."

He started marching her back toward the camp of Armedite soldiers. She knew she had to get out of this, and she started fighting him with every last bit of energy she possessed.

"Let me go!" she screamed.

It was the last thing Reece remembered saying before everything went black, and she woke up shivering on an ice-cold, stone floor.

→

Levi struggled to maintain his focus while his father, Samuel, and the other Guardians discussed the reasons Armedias might have for planning war. Sitting in this meeting seemed pointless to Levi; he hadn't heard a word anyone was saying. He should have never left Reece alone in Simone's care, and as hard as he may have tried, he couldn't suppress the inward feeling that something wasn't right.

Without dismissing himself properly, he stood up, and left the room abruptly. He walked swiftly through the corridors to her room, hoping he was wrong about the danger he believed Reece was in. As he raised his fist to knock, the door to Reece's room opened.

"Jasmeen?" he said, somewhat startled.

"Master Levi," she answered, her eyes wide with fear. "I was on my way to send for you and the emperor this very moment."

Levi maintained his composure. "What has happened?" he asked, as he brushed past her into the room.

"She's not here, sir," Jasmeen said in a shaky voice. "I

went to offer her and Simone some tea, but they were gone." She handed Levi a leather-bound journal, "I found this lying opened on her bed."

"What is this?" Levi said, as he flipped through the pages.

"It's her journal, sir."

As Levi skimmed the pages, his heart nearly stopped when he read her first journal entry. *Impossible,* he thought as he fanned the pages and found the last thing she documented. His fists gripped the leather journal tightly after he read that Simone had offered to help her leave Pemdas.

Levi's heart began to beat rapidly. "Inform the emperor, and tell him that I have sent you. I must see if there is a way I can track them before it's too late."

Levi exited the room hastily, and nearly ran over Harrison in the corridor. "Levi? What has gotten into you?"

Levi shoved the book into Harrison's chest. "Reece may have left Pemdas, and I have to find her."

As Levi started to walk past him, Harrison grabbed his arm. "Hold on a minute," Harrison said, as he stared at Levi in confusion. "What makes you think that?"

Levi glanced down at the journal. "The last page of that journal states that Simone offered to help Reece leave." Levi ran his hand aggressively through his hair. "This was directly after she ordered me out of her room in order to be alone with Simone."

Harrison stared at Levi in disbelief, "Why would you leave her alone with that woman?"

"Harrison!" Levi glared at him darkly, "We have no time—"

"If these writings are true, how could Simone have helped her leave Pemdas?" Harrison interrupted Levi as he flipped through the pages. "There is no possible way—" He stopped himself, and looked somberly at Levi. "Michael," he said gravely, "she used his horse!"

This can't be happening. Levi rubbed his forehead in distress. "I should have let Javian destroy that horse!"

Harrison's expression darkened. "We must locate Reece immediately."

"I will find Reece! You must interrogate the woman from Armedias."

Harrison looked at Levi in confusion. "The priestess? What could she possibly have to do with any of this?"

"Read Reece's first entry. She writes of a nightmare that she had. She describes the exact scenario between me and the priestess on Earth." He stated. "Harrison, I never told her about that confrontation. I only informed her that the Armedite had read into my mind!"

"If what you are saying is true, how could the priestess have gotten into Reece's mind like that? Her mind is protected; our devices can't even alter it."

Levi shook his head. "Her mind may be protected against *our* devices; however, don't forget that the Ciatron were able to use their powers of mental persuasion on her successfully. I believe that the priestess has done the same thing. The priestess took over Reece's mind, and persuaded her to leave Pemdas!" Levi turned to leave. "Just speak with the woman, and do whatever you can to get answers from her. I must go."

"Rest assured, I will get the answers we need from her," Harrison said.

As Harrison disappeared down the steps that headed toward the command center, Levi walked briskly through the corridors. He stopped to ask the palace guards who attended the doors if they had encountered Reece. They informed him that she had taken her usual walk into the forest.

Levi ran quickly in the direction the guards pointed him. There was hope in his mind that they were not too late, and Reece was still in Pemdas. His confidence was shaken when he discovered the fresh hoofprints of a Guardian horse in the soil before him. He knelt down and pressed his fingers along the edges of one of the prints. After examining it, it was obvious that a horse had been in the area recently.

Without wasting another second, he went directly to the stables to see if Michael's horse was still in confinement.

Javian met him at the entry. "Master Levi?"

"Is Michael's horse in his stall?" Levi asked, as he stormed past the stable master and into the large building.

"Of course, sir. Mr. Maxwell has been in charge of that horse," Javian said, as he followed Levi through the stables.

Levi closed his eyes in disbelief when he encountered that the stall for Michael's horse was vacant. He roared angrily as he turned to exit the building. He jerked Areion's reins off the hook and threw them over his shoulder. He bellowed loudly for his stallion, and glanced back at Javian. "Notify Samuel that we need men positioned at every vortex leading out of Pemdas this instant."

As Areion approached the fence, Levi jumped it, and swiftly pulled the bridle over his horse's head. Areion bit down on the silver mouthpiece of his halter forcefully, prepared and willing to adhere to Levi's course of action.

Levi grabbed the reins, a handful of mane, and hoisted himself onto Areion's back. "Go, NOW, Javian! We may still have a chance to stop them!"

Levi charged Areion toward the forest where he had discovered the fresh prints of the Guardian horse. Areion effortlessly jumped over the large fence as Levi directed him to the location where he found the fresh hoofprints. The tracks were fresh enough that Levi knew Areion could easily follow the scent of the soured horse. "Follow them!" he ordered his stallion.

Areion lunged forward aggressively, and they raced rapidly through the forest. Once they were over the protective barriers of Pemdas, Levi halted Areion at the vortex to Armedias. It was painfully obvious that Reece had been taken into the dimension. Areion fought Levi's hold on the reins as he approached the vortex. As tempting as it was to travel through and recover Reece, he knew that their army was on the other side, waiting for the Pemdai to make such a foolish move.

Levi ordered Areion back toward the palace. When he arrived in the courtyard, he jumped off the horse's back and bounded up the steps that led into the palace. Levi charged into the command center, looking for Samuel. The atmosphere of the palace had changed entirely. Imperial Guards and Guardian warriors were combing throughout the palace grounds and rooms in search of any sign of Reece and Simone.

He approached where Samuel stood with a group of Guardians, giving them instructions on where to search for Reece. "Commander." Levi interrupted. "Reece is in Armedias."

"How certain are you of this?" Samuel responded.

"Michael's horse is gone. I followed the animal's fresh trail to the vortex that leads into that land." He stared gravely at Samuel.

"We have dispatched Guardians to be stationed at every vortex that exits Pemdas, I will inform the emperor of Reece's whereabouts immediately." Samuel replied. "We have also received word that Mark Prather was the one to remove Michael's horse from his stable."

Levi inhaled deeply, "Who witnessed this?"

"Javian found one of the stable men, severely injured

behind the stable yard, and it was his report that validated that it was indeed Mark Prather who freed the soured horse from his stable."

Levi's lips pressed into a fine line as he closed his eyes and tried to maintain his focus. "I have no idea how that man was not noticed lurking around the palace." He gazed at Samuel sternly, "However, we waste time trying to deliberate how he and Simone were able to plan this scheme together."

"They both will be dealt with as the traitors they are, Levi. The emperor and I have already discussed this." Samuel returned.

"Very well," Levi answered impatiently. "Where is Harrison?"

"He is interrogating the priestess."

Levi spun on his heel, and walked down to the prison chambers where the priestess was being detained. When he overheard Harrison questioning the woman, he approached slowly, listening to their conversation.

"For as intelligent as the Pemdai are, I'm surprised it took you all so long to figure out that I was controlling that girl from the moment I first arrived here," he heard the priestess say.

"So this was Lucas' plan all along," Harrison said sternly. "For us to imprison one of his mind-warping agents in Pemdas, and have you drive the Key out from our protected realm. Excellent strategy. I must commend him personally, when his heart meets the tip of my sword."

The woman chuckled. "Yes, it had been our plan all along. I couldn't reach the mind of that woman unless I was in the same realm and close to her. Fortunately, I was able to see into Levi Oxley's mind, and it not only ensured that I would be taken captive in Pemdas, but that I would be put under close guard as well. I was very pleased to find that I would be placed in a unit that was in the same location where that girl resided." She laughed. "It's been quite amusing sitting down here tormenting that child's every thought," she sighed softly, "her mind was a lot stronger than I anticipated though."

She focused on the ground, and she seemed to be watching the whole process of terrorizing Reece play out in her mind. "She definitely battled my persuasions." She looked at Harrison with an innocent smile. "If she hadn't fought so hard for her proper mindset, I wouldn't have had to give her such traumatic headaches. Mindless child." She mocked.

Harrison's features darkened. "You are very bold to admit this to me."

"I fulfilled my purpose in coming to Pemdas, as was required of me, and that is all that matters. Your men are outnumbered, and if you go to war at this time, it will result in the demise of your world. I have no fear of your kind."

She looked up and noticed Levi standing in the doorway. Harrison glanced back, but continued to question the woman. "How are you so sure that we are outnumbered, Armedite? You have no idea how large our armies are, nor does your cowardly leader."

The woman smiled. "I not only persuaded the girl to suffer," She paused and giggled. "But I also managed to take complete control of her mind more than once. Levi gave me the information I needed last night, thinking he was talking to Reece."

Levi gritted his teeth together so tightly that he felt his jaw muscle spasm.

The woman smiled sardonically at him. "How is your lip, darling; I didn't make it bleed too much, did I?"

Levi clenched his fists as he fought the urge to end the woman's life in that moment.

"Where is Lucas keeping Reece?" Harrison calmly asked.

Before anyone could say another word, the woman's appearance changed. Her appearance seemed holographic, as did their surroundings. The lights flickered off in the cell as her turquoise eyes began to glow, and she projected a vision of where Reece was being held. Rage coursed through his veins when he saw Reece lying unconscious on the stone floor of a dark chamber with Simone standing over her. He tried to move, but he was paralyzed where he stood.

He watched with fury as Simone knelt down beside Reece. She grabbed her hair, and looked toward four women who entered the room. The women were identical in appearance to the priestess.

"We've done our part," Simone said with an evil grin. "Now," she slammed Reece's head hard onto the floor. "Get into her mind, and give us the information we need."

"In time," the four women said in unison.

Simone's gaze darkened as she stood up, and approached the women. "We need that location to the stone! Open the girl's mind!" Simone ordered as the vision dissipated.

"Who are you?" Harrison questioned in a deadly voice.

The priestess stared dangerously at Harrison. "You'll have that answer soon, brave warrior. I believe I've answered more than enough for you already. Now, go. I'm sure you and your kind are thoughtless enough to avenge that girl's life." She sneered. "It's the death you all long for, isn't it; to bravely die saving all worlds for some ridiculous cause? It is ignorant, and foolish."

"The only thing that was foolish of us was to offer you clemency when we first encountered you," Harrison retorted in a lethal voice.

"Leave us," Levi commanded Harrison.

Harrison looked at Levi in question, and then, with a simple nod of understanding, walked toward the doorway. As Levi approached the woman, she grinned evilly at him.

"Should I be fearful of you, prince?"

Levi's eyes narrowed as she instinctively backed against the wall, away from him. "Only if you fear death." He glared into her eyes purposefully. "Why have you shown us these images?"

She laughed softly. "To make you aware that if you do indeed take my life, then I can assure you my sisters will no longer hesitate to remove the map from that Earthling's mind with whatever force necessary." She went to reach for Levi's face, and he immediately deflected her hand. The woman's eyes darkened. "Our minds are interconnected," she threatened. "We all experience the same feelings, we see the same—"

"I have no patience for such absurd talk," Levi interrupted, "where are they keeping Reece?"

Levi seized both of her arms, causing her to gasp in pain, yet she only laughed in response. This seems familiar, does it not?" she said, with enthusiasm in her voice. Her turquoise eyes glittered as she stared into his. "I believe the last time you laid your hands on me, I was able to damage your mind."

Her eyes became wild, and Levi felt the same jolt of energy he did the day this woman read his thoughts. He let out a breath, and forced his mind to block the energy force that the priestess was delivering to him. Her forehead crinkled in defeat, and her irises turned black.

A tiny smile drew up in the corner of Levi's mouth. "It seems your dark powers have limits."

"It would be unwise to end my life," she threatened vehemently.

Levi returned her intimidating gaze. "What was unwise is

the fact that I did not end your life the first time I had the opportunity."

"Reece Bryant will die. My sisters await my instructions now!" the woman spat.

Levi brought both of his hands up to cradle her neck. "I must disagree," he replied, as he tilted his head to the side, studying her. "You see, with the information that you so proudly confessed to me, I am aware that your sisters will also die when I end your life."

The woman's eyes widened in response and before she could respond, Levi ended her life.

He turned to leave, and found Harrison still standing in the doorway.

"Excellent assumption!" Harrison said.

"We must arrange the strategy to recover Reece without delay. If Lucas was depending on those creatures to remove the map from her mind, my killing them may have bought us enough time to rescue Reece before it is too late."

Chapter 27

eece tried seeking comfort by huddling a dark corner
of the small, damp cell. The stone floor was bitterly
cold, and forced a painful shiver to persistently
radiate throughout her body. Her head throbbed so
significantly that she could hardly keep her eyes open.
Every part of her body ached, and she felt herself
becoming weaker by the moment.

She pulled her legs in close, and wrapped her arms
tightly around them, trying to stay warm. She had no idea
where she was, or how she had gotten there. She was

trembling in fear, and her only hope was that Levi was looking for her.

She ran her fingers over the bracelet on her wrist, and recalled the day that Levi gave it to her. *The Pemdai believe that an arrow represents courage and protection...* She heard his voice as if he were in the dark room with her. She smiled as a tear slipped down her cheek, knowing he would come for her.

The side of her head ached and she could feel that her hair was matted with blood. It felt as though her ribs had been broken, and each breath she took was excruciating.

She was startled when she heard the sounds of footsteps approaching her location. The flickering light of a candle illuminated the area outside of her cell. She could see that she was imprisoned somewhere behind bars. She watched as two shadows approached her location. Keys rattled, and then the door eerily squealed open. She glanced up and recognized the first figure; it was Simone.

Reece pulled herself up, and tried to stand on her feeble legs. She held her balance with one arm on the stone wall.

"You are a wicked woman," Reece managed in a hoarse voice.

Simone gracefully walked over to where Reece stood clinging to the wall for support. As swiftly as Reece saw the evil reflection on the woman's countenance, Simone reached out and slapped her across the face, causing her to fall onto the floor. Reece crawled away from Simone slowly until she bumped against the wall.

Simone looked down at Reece and grinned. "That was for me having to pretend to be regretful for trying to have you delivered to the Ciatron," she sneered.

Reece didn't respond.

"Get up!" she ordered.

When Reece didn't comply, Mark Prather stepped

forward, reached down, and jerked Reece up to face Simone. The man held Reece in a bone crushing grip, and she wailed in pain.

Simone snickered and paced in front of her slowly.

"Reece, I never had any intention of returning to Pemdas after I learned that you and Levi were engaged to be married. Even if I had wanted to continue to be a part of such an abominable society, I couldn't have. Because of you, everyone hates me. You ruined my life!" Simone stalked back and forth as she recounted past events, "Fortunately for me, Michael brought me to Armedias. I soon learned this land and all of its inhabitants despised the Pemdai as much as I did. Imagine my delight when Emperor Lucas and his priestesses informed us about a strategy in which you could be removed from Pemdas with my assistance. They couldn't have picked a more willing subject to help carry out their plan, of course." She cackled menacingly.

Reece stared at her in bewilderment.

"Pretending to befriend you in order to gain your trust would've been impossible if it weren't for the priestess, I'm sure. The only tolerable part of being in your presence was watching her torment you. Watching her tear you and Levi apart before my very eyes was almost as enjoyable as seeing you suffer this very moment.

"She was the reason for my nightmares?" Reece looked at the ground, and then back at Simone in disgust. "She was the reason I trusted you?"

"Amazing, isn't it? You have been her victim the entire time." Simone reached out and ran her fingertips gently along Reece's face. "And you were my victim as well. As vile as I felt walking in the halls of Pasidian Palace again, pretending to be remorseful, it will have been worth it in the end." She cocked her head to the side and smiled. "And here we are, at the end of your pathetic life."

Simone stepped back and nodded to Mark Prather. The man pulled back and plunged his fist into Reece's stomach. He continued to beat her until Simone erupted with laughter.

"Stop, Mr. Prather. We need her alive for the time being," Simone said as Reece collapsed to the floor.

She knelt down and grabbed Reece's hair tightly, bringing Reece's eyes to meet hers. "I want her to be alive," she spoke smoothly, "when she finds out Levi has closed his eyes indefinitely." She giggled. "You see, the Guardians *will* put their existence at risk to save you once again, and we stand ready for them. My Michael leads an army who is prepared to battle and defeat them effortlessly."

Simone released her grip from Reece and stood.

"I will return when I have been assured that the lifeless body of Levi Oxley is being sent to you. All I desire now is to see the look on your face as you see your one, true love…dead."

Reece became nauseated, but said nothing.

As Simone turned to leave the chamber, she stopped and looked back at Reece. "I do wonder…will you beg of me to help you join your beloved Levi when his body is displayed before your very own eyes?" She giggled maniacally, turned, and swiftly left the room.

Reece struggled to breathe, and had no strength left within her to sit up. She managed to slowly drag herself over to the frigid wall. Her arms and legs were numb, but with great effort, she was able to lean up against the wall just enough to breathe easier.

Tears began to run down her cheeks as she tried to imagine Levi's face. His stunning smile appeared behind her closed eyelids, his vivid blue eyes staring at her confidently. She found comfort in his expression, and she would hold on for him.

⟶

Levi, Harrison, and a large group of Guardian men took their seats around a long table, waiting to be debriefed and receive their orders.

"Gentlemen, we are facing a situation that requires us to act more hastily than ever before; however, while we continue to wait for more warriors to arrive, we are at a grave disadvantage," Navarre started. "I have made all leaders of the Council of Worlds aware of the threat that is at hand." Navarre eyed Levi somberly. "Fortunately, we have removed the immediate threat of the priestess and her associates; from what we have learned, Lucas was relying on their talents to unlock the map to the location of the stone." Navarre looked at Samuel. "Commander, inform the men of our plans."

Samuel stood up and called for the lights to dim in the room.

"Gentlemen, we have dispatched scouts to discover how their formations are set up." As he spoke, the room displayed three-dimensional, holographic images that appeared before them. They could see Armedias' army, lined up and prepared for the Pemdai to invade them. Samuel waved his hand toward the men and horses standing at attention. "As you all can see, we do not have enough soldiers to battle the army that awaits us. As skilled as our warriors are, we will be defeated if we go into battle at this very moment."

"That's easy to see, Samuel; however, time is not a luxury we possess. We cannot wait for additional troops to join us," Levi interjected abruptly.

Samuel nodded. "That is true." He looked at Navarre,

"Fortunately, Torserlock, the ruler of the Briedirken dimension, has come to an agreement with the emperor only a few moments ago. They plan to offer their assistance with our first attack."

Torserlock? Levi thought in disbelief. Harrison glanced at Levi with astonishment.

"I appreciate that the Briedirken people are willing to help, but have they forgotten that the dimension of Armedias is protected by a magnetic energy force that will destroy anything of a technical nature? Sir, they will be destroyed if they enter that land."

Samuel waved his hand in front of the holographic screen, and the dimension of Briedirken was displayed alongside a holographic image of Armedias. "They understand that as well as we do. They are offering us safe passage, so to speak, so that we may gain access to Armedias through their world."

Levi studied the dimensions on the screen in front of them. At first he wondered why they would need to travel through the machine-like world of Briedirken, and then it all made sense. *Excellent strategy, Samuel.*

"Gentlemen, while we wait for all of our armies to assemble, we plan to take out Armedias' front lines tonight." The holographic images morphed into a detailed map that Samuel had designed for their first attack. "Their army is using these men to notify them if we attack them."

Navarre stood. "Because there is only one vortex that leads from Pemdas to Armedias, it would be to our detriment if we were to travel through it until their front lines are destroyed. Because Briedirken has granted us access to their dimension, we can now enter in from another vortex without being noticed."

Levi and Harrison instinctively leaned forward, and a tiny smile drew up in the corner of Harrison's mouth when he made eye contact with Levi. Both men were fully aware of the mission that they were about to be given.

"It will be our duty to go in and decimate this first line of defense, and we will do it within the hour," Samuel said. "This mission will be done with furtiveness, and we must take out as many of their soldiers as we can. If all goes according to plan, when daylight reaches the lands of Armedias, their armies will find all of their frontline guards slain. We will attack with the rest of our men at that time. Taking out their front lines is the advantage we need to be successful."

Navarre placed both his hands on the table. "My brave warriors, we have convened this meeting with all of you because you are our finest. We need your skill in order to ensure that this mission is successful. Do any of you object to the assignment you have been given?"

"If I may, Emperor," Harrison said, "Why must we wait until first light to destroy Michael and his army? Let us finish all of this tonight!"

"If we had the manpower to ensure a victory, we would. Even by the morning, we will only have close to a thousand men out of our entire army here. The Armedites planned this well; as of right now, our Guardian warriors are scattered throughout Earth and many other dimensions. They have been alerted of the situation and are headed back to Pemdas as we speak; but as you well know, depending on their locations, that process is not always an expeditious one." Navarre addressed Harrison. "As soon as we have completed our initial attack tonight, you will ride out and gather the rest of our men. I will go over the details of where you will find them later, as they will be reporting all throughout the night. You will command and lead these men into Armedias, and assist us in battle at that time."

"My lord—" Harrison started to argue.

Navarre smiled. "Harrison, I need you to command the rest of the men. I understand perfectly well that you desire to be with us as we battle; however, your skill and command is needed to bring the rest of our warriors in. Your father will be joining you, as he is making his way here now with close to three thousand Pemdai warriors. Hopefully, if all goes as planned, the rest of our men will be crossing into Armedias shortly after daybreak and joining us in battle. We will have the advantage then, gentlemen."

Another Guardian spoke out. "Emperor Navarre, if I may; is it wise that you join us for the first-line attack? It will be extremely treacherous, and you are the Emperor of Pemdas. It is only out of protection for my emperor that I humbly request that you remain in Pemdas, and wait to join the battle with Harrison and the rest of the Guardians."

Navarre stood tall. "I understand your concern, Mitchel." He said as he stared resolutely at the men in the room. "As your emperor, I will not stand by while I send my men into battle outnumbered. I am a Guardian warrior, the same as each of you. Samuel and I have already discussed this concern, and I will not abandon my decision. My warriors will not go into a mission such as this unless I am leading them and fighting by their side." After a brief pause, Navarre nodded to the men.

The group of men stood respectfully in response.

"Gentlemen, prepare to depart for Briedirken within the hour," Samuel ordered as he dismissed the men.

As the Guardians departed the room, Levi remained silent.

"I believe this will be an interesting attack, and one I shall never forget," Harrison said with a laugh. "Even though our horses can travel through any vortex, it is quite thrilling to know that we will be riding our horses through the dimension of Briedirken. I cannot believe we are about to engage in such a unique way of traveling through that realm."

"I am struggling to believe any of this is happening." Levi let out a long breath. Levi usually shared his cousin's excitement when they were faced with such an arduous mission; however, the thought of Reece's confinement and suffering was the only thing on his mind.

Harrison gripped Levi's shoulder before he could head up the third flight of stairs to his room. Levi stopped and looked at him quizzically.

"Do not fear, my friend," Harrison said purposefully. "We will recover her."

Levi looked past Harrison toward the corridors that led to Reece's room. "Yes, but can we recover her in time?" he questioned as he glanced back at Harrison. "I believe that is where my confidence is lacking at the moment."

"Well, regain it quickly, or you might as well stay here. I will not see you fall in battle."

"I'll meet you at the stables," he said determinedly.

Harrison grinned. "That's the spirit," he said, as he turned to leave.

Once he was fully dressed in his combat clothing, Levi made his way quickly to the sitting room where his mother and sister awaited. He spent a few brief moments with them before he departed the palace, and walked out to where Areion awaited him.

The Guardian horses were lined up, fully armored, and prepared to leave. Levi was the first to arrive, and he led Areion off to a location alone. He stood next to his stallion, overwhelmed with thoughts of Reece. Where was she? Is she suffering in anyway? Is she still alive? *Don't give up. I am coming for you.* Levi clenched his hands tightly as his anger burned throughout his entire body. "She must know I will find her," he softly muttered to himself.

Anger and panic coursed through him, but before he allowed the dangerous emotion to consume him, he instantly suppressed it. *I love you, Reece*, he thought, as he controlled his breathing and forced all thoughts about her out of his mind. He closed his eyes and began to meditate on the mission before him.

After a few moments, Levi was in his warrior mindset. The only thoughts he carried of Reece were that of her being the Key; the one the Guardians had sworn to protect with their lives. Any other emotions would weaken him.

He stood in front of Areion and gazed into his horse's fierce golden eyes, letting bloodlust consume him. This is who Levi was; this is who the Guardians were. They were as fierce as the horses on which they rode, and equally as fearless. They didn't fear death, and they didn't carry the weakness of emotion within them. They craved the fight. They thirsted for victory; and most of all, the bloodshed of those who would seek to destroy them and their cause. They were valiant men who were born to train for battle unremittingly.

The sound of footsteps behind him confirmed that it was nearing time to leave. He opened his eyes, and even though darkness was upon Pemdas, he saw everything as if it were daylight. This unique ability was highly difficult for any Pemdai warrior to achieve, and it took many years for Levi to learn how to completely give himself over to this talent. The only way such an interesting occurrence could take place was when the Pemdai mind was being controlled by the bold warrior within. He rose up, and turned to mount Areion. Areion grunted loudly as Levi stepped his foot in the stirrup and hoisted himself onto his stallion's back. Areion was fierce with impatience while they waited for the rest of the men to join them. The men didn't speak as they began to amplify their mental capabilities. From this point forward, they would communicate telepathically. They were ready for their mission, and prepared to return only when the first line of the Armedite Army was slaughtered in its entirety.

They didn't travel far before they entered into the dimension of Briedirken, where they were met by two large machine-like serpents. Levi had to blink a few times to adjust to the extremely bright colors that streamed throughout the shadowy horizon. He had been in this dimension only twice before, and both times he was happy to leave.

The Guardian horses' hooves clattered loudly against the steel surface they were traveling on. Rocketing noises rushed throughout the air above and all around them, and it was clear that the beings in this world were taking notice of the Guardians entering it on their horses. This was most likely the reason for the two machine-like serpents guiding them through the outer boundaries of this dimension. The people of Briedirken were extremely paranoid beings, and they were very untrusting of others. They did trust the Pemdai, but Levi knew these beings might question the reason why such a large group of Pemdai would ride in on their horses.

They were stopped at the entrance to the vortex to Armedias. "May you all be safe, warriors," one of the serpents said.

Navarre nodded. "We are indebted to Torserlock, and to your people."

"Emperor, there is no need to place you and your people in our debt. Your cause is a noble one, and it ensures the balance that each and every one of us requires."

With that, the two machines left, and Samuel gave a silent order to prepare to enter Armedias.

The horses went through the vortex to Armedias

without a sound. Once they were inside the land, the men dismounted.

The plan from here was to split up and attack their enemy in groups. Doing so would leave each Pemdai warrior fighting close to twenty men by himself; but with their enemy unaware of their presence, it would be an easy task for any talented Pemdai warrior.

Harrison and Levi secured a location on the far side of the line. They gave each other a parting glance before they made their way stealthily toward their first victim.

Levi approached his first target silently. The Armedite soldier turned suddenly as he heard something behind him. As Levi quietly stalked his prey, he felt the nervous energy radiate from the man's body. Reading his mind and planning his attack, he sensed the Armedite becoming weakened. Fear was taking over the man's perceptive abilities, giving Levi the advantage. Effortlessly, Levi covered the man's mouth with his hand from behind. Just as the moonlight had shown on the blade he held to the Armedite's neck, the knife bit through the man's flesh, ending his life that instant. Levi dropped his lifeless body without a sound, and continued on. One by one, the Guardians silently took down the Armedite's front line in this manner.

As Levi approached another soldier, he read into his mind and found that he knew the whereabouts of the Key. He held one blade to the man's abdomen, and another under his chin.

"Where is the human?" he snarled under his breath.

The man couldn't think or respond, and his fear was causing him to become ill. Levi saw the soldier's mind beginning to shut down; as the man's thoughts raced uncontrollably, Levi was able to read a fleeting thought of Reece being held in the dungeons of Castle Merstaille. It was the last thought the man had before Levi ended his life.

Within two hours, the Pemdai Guardians were returning to their horses. The entire Armedite front line of defense was destroyed, and their first mission was now complete. Just as phantoms in the night, the brave warriors of Pemdas mounted their horses and made their way back into their dimension without the rest of the Armedite Army knowing they were ever there.

After they crossed into the outer boundaries of Pemdas, the men prepared for the next attack. Before Harrison left the group, he guided Saracen over to Navarre and Levi.

"Well, gentlemen, I am sure that the next time you see me, I will, once again, be saving the day." He chuckled and reached over to shake Navarre's hand. "My Emperor, fighting alongside you tomorrow is an honor I am looking forward to."

Navarre grinned. "Undoubtedly, the honor will be mine, Harrison. Until then, nephew, be safe. Your father will meet you here tomorrow, and the group of soldiers will be with him. From there, he will return to stand in my place at Pasidian Palace in case we do not return."

Harrison nodded in understanding. He then brought his horse over to Levi.

He reached out and shook his hand. "You know I am envious of you; be safe, my friend."

Levi smirked. "Envious of me?" He shook his head. "I must disagree, cousin; tomorrow you will be the one riding over that hill with thousands of our men to save us."

Harrison laughed. "I look forward to it. Make sure you're alive so that you can witness it."

"I plan to be."

As Harrison turned his horse to depart, Levi called out to him. Harrison stopped and looked back. It must have been the expression on Levi's face that let him know what

Levi was about to ask of him.

Harrison's expression became somber and he replied, "You know that I will, cousin; however, you will not fall in battle at the hands of these cowards. Soon enough, Guardian, you and I will have the privilege of storming our horses through the halls of Castle Merstaille to rescue Reece." He grinned. "Until then."

With a shout from Harrison, his horse responded, sending him off into the darkness, and on to retrieve the warriors that were needed to conquer the Armedite Army.

"Be safe, Harrison!" Levi called out.

Chapter 28

Once Navarre and the Guardians returned to Pasidian Palace after their initial attack, they met with the warriors who had been arriving from other dimensions. Not all of Navarre's army was assembled for their upcoming attack, so Navarre knew that their next strategy was crucial. They needed to make the right decisions in order to keep the advantage until Harrison arrived with the majority of their army.

"Gentlemen," Navarre said, "Our next strategy is crucial. As you are aware, since Michael is a trained Guardian he knows our tactical training and strategies. That being said, it is crucial we plan to do something he would not expect."

Navarre stepped back and let Samuel address the men.

"We've decided to mislead Michael and his army by attacking on foot, instead of horseback."

Levi leaned forward, "With all due respect, sir, you're sending us on a suicide mission. We're already outnumbered until Harrison arrives; we need those horses fighting alongside us."

Samuel looked at Levi, "You are correct in this assumption, and that is exactly what we want Michael to believe."

"Keep in mind, our horses will be mentally connected to us, and they will know when we need them."

The men continued to strategize and go over their battle plans in the command center throughout the remainder of the night. The hour before daylight greeted the lands of Pemdas and Armedias, the Pemdai warriors filled the courtyard outside of Pasidian Palace, prepared to depart for Armedias. They sat on their armored horses and waited for their emperor to join them.

Empress Allestaine walked somberly alongside Navarre and Levi as they made their way toward the courtyard. As they exited the palace to where the Guardians waited below, Allestaine turned to Levi.

She brought her hand up to his cheek, and stared intently into his fierce eyes. "My son, courage and strength do not describe the true warrior that is carried within your blood." She kissed him softly on his cheek. "I am honored to be your mother, Guardian. Be brave, my son. I will anxiously await your and Reece's return." She smiled, and extended her hand to him.

Levi bent over and raised his mother's delicate knuckles to his lips. "The honor has always been mine, my lady."

Levi turned and walked down the steps to where Areion awaited him. Effortlessly, he hoisted himself up on the powerful horse, and quietly waited for his father to say his farewells.

"Emperor," Allestaine addressed her husband.

"Yes, my love."

"There is no greater pleasure than to stand in your presence as your empress. Be brave, Guardian."

Navarre nodded, and reached for her hand. He lovingly brought it to his lips, offered her a respectful bow, and then turned to address his warriors. "Gentlemen, you all know very well that we are fierce people. We are trained daily for the battle in which we are about to encounter. Before we enter into battle, I must have you know my wishes as your emperor."

Every man in the group remained quiet, awaiting the emperor's command.

"The purpose of our mission today is not to terrorize, to maim, or to torture. The purpose of this mission is to recover the Key. You must understand; the soldiers that lie between you and the Key do so because they were ordered to. Therefore, I ask that you honor their sense of duty as you fight, and offer them a quick, painless death."

Navarre descended the steps and mounted his stallion. With Levi and Samuel trailing behind him, he guided his horse through the crowd of men. Once at the front of the line, he spun his stallion around to face his warriors. "Today we honor the memory of our fathers and the ancient Guardians. Let mercy and clemency be delivered on each bevel of your blade!" Navarre boomed. He held a tight rein as his horse began to pace in place. "Brave men of Pemdas, it is a great honor for me to fight alongside each of you. Now, let us fulfill our duties as Guardians, and recover the Key!"

Navarre loosened his grip on the reins, and led the charge to Armedias. The horses fell into perfect formation as they galloped away from the palace.

Just before daylight made its way to Armedias, the horses silently carried the warriors through the vortex. Each man quietly dismounted his horse and drew his sword. The horses returned swiftly through the vortex to Pemdas and awaited the next command.

With their horses concealed, the Pemdai warriors marched toward the slain bodies of the Armedites' front line. They stood with their shields and swords drawn, waiting for daylight to make their presence known. Levi stared into the lavender colored sky; Armedias' sun would rise at any moment now. He gripped his sword tightly, ready for the charge.

Exactly as planned, the Armedites woke to find that their front lines had been obliterated. Levi listened closely to the scattered thoughts of the Armedite Army; they were running around in confusion, trying to figure out how the Pemdai made it into their lands unnoticed.

The Pemdai remained motionless as they waited for the Armedites to respond. At that moment, Levi felt the mind of every Pemdai warrior collectively reading the minds of the shaken soldiers below.

The Armedites were in shock as they realized they were not yet prepared to battle. They were relieved when they saw that the Pemdai had not come to fight with their unique horses.

As the Pemdai remained tuned into the minds of the Armedite soldiers, they were able to hear the commands given to them from Michael.

"Ah, the proud Pemdai warriors have finally come to fight and retrieve their beloved Key." He snorted, and pointed to where the warriors of Pemdas stood, waiting. "There they stand on the hill, gentlemen, saving their horses' lives, as they know they are severely outnumbered.

Even though they have taken out our front lines, they understand they have no chance against you. These men know they will die today; but their foolish pride will send them to their deaths, not their honor or bravery. It is amusing that they should choose to spare their horses' lives, and battle us the old-fashioned way. My fellow soldiers, these hopeless men are on a suicide mission!"

This was good; the Guardians' plans were falling perfectly into place.

Michael turned to face his men. "Tell all of our men to dismount their horses, and send them away. If the Guardians choose to fight on foot, we will happily accommodate their wish. Do not be alarmed; our archers will destroy the majority of them before our swords are drawn. Gentlemen, prepare the charge."

Arrogant fool! Levi thought, as he watched the Armedite war horses flee the battlefield. The Pemdai warriors began their march forward, baiting Michael and his army further. Navarre and Samuel were in front, leading their warriors down toward the Armedite army.

Across the valley, the Armedites had their swords drawn, and they began marching toward the Pemdai men. As the Armedites streamed down into the ravine, the first wave of their archers on the castle top from behind them released their bows, sending thousands of arrows sailing through the sky.

"Archers!" Samuel shouted.

At the announcement from the commander, the Guardian horses stormed through the vortex. The line of horses each approached his respective rider from the rear. As the horses passed at full speed, in one swift movement, each Pemdai warrior grabbed a handful of mane, and successfully mounted his horse without breaking its stride.

The Pemdai charged full speed down the hill as the

arrows fell into the grass behind them where they once stood.

Navarre and Samuel's plan was flawlessly executed; the archers could no longer be used, as now the Pemdai were in the midst of their army. Once in their camp, the Pemdai lunged themselves from their horses and fell into perfect rhythm, battling their enemy with sword and shield only. The horses battled violently alongside the warriors, giving them more of an advantage against the Armedite Army. Just as Navarre had requested, the men pursued and killed each opponent instantly, causing them no pain in delivering them to their deaths.

As Levi and Areion fought alongside the Guardians, they were ambushed by a group Armedites who charged in on horseback. They were so encased in the battle before them that they had not seen the surprise attack coming toward them from their sides.

The Guardians fought to mount their horses in order to defend themselves against the invading army. Most were successful; however, Levi and Areion had become separated in the attack, leaving Levi completely vulnerable.

Levi defeated four men before he was restrained on the ground with a blade at his neck. As Levi struggled to roll out from underneath the man who pinned him to the ground, Navarre came from behind and removed the man's head from his body with one swift motion.

As Levi reached to grab Navarre's outstretched hand, he watched as a sword penetrated through the abdomen of his father's armor.

Levi grabbed his father as he collapsed to the ground. When he looked up, he saw Michael Visor wiping the emperor's blood from his sword.

Michael smiled amusingly at him. "Fear not; I will be your emperor soon enough."

Before Levi could respond, Michael mounted his horse, and sheltered himself within an army of men. The moment Michael fled, hundreds of Guardian horses surrounded them; they formed an impenetrable barrier around the fallen emperor, and everything grew silent.

The Armedites retreated hastily, having no way to break through the wall of horses that served to protect the Guardians behind them. The warriors rushed to where Navarre lay, breathing shallowly in the arms of his son.

As the men gathered, Levi called out. "Where is Samuel? The emperor must be escorted back to Pemdas immediately!"

One warrior looked down at Levi remorsefully. "Samuel is dead, sir."

"Areion!" Levi roared.

The horse charged to Levi's side.

"The emperor is still alive; you must get him back to Pemdas for help this instant," Levi ordered as three men approached and helped Levi strap his father into the horse's saddle.

"Go now, Areion!" Levi demanded, before the horse galloped fiercely toward the vortex.

"We have lost Samuel; are there any others who have fallen?" Levi questioned.

"We have lost 37 men in total, sir. Eleven wounded have already returned to Pemdas," a warrior responded.

Levi nodded in understanding. "The Armedites have only retreated because they believe we will give up now that our emperor is no longer among us." Levi stared purposefully at the group of men surrounding him. "Gentlemen, our emperor is still alive, and we will fulfill the duty he has assigned us. Let us not forget; Harrison will be joining us soon with the rest of our army. It's time for us to form a new strategy."

→

As Harrison arrived at the vortex to Armedias with close to thirty thousand men, his father approached him with more troops. With a quick exchange and farewell to his father, Harrison turned his horse, and prepared to lead the charge into Armedias.

Harrison suddenly halted the men behind him when he saw Areion entering Pemdas through the vortex. *Levi!*

"Areion!" he called out as the horse sprinted to him.

King Nathaniel and Harrison quickly dismounted and approached Areion. The men were astounded to find that the fallen man was their emperor.

King Nathaniel unstrapped his brother from the horse and held the emperor in his arms, "Son, I will bring our emperor back to Pasidian. You must join the rest of the warriors this instant!"

Harrison turned and swiftly hoisted himself back up onto his stallion's back. He ordered two men to escort King Nathaniel's return to the palace.

"Gentlemen, let us join our men!" Harrison shouted, as he gave charge.

The mob of warriors responded, and rode aggressively through the vortex into Armedias.

→

Levi knelt on one knee, going over the next phase of their battle plan.

"Sir," a Guardian interrupted, "The Armedites are holding their formation on the other side of the horses' barrier. They're anticipating our retreat."

Levi stood up, "Are their archers still in place?"

"Yes; however, their army is too close to ours to use them."

"Thank you," Levi answered, "Once Harrison joins our army, Michael will find out that he has made a grave mistake by underestimating us."

At that moment, the ground began to shake, and Harrison and his army thundered through the vortex. *Right on time, Harrison,* Levi thought as the men approached rapidly.

"Sir, our reinforcements have taken Michael by surprise," a Guardian announced, "He is scrambling to figure out his next move."

"The coward will most likely flee, but we're not stopping until we've recovered the Key." Levi responded as Harrison approached him.

Harrison slowly dismounted and walked Areion over to where Levi stood. He unstrapped the emperor's sword and shield from Areion's saddle and handed them to Levi. "Emperor Levi, your Guardians and I await your first orders."

Levi's heart wrenched at the realization that his father had not survived. He gripped the handle of his father's sword and forced himself to maintain his warrior mindset. He turned to face his men, who were all standing at attention. When he spoke, there was no edge to his voice. His words were smooth and commanding.

"Guardians, hear me now! Never before has a Pemdai Emperor fallen in battle. This news will spread, and it is sure to insight rebellion against the Pemdai throughout all dimensions. As the protectors of the Key and of Earth, we cannot allow this seed of dissention to take root. You all know very well that there is more at stake now than the well-being of the Key. The order of the universe, and our rightful place within it, lies here on this bloodied ground. We must make an example this day for all worlds to see. We must show them all that pursuit of the Key, and the power that it holds, comes at the highest price."

Levi continued. "Guardians, we must lay waste to this land, and write upon it a memorial for all to see. From this day forward, Armedias will represent defeat. All worlds will soon learn what happens to those who would interfere with our prime objective.

Levi hoisted himself onto Areion, and grabbed the reins tightly. Areion anxiously stamped his feet in place one by one.

"Guardians!" shouted Levi. "If it bears arms, kill it! If it seeks refuge, capture it. If any building is left standing, burn it! Gentlemen, mount your horses! Let everything you do from here be done in the honor Emperor Navarre, the valiant man who fought fiercely alongside you on this day. Let these words be my first orders to you as your emperor."

With Levi's command to mount, the wall of horses broke, and each Guardian horse raced with its master. Harrison mounted Saracen, and guided him to where Levi sat, staring intently at the Armedites who were retreating rapidly toward their castle.

Levi looked over at Harrison. "Commander?"

Harrison nodded somberly. "At your word, Emperor."

With that Levi drew his sword. "Let us finish this."

Chapter 29

The Guardians showed no mercy as they charged brutally into the Armedites' camp, killing anyone who stood in their way. Once the Armedite line broke, Levi and Harrison heeled their horses to the castle in order to retrieve the Key, leaving the rest of the warriors to finish off the last of the Armedite Army. It was an easy feat, as Michael was nowhere to be found, and the Armedites no longer had a commanding officer.

As Levi and Harrison charged the castle, the archer's drew their bows. Arrows flew all around them, but the horses were too quick for an archer to hit his target. With swords drawn, Harrison and Levi rushed to the bottom steps of Castle Merstaille. The men leapt from their horses as castle guards stormed down the steps toward them. They disarmed their attackers swiftly, and killed them with their own swords.

Levi and Harrison took the extra swords, and quickly ascended the steps that lead them into an outside courtyard of the castle.

Another group of Armedite soldiers stood between them and the entrance to the castle. They walked slowly toward Harrison and Levi, swords drawn.

Harrison, go at them from the right, I'm going left, Levi commanded his cousin telepathically. Harrison nodded.

With a sword in each hand, the men split and attacked the soldiers from the side. As the mob of men began to diminish, Levi was disarmed by an Armedite warrior who towered over him. As another soldier came at him from the side, Levi spun into the attack, missing the blade of the Armedite's sword by only inches. He used his momentum to knock the soldier off balance. Levi reached for the dagger at his hip and pinned the attacker to a tree by his neck. Levi didn't have an opportunity to retrieve his dagger before the larger man rushed over to him.

Give me a second, Levi, Harrison said telepathically as he sensed the danger his cousin was in. He managed to maneuver his way closer to Levi so that he could hand him a sword.

"You're all alone, Guardian. Your head will make a fine trophy," the man taunted.

Levi arched his brow, as he knew that his cousin was about to intervene. Harrison managed to remove a sword from his attacker's grip, and tossed it over his shoulder toward Levi, end over end.

In one graceful move, Levi caught the sword's handle,

and delivered a crippling blow to his attacker's calf. He stood over the man, who now lay on the ground, and finished him with a final strike through the chest.

Once the group was defeated, Levi returned to retrieve his dagger, and prepared to charge the castle.

He glanced at Harrison as he sheathed the dagger. "We must split up from here. Find your way to the dungeons; the Key is there. I will handle Lucas and Michael."

"Give them my regards," Harrison said with a grin.

Levi nodded. "As soon as I have finished giving them my father's."

When the men entered the castle, Harrison turned down a hallway in search of a passage into the dungeon, and Levi continued straight into the empty marble halls, searching for Lucas and Michael.

Levi saw two massive wooden doors at the end of the corridor, which opened for him upon his approach. He advanced with great caution, knowing very well that this was most likely a trap. He used all of his mental ability to tune into whoever might be in the room, and to assess the situation.

The room was a vast, open space with carved pillars lining the stone walls. At the far end of the chamber, a group of men stood guard at the bottom of steps that led up to a throne where Lucas was seated.

Lucas was a young man who took his father's throne before he was twenty years old. It was rumored throughout all dimensions that Lucas may have had something to do with his father's tragic demise. Lucas' father was a humble man, and before his death, he and Navarre were extremely close. So close, in fact, that when Armedias grieved the death of Lucas' father, the land of Pemdas did as well. Once Lucas ascended to the throne, everything changed within Armedias, and they distanced themselves from the alliance they had created with Pemdas.

"Emperor Levi," Lucas said with a strange confidence, "may I congratulate you on your new title. You must be elated!"

Levi approached closer, but said nothing in response.

"Ah, Emperor, you and I have so much in common now. We have assumed the throne at a young age; however, the only difference is, I had to have my father assassinated to gain my rightful place. I envy you; your father's blood is not on your hands...or is it?" He grinned.

"Lucas, you will join your father soon enough," Levi responded.

Lucas chuckled. "You didn't answer my question, *Emperor Levi*," Lucas sneered, "Is not your father's blood upon your hands? Did he not die this day saving your life?"

"My father died in pursuit of your death."

Lucas shook his head. "You men of Pemdas believe yourselves to be so honorable and brave, yet...you are not. You are arrogant enough to believe you will defeat me? Soon I will have the stone in my possession, and I'll control all dimensions in existence."

"I'm not interested in your delusions." Levi said as he drew his sword and gripped it tightly. The men at the foot of the steps approached, and Levi responded quickly.

He lunged at the first man aggressively, plunging his sword into his heart. As he withdrew his blade, he pivoted on his right leg, spun around, and with his left foot, knocked another man to the ground before driving his sword into the man's chest. As another man charged Levi's side, Levi lunged around him, clinched his neck in the bend of his elbow, and broke his neck with one swift movement. One man remained, and he stared at Levi in disbelief. Levi gazed intently into the man's widened eyes for a brief moment before he lunged forward and swung his sword across the man's neck.

Before the last soldier's body fell to the floor, Lucas stood, laughing and clapping his hands. Levi stood, catching his breath. Before he could respond to Lucas, a door to his left opened, and Michael and Simone entered. Five soldiers followed closely behind, carrying a slender body wrapped tightly in a white cloth.

As Michael and Simone ascended the steps and took their places at Lucas' side, the soldiers placed the body on a table at the foot of the steps. Levi's curiosity forced him to pause.

Lucas grinned. "You see, Levi…we are fully prepared to recover the map at any cost. Michael, please indulge our friend."

Simone smiled sardonically down at Levi as Michael descended the steps to where the body lay, guarded by the soldiers. As Michael removed the face cloth, Levi's breath halted. It was Reece, pale and lifeless.

A wave of emotion flooded over him when he saw her. He tried with everything that was in him to retain his warrior mindset, but he couldn't. He began to turn numb, and rage began to replace every steady nerve throughout his body. As he stared at the woman he loved, the sword fell from his hand, and he fell to his knees.

$$\longrightarrow$$

Reece was in and out of consciousness, and she knew she didn't have much energy left within her to hold on anymore. She tried with everything that she had, but when her eyes closed and her mind stopped fighting, she was so comfortable. Only then was she at peace.

She was startled awake when loud noises echoed in the vicinity. The sounds of crashing, yelling, and men groaning frightened her. She struggled to understand what was happening, but she didn't have the energy, and she collapsed over onto the frigid floor. Her face stung from the icy temperature; but she couldn't move, and she felt her life slipping away.

She heard a familiar voice call out to her. She tried to push herself to sit up and respond, but she couldn't move. There was a loud uproar directly outside of her cell. She couldn't open her eyes to see who or what it was. She heard a man call out loudly, and other voices argue back briefly before they fell silent. A loud noise echoed through her chamber, and whoever entered it came directly to her side. The man knelt and cradled her in his arms.

The warmth radiating from him forced a violent shiver throughout her feeble body, and she felt something heavy wrap around her.

"Reece," the familiar voice said.

She tried to answer, but couldn't. She felt him rub his strong hands on her face, assessing her condition. He opened one of her eyelids, and said something that she was unable to comprehend. His voice was distant.

It's Levi. I knew he'd find me, she thought. He held her close, and then something pierce the flesh of her arm. A burning sensation jolted through her body, and she sensed her energy begin to peak. She tried to open her eyes to see his face, but her lids were still too heavy. As her energy was returning to her body slowly, she wrapped her arm tightly around his waist, embracing him as firmly as she could.

She twisted in his arms, gripped the back of his head tightly, and drew her face up to his. His head turned somewhat, and her lips were on his cheek. She kissed him softly, letting her lips linger on the warmth of his soft skin.

"Reece—" the voice replied humorously.

She kissed him softly again, and ran her hands along his

other cheek. She heard him laugh quietly in response.

She rested her head against his sturdy shoulder, "I love you so much," she whispered to him.

"Reece, sweetheart, it's Harrison."

Reece was able to open her eyes and take in the image of Harrison grinning sympathetically at her. She felt the blood rush to her cheeks with embarrassment. Even though she was humiliated, she was beginning to feel energized again.

Harrison placed a kiss on her forehead. "If you must know, I love you too, sweet one. I am thankful that I reached you in time."

Before Reece could answer him, Harrison's expression went blank before her. His eyes were glowing, but distant and seeing something else. When his eyes refocused, he looked at Reece with urgency. He stood abruptly, and scooped her up into his arms.

"I need to get you to Levi immediately!" he commanded, as he fled the chamber cell.

Reece hung tightly to Harrison's neck. He said nothing more as he strode briskly through the dark halls of the dungeon.

She buried her face into Harrison's neck when she noticed the lifeless bodies all around them. The scene was gruesome, and she was baffled that Harrison conquered these men by himself in order to retrieve her.

———▶

Anger coursed violently through Levi, and his blood boiled beneath the surface of his skin as he stared at the lifeless body of his beloved Reece. He grasped the sword that had fallen from his hands, and sprang to his feet. He charged at the soldiers who surrounded Reece's body, and within moments, the men lay lifeless on the stone floor.

He walked over to Reece slowly, and ran his hand slowly

across her cold cheek. *My love,* he thought with despair.

"Did your father suffer much as he lay there dying in your arms?" Michael grinned as he walked down the steps toward Levi, "I can say your darling Reece screamed your name only once before she closed her eyes indefinitely."

Rage and fury ignited throughout Levi's body again.

"Pretty strong little thing, she was; but in the end, she was begging me to end her life."

In that instant, Levi swiftly kicked Michael's sword out of his grip, and lunged at him. He grabbed his arm, and thrust his elbow across Michael's jaw. As Michael stumbled backward, he grasped the dagger in Levi's waistband, pulled it from its sheath, and as the men stumbled to the floor, he plunged it into Levi's side.

Levi growled as Michael began to twist the blade into his flesh. He gritted his teeth as he rolled away from Michael, and pulled the knife from his side. Michael jumped to his feet quickly and stood over Levi.

"Get up, prince! I know you have more than that within you. Fight!" Michael growled.

Levi slumped over onto the ground, holding his wounded side, when he noticed that the sword he had kicked out of Michael's hand was within arm's reach. Levi seized the sword, and at the same time, swept his feet under Michael's, knocking him to the ground. As Michael rolled over and brought himself onto his knees, Levi plunged the sword through his abdomen.

As Michael lay on the floor, writhing in pain, Levi plucked his dagger from the floor, held it by its blade, and hurled it at Lucas. The blade pierced through the base of man's neck with such force that it pinned him to his chair. He wrenched the sword from Michael's lifeless body, and stalked up the stairs toward Simone.

Simone stumbled backwards as Levi approached her

slowly. His eyes were wild and fierce, and his voice was deadly.

"I have thought of the many ways I would deal with you once I learned that you had put Reece in grave danger for a second time," he said as he retrieved his dagger from Lucas' neck and shoved his lifeless body from his throne onto the ground. He glanced down at Reece's body, "but it appears that you have already made the decision for me."

Levi grinned threateningly as Simone panted with fear.

He stared intently into her bewildered eyes. "If you should faint, I will wake you. This will not be a simple death for you, Simone."

Simone's lips turned up into a wicked grin. "Levi, who are you trying to fool? You would not take the life of a woman. That is too dishonorable for a man like you."

Levi pressed his forearm firmly against her throat while he brought the blade in his other hand to softly stroke the side of her cheek.

"Honor? I am grateful you have brought that word up. Would you like to talk about all of the honorable men whose lives have been lost because of your hatred and scheming?"

Simone sneered. "Still dealing with the death of your father, Levi?"

Levi's eyes narrowed. "Tonight I will return to Pemdas to give my father his final farewell, and I will have to do so for yours as well."

Tears filled Simone's eyes.

"How does it feel to know your wickedness caused the death of your own father?" Levi snarled.

Simone shook her head, fighting away her tears.

Levi tilted his head to the side. "I'm surprised to see that you feel any emotion at all," he snarled through his teeth.

Simone closed her eyes. Levi withdrew the knife, and

prepared to thrust it into her flesh.

"Levi?" a soft voice called from behind him.

Levi gasped as he looked at the body lying on the table in confusion.

"Levi...don't!" Reece called out louder.

With one arm restraining Simone, he turned and saw Reece and Harrison standing at the bottom of the stairs. *Reece?* It was her, wearing Harrison's cloak over her ragged, torn dress. Her face was somber, and her eyes were focused on Simone as Reece ascended the steps toward them.

Chapter 30

Reece walked slowly and steadily toward Simone with deadly determination. Simone was visibly shaken as Reece approached her.

"Reece, I'm so glad you're here," Simone stammered nervously, "Please don't let Levi harm me."

"Why shouldn't I?" Reece responded indifferently, "After everything you've done to me, you expect mercy?"

"Reece, please!" Simone begged as she fell to her knees and groveled before Reece. "There have been too many individuals slain today! You are too good of a person to allow the man you love to murder me."

Reece shook her head in disbelief. "It's remarkable how fast the tables have turned for you and me, isn't it?" Reece said as she stared down into the woman's frantic eyes, "You're right about one thing, though; I will not allow Levi to have your blood on his hands."

"Thank you, Reece! I knew you would have compassion for me!" Simone said as she slumped back against the wall.

Reece tilted her head to the side as she studied the woman. "Levi, is there a place where people can be taken to be banished forever and live in misery to pay for the horrific crimes they have committed?"

Simone cried out. "No! Reece! I beseech you, please don't send me—"

"Indeed, there is; you need only ask." Levi answered as he sheathed his dagger.

Reece stared down at Simone. "Simone, you're the embodiment of evil, and you cannot be trusted. You have proven that more than once. Wherever this place is that you are so frightened of, I won't ask for you to be sent there."

Simone smiled faintly in relief.

"I will *beg* for you to be sent there." Reece finished.

With that, Harrison strode briskly up the steps to where Simone lay on the ground, weeping. He jerked her up by her arm and marched her out of the room.

Levi took off his bloodstained, leather gloves and brought his hands to Reece's face in desperation. He cautiously ran his long fingers through her hair, and he softly exhaled. He tenderly braced her head in his hands as he stared into her eyes. "My love, you are alive."

As Reece reached to put her arms around his waist, she saw the blood on his side. "Is this your blood?" Reece asked sorrowfully.

"Yes." He answered absently, his eyes still gazing into hers. "Do not fear, I'll be fine." he said as he embraced her carefully, and buried his face in her neck. "I love you so much. I truly believed I had lost you forever. I am so unbearably happy to have you in my arms again."

"How did they manage to create a clone of Reece," Harrison called out as he returned to the room and approached the body on the table to examine it.

Reece shuddered at the lifeless image of herself.

"That is a good question," Levi responded as he reached down and cradled Reece in his arms, "It is anyone's guess as to how they could have found a way to create such a thing, but let's not forget how insane they all were to begin with."

"Very true," Harrison agreed as they made their way out of the room.

"Harrison, see to it that the clone is burned along with the castle," Levi commanded.

"I have already ordered the men to prepare for its destruction once we depart," Harrison replied.

Reece held tightly onto Levi, resting her head against his chest as the men strode quickly through the halls. When they reached the exit, Reece was astounded by what she saw. The horizon was dark red, and smoke hung heavy in the air. Guardians filled the hillside, milling around an area where it appeared a large battle had taken place. Areion and Saracen were fully armored and stood at the bottom of the steps, waiting patiently for their masters' return.

"Emperor!" a Guardian called out. "We have been successful, and the remaining Armedite soldiers have surrendered to your command."

"Very well," Levi responded. "Your commander will remain behind to ensure that these men are brought to our prison chambers until the Council of Worlds decides their fate." Levi nodded to Harrison, and Harrison quickly fled down the steps with four other men.

Emperor? She thought as she searched for Navarre. As they stepped down the steps to where Areion was, Reece looked up at Levi. "Levi, what's going on? Where's your father?" she said, as she studied his dark eyes. His expression was unreadable. "He didn't..." She choked on her words as tears filled her eyes. No matter how hard she tried to repress her emotions, she began sobbing in Levi's arms.

Levi gently placed her feet on the ground, and pulled her into an embrace. "My love, please do not shed tears for my father. He would not want that from any of us at this time."

She looked up at him, and he gently wiped her tears away. He cupped her chin, bringing her eyes up to meet his. "Reece, you must know that my father gave his life for this moment, and we honor him now by bringing you, the Key, back home to safety."

Reece tried with all her power to hold back her tears as she stared up at Levi. She knew that he needed her to be strong. There would be a time for them to grieve the death of the emperor, but now was not that time.

"Emperor," another Guardian called out. Reece looked over to find Mark Prather shackled, being held by two tall Guardian warriors. A Guardian horse stood behind him, his reins gripped tightly under his chin by another Guardian. "We found this traitor trying to escape back into Pemdas."

Reece instinctively shied away from the image of the fiery red-haired man. She buried her face in Levi's chest seeking refuge in him, and trying to remove the memories of this man assaulting her.

She felt Levi's body turn rigid when he noticed Reece's

reaction to Mark. "Harrison." Levi said deeply as he released his hold on Reece. "Stay with Reece while I deal with Mr. Prather."

Harrison walked over to Reece and braced his sturdy arm around her, lending her the support that her weak legs required.

As Levi walked towards the man, Mark dropped to his knees and looked up into Levi's eyes, "Imperial highness, I beg—"

"Silence!" Levi ordered as he gazed down at him. "You are a revolting creature. A pathetic coward and a traitor." Levi knelt down on one knee, grabbed his neck, and brought his eyes to meet his.

Reece could tell he was trying to conceal his hostility toward the man, but from the angle she had standing next to Harrison, and the proximity in which they stood, she could hear every word he said in his low, commanding voice. She pulled Harrison's cloak she wore around her tightly as she leaned closer into him, unsure of what Levi would do to the man.

Levi pulled his dagger from his sheath and Mark Prather collapsed backward fearfully as Levi brought his blade to Mark's neck. "Conspiring against your own people was an extremely unwise idea, Mr. Prather."

"My lord, I beg of you…"

"I have not asked you to speak." Levi growled. "You will be served the same justice as those traitors who remain alive." Mark seemed to calm with a loud exhale, only to find the sharp end of Levi's dagger at his throat. "You have no idea the restraint I am currently using not to end your life at this very moment. You deserve death, but there has been enough blood shed in front of Miss Bryant's eyes." Levi pressed the blade further into his throat, "You, Mark Prather, will suffer along with Simone. You will never again see the light of day for the rest of your useless life. Your bed will be that of a stone floor, and you will be left nothing but the thoughts of your greed and treachery against your world."

Mark's eyes widened in fear again, "I beg you for death. Please! I cannot be sent to the Isle of Dizlaught."

Levi stood, ignoring the man's request and looked at the warriors restraining Mark Prather and the soured horse. "Take the man to the Isle dungeons." He looked at the men holding the horse as he sheathed his dagger. "Destroy that soured animal, the Pemdai will never fall victim to such a beast again."

With Levi's orders, the men departed quickly.

Levi removed his bloodied breastplate and tossed it on the ground. He turned and called for Areion as he approached Reece, "I must get her home," he said to Harrison as he cradled Reece and helped her into Areion's saddle. "She must be assessed and given the proper treatment by a physician. I will see you this evening."

Harrison mounted Saracen, "Your Guardians and I will take care of everything from here." he said as he turned his horse toward the waiting men.

Levi hoisted himself up onto Areion and held Reece in a tight embrace. She leaned into him, fully content she was safe in his arms again.

He gently kissed her on the forehead, "Let us get you home, love." He said as the large group of Guardians parted, allowing an open path for Areion to bring Reece and Levi out of Armedias.

Levi:

Levi rubbed his forehead and gripped it tightly. He slumped back into his chair and ran his long fingers through his hair. He gazed at his desk and the papers scattered over it. How long had he been sitting here going over the words he would say to honor his father tonight?

He stood up and walked over to the windows that looked out over Pasidian River, which was carved through the palace's front lawns. The beautiful scenery was replaced by images that he believed would never leave his mind now...

***

What am I thinking? What am I doing? Levi thought as he pulled away in the midst of their kiss. What made him believe that he could ever truly love this woman, or that she could be the future Empress of Pemdas? He had to find a way to end this pointless relationship. He didn't want to hurt her; it wasn't her fault. She was one of the finest young women of his acquaintance. She had a sweet-natured personality, and she was a beautiful woman; however, Isabelle Hamilton was not the woman for him.

This haunted memory of his past appeared to him as if it were happening all over again. Levi exhaled as his mind continued to hold him hostage to these visions of an earlier time in his life.

***

Isabelle cleared her throat softly. "Levi? My darling, is everything okay? You've appeared to be somewhat withdrawn from me this entire visit." She peered up at him from under her long lashes.

Levi's lips tightened as she reached for his hands, and he resisted the urge to pull them away from her.

"Forgive me. I am not feeling quite myself these days," he acknowledged.

She smiled in relief. "Levi, you know I will always love you with everything that I am. I know something more is bothering you. You must learn to open up to me."

She brushed her soft, delicate fingers along his cheek.

Once again, Levi resisted any abrupt movements, for fear of shattering her heart.

She cleared her throat. "You and your family are leaving within the hour to return to Pasidian, and I do not wish for our farewell to be as such. Please, talk to me." Her voice cracked.

He looked down into her tear-filled eyes and took both her hands into his.

"Isabelle, I do not wish to cause you pain, but I trust that if I do not say this now, I will only bring you further grief."

She inhaled softly as he continued.

"Forgive me; I do not know how to say this, for I fear it will sound heartless—"

"Levi, don't! Please," she begged him.

"I cannot make you happy, Isabelle. I know that our families want nothing more than to see us married; however, I cannot grant their wishes."

"What have I done to push you away?"

"You've done nothing, Isabelle. I am simply not in love with you."

The words were harsh, and he knew it. He led her to believe that she had a future with him, but all he was aiming to do was fulfill his duties as the intended ruler of Pemdas.

Tears spilled out of her eyes. Levi sighed, and cradled her in a gentle embrace.

"Isabelle, we are young. We have our entire lives before us. I am only twenty years of age, and you seventeen. I have recently finished my Guardian training, and will begin serving on Earth within the week."

She sniffed and looked up at him. "Is that what this is about? If it is, I will wait for you. I will wait to start our lives together."

"I am not ready to commit to anyone or anything. I've only ever wished to be a Guardian on Earth. I have selfishly courted you to do what Pemdas desires of me. I may have to be the emperor someday, and I may perhaps have to marry a woman of royalty, but I do not wish to consider any of those thoughts at this time. Please, you must understand. I don't not wish for you to waste your youth waiting for a love that may never blossom for you. Find someone who will love you for the wonderful woman that you are, and will be. I am not that man."

It was finished; however, it wasn't going to come without a price, and Levi knew it. He avoided the speculative gazes that were cast in his direction as his and Isabelle's family became aware that Levi had ended his courtship with the Duchess of Sandari. His mother looked at him with concern, yet said nothing. She and his father loaded into their carriage, and soon after, they all departed the Hamilton's estate.

As he and Harrison rode on horseback alongside the convoy, Levi's thoughts were elsewhere. He thought about his relationship with Isabelle, and wondered why someone so perfectly suited for him did not appeal to him. His entire life he had been surrounded by ladies who were the picture of sophistication, born and bred to be an emperor's wife. However, everything about their intentions toward him seemed self-serving. Would it ever be possible to find a woman who would look into his eyes and love him for the man that he is, and not the title he held?

As charming as these ladies were, it was obvious that they were more interested in what they would receive as a result of marrying him, than they were with him. He laughed at himself inwardly, for he knew that the possibility of finding a woman who would love him wholeheartedly regardless of his station in life was probably nonexistent.

"Hey, daydreamer!" Harrison called out, pulling Levi out of his thoughts.

Levi glanced over to find his cousin with a broad grin stretched across his face. "What, Harrison?" He snapped.

Harrison laughed. "Are you thinking about rekindling the relationship you just blew to hell back there?"

Levi rolled his eyes, and shook his head. "I've got eight more hours to figure out how I will explain my actions to my mother."

"Levi, you are ridiculous! So when are you going to let me in on this epiphany that you had?"

Levi stared darkly at his cousin. "I'm really not in the mood."

Harrison sighed dramatically. "Give me the details; I need to be able to defend you when the gossip begins. I would rather hear it from you, instead of my sister—or worse than that—Simone."

Levi grinned. "I envy you."

"Ha! How's that? Please enlighten me."

"Tell me; how is it that you can walk in and walk out of any relationship you choose, at any time? You leave the girl broken-hearted, and your family is okay with it? More than that, *you're* okay with it? Why can it not be that way for me?"

"Well, first of all, you're nothing like me. Secondly, I don't feel obligated to impress anyone." He laughed and then went on. "And thirdly, I'd hardly call them relationships."

Levi rolled his eyes. "Harrison, I have witnessed more than one woman slap you across your smug face in almost every kingdom we visit together; and soon thereafter, another is in your arms." He looked over at Harrison. "How do you manage that?"

Harrison shrugged and shifted his weight in his saddle. "Well, I look at it this way; all of the times I have been slapped pale in comparison to the marvelous time I had with the woman who slapped me."

"That makes no sense."

"It makes perfect sense to me. You will not find me locked down in a relationship with any *one* woman. I will not let any woman claim me as her possession." He laughed. "That's what they do, you know."

"Oh? How's that?" Levi said, deciding to humor him.

"Well, for example, let's say I am courting Isabelle. She immediately assumes we are intended to be married, and then she waits impatiently for me to ask for her hand in marriage. Then, let's say we attend a ball. At this ball, my eyes are innocently drawn to other beautiful women in the room; and as a result, she slaps me across the face for no reason."

Levi laughed. "I think you are being a little dramatic."

"Absolutely not! Levi, women are possessive creatures. I am only saying; I will enjoy their company and their lovely lips, so long as they understand I am not theirs to possess."

"Perhaps you are right, Harrison; however, I believe you will retract these words one day."

Harrison shook his head. "Nope. There is no woman who will ever steal my heart in such a way. I guard it well."

They reached the palace with plenty of daylight left. After a fresh change of clothes and something to eat, Levi made his way to the stables in order to go to a more private setting.

He stopped abruptly when he noticed his father waiting with his horse in the stable yard.

"Father, I will return after a while. I am in no mood to be lectured," he said, as he walked to where Areion waited.

Navarre mounted his horse and grinned. "Regardless of your mood, son, you are coming with me."

As badly as Levi wanted to ignore his father's command, he didn't want to face the consequence of doing so. Navarre led them to an area that Levi had never been before. The steep and demanding climb up the mountain made Levi curious as to what his father had planned. After they made it to the top, Levi was awestruck by the magnificent sight before him. The panoramic scene swept from Pasidian Palace, all the way to the ocean.

"Why have you not ever told me of this place?" Levi asked as they dismounted.

Navarre smiled and clapped Levi on his shoulder. "I am surprised that with all of your exploring, you have never discovered it for yourself."

Levi laughed. "I am, too."

"Son, my father brought me here when I was a bit younger than you are now to speak with me about what my intended duties as emperor would be when the day came."

Levi's lips tightened. *Here it comes.*

Navarre walked over toward the edge of the mountainside that overlooked the valleys below. "Son, whether you want to accept this or not, it is in your blood. You will stand as emperor over all of Pemdas. Everyone will answer to each and every command you give them. Kings will seek your advice, and they will be at your mercy. Other dimensions will depend on your Guardians and your knowledge. Earth, of course, will always rely upon your best judgment when decisions need to be made on their behalf. You must prepare yourself for this."

Levi rubbed his forehead, agitated about the subject his father wanted to discuss with him.

Navarre regarded Levi with a stern gaze. "Levi, it is

my responsibility to help you come to a better understanding of what being the emperor of Pemdas entails, and to be of support as you cope with the great duty of it."

Levi felt his jaw muscle spasm, not realizing how tightly he was clenching his teeth together. "Father, if this is about Isabelle, please, you do not need to explain to me about being the emperor—"

"Of course this is not about Isabelle." He laughed. "Well, not in the manner you believe. I am aware that you are trying to please your mother and me, but marrying a woman because of her royal lineage is not what we expect of you. On the other hand, it would come in handy for your wife to be as such. I want you to understand that we are not upset over you ending that relationship."

"What?" Levi stared at his father, confused.

"Son, please, these kinds of talks are not in my expertise. Your mother can find a better way to inform you about love and those sorts of things. Just know that we expect you to find a woman who will make you happy," he grinned sympathetically, "as you will greatly need that, when the day should come that you will stand as emperor."

Levi's lips tightened as his eyebrows knit together. "Father, regardless, I don't want this life."

"Levi, you are still young. You need not have any concern. I am not asking you to rule all of Pemdas tomorrow." Navarre laughed.

Levi sighed in relief. He loved his father more than

anything, and couldn't imagine the day he would have to say goodbye to him indefinitely. Navarre was wise beyond his years, and Levi understood there was much to learn from him.

"Well, Father, I will allow you to educate me on how I should approach being emperor one day, as long as you promise me one thing."

Navarre nodded.

"Don't die anytime soon—give me some time to live a normal life first." Levi grinned.

Unexpectedly, Navarre smiled, and brought Levi into a tight embrace. "Son, I plan to be around for a long time, and to hold my grandchildren in my arms." He stepped back and laughed.

Levi arched an eyebrow sharply and exhaled in laughter. He stood tall next to Navarre. "So, Father, what is it you wish to advise me on?"

Navarre put his arm around Levi's shoulders, and together they stared out at the ocean. "You see, Levi, I like to compare the responsibility of emperor to that of an ocean—"

***

"Levi?" Harrison called out.

Levi turned, startled. How long had he been standing and staring out of his office window watching this memory unfold?

He let out a breath, gathering himself. "Yes, Harrison. Is my mother ready?"

Harrison nodded somberly. "She is with Reece, Lizzy,

and my parents. We are waiting on you."

"Give me a moment," Levi replied.

"Very well," Harrison responded, and turned to leave.

Levi brought his attention back to the view outside of his window. He needed to pull himself together. His duty commanded him to guide the grieving residents of Pemdas past the death of their fallen emperor.

He would perform his father's final farewell this night, and he would use every ounce of energy he had to repress his emotions.

With superior command, Levi spun on his heel and turned to leave the room to go honor his father and all who depended on him…just as his duty commanded him.

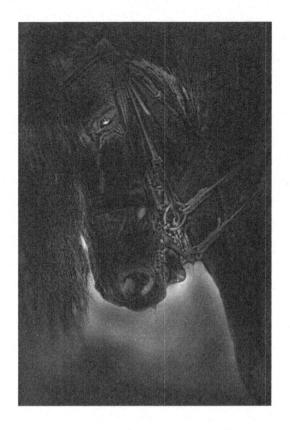

SNEAK PEAK INTO
ANCIENT GUARDIANS: BOOK III

oices, like musical instruments, spoke in unison and perfect harmony. It was the oddest, yet soothing sound. "He will become conscious again," the voices said in unison, "and *they* will come." The female voices finished.

The room became silent.

Unexpectedly, Navarre opened his eyes. He tried to

move, but a strong force restrained him to the hard surface he was lying on. He tried to speak, but no words came out. *Where am I?* He thought, confused.

"His eyes have opened," The voices said in astonishment, "Our plans have methodically worked! Let us give him some time to recover his strength, and then we will proceed to question the emperor."

Navarre struggled to comprehend what was going on, and who was speaking. *What happened? How did I get here?* As quick as a memory flashed into his mind, it vanished; until finally, his mind started to become clearer. He remembered staring into his wife's confident eyes as he said his farewells before his departure for Armedias, knowing he may never see her again.

Then he remembered addressing his warriors, preparing them for a battle in which they were greatly outnumbered. His command to the men echoed in his mind. *Brave men of Pemdas, it is a great honor for me to fight alongside each one of you. Now, let us fulfill our duties as Guardians, and recover the Key!"*

Everything started to come into focus, as if it had just taken place. He led the charge, and their plans were being executed flawlessly. When the Armedite army invaded with horses, and broke their line, the battle became a more of a challenge. As soon as the line broke, Navarre kept close to Levi, knowing he was separated from Areion. His son fought fiercely, but he was overtaken.

"Levi!" Navarre's voice boomed, his voice echoing loudly in the room he was restrained in.

He exhaled when he recalled the last and final memory he had. His lungs weren't taking in air, and he knew his life was ending. He stared up into the intense eyes of his son. Levi remained stern, gazing down at him, and then he was on Areion.

Directly after, everything faded to black. He

remembered nothing else until he woke up in this eerie room, paralyzed and staring up at nothing. The atmosphere of the room was filled with absolute void and desolation.

I've got to get out of here. he thought as he tried to move unsuccessfully.

The harmonized voices laughed, startling him. "Emperor, you will leave, but now is not the time."

Being in such a vulnerable state was highly agitating. He was stunned when he tried to sit up again, his body responded. He tried to swing his legs off of the table, but they were still restrained by the strange energy force. He looked straight ahead and noticed four transparent women. They each had long, flowing, golden hair, and wore long, pale robes. All four women were identical in their appearance, and looked exactly like the priestess that was held captive in Pemdas. He recalled Levi ended that Priestess's life, and therein, all of her sisters. *Why are they still alive? How am I still alive?*

"You are Lucas's Priestesses—where am I? Why am I here? I should be dead!" He demanded.

The four smiled in unison. "You were, for a brief moment; that was the only way we could capture you, and transport you into our galaxy."

"Galaxy? What are you talking about? You reside in Armedias—you are from Armedias." Navarre answered, still struggling to gather his memories.

Their eyes became fierce, and changed from a turquoise color, to a bright crimson.

"We are NOT from Armedias!" They collectively shouted. "We are not from the galaxy that the planet Earth is a part of either. We only used Armedias to set out to find what we were instructed to find—and that is the stone that controls all of the existing realms of Earth."

Navarre's brow furrowed, "That is impossible. No one

can travel out of their own galaxy, never has such a thing been attempted."

Wicked smiles pulled up on all of their faces, "Oh, but *we* can. We can generate ourselves in a particular way to do so. Nevertheless, you are correct, Emperor; no one can travel through different galaxies. Unless, of course, a particular stone was fashioned, by a particular man, and the powers within it could be used. This stone does not only to protect the planet Earth, but it will also open portals to new galaxies."

Navarre was disillusioned by what he was hearing. "You used the stone's powers to open a portal to bring me here? What do I have that you need?"

They laughed, "You see, that is why you are here. We don't have the stone's powers. We have played numerous games with those in your galaxy, trying to locate the one who carries the map to the stone. It was when Movac uncovered the identity of the one who carries the map in her mind that we took over Armedias and their ruler, Lucas."

He recalled Galleta informing him about the length of time the Priestesses where with Lucas. His lips tightened in frustration, "Impossible, all of you took up residence in Armedias years ago."

The women laughed in unison, "I see our sister was successful in manipulating your advisors, Emperor. She is supreme with her skill."

"What!" Navarre's voice boomed in agitation.

"Yes, we have only resided since the Key, as you call her, was revealed to the Council of Worlds." Their eyes narrowed, "We needed a weak leader, one whose mind could be manipulated for our cause. Lucas was perfect, and therefore we used him and his people to give us what we needed. Imagine our utter amazement when we learned that your son was able to see the location. Unfortunately, his mind will not reveal the stone's location, nor will that human child's. After learning this, we needed a new way of opening the portal for our master. The only way to do this was to get the one person who is able to find and use the stone's power to open the portal for us. This, emperor, is why you are here. Your brave warriors will come for you."

"They believe me to be dead!" Navarre shouted angrily.

"Indeed, one last enjoyable torment for your people. You were replaced with a clone the moment we used the energy of the vortex to capture you." The voices laughed, "Our plans were executed so flawlessly that your talented horse could not detect the transfer."

"A clone?" Navarre thought aloud.

"Yes, an exact replica of what you were when you were dead, passing through the vortex. We used our powers to take your body, and at the same time, the clone was transferred onto the horse."

"None of this makes sense." he said as he tried to comprehend what these women where telling him.

"It doesn't have too. All that matters now is that we will have finally achieved what we need," They smiled down at him, "the portal to Earth's galaxy to be opened."

Navarre gazed sternly at the women, "My son will never attempt such a thing. The Council of World's would never—"

They collectively smiled, "Oh, but your son will. He will come for you, and he will bring the stone with him. That, bold emperor, is when our kind will rule over all galaxies."

"There is no way—"

"YES!" Their eyes glowed red, "Yes, Emperor, there is a way!" Their eyes returned to turquoise again and they smiled, "Once your son realizes you are alive, and that there is a way he can open up the portal to a new galaxy, then, Emperor, he will come for you, and we will have our power."

Navarre shook his head, "Your plans will never come to fruition. If what you are saying is true about Levi finding a way to open a portal for inter-galactic travel, he would never attempt it. The Council of Worlds will never allow it!"

They smiled, "See for yourself, Emperor, we will have him soon enough."

At that moment, the dreary walls all around them displayed a snowy mountain range. The air in the room became bitterly cold, as if he were inside the images he was staring at.

His sudden chill was instantly replaced with fear and dread. Aggressively fighting their way through the harsh terrain was a line of fierce Guardian horses with Pemdai warriors upon their backs. There had to of been at least a hundred of them. They wore their guardian regalia and rode their horses in two's. The long trail of horses followed one bold horse and its rider. Navarre studied the rider intently; something was different about the Guardian on this horse.

No! It can't be... he thought in disbelief. Navarre inhaled deeply and swallowed hard, "Reece?"

ABOUT THE AUTHOR

S.L. Morgan was born and raised in California. After 29 years of living in the Sierra Nevada Mountains there, she and her husband began their journeys of moving throughout the United States. She currently lives in Texas, where she and her husband are raising their three children.

In October of 2011, S.L. Morgan became inspired to write her new novel series, "Ancient Guardians." With her passion and love for Jane Austen and other classic romance novels, she was motivated to write a novel series of her own.

S.L. Morgan is currently anticipating five books in the Ancient Guardians series, and is very excited to bring her readers on more adventures and journeys with Levi, Reece and Harrison.

You can also find S.L. Morgan here:
Official Website: www.slmorganauthor.com
WordPress Blog: http://ancientguardiansnovel.wordpress.com/
Twitter: https://twitter.com/slmorgan1
Instagram: http://instagram.com/slmorganauthor
Pinterest: http://www.pinterest.com/slmorganauthor/
S.L. Morgan Facebook page:
https://www.facebook.com/slmorganauthor?ref=hl
Goodreads: https://www.goodreads.com/slmorgan
Ancient Guardians The Legacy of the Key (Book 1)Facebook page:
https://www.facebook.com/AncientGuardiansLegacyOfTheKey?ref=hl

If you enjoyed Ancient Guardians: The Uninvited, help spread the word by leaving your review. It is greatly appreciated and always helps other readers decide whether or not this would be a book that they would enjoy too.

DATE DUE

			PRINTED IN U.S.A.

ROY HIGH SCHOOL
MEDIA CENTER

CPSIA information can be obtained
at www.ICGtesting.com
Printed in the USA
FSOW04n1939061015
11934FS